A DETECTIVE SASHA FRANK MYSTERY

DELIBERATE
DUPLICITY

DAVID ROHLFING

RIVER GROVE
BOOKS

Published by River Grove Books
Austin, TX
www.rivergrovebooks.com

Distributed by River Grove Books

Design and composition by Greenleaf Book Group
Cover design by Greenleaf Book Group
Cover Image: ©iStockphoto.com/Shaxiaozi

Publisher's Cataloging-in-Publication data is available.

Print ISBN: 978-1-63299-306-9

eBook ISBN: 978-1-63299-307-6

First Edition

ACKNOWLEDGMENTS

I would like to thank my wife for her patience during the writing and editing of *Deliberate Duplicity*. Her belief and faith that I could write this book, as well as future books featuring Senior Detective Sasha Frank, never wavered.

I would also like to thank the amazing people at Greenleaf Book Group for their expertise and guidance. Without them this book would not have been published.

CONSTITUTION TRAIL — Bloomington, Illinois

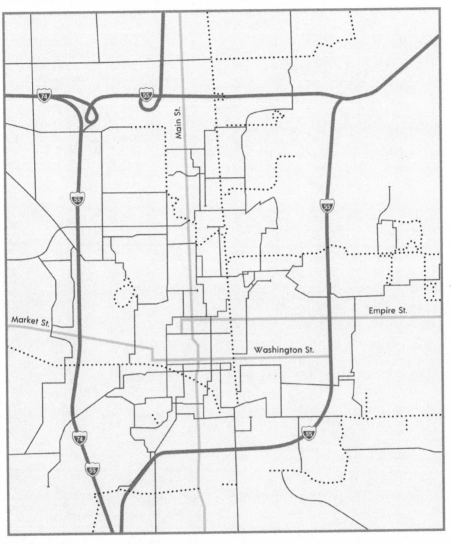

1

DECEMBER 21, 2017

J'Quon Sweeney headed the Adult Supervision unit for the McLean County parole office. As director of the unit, he was not only responsible for the county's parole officers but also directly supervised ten parolees. His office was in the McLean County offices located in downtown Bloomington, Illinois. It was 4:10 p.m., and his last scheduled meeting of this late December day was to start in five minutes. The meeting was with a recently paroled felon currently sitting in the front lobby of his office.

J'Quon grew up on the South Side of Chicago and was the youngest of Elizabeth Ann Sweeney's three sons. He rarely saw his father, Jerome Sweeney. His twin half brothers, D'Jean and T'Jean Adams, were ten years older than J'Quon, and both were convicted felons who had been in trouble since their early teens. The twins had been convicted of robbery and sentenced to three years at Statesville Correctional Facility. When the two were released on parole, they were supervised by Dante Fredericks, a Chicago parole officer. Dante lived nearby and through J'Quon's half brothers became a big influence in their younger brother's life. Although he wasn't his father, Dante spent a great deal of time mentoring J'Quon, guiding him toward sports and away from the gangs that attracted his two half brothers. A rival gang killed them both when J'Quon was finishing junior high.

Dante's influence got J'Quon to focus on football, and through Dante's connections he was able to secure a high school scholarship to Mount Carmel High School. Mount Carmel was an all-boy Catholic high school in the city of Chicago operated by the Roman Catholic Archdiocese. J'Quon excelled in school and especially on the football field. He led his high school football team to multiple state championships while he was a starter, and he attracted multiple college offers to play NCAA Division I football. He then received a scholarship to play football at the University of Illinois. He achieved great success at Illinois both for his scholarship as a student and as a standout 6'5", 255-pound linebacker for the university. J'Quon was twice named to first team all-conference.

Dante was the reason J'Quon wanted to become a parole officer post college. He wanted to focus on helping youth not succumb to the pressures of the street like his half brothers.

At 4:15 he picked up his phone and called to the assistant in the lobby to tell her to send his new project, Charlie Cole, back to his office for their scheduled meeting. J'Quon stood up when Charlie entered his office, shook hands with the parolee, and asked him to please take a seat. He knew instantly where the situation was going. He was going to give Charlie the same advice that he gave each newly paroled felon, although J'Quon knew his advice in all likelihood would not be followed.

For his first meeting with Charlie, he had decided to take a no-nonsense, tough approach and look him straight in the eyes. "I've been going over your file," J'Quon said, "and I think I have a pretty good idea of who you are and what you've become. This is your chance to change the direction that brought you here. Do you understand? Otherwise I see you going back to Menard like the countless others in your position who continued making bad decisions." He waited for a reaction, but Charlie turned to the window and looked down at the traffic on Main Street.

Finally J'Quon broke the silence. "I will help you transition into this community, but it's up to you to also put in the work. You can be sure that I'm going to be watching you and pushing you toward making the right choices. The choices that will keep you from going back into prison. Okay?" Charlie looked back at the parole officer and nodded. J'Quon knew Charlie felt he had no control of his future, but, in fact, his future was totally in his control.

For the next few minutes, J'Quon completed one of the forms required for Charlie to work at the warehouse job, which his office had found at Higgins Moving & Storage. Charlie sat silently looking around the office. The younger J'Quon in the framed photographs hanging on the walls had much more hair.

Many showed J'Quon and others in football uniforms. There were also several trophies, some from J'Quon's time in high school.

Charlie earned his GED when he was in prison at Menard. He couldn't recall going to a single high school ball game, football or any other kind, as a kid. He'd missed out on a lot of things as a teenager due to the decisions he made, but years ago he'd found countless others to blame for his bad decisions. Classic blame-shifting.

Charlie believed he'd been placed on the path he took by his worthless old man, an alcoholic and drug user who swung his fist at him anytime he got within arm's length. His mother, also a drunk and druggie, wasn't much better, at least in Charlie's memory. Both let their three kids fend for themselves. How he and Christine made it out of Chicago's South Side alive was amazing. Their younger brother, Tommy, wasn't so lucky. He joined a local gang and was killed by a rival gang member who was never charged with his murder. It remained unsolved like so many others in Chicago. Christine somehow turned out okay though. She had made good decisions. She'd graduated from college and married an Illinois State Police officer. Unfortunately her husband was killed in a traffic accident while on duty. Christine lived in Normal with her two children, which was why Charlie had asked to be paroled to the Bloomington-Normal community.

J'Quon asked, "Can you start work on Monday?" Charlie nodded. J'Quon straightened up in his chair. "I asked can you start work on Monday, Charlie. I need you to answer out loud and not just nod at me. Show some respect, or at least understand the control I have over your life."

"Yes, I can." Charlie turned back to watching the passing traffic.

J'Quon already knew that Charlie would end up either back in prison or dead. He'd seen countless parolees who couldn't adapt. Many never had a chance. Or at least that was how J'Quon looked at parolees like Charlie. He took one final look at the paperwork to make sure everything was right, shuffled it together, straightened the edges before stapling them, and handed the document across to Charlie. "I need you to sign your name at the bottom of page one, page three, and the last page." He handed Charlie a pen. "You need to write in the date after you sign on the last page."

Charlie signed his name three times without reading the document. He dated the last page below his signature as he was instructed and handed it back to J'Quon. "Here you go." He returned to looking out the window.

J'Quon checked the three pages to make sure that Charlie signed where required and then said, "Mr. Cole, could you look my way, please?" Charlie turned to him. "I need you to focus for a few minutes as I tell you a few important pieces of information."

Charlie sat up in the chair, and the two men stared into each other's eyes. "I'm here right in front of you," Charlie said. "What?"

J'Quon sternly replied, "Charlie, you need to listen up and understand that I'm the only person who gives a damn about you. I'm the only person right now who is helping you find a job. You have to know that no business wants to hire a convicted felon, especially one with your record. Everyone in this state knows that Menard is where hardcore felons go to pay their debt to society for the crimes they've committed. Regardless of that fact, I found a job for you working for Mr. J. W. Higgins. Mr. Higgins is a Christian who believes that people, even people like you, deserve second chances. There aren't many people like Mr. Higgins, and you're not going to mess this up. Do you understand what I'm saying?"

Charlie continued staring at J'Quon, showing no emotion.

"Do you understand what I'm saying?" J'Quon said more loudly.

Charlie glanced away. "Yeah, I understand."

"Today is Thursday," J'Quon said in a calmer voice, "and you start at Higgins this coming Monday. Actually you start at midnight Sunday night. You'll continue living at the halfway house a few blocks from here on West Mill Street. You don't have a car, right?"

Charlie felt that J'Quon was disrespecting him, and he stood even taller in his chair. "You know I don't have the money to buy one."

"Yes, I know," J'Quon said. "That's why people work and have jobs. To be able to afford cars, food, clothes, go out to dinner, and pay rent or buy a home. Luckily Higgins is just a few blocks from the halfway house that you're living in, so you don't even need a car."

"Yeah, I know that. I know you need money to buy things." Charlie glared

at J'Quon. "I'm not stupid. But I'm gonna be making less than twenty thou ·
a year. How am I supposed to survive and buy those *things* you say a job lets
you have?"

"This is the first real job you've ever had," J'Quon said. "Being a convicted felon for committing armed robberies, violent assaults, attempted
murder, and other crimes got you to where you're now sitting across from me
as a recent parolee and former guest of Menard. This is a new starting point
for you. The opportunity to reset your life and become a law-abiding member
of society." J'Quon repeated what he said to every parolee who had sat in the
chair across from his desk. "Your job is to keep yourself out of trouble. Try to
settle into the halfway house and the job you're starting in a few days. Don't
drink, don't do drugs, and save as much of the money you make at your job
as you can so you can get your own apartment and buy a car. I am willing to
invest my time in helping you transition to a person who contributes to this
community and society in general. But again, Charlie, it is up to you and only
you to do all that you need to do to make it happen. If you don't put forth
the effort, then I will be on you like stink on skunk. And you don't want that.
Understand?"

Though he was furious that he was being treated like a kid, Charlie was
smart enough to know that he needed to get along and say all the things that
his parole officer wanted to hear. Today wasn't the time to fight back. "Yes,
sir. I understand. I know that I have to take responsibility for my life and
that starts today. I'm committed to doing whatever I have to, and the job at
Higgins is the start. I appreciate you finding the job for me and Mr. Higgins
agreeing to hire me."

J'Quon had heard the same BS from almost every parolee he'd been
assigned. It was as if the Illinois prison system held seminars for prisoners
being paroled, taught by former parolees, on what to say at your first meeting
with your parole officer. But he knew that he owned Charlie's ass. "That's
great to hear. As you know, I will be checking in on you regularly. We will have
regular meetings that you are required to attend. I can ask you for a urine
sample or require you to have blood drawn to ensure that you're following the
rules of your parole. I'm glad you're taking responsibility, as that is the first

step to resetting your life here in Bloomington. I'm sure you'll do well in your job at Higgins." J'Quon tried to keep a positive tone in his voice. "You should also be aware that I can walk into where you live, where you work, come up to you on the street, anywhere and anytime, to check on you. I can also ask for a urine sample anywhere, not just here. Like I said, it's up to you to keep your nose clean and out of trouble."

"Thank you, sir. Am I good to go now?"

"Yes, you can go, Charlie. I know I'm repeating myself, but you've been given a chance to change your life for the good, and I'm here to help you achieve that. Good luck at Higgins."

They stood up and shook hands, and J'Quon handed Charlie one of his business cards. He followed the parolee out of his office and down the hall. When they reached the lobby, they stopped at J'Quon's assistant's desk to set up a time for Charlie's next appointment. They chose the next Friday morning at 9:30 a.m. Charlie would have gotten off work, and Higgins was just a short distance from J'Quon's office.

"I look forward to hearing about your first few days at Higgins. Have a nice weekend, Charlie."

Charlie nodded, turned, and walked through the lobby door and out to the bank of elevators. Clearly neither liked the other, but Charlie would be the one who would have to bend to the will of J'Quon if he was going to stay out of prison.

J'Quon's thoughts quickly shifted from his meeting with Charlie Cole to the Thursday night poker game that would start at Maggie's in just over three hours. He looked forward to the low-stakes game in the back room of the downtown Bloomington bar with a few of his friends. The game provided the opportunity to share some of the personal and professional BS they each dealt with over the past week. The key rule of Thursday night poker was that whatever was said during the game stayed in the room. It was a safe space to bitch about what was going on in their lives. J'Quon certainly needed it, and he knew others in the room did as well.

2

The Thursday night poker game at Maggie's Bar & Grill was frequented by members of law enforcement agencies in the area, including Bloomington and Normal police departments, McLean County parole officers, officers from the Illinois State Police, plus members of the FBI, DEA, ATF, and other state and national criminal agencies in the area. Other patrons included lawyers who officed in the vicinity and judges who worked at the nearby McLean County Courthouse.

The bar was co-owned by Jimmy Reynolds, a retired Bloomington police detective, and Ron Simmons, a retired attorney whose firm specialized in representing large insurance companies headquartered in the area. Maggie's was divided into front and rear bars separated by a wall with a set of swinging doors that harkened back to the saloons of the Wild West. The front bar was the smaller of the two and rarely had patrons. Most people in the downtown area knew about Maggie's and weren't really that comfortable entering the front door. The bartenders assigned to work the front bar tended to be imposing men who weren't inviting to those not welcome, which was Jimmy and Ron's intent. Patrons who walked in unknowingly got served, but there wouldn't be much conversation from the bartender. Maggie's back bar operated more as a club, and you only ventured through the swinging doors if you were someone known by one of the owners.

One of J'Quon's best friends was real estate attorney Michael Drake, and both were regulars at poker night. A couple of other close friends who were regulars on Thursday nights included criminal defense attorney Jonathan Jennings, who defended some of the recent parolees whom J'Quon was responsible for rehabilitating back into the community, along with Chet Steele, who was a circuit court judge in the area. Jonathan, or JJ, as he was known to his close friends, was a named senior partner in the law firm Jennings, Craft

& Jones, LLP, and Michael was an unnamed partner in one of the largest law firms in the Bloomington-Normal community.

J'Quon had become friends with Michael at the University of Illinois. They had first met when both joined a stock investment club in their sophomore year. They became fast friends. While most club members were making faux stock trades during the year, hoping to win the annual club competition and the trophy that went along with winning, Michael was using the club and its members as advisors for his own stock portfolio. Michael had also helped J'Quon fund a personal trading account, which helped change J'Quon's and his mother's lives.

As a college football standout, J'Quon knew that he wasn't destined for the National Football League. Instead, he was looking toward a future where he could make a difference in a community. Michael graduated at the same time as J'Quon and then entered law school at the university. Since he was going to be at the university for law school, Michael convinced his best friend to stay and work toward a master's in business administration after graduating with a degree from the School of Social Work. They shared an apartment in Champaign while they did their postgraduate schooling, and then Michael persuaded J'Quon to settle in Bloomington, where J'Quon began working for McLean County. They had been very close friends for more than fifteen years.

Michael and J'Quon usually sat next to each other at poker night, and JJ sat on the other side of J'Quon. Others at the table tonight were Special Agent Lee Barnes, who was with the FBI, the Honorable Judge Chet Steele, defense attorney Carly Stutsman, JJ's law partners Gray Craft IV and Sig Jones, Agent Max Duncan with the Illinois Bureau of Investigation, the Honorable Shirley Logan, who was another judge on the circuit court, defense attorney Cindy Cordman, and local real estate investor Jimmy Banks.

Each participant was knowingly playing in an illegal poker game in what Illinois considered a gambling place, a Class A misdemeanor for the first offense and a Class 4 felony for each subsequent offense when determined by the circuit court that the premises is a public nuisance. This was especially ironic when sitting at the table that night were two judges from the circuit court. Each player averaged at least forty games per year. The co-owners,

Jimmy and Ron, had been running the bar over the past fifteen years, and they could lose their food and liquor licenses if they were charged with operating a gambling place. Chances of that happening were very slim, considering the bar's patrons.

As the first hand was being dealt, JJ began sharing the problems he was having with his current on-again, off-again girlfriend, Jodie Paxton. It was his night to receive the bulk of the crude remarks at the table, even from the three women playing. Most of the remarks related to his current relationship with the amazing-looking recent University of Chicago Law School graduate who was planning on working for the local state attorney. JJ had been married and divorced twice before, and everyone at the table figured he'd marry the current girlfriend and divorce her within a couple of years. Just two hours into the game he'd been overserved his usual old-fashioned.

"She's just a friend, and she isn't that special," JJ loudly told everyone at the table. He didn't like the term "girlfriend."

Shirley, who had been married and divorced once, vowing to never marry again, gave her sage advice. "JJ?" He didn't hear her. "JJ!" she boomed. JJ quickly turned to her. "You're a pretty smart boy. Why haven't you figured out you don't need to marry? You can play the field like me. Heck, I'd even let you do me." The entire table erupted in laughter.

Not wanting to be left out of the friendly ribbing, Judge Steele said loudly, "You know what, son?" JJ looked over at the judge. "Right now, that girl may be looking good to you, but I guarantee you that somewhere somebody else was tired of her shit and happy to see her go." That brought even more laughter.

JJ threw his cards into the middle of the table, pushed his chair back, and stood up, unable to take the heat from his playing partners—especially from a female circuit court judge who was over sixty and old Judge Steele. He wanted to cool down before rejoining the game. He went to the bar to order another drink and started to talk with Jimmy, one of the bar's owners.

As Max collected the cards from the hand that Judge Steele had quickly won, Michael said, "Now that's funny stuff. What's new in your world, Quon?" Only Michael called the big man Quon.

Everyone at the table was a friend of J'Quon and admired how much he cared about his job. "Same old same old." J'Quon finished the last of his beer. "You know I deal with losers every day of the week, and today was no different."

"Sorry to hear about your day, Quon," Michael said, "but my day was great. I closed a big deal for the new electric vehicle company coming to town, and I'm feeling great."

Everyone knew he'd been working on finding a property for an electric vehicle manufacturer that was interested in building a facility in the area. The company expected to hire up to a thousand people when fully operational. A new company bringing in that many new jobs made Michael into a local hero. Everyone at the table clapped, and there were a few whistles. Michael stood and bowed. "Thank you. Thank you."

Carly, sitting on Michael's right, said, "Well done! That company is going to be great for the community." Others at the table nodded in agreement.

He smiled, thanked them, and motioned to the dealer that he was heading to the bar. J'Quon followed him. "I'm all ears if you want to talk," Michael said. "Let me get us a couple more beers and then why don't you tell me about it?" As they waited, they listened to JJ telling Ron Simmons about his new girlfriend, though he had just been telling everyone at the table that she wasn't his girlfriend. Michael smiled to himself. He'd bet the farm on JJ marrying the new girlfriend within the year. What a dumbass.

The bartender put the two draft Stellas on the bar in front of J'Quon and Michael. Michael reached out to shake the bartender's hand with a neatly folded hundred-dollar bill between two fingers. "Thanks, Brownie."

The bartender smiled and nodded as Michael thanked him. "Anytime. Thank you, Mr. Drake." Michael was a big tipper. Those on the receiving end of his generosity knew, but his friends did not. That was the way he liked it. He did things for people like Brownie all the time. Two years ago, Brownie had been injured in a motorcycle accident, and Michael had paid what insurance wouldn't cover. He also made sure that Brownie's apartment rent was covered.

J'Quon thanked Michael for the beer, and they clinked glasses. "Tell me what's going on," Michael said.

J'Quon leaned his back up against the bar. "I gotta tell you something I learned a long time ago, man. Once a loser, always a loser."

Michael took a drink of his Stella and smiled. "True. It's hard to dig yourself out of a hole, but there are those who have."

"You're right. If I'm honest, and you know this more than anyone, Dante came into my life because of stupid decisions my twin brothers made. If it wasn't for Dante caring about me, I would probably have followed them into a life of crime and be dead too." J'Quon bowed his head and said a quick prayer for his half brothers.

Michael raised his glass to his friend. "You're my best friend, and I feel blessed that Dante was there for you when he was. I'm here for you now, my friend."

They clinked glasses. "True that. And I for you, Michael."

JJ moved over to where they were standing at the bar and accidently bumped into Michael. "Sorry!"

"No problem, buddy. Can I buy you another drink?"

"No, Ron bought me one on the house." JJ moved between J'Quon and Michael. "What you guys talking about?"

"I was about to ask Quon what kind of loser he counseled today."

J'Quon laughed. "A loser from Chicago. Grew up a gang member and spent his youth in juvy. Then graduated into more serious felonies and was sent to Menard." He shook his head. "I can tell you right now that regardless of what I try to do for him, he's going back. He can't help himself. The dude is about to start a minimum-wage job, and he's not going to be happy with his life." J'Quon shook his head. "There's nothing anybody can do to help Charlie Cole. He's an idiot. And I guarantee you that he's just waiting for somebody to offer him something more than he has now. He'll screw up. I guarantee it."

"There's nothing you can do for this guy?" JJ slurred.

"I'll try, but I don't think so."

Michael stepped back a little from the bar. "Can't you just work your magic on him?"

"Based on the meeting this afternoon, his odds of going back to Menard are as good as JJ getting married to his—" J'Quon and Michael burst into laughter. "Girlfriend!" they shouted. JJ put his hands up in the air, like what?

"Now that was funny," Michael said to J'Quon as they clinked glasses. They raised their drinks to JJ, who raised his own and sheepishly smiled. All three clinked their glasses, and JJ spilled most of what was in his glass onto the bar.

Brownie wiped up the spilled drink. "Do you want another, Mr. Jennings? It's on the house." JJ nodded yes.

"JJ's going to marry his newest girlfriend," J'Quon said. "And Charlie Cole will be heading back to prison. He's like the scorpion and the frog."

"Who's like the scorpion and the frog?" Michael looked perplexed.

"Charlie's like the scorpion in the story about the scorpion and the frog. They're both on the bank of a river. The scorpion asks if the frog will give him a ride on his back across the river. The frog asks why would he do that, and says, 'You'll sting me, and I'll die.' The scorpion replies, 'I would never do that, as we'd both drown in the river.' The frog agrees and lets the scorpion get on his back. Halfway across the river, the scorpion stings the frog. The frog asks the scorpion, 'Why would you sting me? We're both going to die.' The scorpion replies, 'What did you expect? I'm a scorpion.' Charlie can't help himself, Michael. The guy only knows what he knows, and what he knows is life as a criminal. He is the scorpion."

"Yeah, I get it."

"I'll bet the house he's not going to make it, and he'll be back in prison within the year, or he gets himself killed."

"I hope you can influence him to turn his life around like Dante did for you."

"It's my job, so I do too." J'Quon looked at Michael. "You want another beer? My turn to buy."

Michael nodded. J'Quon raised his empty glass to Brownie and signaled for two more. Then he motioned to the dealer that he and J'Quon would be playing the next hand.

As they returned to the table, Michael called out, "JJ, are you going to play the next hand?"

JJ took a long drink of his old-fashioned. "I'm toasted. Deal me out." He finished his drink and asked Michael, "Can you give me a ride home?"

"Absolutely! You're not driving tonight and maybe not in the morning, based on the number of drinks you've had, buddy."

"Funny man. Very funny." JJ looked at his watch. "Let's go!"

"It's only 10:45. WTF?" Michael was ready to leave but couldn't waste the opportunity to mess with JJ.

"Come on, Michael. I'm toasted."

Michael leaned over to J'Quon. "Do you mind following me over and bringing me back so I can get my car?"

"No problem. I'm ready to roll. My cards suck anyway." J'Quon stood up and walked back over to the bar as he finished his Stella.

Michael took one last look at his cards before tossing them into the middle of the table. "Thanks, guys. See you next week." Everyone at the table said their goodbyes or nodded. "Let's go, JJ," Michael said.

JJ turned, stumbled, and ended up on the floor. J'Quon and Michael helped him to his feet.

"Give me your keys." Michael held JJ by the arm.

"Here you go, man." JJ reached into his front pocket.

Michael took the keys and said to J'Quon, "Give me a few minutes before you head over. I'm going to get JJ upstairs and into bed before I leave him. He'll never make it up the stairs by himself."

J'Quon laughed. "No problem. I'll be out front of his house in a few."

Michael and JJ left out the front door, and Michael helped JJ into his Mercedes. "You okay, man?" Michael asked.

"Yeah." JJ covered his eyes with his hand. He quickly fell asleep.

Michael drove past the entrance to the private golf course where he and JJ were members. He turned onto the street where JJ's home backed up to one of the fairways on the back nine of the course. As they approached the garage on the side of JJ's house, the door automatically started to open. Michael thought it was so cool to have the door open as the car approached. He needed to have one of these door systems installed at his house. He pulled into the garage and turned off the car. The garage door was automatically closing as Michael grabbed the keys, got out of the car, and walked around to JJ's door. He glanced around the four-car garage before opening the door and waking up JJ.

Ros, JJ's Australian Kelpie, came from the house through the doggie door. "Hey, Ros. How you doin', girl?" Michael bent down and petted the excited dog with his right hand. "JJ isn't doing too well tonight, Ros. Let's take him upstairs." The dog ran back to the door and began barking.

"Hey, Ros." JJ tried to reach down to pet his dog and almost fell out of Michael's grip.

"Hold on, buddy. Let's get you upstairs." Michael opened the door, and he and JJ followed Ros into the house. She barked happily and danced in circles.

"I'm going to set you down at the kitchen table and let Ros out, okay?" Michael said.

JJ nodded. Michael set him down and opened the side door and let Ros outside. He watched her run around the well-lit backyard. She stopped for a few seconds and then ran back into the house and sat down. He closed the side door and then grabbed several treats from a cabinet drawer. He leaned down to give them to Ros and rub her head. "Let's go, girl."

Michael followed the dog as she ran out of the room. He stopped to help JJ out of the chair and then took him upstairs to his bedroom. Ros was already lying on JJ's bed, waiting for the two to enter. Michael gently set JJ down on the bed, and JJ immediately lay down and rolled over. "I'm going to leave your keys on the bedside table. Your car is in the garage. Quon is picking me up. Talk to you tomorrow, buddy." Michael patted Ros one more time on the head. "See ya, girl." He walked out of the room, down the stairs, and opened the front door. He stopped and yelled back up the stairs. "Your alarm isn't on, JJ." He waited for a response and heard nothing back from JJ. He closed the door behind him and walked down the front steps and got into J'Quon's waiting car.

"How'd that go?"

Michael smiled. "Well, he's in bed. Hopefully he doesn't have an early meeting, 'cause he's going to miss it. I'm going to call and leave a message for his assistant." He looked up Judy's contact number at the office and left her a message that JJ would probably be late getting to the office. "Thanks for picking me up," he said.

"No problem, man. Wow! Was he toasted or what?"

"Yeah, I guess he was. I'm not sure what JJ sees in Jodie."

J'Quon started laughing. "Seriously?"

"Okay, I know." Michael laughed too. Jodie was smart, beautiful, young, and had a great body. Of course he knew why JJ was seeing her. "You know that he's going to marry her, right?" What J'Quon didn't know was that while Jodie attended additional classes on the West Coast before joining the DA's office, JJ was hooking up with a number of women. Always the player.

"Of course I do." J'Quon dropped Michael off at his car and they said their goodbyes.

As Michael pulled into the garage at his home on Sunset, he thought again that he needed one of the automatic openers like JJ had. He got out, reached into his pocket, and pulled out a thin plastic case before he placed it on his workbench.

Inside he looked out the sliding doors to his expansive patio and onto the woods at the back of the property. Spotlights attached to the back of the house highlighted the trees. He walked over to the antique bar that he had shipped from Scotland, opened an upper cabinet, and reached for a heavy lead crystal scotch glass. Michael liked his scotch neat. He poured two fingers of the 1936 Mortlach fifty-year-old single malt scotch. He savored the first sip while thinking about the next chapter in the life plan he'd had since college. He raised his glass to his parents, who died the summer before he began college, and then took another sip of the peaty single malt, thinking that everything in his life was coming together.

3

At 6 a.m. Gentle Bill passed Brian the clothing pack prisoners called dress-out clothes through the narrow bars of his cell. In his southern Illinois drawl, he said, "Morning, son. I know you know that today's your day. Change into these, as the release team will be coming for you within the hour."

Brian nodded. "Thank you."

One of the oldest guards in Menard, Gentle Bill was a giant man at 6'9" and roughly three hundred pounds. He had been working as a guard for thirty-six years and was considered compassionate by the inmates. Few referred to him as a hack, what they usually called the guards. Not many of the hacks could be described as compassionate, a relative term when it comes to describing prison guards. He could knock heads with the best of them if the situation called for it. According to Brian, considering the crap the inmates gave the guards day in, day out, it was no surprise that most of the hacks were SOBs. You got what you gave inside Menard.

Gentle Bill held out his big hand, and Brian reached out to shake it. "Good luck, son. Don't do anything to get your ass back in here." He looked Brian in the eyes with a stare. "Okay?"

Brian again nodded. "Yes, sir. Thank you, sir." Brian had shared the 7' x 9' cell with Jim "High Five" Snyder, a 6'5", 220-pound lifer. When he first was assigned the cell with High Five, his new cellmate had told him that the upper bunk was Brian's. That was almost five years ago. Brian had never asked his cellmate and protector where he got the nickname; he'd quickly learned when he entered Menard that it was best not to ask too many questions of other prisoners. One of the old-timers on the floor named Smokes told Brian that High Five used to play point guard at Southern Illinois University, an NCAA Division I college, before he killed a man with a pool cue in a fight at a central Illinois bar. Smokes said High Five had played a lot of basketball when he first arrived at Menard. He had an amazing three-point shot, which he practiced almost every day on one of the prison basketball courts. One day after making twenty-eight three-point shots in a row from deep in the corner, he trotted around the court, high-fiving everyone who had been watching the display. That was sixteen years ago. The nickname stuck.

High Five got up from the lower bunk. "What you got there, Brian?" He knew full well what Gentle Bill delivered.

"Dress-outs. Gentle Bill told me the release team will be here shortly to take me out." He was hoping High Five hadn't heard Gentle Bill say, "Within the hour." Brian stood in front of the bunk beds at the end closest to the door and opened the brown cardboard box and started changing.

High Five looked over at him. "I heard." He sat on the toilet.

Brian began changing into the sweatpants, sweatshirt, and tennis shoes that had been in the box, hoping that the release team came sooner rather than later. He was afraid that High Five was going to whistle at him and demand Brian give him the same service he'd been providing his protector one more time. Brian spent the next thirty minutes putting the few books and miscellaneous items he had accumulated over his fourteen years into the small cardboard box that had contained his dress-outs. He added the few toiletries he had as well.

Thankfully the release team showed up early. The two hacks responsible for ensuring his smooth exit out of Menard were accompanied by an armed hack named Burns. John Burns.

Burns brusquely told Brian, "Turn around."

Brian complied, and Burns unlocked and slid the jail cell door to the side. Brian looked at High Five, telling him, "Good luck." High Five didn't look at him or say anything.

One of the release team told him to step forward. Brian did as he was told. The two hacks secured the belly chain first and locked it in place. Then they cuffed his wrists and ankles. Brian looked into the cell and thought how great it would be if High Five's next cellmate were much bigger, more of a badass, and even more abusive to High Five than he had been to Brian. That made him smile.

Burns grunted, "Okay. Let's go. Transports a-waitin'."

Brian acknowledged the order with a nod, turned, and started down the hallway. He could only shuffle his way along. As he went by Smokes's cell, he nodded. Smokes nodded back. "Be good, son."

Sweating with nervous anticipation, Brian shuffled through the maze of hallways as he followed the release team member in front of him. The other team member was behind him, and Burns brought up the rear. Brian was told to stop in front of a counter that opened up into the hallway to his left, where a prison clerk sat. The name tag on his shirt pocket said "Hester." He asked Brian to confirm his name and prisoner identification number. Brian gave Hester his name and ID number. The clerk nodded and told the release team to remove Brian's cuffs and belly chain. He handed Brian an envelope with his gate money, a small amount of cash meant to help former inmates make a fresh start, along with a one-way Greyhound bus ticket from Saint Louis, Missouri, to Bloomington-Normal, Illinois. Bloomington would be his new home.

"Mr. Keyes, let me be the first to congratulate you now that you've been officially exited from the Menard Correctional Center," Hester said. "No one here wants to see you back. I suggest you keep your nose clean. Please turn around and wait to hear the buzzer, which will unlock the door behind you, which will allow you to exit this facility. Good luck, Mr. Keyes."

"Thank you, Mr. Hester." Brian turned and faced the door. A loud buzzer sounded, and Brian stepped forward, pushed on the door, and stepped into a small holding room. There were six other prisoners already in the room who were also being paroled. They'd all been in the room once before, when they entered Menard. All were dressed in the same sweatpants and sweatshirt and the cheap pair of tennis shoes they were given earlier in the day. Each was holding a small cardboard box filled with the few possessions they had accumulated while in Menard. One of the release team members handed Brian his cardboard box and then closed the door. The buzzer sounded again, locking the door.

The motley group in the holding room looked like a sports team that was accustomed to losing. As if they were waiting for the team bus to take them on another dreaded road game. A game they each knew they'd have little chance of winning.

One of the two hacks in the room ordered them to walk single file out the door at the opposite end of the holding room from where Brian had entered. As he stepped outside, Brian thought it felt especially cold, even for February in southern Illinois. Two more armed hacks were standing beside the white prison van the former inmates were walking toward.

Brian looked around the fenced-in area, which the inmates referred to as receiving. They were still inside the eighteen-foot-high razor-wire perimeter fence that ringed the Menard complex. The bigger of the two hacks told them to get into the van.

For the past fourteen years, Brian had been living with the thirty-seven hundred or so other convicts at Menard, if you could call what had been his life inside living. Prisoners came and went, most leaving alive. He swore to himself that he wasn't ever coming back. He knew odds were that half the men standing with him at the prison van today would be back in a few years. He would not be one of them. Once he was on the bus to Bloomington-Normal, he would be forever free.

The parolees climbed one by one into the van, which would take them to the Greyhound bus station in Saint Louis. Brian tried not to look at the other six prisoners. If someone thought you were staring at them, chances were they'd confront you. Once they were seated, each of them stared straight ahead, out the windshield.

At this moment, Brian was feeling lucky—very damned lucky to get out of that hellhole without any serious damage done to his mind or body. Damage was most certainly done, as every prison inmate would tell you if they were being honest, but Brian would never talk about it because of the daily humiliation he endured. He wasn't going to miss High Five at all. Brian was alive, and that was cause enough for celebration. But not yet. Soon, though.

A loud thump made the parolees jump. The driver was locking down the van doors in the back. Once locked, the doors could only be opened from the driver's seat or by key from the outside. The side and back windows of the van were covered in the same steel mesh as the cage that separated the parolees from the hacks.

The hack in the passenger seat turned around to address them in his practiced badassed voice. "Listen up! I'm Mr. Collins, and I'm responsible for getting you to Saint Louis, along with Mr. Remington, who's driving us today." Collins looked around to make sure everyone was focused on him. Hacks always had your full focus or there would be hell to pay. Even today. "You know this is your final ride courtesy of Menard. It's gonna take about an hour and a half. We don't want to hear a peep out of any of you. We're not gonna make any stops until we get to the bus station in Saint Louis, where we will let you out. Any questions?" There were a couple of grunts and nods. "Okay. We're off." He turned around, and then turned back to them. "Make sure you've got your seat belts on. We don't want any of you getting hurt now, do we?" Collins and Remington laughed. No one else on the bus did.

Brian guessed everyone on his side of the cage hoped that Collins and Remington had a head-on with an 18-wheeler pulling a full load on their return. He chuckled at the thought.

As the van drove out of Menard, Brian glanced over his right shoulder at the massive stone facade that fronted the prison. He wasn't going to miss that place. He quickly turned to his left to look at the Mississippi River as the van turned right onto Kaskaskia Street, which crossed in front of the prison. The Mississippi flowed slowly south past Illinois and Missouri and then through the states of Kentucky, Tennessee, Arkansas, Mississippi, and Louisiana, where it emptied into the Gulf of Mexico. Once in the gulf you could travel on the water to anywhere in the world. Brian wouldn't be traveling anywhere outside the state of Illinois until his parole officer gave him permission, and he knew that wouldn't be for a long while.

The van turned right onto Fern Valley Road, ending his view of the river. The van drove for another mile, eased into a left turn at the green light, and then onto Illinois Route 3.

The van ride to Saint Louis gave Brian time to think. He always prided himself as being known as a tough guy and someone to be feared while growing up in Roanoke, Illinois. At 5'10" and 165 pounds, he certainly wasn't considered tough at Menard. While in high school he wasn't the biggest kid, but there weren't many who would mess with him. He considered himself the biggest fish in small pond Roanoke. He didn't focus on grades in school, getting more Cs and Ds than any other grade, but he did well enough to be able to play school sports, and he was a star. School sports was always the most important topic of conversations growing up in Midwest small towns. Once he graduated from high school, he quickly found that the attention he enjoyed in the area pivoted to those still in school playing sports.

After graduating high school, Brian had little success holding a job, but he soon found something he was good at—petty crime, small-time thefts that seemed low risk and allowed him to survive.

He and his friends, Todd, Dillon, and Adam, robbed homes and businesses of computers, televisions, Xboxes, motorcycles, ATVs, and construction equipment that could be easily sold. Soon they began talking about moving up to riskier crimes that would have bigger payoffs. After a night of heavy drinking, they agreed that bank robbery would be the quickest path to easy money.

The friends' first bank robbery was very successful. Their second robbery quickly went awry when Brian struck a customer with the butt of his weapon. The man he hit was a seventy-year-old decorated Vietnam War veteran confined to his wheelchair. The man was in the bank with his son, who pulled a concealed weapon defending his father. Brian shot the son, and the four bank robbers fled the bank. Police captured the four a short time later.

One of the friends turned state's evidence on the others after learning that he would only face a minimum sentence if he talked. He also told prosecutors the gang had committed a previous bank robbery.

While Brian had been awaiting trial in county jail, he'd heard about Menard from others in lockup. As the ringleader, Brian was charged and convicted of bank robbery and attempted murder and sentenced to Menard for thirty years. As tough as he thought he was, he was unprepared for what he would face while in prison.

Many of the felons in Menard focused on weight lifting, and there really weren't many opportunities for sports. Most of the prisoners were much bigger and meaner than Brian. He found out quickly that in order to survive he needed to be meaner and find protection. It would take time to rid his mind of the last fourteen years.

4

Yesterday morning, as Charlie was walking home from work, a guy driving a van pulled over and asked him if he'd be interested in making some easy money. The thought of earning some cash interested Charlie, so he agreed to meet with the man, who introduced himself as Fred, at a restaurant a few blocks away from his halfway house at eleven o'clock that night to listen to what he had to say. When he arrived at the agreed-upon time, Charlie was the only customer in the restaurant. He sat at one of the tables in the back corner. A minute later, Fred entered the restaurant and came over to the table. "Okay if I sit down?"

"No one else is gonna be sitting there," Charlie said. He wasn't used to someone being considerate.

After a few minutes of talking, Charlie realized Fred knew things about him that few could know. He knew that Charlie was born and raised in Chicago and had spent most of his teen years in juvenile detention centers before committing serious crimes as an adult that landed him in a cell in Menard. He knew Charlie had been involved in gang shootings and was sent downstate for thirty years before getting paroled after fifteen years. He knew all about Christine, Charlie's sister, and her family. And he knew about Charlie's crappy job at Higgins, that he didn't own a car, and that his future was bleak. Charlie was precisely the kind of guy Fred was hoping to find.

Fred told Charlie that he wanted his help finding someone capable of killing. He said that he was seeking revenge and would pay him big money to find the right person. Charlie couldn't decide if it was a setup or a once-in-a-lifetime opportunity.

Ten minutes before Charlie's shift started at Higgins, he told Fred that he needed to get to work. They agreed to meet again the same time the following evening. Fred would pick him up at the corner a block west of the restaurant. As they shook hands goodbye, Charlie realized Fred had been wearing leather gloves inside the restaurant. He knew the guy must be crazy to want to kill ten people, but the gloves inside were just weird.

As he walked in the darkness, Charlie considered Fred's offer. The money Fred was willing to pay would be more than enough for Charlie to quit Higgins, buy a nice car and house anywhere in the world, and begin a new life with a new identity. But he wouldn't be able to do it alone. His friend Brian came to mind. Brian had been paroled from Menard just last month. He could be interested. Brian's new job sucked and was as much a dead-end as his own.

After he finished his midnight shift, he'd text Brian, who would already be at work at M & M. They had been texting back and forth on burner phones. Christine had reluctantly delivered a phone to Brian at Charlie's behest and conveyed Charlie's message that the phone was a get-out-of-jail gift. The two weren't supposed to see each other or other felons without their parole officer's approval, but with the money Fred was offering, it was worth the risk.

For the kind of money Fred was talking about, he thought he could convince Brian to kill ten people. He needed to think about the best way to present the idea. Should he go straight to the payout and then tell him what he needed to do to get it? Or should he emphasize a new name and identity anywhere in the world with enough cash for the rest of his life? As he pushed his time card into the time clock, Charlie said to himself this was his only chance at a new life, and Brian was going to be his ticket.

5

Charlie took a circuitous route from his apartment to where Brian worked at M & M to ensure that no cops or parole officers were following him. He had taken three different Bloomington-Normal Connect Transit buses and walked several miles to get himself to the covered bus stop bench he had been sitting on for the past thirty minutes. He took deep drags off his Marlboro Red as he watched rush-hour traffic. He chuckled to himself, thinking commuters in the Bloomington-Normal area didn't know heavy traffic. Chicagoans knew traffic. They'd consider this light for a Thursday afternoon.

When the walk sign appeared, he stood up and double-checked traffic before jogging across the street toward the entrance to Twin City Industrial Park. M & M was located on one of the side roads off the main entrance to the industrial park. Brian had agreed to meet him outside the gates of M & M after his shift.

Christine told him that Brian drove an older red four-wheel drive Dodge Ram. Brian's mom had passed away while he was in prison and left him some money. Charlie figured that was how he was able to buy a truck. Lucky guy. Based on his current earnings, it would be a long while until he'd be able to buy something to drive around in.

————

When his shift ended, Brian quickly changed out of his work coveralls and headed out the back door to the employee parking lot. Outside he glanced around for any signs of his parole officer. Usually Sweeney did spot checks on payday, which wasn't until next Monday. When he reached his big Dodge Ram, he walked around as if he was checking out the vehicle, though he was actually double-checking for any sign of Sweeney.

Once he felt confident Sweeney wasn't in the parking lot, Brian climbed into the four-wheeler. He started up the truck, hit the gas pedal several times before putting it into gear, and slowly pulled forward out of the parking spot. As he went through the gate, he slowed down until he spotted Charlie. Brian stopped the vehicle, and Charlie jumped in. Brian hit the gas before Charlie had pulled the door closed. He sped out to the main entrance of the park. Charlie offered a Marlboro to Brian as they pulled up to the red light.

"Great to see you, man," Brian said. "How you been doin'? Christine said you were doing okay."

"I'm doin' okay. I don't have a sweet ride like this big-assed four-wheeler, but that's going to change soon."

Brian took a cigarette, and Charlie lit it for him and then lit one for himself. Driving in the country at this hour would give them the best odds of not being spotted. But they needed to keep an eye out for any dumbass deer wandering onto the road. As they smoked, they quickly caught up with what had happened since they last saw each other in Menard.

Charlie and Brian had cells on the same floor of the cell block in Menard. They'd tried to watch each other's backs, and both had escaped without any major altercations with other prisoners. It helped that each had their own protector, or daddy. Though neither brought it up.

"I gotta thank you again for the burner," Brian said. "It was really great meeting Christine. After all you told me about her, I gotta agree with you that she's awful pretty. But I could tell she was scared meeting me."

"Yeah. Even though she didn't know what was in the package, she really didn't want to deliver it. I finally convinced her, but she told me not to ask again. She *was* a little afraid to go to your place."

"I *did* spend fourteen years in prison for attempted murder." Brian checked his speed and slowed a bit. "I'm lucky that M & M doesn't seem to care about my time in Menard. Sweeney convinced them that I had a good record inside, and I impressed 'em with my welding skills. Who woulda guessed that when I took up as a bird-killer inside I could turn it into a job outside? Of course, the bastards didn't hire me as a welder. For at least six months, I'm working as a probationary gopher making minimum wage while welders are making over twenty an hour."

"You did chew up a bunch of downtime learning welding, and they gave you more leash than me. I didn't go back after that first class. Listening to all that crap about things we needed to do to make sure we didn't come back was a pain in the ass." Charlie put out his cigarette. "What was that word they kept sayin'? Residism? Reshitism?" He laughed out loud.

"It's recidivism." Brian shook his head and glanced over at Charlie. "I figured out it was a way for me to stay under the radar inside, and there's no doubt it's helped since I got out. Sweeney has been pretty good so far. He thinks I'm on the straight and narrow, which I am, unless you've got something for me?"

"I have something; we can talk about it at dinner."

"I recommend you order the horseshoe when we get to the restaurant," Brian said. "It's a mountain of a meal. They start with several slices of thick toasted white bread, add a couple hamburger patties, cover them with French fries, and top it all with a cheese sauce."

Charlie feigned disgust. "That sounds like crap!"

Brian laughed. "Maybe, but you gotta try it, man. It's delicious."

Charlie shrugged and looked out at flat farmland waiting to be plowed and tilled for the coming corn and soybean crops. He hated the flatness of rural Illinois. You could drive hundreds of miles in any direction and see the same landscape. He smiled to himself. Soon he'd be able to live anywhere he wanted.

They stopped in Minier, a town so small you could drive through it while holding your breath. As they pulled into the small gravel parking lot of the diner, Charlie pointed to the side lot and Brian parked in a spot near the back. They scoped the area before getting out and heading for the front door.

Inside, a woman standing behind the counter smiled and said, "Welcome to Cadwell's. You can seat yourself."

Brian mouthed a thank-you, and both he and Charlie looked around the rest of the restaurant. There were maybe fifteen patrons. Brian motioned to the woman that they would be heading to a booth in the back.

She followed them to the booth, carrying menus and water. As she set the glasses on the table, she said, "My name is Shirley. Can I get you anything else to drink?"

Brian and Charlie both looked at the waitress with the big smile before Brian looked down at his menu. "Water's fine," Brian said, his eyes on the menu.

"Sounds good. Would you like to hear the evening's special?"

They both ordered the special, all-you-can-eat lake perch with a choice of two sides.

Shirley left to place their order, and Brian quietly said, "So, what do you want to talk with me about?"

Charlie glanced around the dining room. "Well, I've got an opportunity for you to make some serious cash, and it comes with a new life too."

"Okay. Lay it out."

"I know you've got a job, and when your mom passed away while you were in Menard, she left you some money."

"The job sucks, and Mom left me about fifty thousand. That's how I bought the Ram. I've got some of that cash left, but I'm only making $8.25 an hour. As long as they keep me on, I'm gonna make maybe seventeen a year. Maybe more with overtime." Charlie nodded, wondering if Brian might be willing to take on the job. "I could make forty a year plus OT if I got the welding job."

"Okay, man. The first thing I have to ask is if you'd be willing to do almost anything for a chance to make three hundred thousand in cash, plus get a new identity." Charlie paused to let the information sink in. "The new identity will be rock solid. You can move anywhere you'd like, and you'll get a new birth certificate, social security number, and license. I know you don't have much family, but if you do this, you'll never be able to see the family you have left again."

"I'm listening, but where are you getting that kind of money?" Brian asked, his eyes on Shirley as she approached with a small basket of freshly baked rolls and butter in small gold packets. It had been a while since Brian had a dinner roll, and he immediately reached for one.

Charlie also chose a dinner roll. He tore it in two, opened one of the packets, and spread the butter onto each half. He took a bite. "Here it is," he said and swallowed. "A guy I know has a bunch of money, and he's got a score he wants to settle with some folks."

"Who is he?"

"I can't tell you his name, but he's real, and he has a boatload of cash. He's willing to pay big to get what he wants done." Charlie shoved the other half of the roll into his mouth and chewed while studying Brian. "He wants payback for something these folks did to him a while ago. I don't know why exactly, but I also don't give a damn."

Brian nodded. "What does he want done?"

Shirley called out as she walked toward them: "Here you go, gentlemen. Two specials." She placed the plates in front of them. "I'll bring more rolls when they come out of the oven. And more water. Anything else you need?"

"Nope. We're good." Charlie smiled at the waitress. Shirley was a pretty good-looking gal. He guessed she was about fifty. She returned his smile and headed back to the counter. "It's been a while, you know?" Charlie said as they watched Shirley walk away.

"He has a list of people he wants killed," Charlie said as he had a bite of fish.

Brian shrugged. "Okay. And?"

"He wants ten people dead. He wants them killed in a certain way, and he wants one of them killed every ten days until it's over."

"Holy crap. What did these people do?"

"I told you. I don't know, and he's not goin' to tell me."

"When do I get to meet this guy?"

"You don't. Everything goes through me. He calls it a cutout or something. I work with him, and you work with me. He asked if I knew somebody who could do this, and I told him I thought I did, but he doesn't know who you are. He's never going to meet you, and you're not gonna meet him." Charlie paused. "That's the deal."

Shirley returned with fresh rolls and butter. "How you gentlemen doing? Need more fish yet?"

In unison they both replied, "Not yet."

"I'll be back in a while. The kitchen shuts down in about thirty minutes, so if you'd like more fish let me know."

Brian waited until Shirley had reached the counter. "I've never killed anybody in my life," he said in a low voice. "But if I'm going to take care of the ten people this guy has a beef with, I'm not doing it unless I get a big pile of cash. And I'm going to need more than three hundred thousand."

Charlie took a big drink of water. Maybe if Brian would agree to the job he could get more money. "Can I lay out how you get paid and then let me know what it would take for you to do it?"

Brian nodded.

"If you agree to do this, I've got five thousand in cash for you tonight. Just for sayin' yes." Charlie glanced around the restaurant. "For the first one you get ten thousand, the next fifteen, and each one after that you get twenty-five thousand until the last one. You get a hundred thousand for that one. A nice kicker."

"If—and I do mean *if* I do this—I want half a mil."

Charlie looked incredulously at Brian. "Geez, man. You gotta be kidding me. You seriously want me to ask for half a mil?"

"If the guy wants this done, that's what it's gonna take." Brian gave Charlie a hard stare. "And not one cent less."

Charlie ate the last few bites of fish on his plate and chewed thoughtfully. "I'll ask him. My gut tells me he'll pay. But if I go back with this ask, you gotta promise me you'll do all ten."

"I will," Brian said, looking Charlie in the eyes. "You can tell the guy I want fifty thousand for each one. I'm not going to do it any other way." He picked up another roll, set a pat of butter on it, and watched it slowly melt.

"I'll ask him, and then I'll send you a yes or no on the burner."

"And I want the five tonight." Brian knew he had Charlie and the guy over a barrel. He was happy to have the cutout or whatever Charlie called it. He had no interest in meeting the guy.

"Deal. I'll give you the money when we're back in the truck."

"And you got dinner tonight as well." Whoever Charlie was working with could afford to buy his dinner.

Shirley approached with a platter of fish. "Cook made this fish for you because he's shutting down the kitchen. If you don't want it now, I can put it in a to-go container."

"That's awful nice, Shirley," Charlie said with a smile. "I think I'll have more now while it's hot." Brian nodded. Shirley smiled and left the platter on the table and walked back to the kitchen.

When it was time to pay, Charlie pulled out two twenties and laid them on the check. "Keep the change, Shirley. We'll be back."

She thanked Charlie for the big tip. "You both have a good night," she said.

In the truck, Charlie reached into the pouch on his hoodie. "Here you go, man." He handed Brian a thick envelope. "Let's do this."

6

Shivering in the late-night cold while waiting for Fred to pick him up, Charlie was trying to work up the nerve to ask Fred to pay them both a half million. If he could afford three hundred thousand each, he likely could afford a bit more. A van drove through the intersection and stopped just past the corner where Charlie was standing on the sidewalk near the end of the bridge. Charlie walked over to the van and stepped up to the passenger-side door. He looked in to see Fred sitting behind the wheel. He opened the door to get in. It was nice and warm inside the van, but Fred was again wearing a pair of leather gloves.

Fred pulled the van away from the curb and headed west. Charlie decided he'd wait for Fred to speak first. The two sat quietly in the van until Fred finally talked. "How'd it go with your guy?"

Charlie hadn't looked at Fred since he'd gotten into the van. "He's willing to do it. I didn't go over any of the details other than letting him know how many people he'd need to kill." Charlie assumed Fred would reply, but he silently drove. "I gave him the five thousand in good faith as you told me to." Charlie paused. "He said he'll only do it for half a million. Nothing less." Charlie took a deep breath. "And I want the same as him." After a few minutes, Charlie sheepishly looked at Fred and added, "We don't want to wait for a big payoff. We want fifty thousand after each."

"I'll pay the two of you a total of one million, but you both have to follow the exact plan that I've laid out. If you deviate one iota from the plan, there will be consequences."

Charlie mulled this over. "Okay, but what is an iota?"

Fred chuckled. "It means you have to follow each and every step of the plan with zero changes." Fred turned to look at Charlie. "Do you understand what I'm saying? I need you to know that I'll pay you both what you're asking, but only if it's done exactly as I want it done, each and every step. If you both understand that, then we have an agreement."

"You got a deal," Charlie quickly replied. Thinking he had Fred over a barrel, he made one more demand. "I meant to say we each want fifty thousand up front, before we murder."

Fred assumed Charlie's last demand was something that he had come up with as he was saying it. He could give Charlie a win, and he'd look good in the eyes of the guy he'd chosen to commit the murders. "Well, Charlie, I tell you what. I will agree to give each of you fifty thousand up front and then fifty thousand each after every murder is committed. As you like to say, we have a deal."

"Great!" That was too easy. Charlie wondered if he should have asked for more.

Fred stopped at a red light and then turned left. "I need to ask you a very important question. Now that I've agreed to the additional hundred thou up front, it's up to you to decide whether you want that extra money for just you or if you want to split it with your guy." Fred made a left turn. "It's your call."

"I'll give that some thought and let you know," Charlie replied. Inside he was smiling.

Fred pulled into the parking lot of a restaurant that served what many said were the best fried pork tenderloin sandwiches in town.

Charlie wasn't sure why Fred had pulled the van into the parking lot of some restaurant on the east side of Bloomington. It was well after 11 p.m. on a Thursday night, and the lot was packed.

For the next thirty minutes, Fred went over the details that had to be repeated exactly for each of the ten murders. Fred handed Charlie a sheet of paper detailing the plan to be followed and an envelope that contained the keys to a large shed on the west edge of Normal. Inside the shed were parked ten vehicles—a different one to be used by Brian to drive to each killing. The name of the victim Fred wanted to be killed, along with items required to follow Fred's plan explicitly, would be found inside each.

"You now have everything you need. We won't meet again unless I feel we need to. I will text you the address of the shed before the first killing. I will also text you where you can pick up the cash you require before you start and then text you again the location of the cash for each murder. Understand?"

Charlie nodded. Fred had just answered the question he was going to ask. "I need to get to work," he said.

Fred got Charlie to Higgins a few minutes before he needed to clock in. He stopped a block away. "We good?"

"Yeah, we're good." Charlie opened his door and got out of the van, and Fred pulled away. Florida was going to be nice, maybe even Panama or Costa Rica. Warm weather year-round and plenty of girls. It all sounded good to him as he quickly walked toward the entrance of Higgins. Based on Fred's plan, he should be able to enjoy the good life in a little over three to four months. "How sweet is that?" Charlie said out loud as he opened the door and walked into work a minute before midnight to start his graveyard shift.

7

For two nights in a row Charlie and Brian sat opposite each other in the same back booth at Cadwell's. Brian had convinced Charlie to try the horseshoe, and to Charlie's surprise he liked it. "I got a new favorite meal," he said. "This might be better than a Chicago dog. It sure fills you up more."

"I told you. Whoever thought this thing up got it right. 'Course it could cause a heart attack." They both laughed. As Shirley cleared the table, Charlie and Brian ordered two slices of cherry pie à la mode and coffees.

As they ate, they talked about J'Quon. So far both of them were playing nice with their parole officer. They compared their meetings with him since leaving Menard. All in all, he was an okay guy, although he'd been a pain in the ass the first couple of weeks. They both thought he had mellowed out quickly since they were keeping their appointments with him and their noses clean. With what they were planning, they didn't need J'Quon sniffing around their business. They'd make sure to keep their noses clean.

The pie Shirley recommended couldn't have been better—warm and home-made, with vanilla ice cream on the side. She picked up their plates and refilled their coffee after they told her they were going to sit and talk a bit.

Charlie laid out Fred's detailed plan. He also made it clear that from this point on, they would only communicate with each other by text. They were not to see each other until after the last murder had been successfully committed.

"I guess that makes sense," Brian said.

"Good. We gotta stick to the plan."

Charlie scanned the sheet Fred had given him. "I need to know what size clothes you wear."

"Funny question. What kinda clothes?"

"Sweatpants and sweatshirt. Shoe size too." Charlie added, "Funny, just like Menard." They both laughed.

Charlie noted the sizes. "There will be two stun guns, two clear plastic bags, four zip ties, a pair of scissors, a Ziploc bag, a tube of Super Glue, and a roll of duct tape. This is a little weird, but he wants you to use the glue to keep their eyelids open." Charlie shook his head, thinking that Fred was a crazy bastard.

"What the hell?" Brian's eyes widened.

Charlie shrugged. "I don't know what to tell you. I'm just telling you how he wants it done. You can't deviate from the plan. Not one iota." Brian nodded, and Charlie felt a little disappointed Brian hadn't asked for the meaning of "iota."

"Interesting dude, this Fred. I gotta tell you that this guy must really be pissed about something these people did to him, or he's just f-ing crazy." Brian shook his head.

"Yep. But you're still gonna do it, right?"

Brian laughed. "For a half a mil I'd do you too, Charlie."

Charlie whispered, "Screw you." He smiled. "I'd do you for a lot less." They laughed, but they knew that if Fred asked either of them to kill the other for the kind of money he was throwing around, they'd probably do it.

Shirley returned to check if they'd like more coffee. "I think we're coffee'd out," Charlie said. Brian nodded.

"Okay, boys," she said as she dropped the check. "See you again soon."

"You betcha," Charlie said.

"Thanks, Shirley," Brian said.

As she turned and walked back to the counter, Charlie said, "You know she's growin' on me. She's a fine-lookin' woman."

Brian chuckled. "It wouldn't matter what she looked like for you, would it, Charlie?"

Charlie dropped a fifty-dollar bill on the table, and they headed to the door. Charlie stopped by the counter and said, "Money's on the table, Shirley.

Thank you much, darlin'." He hoped for more than a smile and a nod from her, but that's what he got.

———

On the ride back, neither of them said anything for a mile or two until Charlie broke the silence. "You have to get a few pictures taken for a new driver's license and a passport. FedEx is someplace you can get your picture taken, and they're open late tonight. Be sure to get several sets. If you get them tonight, I'll get them from you tomorrow night after you get off work."

"I can do that."

"You know I'm going to get a license from either Texas, Alabama, or Florida. I'm gonna buy a boat and fish."

"So you said." Brian was thinking about where he'd go after the plan had been completed. "I'm thinking Idaho or Montana for me. A half mil will go a long, long ways out there. I'm going to get me some land out in the woods and hunt and fish. Hopefully find me somebody like Shirley. Only younger." He laughed.

"Besides the state, I need a town you want to use too. The guy I'm using will look up on the internet an apartment address in the town and state you use for the license and passport." Charlie looked at Brian, wanting to make sure he knew who was the boss. "Just let me know."

"Yep. I don't think we should go back to Cadwell's. Do you want to grab something to eat tomorrow night?"

"No. Just text me when you're headin' my way after you get off work. Meet me at the corner by Business 51 where you dropped me off the other night, and you can tell me then. Write it down so I won't get it wrong."

"Deal."

———

In his room in the halfway house, Charlie cracked open a window. Even though it was cold out, he wanted to smoke a cigarette. He lit a Marlboro

Red and pulled a chair over near the window. He took a big drag. Life was going to be good.

Sitting in the chair blowing smoke out the window, Charlie thought that what was left of his family would certainly be better off if he left. He knew his sister would never say it, but Christine didn't want him around either. When he had last seen her, he told her that he loved her very much, but her kids would be much better off growing up without him around. It was obvious that he was a bad influence and a good-for-nothing uncle. He told her he was going to stop seeing her and the kids. She had gotten emotional about his decision but understood that it was best for everyone. He hadn't seen much of Christine since he was a teenager anyway, and he'd only just met her two kids after getting out of Menard. His new life would benefit everybody. Yep, life was going to be good.

8

MARCH 31, 2018

Charlie's alarm had gone off a few minutes ago, and he was about to get out of bed and get ready for work when his phone buzzed: "Need to talk ASAP." Crap. They were not supposed to talk to each other, only text each other and only when needed. He replied: "OK. 30 minutes." If Brian needed to talk, something must have gone wrong, and that meant Charlie might have to reach out to Fred. He was not looking forward to that. Charlie sent another message: "Same place."

———

When the Dodge Ram stopped at the designated intersection, Charlie came out from the shadows of the bridge where he had been briefly standing, opened the door of the pickup, and got in. The light changed to green, and Brian quickly accelerated. Charlie looked over at him. "What's up, man? Did everything go okay?"

"I know. I know. We weren't supposed to meet again." Brian was excited as he continued south, looking in his rearview mirror to ensure they were not being followed. "I just needed to talk with you about what happened. It was freakin' crazy, man."

"What do you mean 'freakin' crazy?'" Charlie was getting worried that something might have gone wrong.

"I killed them! It went just as we planned. Or he planned. Whatever. Everything went perfectly!"

Charlie leaned over to look at the speedometer and saw that Brian was going about ten miles over the speed limit. "Slow down, Brian! Last thing we need is to be stopped riding together. Sweeney would have our asses back in jail so fast." Brian quickly slowed.

A few miles later, Brian pulled into the parking lot of a closed doughnut shop, killed the lights, and left the truck running. "Listen, man. Everything is cool," he said. "I did it. I killed 'em both. That is why I am freakin' out, man. It was so easy."

"I thought something was wrong," Charlie said. "You scared the crap out of me. Tell me how it went." He only had about forty-five minutes until his shift started, but he understood that Brian had to talk, and the only person he could talk to was him. "Tell me!"

"Well, I went to the garage to get a vehicle, as Fred planned. The first vehicle was a Ford pickup, and there are nine other vehicles there, just like you said there would be." Brian was talking fast. He took a deep breath and tried to calm down. "I opened the five-gallon bucket marked #1 that was in the bed of the pickup. When I looked inside, all the other things I needed to follow Fred's directions were in there. And there was the envelope with the specific instructions to follow, just like he said."

"Okay. So, everything was just like he said. Great!" Charlie lit a cigarette to calm his own nerves.

"Sorry, I just had to talk with you. Everything went just like you said he said it would. Can you give me a cig, man?" Charlie handed Brian a cigarette and his lighter. Brian lit the cigarette, took a deep drag, and handed the lighter back to Charlie. "Listen. I just wanted you to know that this guy is genius. After I changed into the clothes, I drove the pickup truck to the parking lot off GE Road and walked over to Clearwater Park. It was easy to find the house. I hid behind the tall bushes he said would be beside the garage. When they opened the garage door to park their SUV, I followed them in and circled around the backside of the other SUV. They closed the garage door and never saw me. When they got out of the SUV, they walked toward the door leading into the house, and that's when I came around the front of the other SUV and tased 'em. The wife was driving, so I was closest to the husband, which was how the guy said it would be." Charlie lit up another cigarette, and Brian cracked the window.

"You're jacked up, man. Is this why you wanted to meet?"

"Guess so. I don't know. I beat up guys before, and I shot the one guy in the bank robbery, but this was just crazy. I hit the guy in his right shoulder with the Taser, and he dropped like a rock. The wife turned her head, and I hit her with the Taser. The two of them were on the ground shakin'. I got the husband on his stomach, and I tied his hands behind his back first, then the wife, and then I tied up their feet. When the wife dropped, she hit the back of her head on the bumper of the SUV. Crazy, man. I placed a bag over the husband's head and duct-taped the bag to his neck and then did the same to the wife. I gotta tell you, seeing the look on their faces was priceless."

Charlie thought Brian was nuts. After the first two murders, it was like he was hooked. Like when alcohol was not enough, and his mom moved to crack and got addicted. He slowly tried to move as far away from Brian as he could. Once he got out of the truck, he never, ever wanted to see his friend again. "Did you put tape over their mouths to keep 'em quiet?"

Brian was beginning to calm down. "Yeah, I did. Did I not say that?" He took a drag of the cigarette. "It took a couple of minutes for them to die. The guy went first. Once I knew they were dead, I removed the tape and bags from their heads; then I took the scissors and cut off the zip ties and all their clothes. I saw there was a little bit of blood on the wife from where she hit her head from the fall. I got the Super Glue and did as the guy wanted. That was freaky, man. I had to hold each of their eyelids open for the glue to dry. Pretty quick, though. Then I took off their wedding rings. The wife had on earrings, and she also had a toe ring, so I took them too. I also got their driver's licenses out of their wallets as he wanted. I put all that stuff into the Ziploc bag. I dragged the husband outside through the door leading out to the pool. I opened the gate in the backyard and dragged him out to the tree right behind the house and propped him up against it like he wanted. I went back in and got the wife and then dragged her out and put her next to the guy. That all took maybe twenty minutes. What freaked me out the most was the little bit of blood on the bumper and garage floor." He looked at Charlie and put his hands up. "Like, what the hell do I do now?"

"What do you mean?"

"I was supposed to follow his directions. I wasn't sure what to do about the blood."

"What do you mean you weren't sure about what to do?"

"Should I leave it? Clean it up? I did everything he asked, but I was supposed to not deviate *one iota*. Since the blood was not in his plans, I decided to clean it up the best I could. I saw a bag of rags and a bottle of chlorine on a shelf in the garage. And that was the cleanest garage I ever saw." Charlie nodded. "I took some chlorine and one of the rags and cleaned up the blood on the bumper and the garage floor. There was a little bit of blood on the floor of the room I dragged her through, so I cleaned that up too." He turned and pushed what was left of the cigarette out the cracked window. "Then I poured Clorox where the blood had been on the floor in the garage. I double-checked that I hadn't left any of the jewelry or zip ties or used rags or anything in the garage and made sure the side door would be locked from the inside and then closed the door behind me. It was so cool, man. I almost can't wait another ten days to do it again."

"I can see that." Charlie knew Brian was certainly the right guy for the job. Charlie had grown up in a tough environment walking the streets of Chicago, so he saw more crap in a single day than Brian had seen in his lifetime, up until stepping through the gates of Menard. But the poor bastard caught up quickly. Menard turned him into a monster, and Charlie was now afraid of him.

"I just had to tell you what a high tonight was."

"I get it, man. But from now on, we cannot meet face-to-face again. Okay?"

"Sure. Sure. I know."

Charlie checked the time. "Can you drop me back at the bridge? I gotta get to work."

"Sure. Thanks for meeting. I just had to see you, man." Brian turned on the headlights and put the truck into drive. He pulled onto the highway and drove back to where he had picked up Charlie.

With his hand on the door handle ready to get out, Charlie cautiously looked across the seat at Brian. "Go home and get some sleep, okay? I'll text you with where you can pick up the cash in the morning." They bumped fists. Brian nodded, but Charlie guessed that it would be a sleepless night for the guy. Like a wild animal that got its first taste of blood, Brian wanted to kill again.

Charlie opened the door and quickly got out. He watched as Brian pulled away from the curb and then checked out his surroundings to make sure no one was around. He texted Fred: "One down, nine to go. No problems." The reply was quick: "Ok. $$ in morning." As he started his quick walk to his shift, Charlie thought about his new life and all the money he would have to spend on it. Life was going to be good.

9

APRIL 1, 2018

I t was a few minutes after 6 a.m. on Sunday, and Sasha Frank had been lying in bed awake for maybe an hour as countless random thoughts surged through his head. His partner, Janet, was sleeping next to him in the bed they'd shared for almost ten years in their home on the southeast side of Bloomington. He loved lying quietly next to her early in the morning and watching her sleep.

Sasha had three grown children with his first wife, Julie. They divorced after fifteen years of marriage. They got along a lot better since splitting up. He saw her and her husband, Dave, at birthday parties, soccer games, baseball games, and other events that today's grandparents go to for their grandchildren.

Sasha and Janet had been living together since shortly after his divorce from Karen, his second wife. Karen was fun for about three years, before she wore him out with her serial cheating. At the same time, she was overly needy and selfish. He hadn't seen Karen since she moved to Las Vegas after their divorce. Thankfully they hadn't had any children.

Janet had also been married before, for almost twenty years to a local businessman who committed suicide after hiding financial ruin from her and bankrupting his regional body shop business. They'd decided early on not to have children.

Sasha's phone rang. "Frank," he said.

Janet frowned, rolled over, and pulled the covers over her head.

"Good morning, Sasha," Todd Douglas said. "Sorry to wake you."

"You didn't, Todd. Hold on one second." Sasha got out of bed and quickly walked down the hallway that led from the bedroom to the kitchen. "What's up?"

"We got a call about twenty minutes ago from an early-morning jogger. The guy told 911 he found two naked bodies on the trail near the northeast corner of Clearwater Park. Man and woman. I sent Jenkins and Darby over to check it out. They confirmed that there were two bodies and then immediately started securing the area."

Sasha stopped when he reached the kitchen. "Geez."

"Yeah. No kidding."

"Any apparent cause of death? Deaths?"

"Nothing. The patrolmen said there were abrasions on the heels of both victims, and they're assuming the bodies were dragged there. There was redness on their wrists and ankles like they'd been tied up. And redness encircling both of their necks."

"Have you called the ME?" Sasha took a glass out of the cupboard.

"No, I called you right after Jenkins radioed me with the report. She'll be my next call, if you're okay with that."

Sasha filled the glass with orange juice. "Wait until I get there and access the scene. Beff will start driving me crazy the minute she arrives."

"Roger that. Can I call Jenkins and Darby to let them know you're on the way?"

"Yep. Make sure they cordon off as big an area as they can. And get enough guys over there to help them lock down and secure the area from any prying eyes. Erect pop-up screens to hide the bodies from view." He downed most of the juice.

"Will do." Todd laughed. "You know, all the local guys from the FBI, ATF, IBI, along with any others from the alphabet soup are going to start showing up. News media too."

"That's exactly why I want the area cordoned off. Keep them all out. Tell Jenkins it's his responsibility to ensure that no one—and I mean no one—gets into the scene before I get there. I'll be there as fast as I can."

Sasha quietly walked back to the bedroom and into the bathroom. He quickly applied deodorant and brushed his teeth, and as he was stepping out, Janet sat up and frowned. "What's going on?"

"Good morning, sweetheart." He reached back into the bathroom to grab what was left of the juice. "Our plans for this afternoon have to be post-poned." He sat on the edge of the bed beside her and gave her a soft kiss before handing her the glass.

"Why? What's up?"

"That was Todd at dispatch. It's a double homicide."

"Seriously?" Without letting him answer, she said, "Where? When was the last time someone was killed around here?"

"They found them over at Clearwater Park. Ashley Cummins was the last one?"

"That's right."

"Along with all the drug dealers." Sasha stood up, and Janet got out of bed and walked into the bathroom. He dressed in the walk-in closet and then headed for the bathroom. Janet had just flushed the toilet and was turning on the shower. "It's April Fools' Day," he said as he ran his electric razor over his cheek. "You don't think they're pulling my leg on it being a double homicide, do ya? They've pulled crap like that before, and they know I'm thinking about retiring."

"You're nuts thinking anyone would joke about a double homicide. Even if it is April Fools'." She took off the old Saint Louis Cardinals T-shirt she wore most nights to sleep and then opened the shower door to step in.

Sasha pulled her close, giving her a big kiss. "Have I told you lately how amazing you look and how much I love you?"

"Several times last night, if you remember. You need to get the heck out of here. You're wasting time, and you know it." Janet gave him a kiss on the cheek and stepped inside the shower. She waved goodbye before turning on the water.

———

A few blocks from their house, Sasha turned on his siren and lights. The blue lights embedded in the front and rear bumpers alerted traffic ahead of him to get out of the way of his unmarked SUV. What little early Sunday morning traffic there was pulled into the right lane and slowed as he sped past, electric razor in hand.

Sasha was the oldest child of a retired FBI agent and a former Soviet Union embassy employee in Washington, D.C., who defected to the United States. He was born in 1962. His father, Edward Joseph Frank, and mother, Alyona Anya Vasilevskaya, met during the beginning of the Cold War between the Soviet Union and the United States in 1960. His father was assigned by the FBI to turn his mother, who was an attaché at the Soviet Embassy in Washington, D.C., so she could provide the United States with intelligence as the Cold War was beginning to heat up. The Cuban Missile Crisis was about to take place, and the FBI was tasked with finding out as much as they could about what was happening inside the Soviet embassy.

The detective was named after his maternal grandfather, Sasha, a World War II hero who was the commander of an elite Soviet Union Rifle Division that was key to winning the long-fought Battle of Berlin. He and the men under his command were snipers responsible for killing thousands of German soldiers during the final battle, which led to the fall of Berlin and helped end the war. Sasha's namesake was one of a number of Soviet officers who achieved the highest state honor for distinctive service to society during the war. He was recognized as a hero of the Soviet Union. It seemed ironic to Sasha that his mother was considered a traitor to the Soviet Union, but a heroine in the United States.

Edward fell in love with Alyona while he was the case officer handling her defection and subsequent debrief. They married one year later. The FBI didn't believe the Soviets would target Alyona for death, as she was a low-level employee, although she provided a great deal of valuable information on the inner workings of the embassy. She gave the FBI a better understanding of who did what inside the embassy. To make Alyona a less visible irritant to the Soviets, the FBI wanted to get her far from Washington, D.C. Edward was offered and accepted a promotion to head the FBI field office in Springfield, Illinois.

Sasha was born and raised in Springfield, and after finishing high school he went to Illinois State University and received a bachelor's degree in law enforcement in 1984. After graduation he joined the Bloomington Police Department. A thirty-four-year department veteran, he was the only senior detective on the force.

Since joining the department right out of college as a patrolman, he had enjoyed early promotions, moving up in rank. Before becoming a detective, he'd served as a sergeant. He'd worked in street crimes, undercover in vice combatting prostitution, gambling, drugs, and pornography, and he had been the department's first K-9 officer. He'd considered retiring when he hit the thirty-five-year mark, but Janet was nine years younger, and she wouldn't be eligible for retirement for another six years, based on her time working for the City of Bloomington as the manager of the 911 Central Emergency Dispatch Center. What would he do all day while she was at work? Besides, if he further delayed retirement it meant more money for them long-term.

———

Sasha turned off his siren as he pulled the SUV into Clearwater Park. There were ten or so patrol cars, two ambulances, a fire truck, and several other vehicles, which he figured included a few of the alphabet folks. Obviously this was no April Fools' joke.

He headed toward the entrance to the park, where a single police officer was stationed in the middle of the drive. He'd been to the park a few times with his grandkids so they could play. The playground was about halfway in, and the pavement ended about a third of the way to the playground. It hadn't rained the past week, so he was expecting—hoping—that he could drive past the end of the pavement. Sasha rolled down his window and introduced himself to the officer standing guard in the parking lot.

"Hi, Detective. I'm Denise Walker." They shook hands. "Ben told me to expect you. Are you familiar with this park?"

"Yes, I am." He glanced out the windshield to the paved path that stretched out in front of him.

"Great. Ben, I mean Officer Jenkins, is stationed at a pavilion just west of the playground. He's parked next to a CSI truck. He told me to tell you that each entrance to the park is sealed off, and he has officers positioned in other areas along the perimeter. So far, we've had no issues with residents or press being nosy."

"Thanks, Denise. Nice meeting you."

Denise stepped back from the vehicle as Sasha slowly pulled forward.

He drove slowly down the path, reacquainting himself with the landscape and mentally taking notes as to the layout. When the pavement ended, he continued to drive on the grass toward where he knew he'd find Ben. He passed a sanded volleyball court and three basketball courts on his right and an open field on his left, which was used for games and practices for youth football and soccer. In front of him, several police officers had lined up along the west border of the park.

The CSI truck was parked beside the pavilion. Ben had done exactly what he had been trained and instructed to do—keep everyone outside the established perimeter of the crime scene.

Sasha got his SUV as close as he could to the large vehicle emblazoned with *CSI*. He kept his SUV running according to protocol and got out. He made a slow 360-degree turn to get a complete view of the park and the surrounding homes. It was just beginning to be daybreak. People were standing in their backyards, trying to see what the commotion was about. He walked toward Jenkins, who was stepping out of the back of the CSI vehicle.

"Morning, Ben," Sasha said. He was glad Ben had been first on scene. Ben Jenkins had been a member of the Bloomington Police Department for four years. He joined the force after spending six years in the U.S. Marines. Ben had served as a soldier for a year in Iraq and another one in Afghanistan. For the last two years of his military service, Ben had been an officer in the USMC Security Division, providing protection at the U.S. Embassy in Iraq and Afghanistan. Sasha knew that Ben had asked for the assignments. Ben's psychological evaluations always came back above normal, so he was never denied requested posts. They didn't come any better.

They shook hands. "Morning, Detective. I've got a black coffee for you if you're interested."

Sasha took the coffee and nodded. "Walk me through what you found."

They walked to the front of the CSI truck and stopped where no one would be able to hear them. "You know that 911 got the call just before 6 a.m. from the guy who found them? Less than an hour ago. By the way, how's Janet?"

"She's fine. She's always fine."

"Cool. Tell her hi." Ben looked down at the tablet he was holding and read from his notes. "The gentleman who found them is forty-two-year-old John Salazar. Darby has secured the phone, keys, and ID Salazar had on him. He's inside the truck. Darby is trying to keep him calm. I asked him if there was anyone he wanted to call, as I expected that he would be with us a while. We let him call his wife to let her know what happened and that he's with us at the scene. I also let her know we would drive him home when we're done with him.

"He's a local insurance agent. He was out for an early-morning run. Salazar lives over on East College just west of Stone Mountain Boulevard. Nice area. He says he usually runs a little over four miles, three or four times a week. He always takes the same route from his house across the street from Tipton Park. He says he crosses the street and runs the Constitution Trail south along Airport Road, turning west on GE Road to North Hershey, where he crosses GE and heads back east to the section of the trail that leads back into Clearwater Park. He circles the park before backtracking the route to then return to his house. He says it normally takes him about thirty minutes, maybe a little more. All in all, not a bad time."

Sasha nodded. "What else?"

"He entered Clearwater Park and took a right at the entrance, which takes him around the perimeter. He says a couple hundred feet from returning to the point where he entered the park, he saw something propped up against a tree. He noticed out the corner of his eye that it looked like something was somewhere it shouldn't be. He said it was like seeing a deer out in a field when you're driving on a country road. You know, driving and not looking, but somehow you see it."

Sasha nodded.

Ben glanced at his notes again. "Salazar slowed down and came to a stop on the path about twenty-five feet or so from the victim. He said it wasn't light out, but with the park lights still on he could see that it was a person who appeared to be sitting on the ground with their back up against the tree, naked. That's victim number one. He shouted and got no response. He shouted again before walking toward the victim, a man. Then he saw victim number two. A woman, also naked. He vomited. Doesn't appear he got any of it on either victim, but ME will confirm."

Sasha nodded again. "And?"

He looked at his notes again. "That's when he called 911. He was freaked out, as you would kinda expect. He says he's never seen a dead body before, other than at a funeral. He's calmed down a bit, but he's still freaked. I told Darby to wrap him in a thermal blanket, give him a bottle of water, and get him into the back seat to warm him up. I did a quick visual to confirm that they were both dead right there. I got within five feet of them. The eyes of both were wide open. When I shined my flashlight into their eyes, there was no response."

"Got it. And?"

"I radioed Todd and told him what I'd found. He told me that he was sending more troops over and I should secure the scene. I set the perimeter at 250 feet from the victims and positioned the officers who had arrived every couple hundred feet around the perimeter, telling them to let nobody in without my okay. No one should be inside the path that surrounds the park. You'll see that I taped off the area from the fences behind the house and at least fifty feet around where they were found. We also put up the screens you requested. Once the CSI truck got here, we got Salazar inside the truck and they got him hot coffee. He's inside there now. That's all I've got, Sasha."

"You started the log, but I'm taking charge of the investigation, so please make note of that now."

Ben nodded. "Sounds good."

Sasha got out his radio. "Todd?"

"Yes, Sasha."

"Please call in the ME."

Todd radioed back. "Will do. She may already be aware, as I got a call from her office a few minutes ago. Somehow, they got alerted that something was going on. I told them I was awaiting a call from you."

"No problem, Todd." Sasha turned to Ben. "Why don't you show me the bodies? After that we'll get with the ME and then I'll talk with Salazar. Do you have a CSI kit in the truck?"

"Yep. I'll get you one."

"I've got one. It's for you. You're with me."

"Roger that." Ben went to the CSI truck and returned with an extra CSI kit. "Okay. Show me."

They stopped where the crime scene tape was stretched across the path, about fifty feet from the bodies. They ripped open their CSI kits, and Ben watched Sasha pull out the coveralls and put them on. Sasha then put on the hair cover, booties, mask, and latex gloves. Ben followed the same procedure. They tossed the empty packages onto the paved path and began walking toward the bodies. Sasha stopped and turned to Ben. "Stay behind me." Ben nodded.

They shined their flashlights directly at the crime scene. A male victim was in a sitting position with his back against the tree trunk. Past the tree was a six- to seven-foot-high fence that looked like it ran across the backsides of two homes on the northeast corner of the park. There was a closed gate in the fence of the second house from the corner.

Sasha stopped when they had almost reached the tree. He'd spotted the second body, just as Ben had described. Sasha began the process he used in any investigation. He thought about the basic crime scene questions of who, what, when, where, how, and why. The same questions news reporters utilized, except that for Sasha the means, motive, and opportunity were key to solving the crime. Motive always involved revenge, greed, or need. What was the impulse behind this? He was confident that all questions would be answered over the next few hours, days, and weeks. Hopefully not months.

It was first light, but the flashlights provided them the opportunity to focus more closely on specific details. Obviously both victims were naked, as Ben had reported. He first pointed his flashlight at the head of the male victim, who looked to have been in his middle- to late thirties. It was hard to tell how tall he was, maybe a little less than six feet tall. He had neatly trimmed short black hair. His face had a five o'clock shadow. The man's eyes were wide open and bloodshot. The victim's neck was ringed with redness just below his Adam's apple. He had a great deal of body hair. There was also redness around the victim's wrists. He moved the flashlight beam to the man's ankles and saw redness there as well. The abrasions pointed to his being tied up at some point, but there was no evidence of restraints at the scene. Cuts and dried blood were on the victim's heels. Perhaps he'd been dragged to the tree?

Sasha turned his focus to the woman propped up against the tree and leaning into the man. She appeared to be six to eight inches shorter than the man. Again, it was hard to tell by the way they were positioned. Her head was resting on the man's left shoulder. Sasha thought it looked like they were sitting up in bed watching a movie together, as her eyes were also wide open and bloodshot. She had short blond hair and the same redness around her neck, wrists, and ankles. She also had visible abrasions and dried blood on the heels of her feet.

Sasha pulled out his phone and took face pictures of both victims. He motioned Ben to step back away from the bodies and took full-body shots.

"Ben?" Darby called on the radio. "ME's arrived. Can I bring her over?"

Ben looked at Sasha, and he nodded back his okay. "Yes, Darby. Is she by herself?"

"Her team is with her, but she says she will be alone for a first look before the team heads over. We're heading your way now. I've assigned Officer Davis to stay with Mr. Salazar."

"Roger that, Darby. Thanks."

Sasha knew the ME very well. Her name was Elizabeth Turner, and she went by Beff. One of her younger siblings couldn't pronounce "Beth" as a child, so "Beff" stuck even forty years later. Beff was forty-four years old, a medical doctor and forensic pathologist with an impeccable record as the ME for McLean County. She'd been in the role for the past six years and was highly respected within the city, county, and state law enforcement communities. She was married to a local attorney, and they had one child. Sasha and Beff had worked together on two previous investigations. Both were deaths that involved work accidents. One was an employee electrocuted attempting to repair an outdoor sign, and the other was an employee at a local grain elevator who had suffocated while working in one of the company silos. Sasha occasionally saw her at city functions, but other than those occasions, they rarely interacted.

Sasha asked Ben to give her a brief update on what transpired with Salazar, and then he would give her his update on what he found at the scene. She'd probably want to see the crime scene by herself before waving both—or maybe just Sasha—over to further confer. Sasha mused that she may not even be interested in their input. Once she was done with her review, she'd radio her team to come over with the equipment they would need to fully document the scene before having the bodies removed for further investigation and autopsies.

"Hi, Sasha. Long time no see," Beff said. "We have to stop meeting like this." She laughed.

Sasha took off his right glove, and they shook hands. "True. Very true. But here we are. You've already met Darby. I'd like to introduce you to Officer Ben Jenkins." Beff nodded, and the two shook hands after Jenkins removed his right glove. "Jenkins and Darby were first on scene after 911 received the call from Mr. Salazar, the man who found the two bodies while out for a morning run. Do you want Ben to provide you further information?"

"I would rather not. At this time, I'm only concerned with the work my team and I need to do. We'll be taking pictures, ensuring that we secure the evidence on scene and that it is collected before we move the bodies for autopsy. We will make determinations with the evidence and facts we find. We can compare notes at the autopsy. I assume that you'll want to attend?"

At first Sasha was annoyed that she wasn't interested in any information other than what she and her team assembled. But then he realized he'd also prefer to rely on information he found relating to the investigation, with input when needed from others. Beff's input after she completed her part of the investigation, based on evidence she and her team found, would be key to the overall investigation and solving this crime. "That makes sense, Beff. Let me know if there's anything you need from us. We will stay here on scene. I look forward to your letting me know whatever you can before you head back to the barn for the autopsy. That could give us a faster start to the investigation." He hoped his use of "us" would help make Beff believe it was a team effort.

Beff nodded. "Absolutely. My team will take hair, DNA samples, and evidentiary swabs from the three of you along with anyone else in your department who has been within fifty feet of my crime scene. I'd also ask that you give the items you wore from each of your CSI kits so they can be bagged by my team. They'll do that before you leave, please."

She pulled out a pair of latex gloves she had in the right front pocket of the head-to-toe CSI suit she was wearing over her street clothes. She then pulled the cord on the hoodie, leaving only her eyes exposed. Next she put on a pair of goggles. She wouldn't be adding any forensic material to the crime scene. After taking one quick 360-degree view of the surroundings, she looked at Sasha. "I do have one question. Do you know who the victims are?"

"Not yet. Both are naked and there are no IDs visible at the scene. We'll canvass the neighborhood surrounding the park to see if anyone can ID them from description. If not, I have headshots."

"Thanks, Sasha. I'll let you know when we're done and ready to transport. I'm guessing we'll be working the crime scene for the next two hours, absolute minimum."

Beff met her team walking up with equipment they'd use to investigate the scene. She talked to them in a low voice. Sasha assumed she was telling them what each was responsible to process at the crime scene. She finished giving them instructions and turned to walk toward the two victims. Her team immediately started getting their equipment ready so they could begin their individual tasks once she signaled them to join her.

Sasha watched Beff walk slowly to where the victims were positioned. He turned to Darby. "Stay here and make sure no one comes into the area until the ME and her team are finished with their investigation and are ready to transport the bodies. If anything seems hinky, let me know ASAP. Okay?"

"Yes, sir."

"I'll send someone over with some coffee for you." Sasha looked at Ben. "Beff's team needs to collect potential evidence from us, and then we'll talk to Mr. Salazar." The forensic team took DNA and hair samples from each of them. They also took the overalls, booties, gloves, mask, and hair covers they'd been wearing and placed them in individual evidence bags. Forensics would use what was collected to exclude possible contamination they left at the scene.

10

M r. Salazar was sitting in one of the command chairs of the CSI vehicle alongside Officer Davis. The CSI team had already taken DNA and evidence swabs from Salazar, who was wrapped in the thermal blanket he'd been given when the officers arrived. It wasn't really that cold out, but in running shorts and a long-sleeved T-shirt, Salazar needed the thermal blanket, even inside the truck. He probably was still experiencing shock as well. Salazar was holding a cup of coffee and staring blankly at the floor of the truck.

Officer Davis stood and shook hands with Sasha. "Morning, Detective."

"Good morning, Billy. Good to see you. Do you mind taking a cup of coffee over to Darby?"

"No problem." He poured coffee into a Styrofoam cup and left the truck.

"Are they keeping you warm and that coffee cup refilled, Mr. Salazar?" Ben asked.

"Yes, they are. Thanks." He looked pale.

"I'd like to introduce you to Senior Detective Sasha Frank. He will be leading the investigation into what's happened. He has some questions for you. Are you comfortable talking with him now?"

Sasha stepped over and reached out to shake Salazar's hand. Salazar remained seated and shook Sasha's hand. "It's nice to meet you, Mr. Salazar. Can I call you John?"

"Yes, Detective."

"I understand from Officer Jenkins that you were out for a run today and came upon the two victims." Salazar nodded. "I know that you've answered a number of questions Officer Jenkins asked, but I'd like to ask you some questions and hear your story from when you first saw the bodies in the park this morning. Would that be okay, John?"

"Sure." Salazar sat up straighter in the chair.

Sasha took out his phone to record the interview. "I want to inform you that I will be recording your statement. This is standard procedure." Salazar nodded. Sasha opened the recorder app on his phone and started the interview. "It is 7:23 a.m., April first. This is my first interview with John Salazar regarding what he encountered today at Clearwater Park located on the east side of Bloomington. Could you please state your name for the record?"

Salazar shifted in his chair. "My name is John Salazar."

"Let's start with your telling me when you got up this morning."

"I run three or four times a week. I set my alarm for 5:35 a.m. I'm normally out the door of my house within ten minutes after waking. I have an app on my mobile that tracks my run each day. Today was like any other day." Salazar paused. "At least up until I found the bodies."

Sasha and Ben could tell that Salazar was picturing the scene in his mind. He shuddered. "I know this is hard," Ben said. "Please go on."

"I keep at a pretty good pace during my run. I was making good time when I entered the park from GE Road. I ran the path around the park, and it was after I passed the playground that I first noticed something that seemed out of place. As I got closer, I slowed down and saw what looked like a person sitting with their back up against a tree. I stopped on the path about thirty or so feet away from the tree. The person looked naked. I yelled, 'You okay?' I got no response. So I yelled again. Still no response. I slowly walked toward the tree, and when I was maybe ten or so feet away, I could see it was a man. He was kinda looking off to the side, so I circled around so that I could see his face. That's when I noticed the woman. It scared the hell out of me, and I stepped back and yelled at them again. Neither of them moved." Salazar fidgeted in his chair and took another drink of coffee. "I stepped closer, and that's when I could see . . . could see that their eyes were both open and looking at me. They really weren't looking at me. I backed away from them fast, turned and vomited. I walked back to the path and called 911. I waited on the path until the two policemen showed up."

Sasha was pleased with Salazar's ability to recall his experience. His statement matched what he had told Ben earlier. When the case went to trial, he should be a great witness.

Salazar looked straight at Sasha. "They were both naked, sitting on the ground, leaned up against the tree. Their eyes were wide open. It was like, like they were staring at something out in front of them, but they weren't. They were both dead. It really scared the hell out of me."

"Did you touch either of the bodies?"

"Hell no!" Salazar quickly replied, shuddering.

"I needed to ask. You didn't take any pictures with your phone, did you?".

Salazar glanced over at the plastic bag containing his belongings that was sitting on the counter on the other side of the truck. "No, sir. And you can take a look if you'd like." He took another drink of coffee.

"Yes, I would like to confirm what you've told us about taking no pictures. This is just part of our investigation. At the same time, Mr. Salazar, I'd like to also confirm that there aren't any texts, social media postings, or email related to what you encountered this morning. Would you allow us the opportunity to confirm all of that? If you do, we will be able to give you back the items in the evidence bag."

"That's fine. I'm telling you the truth," Salazar replied, obviously annoyed that Sasha inferred he might be hiding something.

"Please understand that this is normal protocol. We must ensure that what you've told us is absolute fact. I'm not questioning that you're telling the truth. When we go to trial to convict whoever committed these two murders, attorneys for the murderer will probably ask you questions about your actions after finding the bodies. We don't want to give anyone the chance to say we didn't cross the t's and dot the i's. This is nothing more than that. We will be able to show that we have absolute proof that you're telling us the truth," Sasha said in a manner that would leave no doubt that he did indeed believe Salazar. "I hope you understand that."

"Okay. Sorry. It's just that—"

Officer Davis returned to the CSI truck and stood silently next to Ben.

Sasha quickly added, "Mr. Salazar, we absolutely believe you." He looked at Ben. "Could you please hand Mr. Salazar his phone?"

Ben reached over and picked up a package containing a pair of latex gloves that was sitting on the counter. "Certainly." He put on the gloves, picked up the evidence bag, opened it, and handed Salazar his mobile phone.

Salazar quickly keyed in the six-digit security code and held the phone out to Sasha. Sasha opened a package of latex gloves and put on just one glove for his left hand.

Sasha took the mobile phone from Salazar. "Thank you, John. We are ending the interview with John Salazar at 7:49 a.m." Sasha stopped the recording using his right hand. He looked at Salazar. "We will be right back." Sasha turned to Billy. "Could you please stay with Mr. Salazar?" He put on a glove on his right hand.

"Yes, sir."

Sitting at a table in the pavilion, Sasha touched the icon for photos. It didn't open. Trying again, he quickly realized that the latex gloves he was wearing wouldn't allow him to operate the phone. He laughed to himself. He knew that wearing gloves wouldn't allow the capacitive sensor to activate. A small electrical current that runs through our bodies gives us the sense of touch. A phone screen uses that small electrical current to open apps. He'd learned that at a law enforcement symposium he'd attended in Chicago a few years ago. "Can you ask one of the CSI techs for a stylus?" he asked Ben.

Ben went to the CSI vehicle and quickly returned with a stylus.

Sasha took the stylus and touched the photos icon. He scanned the pictures and saw that the most recent pictures were from two days ago and appeared to be a number of inside and outside pictures of a house. The house was not furnished. Not that they'd have anything to do with the investigation, but he'd ask Salazar what those were. Sasha next tapped the stylus on the messages icon and saw that the last text was to Maria Salazar. "Is Salazar's wife's name Maria?"

"Yes."

Sasha tapped on the mail icon. Salazar had two email accounts. One personal and the other business. He scrolled through the inbox of the personal email. There was nothing noteworthy. He moved to Drafts and there were none. He looked in the Sent folder, and the most recent was from last night to a friend whom he had forwarded an ESPN article to on the Chicago Cubs spring training. Sasha grew up a Saint Louis Cardinal fan. He hated the Cubs. The most recent folder in the Trash folder was from last night. The original email from ESPN. He also didn't find anything in the business email folders. He checked Recents in the telephone icon; the last three calls were marked missed and were from his wife, probably wanting him to call her again to find out where he was. The next was the call to his wife letting her know he wouldn't be home from his run as usual. Before that to 911, and then some calls from last night. Sasha pulled out his iPhone and with the stylus tapped on the camera icon. He snapped a picture of the list of recent calls. He checked voicemail, Facebook, and LinkedIn. Nothing. There weren't other apps on the phone that looked like they'd allow sending pictures, but he'd have a CSI tech fully check out Salazar's mobile.

"He's not going to like it, but we're going to have to take the phone into evidence even though there isn't anything of interest on it," Sasha said. "I'll explain that to him."

In the CSI truck, Billy and Salazar were talking baseball. Geez, both Cubs fans. Sasha couldn't imagine.

"Hello again, Mr. Salazar," Sasha said. "I'd like to ask you a question about the pictures of the house on your mobile. Can you tell me who owns this house?"

"I'm an insurance agent, and one of my policyholders called me to let me know he and his wife bought a new house. I have to take pictures of the outside of the home to underwrite the policy. He asked me to take pictures of the inside too."

"I apologize, but I'm going to have to take your phone into evidence." Salazar looked blankly at him. "There aren't any phone calls you made other than those related to our investigation, but I will need to keep it until the district attorney says I can return it to you. I apologize for the inconvenience, but I hope you understand. I'm sure you've backed up your phone, so you'll just have to get a phone to replace this one and download the backup. If you haven't backed up recently, CSI will back it up and inform you when they've done so. Again, I apologize for the inconvenience."

Salazar nodded. "Okay, I guess."

"Thank you for understanding. There are three voicemails on the phone that appear to be from your wife that you evidently haven't played. Do you mind putting your phone on speaker and playing those for us all to hear now? I'd appreciate it if you'd start with the first before moving to the second and finish with the most recent voicemail. Okay?"

"Certainly."

In the first message, they heard Maria Salazar ask her husband if he was okay. The second message came a few minutes later, asking the same question. In the last message she asked her husband to please call her as soon as he could, as she was very concerned for him. After the last voicemail finished playing, Salazar handed Sasha his mobile phone.

"Thank you, John. I'm going to have Ben take you back to the police station and ask that you write down what you've told us. This will be your official statement for the record. If you remember anything, regardless of how minor it might seem, please add that and note that it was something new you remembered. Can you do that for us?"

"Yes, I can." Salazar paused. "But could I go home first to see my wife and change clothes?"

"Absolutely." Sasha turned toward Ben. "Could you please drive Mr. Salazar to his home before you take him to the station? Once Mr. Salazar has provided us a written statement, you can then take him back home."

"Certainly, Detective."

"Can my wife go with me to the station?"

"No, I'm sorry, she can't. I hope you understand." Sasha was firm and waited for Salazar's response.

"Okay."

"You're under no obligation to do what I ask, but we would appreciate it very much if you would not talk with anyone about what you saw today. When we find a suspect and then prosecute that person for these two murders, anything that you may have said to anyone else could be used by the defense to destroy your testimony and credibility to the jury. I hope you understand."

"I understand, Detective. I won't talk to anyone other than my wife."

"Yes, but please don't talk with anyone else. If you need to talk to a doctor, priest, pastor, rabbi, imam, or some other religious or professional person to help you through what you've experienced today, please do that. We encourage you to do so."

"Are you ready to go, sir?" Ben asked. Salazar nodded, stood, and reached out to shake hands with Sasha. Salazar looked as if he was ready to let go of pent-up emotions. They walked over to Jenkins's police cruiser, Ben opened the passenger front door, and Salazar got in.

———

It was getting close to 8 a.m. A lot had transpired since Sasha received the initial call from Todd less than two hours ago. He turned to walk back to the CSI van. He'd ask one of the technicians to print out copies of the two photos he'd taken of the victims. Then he'd call Todd and ask him to assign four patrolmen to meet Sasha here at the CSI vehicle, where he'd tell them to canvass the residents surrounding the park to see if any of them recognized the two victims. He stared at the picture of the female victim and asked out loud to himself, "Who are you, and why did someone do this to you? I promise you that I will find the person who did this, and they will be brought to justice." He planned on keeping that promise.

11

Beff turned on the camera and microphone built into the goggles she was wearing. "Testing. Testing. Are you getting the video and audio transmission?"

Steve Hudson had been working with Beff for the past five years and was one of her most experienced employees. "All's good."

"I'm going to start now."

She moved slowly toward the bodies, shining her flashlight on the crime scene. "My name is Elizabeth Turner, and I'm the medical examiner for McLean County, Illinois. Today is April first, and I'm at the northeast corner of Clearwater Park in Bloomington, Illinois. I'm investigating the discovery of two bodies, one male and one female." The equipment would provide her, her team, and the prosecutors with documentation of the initial stages of her investigation, but she thought narrating the investigation might also be helpful.

"Both bodies are naked. Their buttocks and legs are positioned on the ground with backs leaning against the trunk of the tree. Once we've moved the bodies to the autopsy room, we will be able to determine whether these two were placed here pre- or post-mortem, but my initial belief is that they were positioned at this location post-mortem." She shined her flashlight at the male. "The male is positioned against the tree trunk, and the female is positioned so that she is leaning against the male's left shoulder. The eyes of both victims are open, and it appears that glue has been applied to the eyelids to hold them open. I estimate that the male is between thirty and thirty-five years of age. The same for the female. There are obvious signs of redness at the ankles, wrists, and necks of the two bodies. The redness on the ankles and wrists suggests that the bodies were tightly bound before death. Small cuts visible on the ankles and wrists suggest that the restraints may have been thin, possibly plastic. It appears that both wore rings, as there are marks consistent with those that wear wedding rings on their left ring fingers. Neither are currently wearing rings. The female also may have worn a ring on the second toe on her left foot, as there are similar markings there. There is evidence of abrasions and blood on the heels of both bodies." The two were probably dragged to this site from somewhere close.

Beff turned to her team. "Are you ready to approach the scene?"

"We're ready," Steve said.

"I'll let you know shortly when you can start." Beff turned back to the bodies. "I'll now take initial readings of body temps." She removed a thermometer from a side pocket of her suit and read the temperature it showed, then placed it under the right armpit of the male. She waited approximately two minutes. "The male's body temperature is 42.9 degrees Fahrenheit. Steve, what is the current outside temperature?"

"The current ambient temperature is 42 degrees Fahrenheit."

"After a human life ceases, the body loses its average normal temperature of 98.6 degrees Fahrenheit until reaching the environmental temperature of its location. Since the body temperature has reached the current outside temperature, I should be able to determine an approximate time of death when we get back to the lab." She put the thermometer into a plastic evidence bag and then removed another thermometer from her side pocket and placed it under the left armpit of the female. "The female body temperature is 42.1 degrees Fahrenheit. We will take rectal readings before we transport the bodies."

Beff moved the light over the female body. "I'm seeing clear signs of livor mortis on the female body located on her left leg and buttock above where the body is touching the grass. Livor mortis begins appearing within the first thirty minutes after death and generally is not initially visible for approximately two hours. The color intensifies over time. The intensity of the coloration I'm observing suggests that the female died at least eight hours ago. Possibly longer." She shined the light up the back of the female and to her head and noticed the red ring that encircled her neck. The female had short blond hair. Beff thought that if she had seen the woman on the street, she would have stopped her to ask where she got her hair styled. She pointed the flashlight at the ground. "As you can see, there are impressions in the soil near the tree that appear to be from a boot or shoe. Our photographer will get clear photos of the impressions." Beff waved her hand, and the photographer gave her a thumbs-up.

"There's a small trickle of dried blood on the lower left portion of the back of her hairline above the redness that encircles the neck. I'm going to use a small probe to see if I can determine the source." She began slowly investigating the area. "There are clear signs of a small laceration and swelling on the upper left side of the skull. There is a small amount of blood matted in the hair, and I can see dried blood on the tree trunk where the head is resting against it."

Beff shined the light into the female's eyes. "As you can clearly observe in the eyes of the female, there are obvious signs of subconjunctival hemorrhaging. The bodies have redness around the neck, which denotes that they may have been strangled or were denied oxygen in some other manner to cause death. Loss of oxygen can cause the rupture of blood vessels or subconjunctival hemorrhaging." She moved the light to the male. "You can clearly see the same subconjunctival hemorrhage that has occurred in the male. I believe that we will find that the male and female died due to the loss of oxygen either by strangulation or some other means." Beff turned toward her team. "It's time to begin working the scene so that we can transport the two bodies back to the lab as soon as possible."

She stepped back from the two bodies as her team moved forward in a coordinated manner. The evidence photographer began taking countless photographs of the overall scene and individual bodies as she had been trained. She also photographed specific crime scene evidence found by the others on the team. She took a number of pictures of numerous impressions made in the soil, and for each photo she placed a device on the ground to show the dimensions of the impression.

Beff was proud of her team and the work they did. They collected grass, tree bark, and soil from the scene, along with evidence captured on tape and countless swabs of both bodies, placing each piece of sample evidence into bags that were cataloged and then logged into a laptop computer.

The team also took detailed measurements of each body, the area around the tree, and the tree trunk. Shortly after they began the investigation, they measured and outlined an area ten feet in circumference surrounding the immediate crime scene.

When the team completed their collection of evidence, Beff stepped forward to move the bodies. With the help of Steve, she began with the female body. The body was in rigor mortis. Beff turned it slightly, and she took another body temperature reading and asked one of the team to note it for the record. She asked Steve to hold the body still so that she could look more closely at the laceration she had found on the back of the victim's head. She shined the flashlight and lightly probed the immediate area around the wound and asked one of her team to step over to take evidence from the area. It was too early to determine if the wound occurred before or after death.

"I'm done, Steve," Beff said. "Let's put her in the bag." Both were very respectful while placing the corpse into the body bag. As they were moving the male, Beff said, "Help me turn the body on its side. I see redness just below his left shoulder on his back." She used her fingers to brush the thick body hair out of the way for a better look. "There are two small holes here, and both show obvious signs of redness. I believe that these are wounds caused by a Taser, possibly used to subdue him prior to having his wrists and ankles secured." The evidence photographer moved into position to take several pictures, and then Beff took a body temperature of the male. "Let's put the body into the bag, and then let's take a better look at the female before we transport. Okay?"

Beff found the female had similar holes on her back. "I don't know how I missed this wound on her back under her right shoulder. I believe that she was also tased."

12

Beff was removing the last of her gear when Sasha approached with coffees. It looked like there was more than enough for her, her team, and Darby. How thoughtful, she thought. "I'm sure hoping that one of those is for me."

"You know it. What's your fancy, Beff? Black? Milk or sugar or both?"

"Check with my team and Darby. I'll take whatever is left. I'm not picky."

Sasha distributed the cups and returned to Beff. "Well, I hope you like coffee with cream and sugar, because that's all that's left."

"Perfect. Just the way I like it."

"I bet it's not. Would you like to share what we each have learned since we last spoke?"

"Do you want to go first or should I?" she asked.

"You go first."

Beff sipped the coffee. She had never had it with cream and sugar, and she hoped this would be the last time. She shared a detailed description of her findings and finished with "I hope to have more details once the autopsies are complete." She took another sip of the wretched drink and asked, "Do you want to attend the autopsy?"

"I don't think so. It will be someone working with me."

"That works. So what do you have?"

"We have tentative identification of the two bodies, and if we can confirm their IDs, the two live in the house directly behind you." Sasha lifted his coffee cup and motioned toward a two-story house on the edge of the park.

"Seriously?"

"A resident two doors south told us that the two are husband and wife. Tentatively identified as thirty-five-year-old Warren Zumwalt and his thirty-four-year-old wife, Maria, maiden name Matthews. The neighbor says they have no children. We should learn more when we get the warrant to enter the residence." Sasha looked at his watch. "We should have that shortly."

"We have checked social media accounts and believe that it is indeed the Zumwalts' house. I have officers riding over to get confirmation and provide notice to those whom we believe are family members, possibly siblings. We should have confirmation shortly."

"Sounds good. Let me know when I can send a team over to the residence so we can help with collecting evidence, and let me know who you'll be sending over as an observer as soon as you can."

"It will be Detective Chris Watkins. Do you know Chris?" Beff didn't acknowledge the question. "He's a good guy. He'll be helping me with my investigation. I will let you know if for some reason it's not him. Okay?"

"Deal. I look forward to meeting him." She finished her coffee.

"I'll take that." Sasha reached for the empty cup. "I'll make sure next time to have a black coffee for you . . . but hopefully there won't be a next time."

————

Chris greeted Sasha with good news as he entered the CSI vehicle. "I've got a patrolman waiting at the judge's office to bring us the warrant that Judge Carlton signed off on," Chris said. "We should have it in ten minutes or so."

"Great! I need you to head over to the ME's office to observe the autopsies on Mr. and Mrs. Zumwalt." From this moment until the SOB who killed the couple was found and convicted, Sasha would make sure everyone used the names of the victims to humanize the crime in the community. "Beff will be recording the autopsies so I can see them later, but I want you there to ask any questions you feel are appropriate while she's conducting them. Okay?"

"Certainly."

"And if you find out anything that you believe I should know, call me ASAP. I'll be at the Zumwalt residence."

13

Sasha was standing beside Officer Scott Buckley, who was attempting to pick the lock on the side door of the garage at the Zumwalt residence. His radio came to life. "Detective Frank. Come in, Detective Frank." Sasha keyed his radio. "Frank here."

"Could you come around back and meet us at the gate? You've got to see this." Sasha told Buckley to keep trying to pick the lock, but not to enter until he returned. He jogged around the front of the house, through the next-door neighbor's yard to the south, and entered Clearwater Park. He ran to the opened gate, guessing that someone must have gone over the fence. Inside he saw the patrolmen standing in the grass next to the concrete surround of the Zumwalts' pool. He walked over to where they were standing. "What's up?"

One of the patrolmen pointed at the concrete. "We thought you'd want to see this."

What looked to be blood trails ran across the concrete. It certainly appeared that the couple had been dragged from the back of the house, across the concrete, and out the gate at the back of the property to the tree.

Sasha called Chris Watkins on his mobile phone. "I wanted to let you and Beff know that we've discovered what appears to be dried blood on the concrete pool surround at the Zumwalt residence. There are two distinctive trails that lead from the pool to a back door of the residence." Sasha heard a voice come across his radio. "Door's unlocked, Detective."

"Thanks, Sasha," Chris said. "Beff is currently working on Mr. Zumwalt, and she hasn't found anything that we don't already know." Beff signaled Chris that she wanted to say something. "I'm going to put you on speaker."

"It's early, but I believe that Mr. Zumwalt was suffocated and not strangled," Beff said. "I have found what appears to be tape residue on his neck, leading me to believe that a plastic bag was put over his head and secured with tape, effectively cutting off his oxygen supply and causing death."

"That's great info. Have you sent a forensic team out this way?"

"They should be there shortly."

"Great. I'll talk to you if I find anything at the Zumwalts'."

"Roger that. Later." Chris ended the call.

Sasha told the two patrolmen searching the backyard that someone from the forensic team would soon be there to take pictures and collect evidence. "I'd like one of you to stand guard at the gate and the other to stay with the forensic team."

Officer Phil Ashcroft stepped closer to Sasha. "I'll move to the gate, and Johnson can stay here with the forensic team, if you're okay with that."

"That works. Thanks"—Sasha glanced at the patrolman's name tag—"Officer Ashcroft." He had never met Ashcroft or Johnson.

Sasha returned to his SUV and removed a CSI kit from the back. He opened the kit and put all of the items on except the booties and latex gloves. He headed for the side garage door. Buckley was standing there with two other officers when Sasha walked up. "Do you want us to follow you in, Detective?" Buckley asked.

"No, I don't want any of you to possibly disturb the scene. I'll do a quick recon of the house. Good work getting this unlocked." Buckley nodded, and Sasha put on the booties and latex gloves, pulled out his flashlight, drew his service weapon, and turned the doorknob. He shined the beam from his flashlight into the garage, wincing at the distinct odor of chlorine.

A Hyundai Santa Fe SUV was parked a few feet away from him. Janet had a 2018 Santa Fe the same color blue as this one. Maybe this one was the same year. Another vehicle was parked on the other side of the SUV. He slowly entered and scoped the space with the flashlight beam. It might have been the neatest garage he'd ever seen. Certainly, it was neater than his own.

He closed the door behind him and saw to his left a riding lawn mower parked against the wall. The yard didn't seem big enough to require a rider, but it seemed everyone wanted a rider nowadays. He shined his flashlight across the ceiling and spotted a dropdown stairway that would lead to a storage area above the garage. He'd be sure to point that out to the forensic team.

A storage system stretched across the back wall. He could now see that the other vehicle was another Santa Fe SUV, this one red. There was a space of about eight feet between the SUVs. The fingertips of a golf glove hanging from the ceiling rested on the windshield of each car, apparently there to alert the driver when to stop.

He headed toward the door that he guessed would take him into the house. As he crossed in front of the red SUV, he kicked something and sent it sliding on the concrete floor. A shoe. Its mate lay between his other foot and a pile of clothing—two pairs of slacks, two bright blue shirts, four socks, undergarments, two jackets, and another pair of shoes. He bent down and looked closely at one of the shirts. "Warren" was stitched in white across the left front breast pocket. Below the name was a bowling ball patch.

Sasha turned the doorknob, and the door opened into what appeared to be a combination laundry and mudroom. A full-size washer and dryer were on the wall across from him, and along the wall to his right hung coats on hooks. The floor was gray linoleum. Along the far wall was a wooden door with a window on the top half with closed blinds. He pushed open the door to his left and saw a shower stall inside. It must have been for swimmers leaving the pool. He stepped fully into the room and saw an opening leading to the kitchen.

He flipped two light switches, illuminating the room he was in and the garage. He closed the door behind him and walked through the opening that led to the kitchen, his gun drawn. He quickly passed through the neat and orderly kitchen into the family room. A pair of sliding doors led out to the patio and pool area. Next there was a formal dining room, followed by a living room and a two-story front entry foyer. Nothing seemed out of place.

He climbed the stairs that led to the second floor and walked through what he assumed was the master bedroom, en suite bathroom, and two walk-in closets. He moved on to check a hall bath, two guest bedrooms and closets, then onto another room with two desks. Two large computer monitors sat atop one of the desks. One of the Zumwalts could have been a gamer. The screen-saver program rotated through pictures of the couple's wedding photos, them at the beach, hiking in the mountains, riding horses, and posing with family and friends. The pictures were confirmation that the two bodies found in the park were unquestionably Warren and Maria Zumwalt. Sasha said a quick prayer for their souls. The upstairs was as neat and orderly as the downstairs.

"Detective?" Sasha keyed his police radio. "Yes, Buckley."

"The ME team wants to know if they can enter the property."

"I'll come to talk with them when I'm done."

Sasha returned to the mudroom and opened the door that led out to the patio and pool area. Looking out onto the concrete patio that extended maybe fifteen feet or so before the pool cover, he saw similar markings to the ones they found on the pool surround.

Two members of Beff's forensic team were taking pictures and processing the blood evidence that his officers had found a short time ago. He checked the door handle and found that the lock was set; no one would have been able to enter without a key. He shouted out to the officer watching Beff's team members work the scene. "Officer Johnson!" Johnson looked toward him. "This door was locked, and I'm going to keep it that way. I'll let the rest of the forensic team know." Johnson gave him a thumbs-up.

He made another quick circle around the interior perimeter of the garage with the flashlight, but he found nothing. The chlorine stung his nostrils and eyes, and his throat was beginning to burn. He was ready to be done with the garage and back in fresh air. As he was giving the clothing a second look, he wondered why chlorine had been needed if, as Beff believed, the Zumwalts had been suffocated. Maybe blood had spurted from the laceration on Mrs. Zumwalt's skull?

As he stepped out of the garage, squinting in the sunlight, he noticed a neighbor standing in her upstairs window watching the cluster of people outside the Zumwalt house. He nodded at her, and she quickly backed away from the window and closed the curtain. Sasha would have someone interview her to see if she saw or heard anything suspicious.

The forensic team was anxious to get into the residence and start processing

73

the scene. Sasha filled them in on what he'd seen and then told them they could go in but asked them to be respectful of the Zumwalts.

He stretched and breathed deeply, and Buckley offered him a cigarette. He didn't smoke but took one anyway. He asked the officer whether he had noticed if there was any evidence that someone else had tried picking the lock before he had this morning.

Buckley took out his lighter and handed it to Sasha. "No, sir, I did not." Sasha nodded, lit the cigarette, and handed the lighter back to the patrolman.

"No, you didn't see any evidence that someone had previously attempted to pick the lock, or no, you didn't think about it until I asked you?"

Buckley smiled. "No, Detective. That was the first thing we were taught to look for when I learned how to pick locks at the State Police Academy training seminar that I attended last year down in Springfield. There was no evidence of prior tampering with the lock, but if there had been, I would have brought that to your attention, and we would have taken photographic evidence showing that fact. If you look now, there aren't any signs that I picked the lock." Sasha nodded. "I'm that good." They both laughed.

"Thanks for the cigarette, Buckley. Let me know if the folks inside want to talk. I'll be in my SUV. I need to write up what I saw inside the house."

As he walked around to the driver's door of his SUV, Sasha scanned the residential street. A few people stood outside in small groups talking. Several vans marked with area television stations were parked at the far end of the street. Police cruisers were parked several houses down each direction and blocking the street to make sure no one got too close. He opened the door and sat down in the front seat. He plugged his phone and radio into their charging ports and then reached for his laptop sitting in the front passenger seat. He looked out the windshield of his SUV at the Zumwalt house and shook his head. "I promise I will find the SOB who did this," he said aloud. He sighed and started typing his initial report.

14

After driving John Salazar from the station to his home, Officer Ben Jenkins returned to the crime scene. He chatted briefly with the patrolmen blocking the road before turning into the driveway where Sasha was parked.

Ben got out of his cruiser holding two cups of black coffee and walked over to Sasha's SUV to give him an update on Salazar. As Ben approached, Sasha opened his door. "Coffee?" Ben asked. Sasha nodded and reached for the cup.

"How's Salazar holding up?"

"He's calmed down a great deal since you last saw him. When his wife came out to see him when I took him to his home to change clothes, he had a brief emotional meltdown. Not a typical day for the average citizen of this town that's for—" Ben jerked his head to the left, startled by the forensic team coming out from the other side of the arborvitae. "Sorry, Sasha. They surprised me."

"Could you step back, Ben?" Sasha asked. The officer stepped back from the SUV, and Sasha got out. He started to walk around the front of the vehicle and motioned Ben to follow him. Sasha hadn't paid attention to the two arborvitae when he first arrived at the residence. As he approached them, he could see that the ground around the trees had been mulched. There was a stone pathway that went around the trees to the side door of the garage that he had entered a short time earlier. He walked along the path, peering at the ground behind the trees. Mulch didn't cover the ground on the backside of the evergreens. He could clearly see defined footprints in the dirt. "You see these?" he asked Ben. "I want you to tape this area off ASAP. Okay?" Ben nodded and turned to go back to his cruiser to retrieve crime scene tape. "I don't want anyone to accidently step on these footprints," Sasha shouted at Ben as he walked away. "And we need to get forensics to take pictures and cast moldings too!"

Ben returned with the tape and secured the immediate area where Sasha found the footprints. "Do you think these were left by the perp?"

"I don't know for certain, but it seems probable. Let's assume the Zumwalts were at bowling league last night. They returned home, opened the garage door, and pulled in. The perp was hiding behind the two evergreen trees and entered through the open garage door, surprising the Zumwalts upon their return, maybe tasing the husband first and then the wife. Then the perp tied them up while they were incapacitated. And then suffocated them, as Beff thinks." Ben nodded. "After killing the Zumwalts, he removed whatever he used to tie them up, which I didn't see in the garage. Then he cut off their clothes and dragged them through the mudroom, past the pool, and out the back gate to pose them together next to the tree in the park."

"Do you think one perp could take out the two of them?" Ben asked.

"If armed with two Tasers, which must be the case, since both were tased. If you then assumed that the Zumwalts weren't armed and that they'd be incapacitated for at least thirty to sixty seconds after being tased." Even if his theory was right, it didn't provide Sasha anything else to go on.

Maybe he'd be lucky, and the case was going to be easy to solve. If a member of the Zumwalts' family or a friend would be able to provide him with the name of someone who had a grudge against one or both of them, that would be a game changer. At least that was what he was hoping for.

Sasha walked back to the open door of his SUV, got in, closed the door, and began working on his report again. He'd give Beff thirty more minutes and then give her a call asking for an update. He'd only been typing on his laptop a few minutes when his phone started ringing.

"Hi, Sasha," Chris said. "I'm on speaker phone with Beff."

"Hi, Beff." Sasha quickly reached for a notepad.

"I've finished the autopsies on the Zumwalts," Beff said. "I can confirm that both died from asphyxia, as I believed. Asphyxia, as you know, is a deprivation of oxygen in the lungs and buildup of carbon dioxide in the blood. In this case, the asphyxia was not caused by either strangulation or being choked, in my professional opinion, as there were no signs of deep tissue bruising to the front or back of the neck, nor were there any signs of bruising on the trachea or the larynx." Beff paused to look at her assistant's handwritten notes. "There were no signs of petechiae or capillary bleeding present on their skin, and no mucous membranes present in the whites of the eyes, which also confirms that there was no excessive pressure applied by the killer."

Sasha breathed a heavy sigh. "How long did it take for the killer to cause asphyxia and for the Zumwalts to die?"

"Based on neither body showing signs of petechiae, I would say they died in under three minutes. There was tape residue on both of their necks. Based on the evidence collected during the autopsies, it is my professional opinion that both were suffocated with a plastic bag that was secured with tape. Based on the residue and pattern, probably duct tape." Beff paused for a few seconds, waiting to see if Sasha would ask any follow-up questions. He didn't. "In conclusion, in my opinion and based on the evidence, the Zumwalts were both incapacitated by the Taser. Taser voltage is approximately twelve hundred volts after the skin is penetrated, and that voltage would have rendered them unable to resist. Evidence shows that both were bound by the wrists and ankles with some form of plastic restraint, as there are abrasions and bruising on both of them. At some point after they were both restrained, they died of asphyxia."

Sasha quickly analyzed what Beff explained. "You feel very confident with your findings?"

"Yes, I am." Beff looked at Chris and mouthed, "Do you have anything you want to add?" Chris shook his head. "That's all I've got for now, Sasha."

"Did you find any signs of injuries post-death?" Sasha wasn't sure what to ask. He hadn't been involved in a case like this previously.

"I failed to mention the abrasions and cuts that were found on both of their heels. Based on what Chris told me, your officers found blood evidence on the concrete patio surface outside by the pool. My team called, and they also found blood evidence on a loose screw at the threshold of the door leading out to the patio from the house. Those would be the only traumas post-death in my opinion."

Sasha thought the ME was clear and concise in her report of the findings of the autopsies. "Anything you can add, Chris?"

"No, sir. I was here for most of the two autopsies."

"Beff? Did you find any additional evidence on either of the Zumwalts? Meaning any other hair or fibers, etcetera?" Sasha asked.

"I obviously combed both bodies for any evidence and took a number of samples. Those will be tested by the lab. I took soil samples and other organic materials from the back of their legs, buttocks, and backs, but nothing that looked out of place considering where they were found."

"Let me know if the lab finds anything," Sasha said.

"No problem. I'm sorry that I didn't find something more tangible that would help you in your investigation." Beff looked over at Chris and tapped her watch.

Chris looked at his watch. "Do you need me back now?"

"No hurry. Why?"

Beff answered: "If Chris can wait twenty or so minutes, I will be able to send a transcript of the autopsies with him, as well as videos and pictures."

"I'm probably going to head back shortly to the station to finish up my report and talk with the chief," Sasha said. "See you over there."

"Any other questions or thoughts, Sasha?" Beff started to take her autopsy gown off.

"No, Beff. I'll check back with you later. Thanks again."

"Sure thing. We should grab a drink sometime. Sometime soon with Janet and Drew would be nice."

"Yes, it would. I'll check with Janet and let you know." Sasha knew that Janet wasn't really a fan of Beff's, so he was hoping that Beff was just being friendly. He would call and ask her if she'd like to have coffee or meet for lunch to talk about the case in the next few days.

15

Charlie wasn't sure why, but he was feeling extremely nervous about seeing Fred, who had texted a few hours earlier requesting a meeting. It was dark out, and with no streetlights under the bridge, he could stand on the sidewalk and not be seen. There was normally little traffic on the street, especially after businesses in the area closed. Tonight was no different.

At eight o'clock sharp, Fred pulled up in a white panel van and stopped where Charlie was standing under the bridge. Charlie had never seen the vehicle, so he stepped up to the passenger-side door and peered in. He opened the door and sat down in the passenger seat.

Fred turned off the van's engine. "Thanks for meeting with me. How's it going?"

"It's going okay."

"Great. I wanted to ask you how you thought Brian was dealing with last night. Is he doing okay, and do you think he can continue with the plan?"

"I think he's doin' okay. And I think that he can commit all the killings. I need to tell you that I met with him last night." Charlie waited for Fred to react, but he didn't. "I know we're not suppose' to meet, but I got a text from him around eleven o'clock tellin' me that he needed to meet. Urgently. I agreed to meet him, as he sounded desperate. I figured it was important."

"I understand. I probably would have done the same thing under the circumstances."

"I thought that maybe something went wrong, so I thought we both needed to know what. But nothing went wrong. Everything went according to your plan."

"Then why did he need to meet with you?"

"He was totally wired. Totally. He was so jacked up he just needed to release some steam. I was the only one he could talk to. I can tell you that he enjoyed killin' them. He'll kill anybody you'd want killed."

"Okay." Fred paused. "So there is no problem?"

"No. No problem. Brian's gonna follow your plan. Like I said, he'll kill anybody. He scared the hell out of me last night, and I'm even more scared of him now."

"That's all I wanted to hear." Fred was dressed in all black and was also wearing black leather driving gloves. His right hand had been on the steering wheel since Charlie had gotten into the van, and his left hand had been resting on the driver's door armrest out of view. Fred moved his left arm across his chest and shot Charlie in the left side of his neck with the Taser.

Charlie's skeletal muscles froze. Fred pulled him into the open space between the driver and passenger seats in the front of the van and then into the open area behind the two seats. Fred reached for the two zip ties in the front pocket of his hoodie and secured Charlie's hands and feet behind his back, then took a piece of duct tape and put it over his mouth. He pulled a clear plastic bag over Charlie's head, securing the bag around Charlie's neck with duct tape. Fred retrieved the burner phone Charlie had been using from his coat pocket, started the van, and headed toward the interstate.

———

Fred was heading about sixty miles southwest of Bloomington, and it would take him a little over an hour to make the drive. He exited off the interstate north of Springfield and then turned onto a county road a few minutes later. After driving a couple of miles, he stopped at a metal entrance gate. He opened the gate with the remote that he brought with him. He then headed down the long lane that led back through the surrounding woodland. He drove past a large pond, which at one time had been a gravel pit, then on toward the middle of the property where a cabin and machine shed stood.

The woodlands and cleared acres together covered one square mile. The

640 acres were surrounded by four county roads. The property was very secluded, which was why Fred had it purchased twelve years earlier. To this day there was still only the one road, which led to a gravel pit.

There were over a hundred trail cameras installed on the property, which are typically used by hunters to record and track wild animals. The cameras can record twenty-four hours per day and are activated only when an animal or human enters the area the camera is set to cover. Although there were many wild animals that lived or roamed through the property, rarely did any humans attempt to walk through the woodlands. There were countless posted signs warning of no trespassing and the existence of the cameras. Anyone who ventured onto the property was warned of prosecution if they were caught trespassing. Each year Fred made large donations to county and state law enforcement agencies so that those on patrol in the surrounding area kept a constant watchful eye on the property. Any activity recorded by the cameras was instantly uploaded to the cloud. Fred had employed someone to immediately review any video attached to an email that alerted movement on this property, as well as other properties he owned.

When Fred visited the woodland property, he was able to disable a set of linked cameras, which recorded movement on the lane, around the pond, cabin, and machine shed areas, leaving only the remaining interior and perimeter of the property covered.

He parked the van in the machine shed next to a liquified petroleum gas commercial incinerator mounted on a trailer. It was easy to slide Charlie out by pulling the tarp he had laid in the back of the van before the murder. Charlie's body tumbled to the concrete floor.

Fred positioned an overhead electric chain hoist to where Charlie was lying and reached for the four corners of the tarp. He secured the hoist hook into the four steel ringlets at the corners of the tarp. He pushed the lift button on the remote, which lifted Charlie up eight feet, and again used the remote to reposition Charlie's body over the incinerator. Slowly he lowered the body into the opening. He detached the hook from the tarp, then engaged the remote to move the hoist away from the incinerator. He closed the door of the incinerator and then fired up the LPG unit. He watched the temperature gauge quickly move to his desired temperature.

His plan had gotten off to a good start. A very good start.

16

It had been nine days since the Zumwalt bodies had been found. The tip line that had been activated the day of the murder initially offered several leads but none that were substantive.

The Zumwalts had led an unassuming and low-key life in the community. In the past nine days, Sasha and his team had interviewed over twenty family members, along with close to fifty friends and coworkers of the couple. They'd found no one who could provide any clue as to why the couple had been murdered. What was clear was that Warren and Maria were both well liked by those who knew them. Everyone interviewed told the team similar information. The childless couple married right after they graduated from college almost twelve years ago, and they led an active lifestyle. They enjoyed success in their careers, which gave them plenty of time for travel and sports. No one had come forward with any information that suggested a motive for murdering them.

––––

Sitting at his desk at the police station, Sasha began his morning with his usual cup of black coffee. Since the investigation began, he had spent each morning looking at his murder book. He and the team had compiled crime scene photos, his notes and those of others involved in the investigation, and transcripts of all of the interviews that had been conducted. The book also included Beff's autopsy reports and her team's forensic report of the evidence found where the Zumwalts had been posed in the park, along with the evidence found in their home. There were also numerous crime scene sketches made the day of the murder. What was missing from the book were witness statements, but no one had come forward.

He reread the bios of Warren and Maria. Absolutely nothing popped out. The couple led a fairly boring life in Bloomington. Both had grown up in the area. Warren had gone to high school in Normal, while Maria had attended a local Catholic high school. They met at the University of Illinois and were married the summer after they graduated college. Each found good jobs in the area, Warren in IT at the headquarters of an insurance company and Maria a job for a national big-box retailer. Warren had recently been named a director in the IT department, while last year Maria became the general manager at one of her employers' locations in town. Neither had ever had a run-in with law enforcement. Not even a traffic ticket had been issued to either of them. They were both active in their local parish and in local charities. The Zumwalts led an exemplary life.

Sasha stood up and stretched. He grabbed his coffee cup and walked down the hallway to the kitchen. He picked out a dark roast blend from the basket of coffee pods and brewed the coffee. He was steps away from his office door with the steaming cup of coffee when Chris Watkins rushed up to him.

"Hey, 911 just got a call from two city workers clearing brush on the Constitution Trail over by East Empire Street," Chris said. "They found a male propped up against a tree. Obviously dead, naked, and with his eyes wide open."

"Crap!" Sasha walked around Chris and headed to his desk. He poured the coffee into his to-go mug and grabbed his jacket. "Call dispatch," he told Chris, "and tell them to make sure that the first officers on the scene cordon off the immediate area. Was the body found north or south of Empire?"

"North."

"Have dispatch send officers to block the trail from East Empire to East Emerson. No one in or out. Got it?"

"The trail doesn't intersect with Emerson at street level," Chris said. "It goes over Emerson on an old railroad bridge that's been converted into a walking bridge."

"Have them block anyone from heading south at the bridge then."

"Got it. What do you want the first on scene to do with the two city workers?"

"Tell the officer to get them both into a cruiser and wait for us to get there to take their initial statements."

"What about Beff?"

"Same as last time." Sasha knew Beff would hear about the body soon enough, but he wanted a little time at the scene before she showed. "We try to keep her at a distance until we get a chance to look over the crime scene first. Okay? Let's get out there."

———

A police cruiser with its lights flashing was parked on the sidewalk at the entrance of the trail at Empire. With oncoming traffic coming to a stop, Sasha and Chris maneuvered their SUVs onto the sidewalk that ran parallel to the street, where another police cruiser blocked the entrance to the trail. The officer got into his vehicle and backed it up so that the detectives could turn into the entrance to the trail.

Sasha drove slowly onto the paved surface of the trail. A six-foot-high chain-link fence ran along both sides of the trail, and he could see the lights of a police cruiser flashing about five hundred feet ahead. The chain-link fence ended where he parked behind the police cruiser. Chris pulled up behind him.

Two men were sitting in the back of the cruiser, and a police officer was standing at the driver's door, looking at Sasha. "Morning, Officer," Sasha called as he got out of his vehicle. "I'll be right there." He grabbed a CSI kit and flashlight out of the back of his SUV and waited for Chris as he gathered equipment. They walked over to the officer. "I'm Senior Detective Sasha Frank and this is Detective Chris Watkins."

"Detective Frank. Detective Watkins. I'm Terry Eberhardt. Nice meeting you both." The three men exchanged handshakes.

"Will you walk me over to the scene? Detective Watkins is going to briefly talk with the two workers in the back of your cruiser."

Officer Eberhardt led Sasha past the front of his cruiser. "I've already taped off the crime scene."

"Excellent. Please tell me everything that has happened since you arrived."

"I arrived at the scene and parked my cruiser at 8:01 a.m. Dave Townsend and Joshua Evans, the city workers, were both standing at the back of their truck and were noticeably upset. They had been assigned to clear heavy brush from around the trees along the trail. They told me that they arrived around 7:30 a.m."

"That's their truck up ahead?" Sasha pointed at a city pickup truck parked in the grass between the trail and forested area.

"Yes, sir. They told me that right after they arrived, they got out and dropped the tailgate of the truck. They both had a cigarette before starting to clear the brush from around the trees along this section of the trail."

"Did they both tell you this or did one tell the story?"

"Evans did most of the talking. I think he's senior to Townsend."

"Okay, go on."

"They finished their smoke break and started pulling out the equipment they use for clearing brush. The two of them said they each headed in different directions on the west side of the trail. They cut fifty or so feet of brush and then use rakes to make piles of brush. As soon as they finish a section, they call in another city vehicle that picks up the piles and hauls them away." Eberhart turned away from Sasha and pointed to a huge oak tree that looked maybe fifty to sixty feet north of where the pickup truck was parked. "See that big oak past the pickup truck? Townsend was clearing brush from around that tree when he found the body.

"Townsend said that he gave out a shout as soon as he saw the body. Evans said he heard Townsend over the sound of the bush whackers and came running, thinking that Townsend had somehow gotten injured. He found out that Townsend was okay but there was a dead man leaning against the oak tree, naked. It appears his eyes are glued open. There are drips of dried glue beneath his eye and on his cheek. Almost looks like dried tears. Evans called 911 to report the body."

"The call came in around 7:55 and you arrived here at 8:01? You were on patrol somewhere close by?"

"Yes, sir. I was driving through the university. Illinois Wesleyan. My normal routine for this time of day. I got here pretty quick."

"What's happened since you arrived on scene?"

"Like I said, when I arrived the two were standing on the trail behind their truck waiting for me. I asked them to point me toward the body and told them to stay put. Then I walked over and saw the body." Eberhardt paused again. "I checked to see if the man was indeed dead and felt for a pulse on the right side of his neck. There was no pulse, and he was cool to the touch. He was obviously deceased."

"Did you only touch his neck?"

"Yes, sir. I only touched his neck, and I had on latex gloves. I marked off the area with crime scene tape, except for an opening to access the scene."

"Thank you, Officer. Well done. You stay here. I'm going over to the body. Please tell Detective Watkins to join me when he's finished with the two city workers."

Sasha changed into the CSI gear and headed toward the crime scene. He passed the two piles of brush, and then the tree trunk of the oak came into view. It was at least eight feet in diameter, one of the largest oak trees Sasha had seen. The limbs extended out over the trail and into the backyards of two nearby homes.

He moved to his left around the trunk of the tree, trying to not disturb the scene. He stopped at first glimpse of the right foot and partial leg of the man. He moved around the tree until he could see the body sitting on the ground leaning up against the tree trunk.

The scene was very similar to what he had encountered at Clearwater Park. The man was naked, and his right leg was crossed over his fully extended left leg. His hands were folded neatly together in his lap covering his genitals. It was as if the man was embarrassed being found naked in public. His eyes were wide open.

The man had a muscular build, short blond hair, very little body hair, and several tattoos. There was a braided barbed wire tattoo around his right bicep, and on his left upper chest he had a Celtic cross. There was a compass tattooed on the top of his left foot.

Sasha estimated that the victim was about six feet tall. The man wasn't wearing any jewelry, unless he was wearing a ring on one of the fingers of his left hand, which was covered by his right hand. Both wrists and ankles showed visible signs of abrasions, just as with the Zumwalts. There was no visible blood or wounds, although, like the Zumwalts, there were visible abrasions on the right heel. The man's left heel wasn't visible.

Though the sun had been up for two hours, Sasha scanned the ground with the beam of his flashlight. He spotted marks that looked like a single tire tread. There were also shoe or boot prints visible. He followed the track in the dirt to the backyard of a gray house that backed up to the trail. The tire tracks ended where the grass in the backyard began. He wondered if the man had lived in the house.

He returned to the body and squatted down to get a closer look and heard Chris approaching. "Try to stay at least ten feet away from the tree," Sasha said. Chris came up behind him. "I'm sure we're looking at the third victim," Sasha said. "There are at least five pieces of similar evidence that point to that probability."

Sasha stood up and shined his light on the body. "I haven't gotten close enough to see if there are marks from a Taser, but I don't see any visible puncture wounds." He shined the light on the neck of the body. "It's hard to tell from here, but it looks like there could be some tape residue around his neck, similar to what we saw on the Zumwalts."

He guided the light around the perimeter of the body. "Will you reach out to Beff and bring her up to speed?" Chris nodded. "Then take a picture of the body and get a couple of officers to start knocking on the doors of the houses in the neighborhood to see if anyone can identify him."

"Will do. Anything else?"

"Call dispatch to send a couple of officers to stand guard over the body until Beff transports it to the morgue. I'm going to walk back now to tell Eberhardt to stand guard until the extra officers show up. Then I'm going to do a field interview of the two city workers. Once the extra officers are in place, I'll have Eberhardt take the two back to the station. I'd like you to interview them. Separately of course. Sound good?"

"Sounds good. I'm heading back to the station now." As Chris turned to walk back to his SUV, he pulled off his latex gloves and put them in his back pants pocket.

Sasha turned his focus back to the crime scene and shook his head. He said out loud, "I'm so sorry for you and your family. I promise you that I will work day and night to find out who killed you." He recalled he made the same promise to the Zumwalts and had zero evidence that pointed to any suspect. "I promise you I will make this right for you."

He took another quick look at the crime scene while praying that Beff's team would find evidence that would lead him to a suspect. Three murders in ten days had taken place in a community where murders were a rare event. The pressure on him to find answers would grow exponentially once the media learned of the latest murder.

He asked Eberhardt to watch over the crime scene. The two city workers were still sitting in the back of the cruiser, and Sasha wanted to talk to them both before they would be taken to the station to be further interviewed by Chris.

He opened the passenger rear door and asked them to step out of the cruiser. Dave Townsend got out of the opened door, but Joshua Evans couldn't open his door, as the cruiser didn't allow passengers to open the rear doors. Sasha leaned in. "Mr. Evans, do you mind sliding across the seat to get out?" Evans did as he was requested.

Sasha introduced himself and shook hands with them. "I'd like to talk with you both about what you discovered this morning. I'm going to record our conversation." Both city workers nodded. He got out his mobile phone and opened the recorder app and turned it on to record the interview. "It's 8:43 a.m. on Friday, April tenth, and I'm recording this conversation with two City of Bloomington employees. Would you both provide me your names, home addresses, and what your jobs are with the city?"

They provided the information asked and began describing what had started out as a routine morning. "But then I saw what I thought was a naked guy lying on the ground," Dave said. "I saw he was leaning up against the tree. I turned off my bush whacker and asked if he was okay. I walked over to him and asked again. Then I touched his right shoulder. He didn't move. I called out for Josh."

"Did he feel cool to your touch?"

"I was wearing my gloves, so I don't know. I spent a tour in Afghanistan, so I've seen dead bodies before."

"Thank you for your service. Please go on."

Dave nodded his thanks. "His eyes were open. Josh came over and saw the body, and he said we needed to call 911. So, we did."

"Thanks, Mr. Townsend. Mr. Evans, did you touch the body?"

"No, sir, I did not," Josh said. "I've never seen anything like that. No way I was touching the guy." Josh shuddered. Both he and Dave lit cigarettes.

"Do you have anything further to add to what your coworker has already told me?"

"Not really. I just called 911, like he said, and then we walked over to the truck and waited for the officer to arrive. It only took a few minutes before he got here."

"Have you seen anyone else since you arrived this morning? Other than the officer who was first on scene?"

Josh answered, "No."

"I saw a guy standing on the back steps of that white house over there." Dave pointed at a house that was across from where their truck was parked.

"The white house with the green shutters?" Dave nodded yes. "The man was just standing there?"

"He was watching his dog in the backyard. Some kinda little dog that went out to pee, I guess. I'm sure he saw me, but when the dog was done it ran back to him and the man let the dog in; then he closed the door."

"You think he saw you?"

"Yes, sir. I am sure he looked over at the truck. I think he saw the two of us get out." Dave looked at Josh for him to agree and confirm what he'd just said.

"Sorry. I didn't see the guy. I can't tell you if he saw us or not."

"Thank you both. I'm ending this interview recording at 8:53 a.m." Sasha saved the recording in the app and forwarded it via email to Chris, who would review it before he interviewed the two back at the station.

Two police cruisers pulled up and parked on either side of Sasha's SUV. He recognized one of the officers as Jedediah "Jed" Cummings, a twenty-year veteran on the force who often took new patrolmen under his wing to teach them the ropes. He reached out his hand as Jed walked up to him.

"Good morning, Sasha. Caught another one?"

"Sadly, yes. Mum's the word, but it looks identical to the murder of the Zumwalts ten days ago. Or it's a copycat. Too early to tell." He turned to shake hands with the young patrolman who accompanied Jed.

"Detective Frank . . . sorry, Senior Detective Frank," Jed said, "I'd like to introduce you to Officer BJ Thomas." The young officer and Sasha shook hands. "He's been with the force a little over a year, and we've been assigned to your investigation."

"I hope Jed is passing along all his expertise. He's the real deal."

"Jed has helped me look like a veteran." BJ laughed. "Or so he tells me."

"You can learn a lot from him, so keep close, watch what he does, and copy his moves. Except on the dance floor. He danced last summer at his daughter's wedding, and we were all embarrassed for him." Sasha laughed. "As was his daughter."

"Hey there, Detective. Shawna watched her mom and me practice our moves, and we got her seal of approval. If I recall, it was you and Janet, well, *you* that looked amateurish out there."

"Janet tries to make me look good, but it's not really possible." The three laughed. Sasha quickly turned serious. "Listen, I'm going to ask the two of you to stand guard over the scene until the ME transports to the morgue." Jed and BJ nodded. "I'm not sure how long they'll be on scene, but if it goes past lunchtime, I'll have someone relieve you guys. Sound like a plan?"

"We can stay here as long as you need us, Sasha."

"I'll be staying in the vicinity until the ME departs. I'm going to leave you to it. If you need anything, let me know." The two officers nodded and started moving toward the crime scene.

Sasha waved Terry Eberhardt over, and they walked back to the police cruiser, where the two city workers were waiting and smoking cigarettes. Sasha thanked them again, and then they climbed into Terry's car so he could drive them to the station. Sasha opened the door of his SUV and picked up his coffee mug. The coffee was stone cold, but he drank it anyway. Today was going to be a long one.

He watched Terry slowly make a U-turn on the trail and drive past Jed's cruiser.

Sasha sat back in the driver's seat of his SUV and called out on his radio. "Dispatch? Detective Frank calling dispatch."

"Hi, Sasha. This is Will."

"Morning, Will. We're going to need to keep the officers blocking the entrances to the trail at East Emerson and Empire Streets until after we transport the body and CSI finishes their investigation."

"Roger that, Sasha."

"I can see that there is still an officer in place at the entrance to the trail at Empire, but could you let me know the status of the officer at the entrance on Emerson?"

"I checked on them at 9 a.m., and both reported that they had turned back a number of civilians. Media was located at both entrances. I told them that no one is allowed in until you give the say-so."

"I can see that our state and federal friends are parked in a business parking lot on Empire."

"I'm taking some heat from them, but I told them that until the ME gives us a green light no one is allowed into the scene. Also there's a CSI vehicle that is ready to get into position, but they radioed in to say that there was a police cruiser and an unmarked SUV blocking the trail."

"The SUV is mine. I'll have everyone here pull forward and off to the side of the pavement now so they can reposition nearer the scene. The cruiser is Terry Eberhardt's, and he's transporting the two city workers back to the barn to be interviewed by Chris." Sasha put his SUV into drive and drove around BJ's cruiser and parked several car lengths ahead. "You can green-light CSI into position as soon as Eberhardt exits onto Empire."

"Thanks, Sasha. I also wanted to let you know that two officers have begun the canvassing of the street west of you."

"Great."

"I've also positioned officers at the intersections of the street that parallels the trail to your east, along with officers positioned at each of the streets that intersect it."

"Thank you for taking that initiative, Will. I should've asked you to cordon off the area on my way over here. I wasn't thinking." Sasha really appreciated the longtime lead dispatcher who directed calls to the force for the day shift. Will had the experience to be a backstop to everyone in the field and make the right decisions in the heat of the moment.

"No problem. We're a team. I'm just doing my part."

Sasha glanced in his rearview mirror. "CSI is moving into position."

"We had already alerted CSI to move into position once you relocated your SUV." Will laughed. "Just being proactive. As soon as—"

"Will?"

"Yes, Sasha."

"Let me know if the canvass develops any leads, okay?"

"I was just starting to tell you that as soon as I get an update from the officers canvassing the neighborhood, I'll reach out to you."

Sasha reminded himself that he needed to listen more and talk less. Janet told him that all the time.

17

asha watched Beff's SUV stop behind the CSI vehicle. She got out, smiled, and waved to him.

"Morning, Beff." Sasha walked over.

"Morning, Sasha. It looks like we caught another one?"

"Looks like it. Would you like me to give you a brief update?" Sasha reported what the workers had told him and described the crime scene and the victim.

"We need to get impressions of the footwear from the city worker that touched the victim," Beff said.

"I'll alert Chris."

Beff turned to Steve. "When they return, be sure that we get those impressions."

Steve nodded. "I will make sure that they do."

"I'll get suited up and take a look at the body." Beff walked to the back of her SUV, opened the hatch, reached in, and pulled out her CSI suit and began pulling it on. She then donned the camera and communication equipment she wore while investigating the Zumwalt crime scene.

Sasha sent a text to Chris: "Return Evans and Townsend to the scene. We need to gather potential evidence from them."

———

Sasha followed Beff and her photographer, Debbie, to the crime scene, stopping twenty feet away, close enough where he could see what was going on but not be in the way. Beff turned on her camera and slowly approached the tree. He watched as Beff eased around the body, recording her observations and indicating different spots she wanted Debbie to photograph.

Sasha's radio vibrated, letting him know that someone was radioing him. He walked a few steps away and plugged in his earbud.

"I've finished the interviews with Townsend and Evans," Chris said, "and they've provided their written statements. They haven't provided any new information. I'm having Eberhardt transport them back to you, as per Beff's request."

"Thanks for the update. Will you head back out here to coordinate with the officers doing the neighborhood canvass?" Sasha turned and saw Beff inserting a thermometer under the victim's right armpit.

"I'll be heading out there shortly."

Sasha removed the earbuds and walked back to see Beff was looking at her watch, timing how long the thermometer was in place.

"Do you know the outside temperature?" Beff asked.

"No, do you want me to check?"

"Sorry, Sasha," she said without looking up. "I thought you were Steve." As she spoke, Steve walked up behind Sasha carrying a temperature gauge.

"Outdoor temperature is 50.2 degrees Fahrenheit," Steve said.

"The current time is 10:02 a.m." Beff pulled the thermometer from under the victim's armpit and held it where the camera would also catch the reading. "I've got an algor mortis reading of 54.2 degrees Fahrenheit. A body's temperature declines 1.5 degrees Fahrenheit every hour after death, but the reading doesn't give me an accurate view as to the time of death due to the outside temperature being 50.2 degrees. I'll take a rectal when we are ready to transport."

"Do you have any approximate time of death?" Sasha asked.

"I understand your desire for information, but it'd be a guess." She touched the body. "Based on body temp and rigor mortis, approximate time of death occurred sometime after 8 p.m. yesterday." She paused. "But the outdoor temperature is obviously a factor, so death in all probability occurred around ten to twelve hours ago. But that's purely speculation at this point."

"Although there were a couple of 'buts' in that answer, that gives me something until you have better information," Sasha said. He turned and walked away from the tree, back to his vehicle. He was getting increasingly frustrated. He sensed that this killing would provide few if any clues as well.

A call interrupted his thoughts. He answered, and Will started talking excitedly: "I just heard from Officer Williams. A resident who lives on the opposite side of the street from the houses that back up to the trail has tentatively identified the picture as Greg Bauer. The neighbor told Williams that Bauer lives in the gray house across from him and works in the service department at a car dealership."

Sasha turned back to look at the gray house near the oak tree. "Okay. Anything else?"

"The DMV has his age at thirty. Born February 2, 1988. That's Groundhog Day. The neighbor says that Bauer is a divorced father of two and his ex moved with the kids to Arizona last year. He doesn't think that there are any local relatives. That's all we have as of now. I've sent an officer to the dealership to get a confirmation on Bauer."

"Good idea to get backup confirmation from the employer," Sasha said. "As soon as you hear back on the second ID, call for a warrant to gain access to Bauer's home"—he looked at a garage in the backyard of the house—"and there's a detached garage that needs to be included in the warrant. I'm going back to the scene and wait for Beff to finish. Text when you get the confirmation on the ID and the warrant approvals."

"Will do, Sasha. You'll get a text from me when I hear."

———

As he approached the crime scene, Beff called out, "We've found a Taser wound on the victim's back right shoulder. I also found tape residue on the back of his neck."

"Greg Bauer."

Beff looked confused. "Greg Bauer?"

"We've got a tentative identification as Greg Bauer. He lived in the gray house right behind you. How much longer before you transport?"

"As soon as Steve tells me the team has everything they need. Probably an hour. Maybe two."

Sasha walked around the tree to get a better look at the house. It was an older well-maintained two-story home with a detached garage about one hundred feet from the residence. There was a screened-in back porch that opened out to a brick patio area where a few pieces of outdoor furniture were arranged around a firepit. It was a nice-looking place. A text came in: "Service manager confirms it's Bauer."

"Who did you piss off?" Sasha said out loud to no one. He shook his head and wondered how Bauer was connected to the Zumwalts. Or what connection Bauer and the Zumwalts had to the killer.

Another text came through: "Search warrants approved."

————

Police cruisers were parked on the street in front of Mr. Bauer's home, and three officers were standing on the sidewalk in front of the house with a civilian. The four of them watched Sasha pull into the driveway of the gray house. He stepped out of his SUV and walked over to where they were standing. "Good morning, gentlemen." Sasha recognized the three officers as Warren Williams, Al Lester, and Brett Griffin. All had served as officers on the Bloomington Police Department for at least ten years.

Warren Williams reached out and shook Sasha's hand. "Morning, Senior Detective Frank." Sasha nodded. He knew that Warren had formally addressed him because he was going to introduce the civilian standing with them. "I'd like to introduce you to Mr. Simon Parnell."

"It's nice to meet you, Mr. Parnell. I'm sorry about the circumstances, though." Sasha and Mr. Parnell shook hands. He thought that the short, bald-headed man looked to be in his late seventies or early eighties. He was wearing a Butler Bulldog sweatshirt. Mr. Parnell smiled.

"Mr. Parnell lives across the street, and he identified the photo I showed him as Greg Bauer, who owns the house we're standing in front of now." Warren motioned toward the gray house. "Mr. Parnell tells us that Greg has lived here for the past seven years, the first six years with his wife and two children before they divorced. Mr. Parnell tells us that she and the kids moved to Arizona a year or so ago. Mr. Parnell tells us that his understanding is that Greg now lives here alone."

Sasha nodded. "Thanks, Officer Williams." He turned to Mr. Parnell. "Sir, can you tell me the last time you saw Mr. Bauer?"

"I believe I saw him arrive home last night around 8:30 p.m. or so. I was out walking our dog and was down the street." Mr. Parnell pointed north down the street. "Greg always parked his car in the garage. When Pepper and I got to the front of my house, the garage door was already closed."

"Pepper is your dog?" Sasha bent down and petted the small dog. Mr. Parnell nodded. "Did you see Mr. Bauer inside the house last night?"

"I don't think so, Detective, but I don't really recall. I'm not in the habit of watching my neighbors."

"I'm sorry, sir. I didn't mean to suggest that you were being nosy. I was just asking if you happened to have noticed him inside his home after he returned home. Nothing more than that."

"I'm sorry, Detective, but I don't think I've made myself clear. I'm not saying I actually saw Greg last night. I saw his car arrive home. It was obviously dark at 8:30 p.m., and there isn't a streetlight in this area."

"I misunderstood what you were trying to tell us. Do you mind if I ask you a few more questions, sir?" Mr. Parnell nodded. "Do you know if Mr. Bauer had a girlfriend?"

"My wife and I weren't close friends with Greg. We'd wave at each other, or we'd say hello and talk to one another when we saw each other at neighborhood get-togethers or on the street. Nothing more than that."

"I understand, sir. Did you by chance notice anyone stopping by to visit Mr. Bauer? Male or female?"

"I can't really say that I saw anyone. Mind you, I wasn't really paying much attention."

"Thank you very much, sir. I'm going to ask Officer Williams to walk back with you to your home, and if you don't mind, I'd like him to ask your wife if she recalls anyone recently visiting Mr. Bauer. Is that okay?"

"Why, of course, Detective. She certainly may know or have seen something."

Sasha watched the two of them walk down the sidewalk to the driveway and then across to the driveway that led up to the side entrance of the Parnells' front porch.

He then shook hands with both remaining officers. "Al, Brett, did you by chance talk to any other neighbors who recognized the photo you showed them?"

"Just Warren and I were knocking on doors. I stopped at several homes, Sasha, and no one was at home. Al joined us once Mr. Parnell provided Warren an ID of the vic."

Sasha shook his head. "The man's name is Greg Bauer. Greg Bauer."

Brett nodded. "Sorry, Detective."

"I would appreciate it if you'd stand guard out front, Brett, while Al canvasses the other homes on this side of the street. Let me know if Warren learns anything from talking with Mrs. Parnell. Once he's back, if you'd ask him to canvass all the homes on the other side, I'd appreciate that very much. Okay?"

"Yes, sir."

"I'm going to check the garage and house. The ME's team should be showing up shortly. Please keep them outside until I come back."

Sasha waited for confirmation of his request and then walked back to his SUV and opened the back hatch. He reached in for another CSI kit, tore it open. "Let Chris know I'm going to look at the garage first and then come back to the house," he told Brett as he pulled on the coveralls. "Tell him to stay outside, please." Brett gave Sasha a thumbs-up. Sasha reached for another two CSI kits. He'd search the garage first and then change into a new one before he entered the house. The extra kit was just in case. He also grabbed a couple of garbage bags.

As he started to walk up the driveway toward the garage, he took in the front of the gray two-story house. There was a large front porch with a side entrance that led out to the driveway. There was a three-foot-high privet hedge that ran the length of the south side of the driveway from the sidewalk to the paved alley near the garage. The bricks in the driveway must have been replaced sometime recently, as the driveway was flat. He grew up on a street with a lot of brick driveways, and none of them were flat. There were dips and bumps caused by the annual freezes and thaws during Illinois winters.

The sidewalk at the back corner of the house led to the back porch and patio area he had seen from the trail. A basketball backboard and hoop hung above one of the two garage doors ahead.

He crossed the paved alley and stopped outside the garage. He pulled on the booties and put on the mask before pulling on the latex gloves. He then pulled on both garage door handles. Neither door budged; they were either locked or were operated by electric door openers. He walked to the corner of the garage and stuck his head around the side. Another privet hedge was planted on this side of the garage. The hedge appeared to end at the back of the property line with the trail. He walked back across the front of the garage and around the corner and spotted a side entrance door. The wooden door looked original, with an ornate stained-glass window in the upper half. He tried the handle. It was unlocked.

He motioned to the officers that he was going to enter the garage. He pulled his gun out of its holster and turned on the flashlight while slowly pushing open the side door. The floor of the garage was covered with the same brick as the driveway. He stepped a few feet into the garage and shined the beam of the flashlight across the top of a red car and onto the opposite wall. Assorted ladders and yard tools hung from hooks on the wood-framed wall across from him. He could now see that the car was a Ford Mustang convertible. Red with a black top. Nice-looking car. It wasn't new, but it wasn't that old either. He wasn't sure of the year. The light beam illuminated water hoses, folding lawn chairs, and sports equipment hanging neatly on the walls.

He pushed the door fully open and continued searching with the beam. Storage shelves and a tool bench that ran along the north wall. He lowered his flashlight and saw what looked like a pile of clothing on the floor near the left front fender of the Mustang.

He returned his gun to the holster as he slowly walked toward the clothing: a pair of ankle-high slip-on boots, socks, slacks with a black leather belt still in the loops, a long-sleeved red shirt that had a logo on the left front pocket, and a light blue jacket. All the clothing showed evidence of being cut with scissors. There was a billfold sitting inside the left boot and a mobile phone inside the right boot. "That's interesting," he said out loud. He noticed something sticking out from under the jacket, and he lifted the jacket slightly with the toe of his left foot. Underneath was a single unused zip tie. It looked to be about twelve inches in length.

Sasha shined the light across the hood and roof of the car, then up to the garage door opener. He then focused on the garage door opener buttons attached to the wall beside the door he had entered. He opened the Mustang's driver's side door, leaned in, and did a quick search of the inside of the car. In the console between the front seats were registration and insurance documents listing Gregory A. Bauer at this address. There were also several packs of condoms inside the console. Mr. Bauer was a player.

He closed the driver's door and looked back at the clothes on the floor. He walked over, bent down to pick up the billfold from the boot, and looked inside, but he couldn't find Mr. Bauer's driver's license. Another similarity to the Zumwalts. Their driver's licenses never turned up.

Sasha walked back to the side door and noticed that there was not a keyed lock installed on the door, just a deadbolt on the inside. That meant the only way to enter the garage was to use the door opener. That was odd. What would you do if there was a power outage? Mr. Bauer wouldn't have been able to open the garage door from the outside. Did that mean that he never locked the side door?

Sasha stepped outside. When Mr. Bauer returned home, did he open the overhead garage door with the side door deadbolted or unlocked? Was the killer already inside the garage lying in wait or did he enter the garage from the outside when Bauer returned? He assumed Mr. Bauer had been driving the Mustang last night. There was really no way of being absolutely sure based on what Mr. Parnell had said earlier.

He walked around the front of the garage and saw that there was really no place for someone to hide inside the garage. Perhaps the killer had hidden on one of the sides of the garage? He stepped outside and looked around for lights. One light was positioned above the side entrance to the back porch, and another was above the side door of the garage where he was standing. The distance from the house to the garage was at least one hundred feet, with only the two lights to illuminate the entire area.

He stepped back inside the garage and found two light switches on the right side of the doorjamb and flipped them both up. The inside garage lights came on, illuminating the garage in pale-yellow light. He stepped back outside and saw that the outdoor light did not light. He reached up and turned the bulb slightly, and the light came on. He'd ask Beff's team to run prints on the bulb. He flipped the two switches off and pushed the overhead door button marked "North," and the door started to open. He looked up at the motor box and saw that the light hadn't come on. He pushed the button to stop the door and hit it again, and the door started to close. He then tried the other button marked "South." The door started to open. Again, no light. He hit the button two more times to close the door. Sasha needed to tell Steve's team to check both bulbs to see if they were out or unscrewed as well.

After finishing his initial inspection of the garage, Sasha was ready to move to the house. At the side door of the back porch, he removed the booties, mask, hair cover, overalls, and gloves and placed them in one of the garbage bags, pulling the tie closed. He donned the contents of another CSI kit before opening the door and walking into the screened porch. He tried the knob of a door that led into the house. It turned but didn't open. There was an old-style skeleton key–type lock below the knob. His family home in Springfield had a similar type of lock. Like many families living in the Midwest when Sasha was growing up, there was always a key hidden under a rug at the back door. Certainly that was a different time. He bent down and lifted the rug. No key. He reached up and ran his fingers along the top molding of the doorframe. Bingo! He slid the skeleton key into the lock, turned it, and heard the lock click open.

He pulled his gun from its holster and slowly pushed open the door, which opened to a large eat-in kitchen. The interior was well lit by the large windows typically found in older homes. He moved through the ground floor room by room—the kitchen, a formal dining room, a family room. A short hallway contained a doorway that opened into a half bath, next into a living room at the end of the hallway that was at the front of the house. He saw a front door in the living room that had a stained-glass window similar to the one that he'd seen in the side garage door. The door led out to the front porch.

There didn't appear to be anything out of place or of interest on the first floor. He moved back to the stairway at the end of the short hallway that led up to the second floor. The upstairs had two bathrooms and four rooms that were once probably used as bedrooms. Mr. Bauer was using one as a bedroom for himself. Nothing looked out of the ordinary. Sasha moved to another bedroom that had animal wallpaper and bunk beds. Another bedroom contained twin beds and looked very tidy. The fourth room was full of assorted adult and children's sports and exercise equipment. Nothing at all looked out of place upstairs. Just like at the Zumwalts'.

Back in the kitchen, he opened a door and walked downstairs to a semi-finished basement, which included a laundry room, a room with a Ping-Pong table covered with boxes of Christmas decorations, and a utility room. He headed back up the stairs and stood in the kitchen. He was thinking that the killer had probably not set foot in the house.

He walked out the back door and onto the porch. He closed and locked the door, then returned the key to where he had found it. He walked around the screened-in back porch and saw nothing of interest. Back on the flat driveway, he removed his gear, stuffed it into the second garbage bag, and pulled it tightly closed. He walked around to the patio and firepit area behind the house and onto the grassy yard. He slowly turned 360 degrees to take in the entire yard. He then headed to the tree where Mr. Bauer had been found. From his position he couldn't see the base of the trunk of the huge oak tree because of the hedge that ran along the back of the property parallel to the trail.

He didn't see any visible tracks in the grass. He returned to the side door of the garage. At the edge of the brick sidewalk, he noticed that a couple of the edging bricks had been moved out of place. He looked back to the opening to the trail, and an idea came to him. He opened the third CSI kit and put on all of the required items before opening the side door of the garage. Sasha entered and turned on the lights. He turned on his flashlight and walked around the back of the Mustang and shined the light across the wall where the ladders and yard tools hung. Below, a wheelbarrow leaned against the wall. He hadn't noticed it earlier.

Had the killer used the wheelbarrow to move Mr. Bauer from the garage to the oak tree where he was posed? Beff had estimated that Mr. Bauer was well over six feet tall and weighed about 220 or so pounds. He was a fairly big guy. Assuming that there was only one killer, Mr. Bauer may have been too heavy for the killer to move on his own. The wheelbarrow would have made the task manageable once he got Mr. Bauer into it. Did the killer know the wheelbarrow was in the garage, or was it a convenient tool that made his job easier?

———

Sasha joined Officers Williams, Lester, and Griffin on the front sidewalk just as Chris pulled up in his SUV. Sasha raised two fingers to his lips, pretending to smoke. "Spare one, Warren?" Warren handed him his pack of menthols and a lighter. Sasha blew out the smoke that he hoped would calm him. "I did a quick search of the garage and house. There's a red 2015 Mustang convertible parked inside that is registered to Mr. Bauer. Could you go back and confirm with Mr. Parnell that that was the car he saw at 8:30 p.m. last night? I'm sure that it is, but let's double-check." Warren nodded and headed across the street to Mr. Parnell's house.

Sasha motioned for Chris to walk with him up the driveway toward the garage. "I found what would appear to be Mr. Bauer's boots and clothing lying on the garage floor just like we found at the Zumwalt home." He stopped about midway to the garage. "In one boot was his billfold, and the other boot contained his mobile phone. I looked inside the billfold, but I didn't find his driver's license. I also looked in the console of the Mustang, and there wasn't any ID in there either."

"So there's really no question that this is the same killer then?" Chris saw Sasha nod yes. "Anything else, Sasha?"

"Yes. Mr. Bauer was a big guy, so a single killer may have had trouble moving him from the garage to the tree. I saw a single tire track on the ground back where the grass ends in the backyard and the trail begins. Inside the garage I found a wheelbarrow. I think the killer used the wheelbarrow to move Mr. Bauer out of the garage to the trail." Sasha motioned with his right thumb toward the back of the house. "There's a couple of edging bricks outside the side door of the garage that have been moved. I'm thinking the killer put Mr. Bauer into the wheelbarrow and then wheeled him out the side door, turned toward the backyard, and with the heavy load dislodged a couple of the edging bricks. The killer probably wouldn't have noticed." He put the cigarette out on the steel casing of his flashlight. Once he was assured that the cigarette was out, he put the butt into his jacket pocket.

Chris looked back toward the garage. "So, the killer used the wheelbarrow to move the body?"

"Mr. Bauer. Yes, I think so."

"Sorry, Mr. Bauer. Then the killer returned the wheelbarrow to the garage? The killer seems to be unconcerned about time or being seen."

Warren rejoined Al and Brett and then gave Sasha a thumbs-up, confirming that the red Mustang was the car Mr. Parnell had seen. "So far, the killer seems to be able to come and go unseen. Since the wheelbarrow was used, I think we're dealing with a single killer."

"Before I forget, I spoke with Beff, and she has started the autopsy. She said she'd let us know if she finds anything of interest."

"I'm kinda surprised that CSI or Beff's team aren't here yet."

"They should be heading this way."

Sasha looked back at the house. "I don't think the killer stepped foot inside the house. The overhead garage door is electric. Mr. Bauer must've opened and closed it, then stepped out of the Mustang. He was probably shot with the Taser immediately. I'm guessing the killer was hiding on the north side of the garage, by the side door, until the garage door opened. The side door was probably deadbolted from the inside. Once the overhead door was open, the killer could have followed the Mustang inside, and with the bulb out on the overhead motor box, it would have been too dark for Mr. Bauer to see someone follow him in."

"Makes sense," Chris said.

"The killer could have quickly subdued Mr. Bauer. Once the killer returned from the trail with the wheelbarrow, he exited out the side door without bothering with the deadbolt. Easy peasy."

Chris's mobile phone rang. "Watkins. Yes. Thanks, Luke. Later, man." He looked at Sasha. "The ME's team just passed the cruiser down the street. They'll be here in seconds."

Sasha nodded. "Is that Adam Simmons's son, Luke, down the street? Geez, he looks like his dad."

"Yes, he really does. Luke was a freshman at Bradley when I was a senior."

They watched a van from the ME's office pull up and park out front. Debbie was driving, and Steve followed in another vehicle.

Steve walked up to where Sasha and Chris were standing and shook hands with Chris. He nodded to Sasha. "Anything interesting over here, guys?"

"Yes, there is. Please see if you can pull any prints off the light bulb on the outdoor light by the side door of the garage. I also opened and closed the overhead doors a few feet to check the motor box lights. Neither light came on, so you might want to check to see if those lights are out or if someone unscrewed them."

Steve looked down the driveway to the garage in the back. "Was the outside light working?"

"It does work. But it was either loose or unscrewed. There's a wheelbarrow in the garage I think the killer may have used to move Mr. Bauer from the garage to the tree."

"Okay. Will do." Debbie and two other team members were standing by the vans smoking cigarettes. "Come on, guys! Let's get a move on it." He turned back to Sasha and Chris and shook his head.

Chris laughed. "Be careful to not push them too hard, Steve. You know the local unemployment rate is low, and nowadays there are plenty of places that would treat them much better." He was only slightly kidding.

Steve watched his team getting their gear ready. "Yeah. Yeah, I know. Still, they drive me crazy." He looked at Sasha. "Anything else?"

Sasha motioned over to the house. "I did a quick search of the house. I don't think the killer went inside. There's a skeleton key to the back door hidden on top of the doorframe."

"Skeleton key? You're showing your age." Steve and Sasha started working for the City of Bloomington around the same time. Both were ready for retirement so they could spend more time with grandchildren. The two had a bet as to who would retire first. The one who retired first had to buy the other a bottle of thirty-year-old single malt scotch. "I'll let you know if we find anything interesting, my friend."

18

The police and ME's office had withheld the more salacious details of the murders of the Zumwalts from the public after they had conferred with the IBI and FBI. They had only told local media that the Zumwalts had been found together at the park, naked and murdered by suffocation. The media demanded more details, but as of today the facts that the Zumwalts had both been shot by Tasers, had been suffocated with plastic bags secured to their necks with tape, with their eyelids glued open, their hands and feet at some point had been bound with zip ties, some personal effects stolen, and that they had been posed after they were killed were being kept from the public. Sasha found it remarkable that none of those details had been leaked to the press. After Mr. Bauer's death, he expected that some of those details would most assuredly get out.

After Sasha pulled up to the ME's office, he parked in one of the designated police department spots. He leaned his head back on the headrest and rubbed his temples. For the past week he'd been experiencing an intermittent headache that he couldn't shake. A combination of too much caffeine, too little sleep, and carrying more stress than ever before in his life was taking a physical and mental toll on his body. He gathered his notepad, phone, and radio and got out of the SUV.

Chris greeted him inside the door with a cup of coffee. "Evening, Sasha."

"I'm not sure I need this, but thanks. Anything you want to tell me before we talk with Beff?"

Chris motioned for Sasha to follow him back outside the front doors of the building. "As you know, the similarities to how the Zumwalts were killed are consistent with Mr. Bauer's murder. There's one additional piece of evidence Beff found that is interesting. I'm not sure what it could mean to the investigation, but she found evidence that he had unprotected sex with an unidentified female sometime prior to his death. Probably only hours before he was killed."

Sasha took a sip of the coffee and thought that the coffee the ME's office had was certainly better than what was offered back at the station. "That's it? Nothing else?"

"You already know that although Mr. Bauer's eyes were also glued open, it's clear that the job was done hurriedly. Everything else was very similar. What do you think about his having sex?"

"I'm not sure if it is important or not."

"Beff is going to run the DNA on the vaginal secretions. If the DNA is in the database, we could at least identify and interview the female to help determine a timeline in Mr. Bauer's movements after he left work."

"What did we find out at the dealership?"

"He left work around six in the evening, based on the interviews with his boss and coworkers. That was the normal time he'd get off. If the neighbor is correct on the time Bauer got home at around 8:30 p.m., then we don't have any idea of what he was doing during those two and a half hours, other than having sex. The dealership may be closed now, but we need to ask if anyone was aware of a girlfriend or someone he was meeting after work."

"Check to see if you can find that out tonight."

———

Sasha walked down the hallway and found the door to Beff's office open and saw her sitting at her desk looking at her computer screen. He stopped before entering and rapped his knuckles on the doorframe. She looked up over a pair of reading glasses. Sasha smiled. "Your coffee tastes better than ours. What's up with that?"

Beff laughed. "We only have the best here." She leaned back in her chair. "Would you like to know our secret?"

"Absolutely."

"You can't tell anyone I told you, okay?" Beff stood up and walked around her desk.

"Mum's the word."

"All the coffee drinkers chip in the difference between what the county budgets for us to spend for coffee and the cost to upgrade. The cost is around forty dollars a year per coffee drinker."

"That wouldn't work at the station."

Beff was surprised. "Why not?"

Sasha stepped into Beff's office. "Coffee drinkers like the same kind of coffee at the station that they drink at home. Yours tastes too good."

Beff laughed. "So, you really like it."

"I just said it's good."

Beff turned around and walked back to her desk and sat down. "Well, you can drop a quarter in the can if you have another cup."

Sasha walked over and sat down at one of the chairs in front of Beff's desk. "Are you ready to go over what you found?"

She leaned back in her chair again. It had been a long day, and she had been on her feet for most of it. "There's not much to tell you. Did you talk to Chris?"

"Yes, but I want to hear it from you, if you don't mind." Sasha put his coffee cup on the top of her desk. She tossed him a coaster.

Beff leaned forward. "The similarities to what I found in the autopsies of the Zumwalts are amazing. Start with the Taser wounds on his upper back, just below the right shoulder."

"I believe he got out of his car, and the killer probably approached him from behind and shot him."

Beff nodded. That information really wasn't relevant to her. "Next the body shows similar abrasions present on both wrists and ankles, again like those found on the first victims." She knew that not saying the names of the victims annoyed Sasha, but she didn't care. "He had a pierced left ear."

"I didn't see that."

"Technically the piercing is called a cartilage piercing. It's located in the transparent tissue at the top of the ear." Beff pulled her hair back to show Sasha on her ear where it was located on Mr. Bauer. "It was a single hole. In that location, a person most often wears either a ringed loop or a barbell hoop. There was redness apparent, which could be the result of someone unaccustomed to removing the adornment having taken it out, or it's possible that the piercing never properly healed. This condition often presents with this type of piercing."

Sasha nodded. Chris walked in and sat down in the chair next to him.

Beff nodded hello and continued. "Next, there was tape residue on the back of his neck, at the kyphosis. The previous two victims both had residue present in multiple places on their necks, but the only residue with today's victim was on the kyphosis." Beff saw that Sasha wasn't familiar with the term, so she turned her head and touched the base of her neck. "It's the small bump or hump located at the base of your neck at the top of your back." Sasha reached around and felt the area on his neck. "Feel it?"

"Yes. Why do you think tape residue would only be present there?"

Beff shook her head. "That's hard to say. It could be that the position of the body at the time the killer placed the plastic bag over his head did not require him to use as much tape. I'm not sure. I just wanted you to be aware." Sasha nodded. "There was also redness on the front of his neck. Together these could be signs that the killer pulled the bag tighter and didn't need to use tape to secure it like with the Zumwalts. Between you and me, I think it was probably the position of the body that allowed the killer to gain better control over the victim. And that there was only one victim the killer needed to be concerned with could also be the reason."

Sasha nodded. "That's a good point."

"The killer may have been able to quickly gain control over Mr. Bauer before he recovered from being shot with the Taser and being bound. The abrasions at the wrists and ankles were not as severe with this victim. It is possible that he died quickly. Death was a result of suffocation." Beff looked at her notes. "There is no question on that."

"That was all good. Thanks." Sasha looked at Chris, who nodded to him, implying that he had found out something. Sasha mouthed, "One second." He asked Beff, "What about the evidence that Mr. Bauer had sex prior to his death?"

Beff looked at her report again. "Vaginal secretions on his genitalia. He had unprotected sex within a few hours before he died. Do you know Gloria Redman?"

Chris shook his head, and Sasha shook his head and said no.

"She's my serologist. I asked her to check with the FBI's CODIS, as it's possible they may have the DNA we found on Bauer in their database. You know CODIS contains the DNA of persons arrested for crimes, those convicted of crimes, as well as the DNA collected at crime scenes that has never been matched and remains unidentified?"

Sasha was annoyed. "Yes, we know that."

"It's going to take a few days to get a report back from the FBI. I just wanted you to be aware that we're checking that."

Sasha nodded. "Okay. Good luck with that." He then gave Beff an update on what they had learned. "Bauer got off work at 6 p.m. last night. I doubt he had sex at work, so between the time he got off work and arrived home around 8:30 p.m., he had sex. We sent officers back to the dealership a few minutes ago to see if we could find out anything more." Sasha turned to Chris. "Can you tell us what you found out?"

"His manager was still at the dealership, as were a couple friends. The manager didn't know anything." Chris paused for a few seconds. "When dispatch sent out the request, two officers responded. After they spoke with the manager and the others, they were standing out by their cruisers having a cigarette when one of his friends they had just spoken with walked out. The friend was evidently hesitant to tell them something he knew about Bauer in front of the others. The friend's name was Taylor Cummins. He told them that since Bauer's wife and kids moved out to Arizona, he was pretty active looking for hookups on dating apps."

"Seriously?" Sasha shook his head.

Beff leaned back in her chair and laughed. "I've got a few girlfriends that use apps for the same thing while going through a divorce. They use it because it can be very anonymous."

"I have to admit I've used it a few times," Chris said, "but not for hookups. I use it to meet people. You can be anonymous or not. It's just not for sex."

Being a private person himself, Sasha wondered why Chris was voluntarily providing this information. "Do you think we can find out who he was with on the app?"

"We'd have to check if they've gotten into his mobile phone yet. We'll probably have to get a court order to look at any of the information on the app," Chris said. "How would you like me to proceed, Sasha?"

"Check to see if they've gotten into it yet. Earlier this afternoon we were checking with his mobile service provider to see if we could get his call and text details, also to see if they could provide us with tracking his movements in the hours or maybe days prior to his death. Beff, is there anything else?"

"The last thing is that we found a variety of fibers, animal hairs, and other contaminants on the body. Those are being analyzed now." Beff picked up a report and quickly scanned the first page. "You told me the victim's clothing was found on the floor of the garage, Sasha. You also said that you thought he may have been transported in the wheelbarrow you found in the garage." She looked up at him.

"Yes. Haven't you talked with Steve?"

"Yes. But right now, I'm talking with you and want to reconfirm what you saw at the two scenes." Beff looked back down at the report she was reading.

"Yes, I believe that is how the killer transported Mr. Bauer from the garage to the tree. That is of course assuming that he was confronted by the killer in the garage, Tased, bound, suffocated, and then moved to the tree. I believe that to be the case, so, therefore, there are two crime scenes, just like the Zumwalts'."

Beff leaned back in her chair. "I believe we have evidence that will show that he was moved from the garage to the trail in the wheelbarrow you found in the garage."

Sasha nodded. "Then we are in total agreement, Beff."

"Mr. Bauer has no family members nearby and possibly no living relatives, based on a call with his ex-wife, so we're waiting for a positive identification from records from the military branch that he served. He was a veteran who served two tours in Afghanistan. Sad way to die after living through that hell." Beff mouthed a quick prayer and crossed herself.

"We have had six different civilians ID the picture we showed them of Mr.

Bauer's body," Sasha noted. "A neighbor, Mr. Parnell, his boss at the dealership, and four coworkers. Have you accessed any local dental records?"

"No, we're still awaiting that information, but the military records provided us all we need to provide a positive ID. The ex-wife will evidently be returning at some point, but she provided the name of an attorney who represented her ex-husband in their divorce. That should help you possibly find out more information."

"If you can provide that information to Chris, he'll check with the attorney first thing tomorrow. Thanks, Beff. Is that everything?"

"Yes, that's it for now." Beff stood up and then stretched. "I'm going to get out of here and call it a day. Others are working on different aspects of the evidence we collected, so as I find out more, I'll make sure you and Chris are updated."

———

Outside, Sasha lit up a cigarette. "Do you agree with what Beff said?"

"When did you start buying your own cigarettes?"

"This afternoon. Do you agree with what Beff said?"

"Yes. It's not sagacious. She just recapped what we believe."

Sasha looked at Chris with disbelief, then laughed. "Sagacious? Geez, Chris. You look that up in your thesaurus this morning?"

"I was kidding. How about I don't think what she said was insightful or helpful. We already know what we know, and we already knew what she told us."

"I agree. Beff isn't happy with me, and I think she was stating the obvious, as she's as frustrated as we are that she and her team couldn't find anything that is helping us find a suspect." Sasha put his cigarette in the receptacle that he was standing next to and took out a piece of gum. "Let's go back to the station for a couple of hours before calling it quits for the night." He pulled out his mobile phone and walked to his SUV. "I'm going to give Janet a quick call. See you there shortly."

Janet answered on the first ring. "Hi, sweetie. How's it going today?"

"I just told Chris it's like déjà vu all over again. Or maybe it is Groundhog Day. Are you still at the center?"

"Yes. I'm trying to finish up some reports tonight because I have a dentist appointment first thing in the morning, and he told me that I'll be numbed up for a few hours."

"I forgot about that. I'm heading back to the station for a little while. I'll try to be home by nine. You want me to pick something up?" Sasha started his SUV, backed out of the parking space, and headed back to the station.

"How about Chinese?"

"That works. I'll let you know if I'm running late." He dialed the chief's mobile number.

The call was answered on the first ring. "Chief Boyer."

"Good evening, Chief. Do you have a few minutes to talk?"

"There is nothing as important right now as this call. What can you tell me?"

Sasha sighed as he pulled into the station and parked. He stayed in the car as he updated the chief.

"There's no DNA evidence other than the victim's?" the chief asked.

"They're testing collected evidence now. Hair samples, fabrics, and other contaminants found in the garage and on the tree where he was found posed. Beff's comments were that the lack of evidence is similar to what was found with the Zumwalts."

"So that's a no?"

Sasha could tell by the chief's tone that he was annoyed that there wasn't something more. "Yes, but Beff did find DNA on Bauer that suggests he had sex with an unknown female between the time he left work and arrived back home. That's been sent to CODIS to see if there's a match in the database. I think that's a longshot, though."

"The media is all over me," the chief said, "and if we don't find something to move this investigation forward, they're going to start working on the mayor. Neither of us needs that."

"I understand. As per Beff, we will know more either later tonight or in the morning. When I hear from her, you will be my first call."

———

Sasha went into the station to meet with Chris. "How can we find out who the woman is that Mr. Bauer hooked up with?" he asked.

"I'll check to see if his pictures show up in any of the dating apps. I'll also see if the Zumwalts were active on any sites. Are you thinking this could somehow be a motive?" Chris asked.

"I don't know. Right now, I think it's a distraction. But who knows?"

"I guess it is possible that the Zumwalts and Bauer could have pissed off somebody they met online." Chris sat down. "We could work on that angle. That's if you think it's worthwhile."

Sasha sat down. "I think we have to drill down on this theory. At first, I thought it sounded nuts, but after giving it some thought it is plausible."

"I agree. I'll ask Steve to see if he's gotten into Bauer's mobile phone yet. I'll check into that ASAP."

Sasha was really feeling tired. He thought it was probably the stress. Leaning back in the chair, he rubbed his temples again and then sat up. "Chris, get a listing of all the phone numbers Bauer called or texted in the past ninety days. Then take that listing to see if any of Bauer's numbers match the ninety days for calls and texts to numbers that the Zumwalts had on their mobiles."

"Good idea. I'm not seeing them traveling in the same circles, but we can look at calls, texts, and other social media activity. I can also have officers check with the dealership to see if the Zumwalts ever had any work done on their cars. That's probably a dead end, because the dealership where Bauer worked doesn't sell the SUV model the Zumwalts were driving. But regardless, I'll have that checked on."

"I agree with you that we're probably not going to find anything, but it'll show the chief we're turning over every stone." Sasha stood up and stretched. He looked at his mobile and saw it was almost nine o'clock. Crap, he was going to be late getting home with dinner.

"I'll start the ball rolling, but it's possible nothing is going to get started until the morning. That okay?" Chris followed Sasha out of the interrogation room.

"That works. Go home and get some sleep. It's been a long day." The two walked over to their desks. Sasha quickly called the Chinese restaurant and placed a to-go order of kung-pao chicken, shrimp fried rice, and egg rolls. It would be ready by the time he got there, in under ten minutes. He loved the efficiency and ease of ordering at Chinese restaurants. Plus, the food was great.

He dialed Janet, and she answered on the first ring. "I'm on my way. I should be home in fifteen minutes or so."

"I'll be right behind you. I'm leaving the office now."

He laughed. "Here I thought I was running behind."

"I bet you a dollar I'm home before you, mister." The two regularly bet on almost anything. The loser of the bet had to write down the date, say that the winner won and why, then sign the bill.

When Sasha told people about the genesis of their betting, he'd say that when they were first going out, he'd purposely lose the bets. Janet vehemently disagreed, saying that he only said that because he lost so many bets. She had a drawer full of dollar bills to prove it. Now he tried to only bet her when he knew he was going to win. He wasn't going to lose tonight. He put on his lights and siren as he headed to pick up his order.

He smiled to himself and began feeling a little better about his day. Talking with Janet could always put him in a good mood, and he couldn't wait to tell her how much he loved her. Tonight he was going to try to put the investigation out of his mind and focus on the two of them.

19

I t was Friday morning, and Sasha and Janet were lying in bed talking about the coming weekend. Sasha's oldest daughter, Emily, who lived nearby in LeRoy, called last night to let her father know that his oldest grandson, Aiden, had baseball tryouts on Saturday. Aiden had asked that his granddad be there since his father, a commercial airline copilot, was on a four-day line and could not get his schedule changed.

Sasha had been working eighteen-hour days since the Zumwalt murders three weeks ago. The chief kept reminding him that he was getting nowhere fast. With the mounting pressure, Sasha wasn't sure he could afford to take a couple of hours off to go watch Aiden try out.

Janet was insistent that he attend. She was going to be there, so Sasha had damn well better be there. "What is it you don't understand? Aiden asked for you to be there."

"I know. I know. You know the pressure I'm under right now. The mayor is on the chief, and the chief is on me."

Janet got up out of bed and said, "Matte glossy?" She went into the bathroom.

He shook his head. "Matte glossy" referred to another one of their early dates when they were looking at some pictures, and Janet made a comment about one of them. For some reason Sasha thought Janet didn't understand the difference between the matte finish on one photo and the glossy finish on the other photo, and he started explaining it to her. After that, when one of them said something to the other that should be blatantly obvious, they used "matte glossy" as a way to point it out. "Okay. You're right. I'll make it work." Without responding, Janet turned on the shower, a clear sign that she wasn't impressed with the time it took him to make the right decision.

Emily would be up getting ready for work and getting Aiden off to school. He texted her: "I will be there Sat. let Aiden know. ♥ Dad."

Sasha was dreading his day, as he had another face-to-face meeting scheduled with the chief, and for the first time the mayor would be attending. The pressure to find the killer was understandably building. Murders were rare in Bloomington, so having three occur in just ten days was causing fear in the area, especially for residents who lived on Constitution Trail.

His phone started to ring, and as he answered, Janet's phone started ringing as well. A desk sergeant never calls a detective at this hour unless something is up. Todd's tone suggested it was bad news.

"I'm sorry to tell you that 911 had a call a few minutes ago." Sasha sat up in bed with his left hand on his forehead. "A man on his way to work pulled onto North Robinson Street a block east of Locust, and his headlights shined on someone sitting by a tree on a section of the trail."

"Damn it."

"He drove his car forward and put on his high beams. He clearly saw a naked female. He stopped and got out to check on her." Todd paused. Sasha walked over to Janet's mobile phone and saw that there was a voicemail message. He carried it into the bathroom. "The female was his next-door neighbor. Told 911 her name is Stephanie Davis. A twenty-eight-year-old who lived by herself in the home directly across Robinson from where he found her. Her eyes were open, Sasha. The 911 caller is a nurse and confirms that she's deceased."

Janet was washing her hair when Sasha tapped on the glass door of the shower. She opened her eyes and saw him pointing at her phone. He placed it on the bathroom counter. "I'll get over there as quick as I can. Please wait fifteen minutes before calling the ME. Get Chris on the phone and let him know I'm heading there now."

"Will do. I have already dispatched four officers and cruisers. The first is already on scene, and I told him to tape off the area. One of the officers is stopping by the station to pick up a couple of pop-up screens to hide the body from view, as there are a lot of homes in that area."

"Good idea. Thanks."

"The guy covered her with a blanket."

"I'll be on scene as quick as I can. Since we know her name and home address, get a search warrant ASAP."

"That was already on my to-do list."

There was no time for a shower. Sasha went into the closet and started getting dressed. Emily texted back: "♥ ♥ GREAT! ♥ ♥ 8:30." Crap, he may have to cancel.

Janet was standing there wrapped in a towel listening to her voicemail. "Another one? What the hell?"

"This time a twenty-eight-year-old female. On the trail on Robinson near Locust. That's just a block or so from the David Davis Mansion. Her last name is Davis. Weird coincidence."

"This is obviously a serial killer, Sasha."

He nodded. "I've resisted so far, but I'm going to call in the Illinois and federal bureaus for more boots on the ground. They've already been looking at the evidence we've found to see if they could find something we missed." Sasha closed his eyes and shook his head. "My meeting with the mayor and chief just ramped up in intensity. I'll call the chief on my way to the scene. I gotta get going."

"Sorry, Sasha." Janet gave him a big hug. "I pray that this time the killer left something that will lead you to him."

"From your lips to God's ears." He kissed her on the forehead.

———

The chief answered on the first ring. "Morning, Sasha. You sound like you're in a hurry to get somewhere."

Sasha could barely hear him over the siren. "I'm on my way to the scene of what appears to be another murder on the trail." He assumed the chief would react, but there was only silence, so he shared all that he knew.

"What the hell is going on?"

"I don't know, sir. I'm going to call in the IBI and FBI for some on-the-ground help." He'd decided to involve the two bureaus to provide him-self some cover. He didn't think they would find anything he, his team, and the ME hadn't already uncovered, which he knew was precious little.

"I agree, it's time to bring them into the investigation. I'm going to give the mayor a call. After you've had a chance to do your initial review of the scene, I'm going to suggest to the mayor that he and I head over. It will help appease him, and it will also give him a chance to be our face of calm and assurance to the media and, more importantly, the community. The pressure just rose exponentially on everybody."

Sasha clearly heard what the chief was suggesting. Elected officials, who were already hearing serious concerns from voters, were going to start scream-ing for the killer to be apprehended. "I'm not sure bringing the mayor into the investigation is a good idea, Chief."

"Why? He can take on the media."

"I think he'll probably put the blame on us."

"The blame is on us, Sasha. We're responsible for finding the killer, not the mayor. What don't you get?"

"What I meant was that I'm not sure having him come out to the scene is a good idea."

"I'm calling the mayor now. Expect us out there by ten o'clock. Understand?"

"Yes, sir," Sasha said just before the chief disconnected the call. Maybe he pushed back a little too hard. The chief was right, of course, but having to babysit the mayor wasn't something Sasha wanted to be doing today. He turned off his siren and lights as he slowed and stopped at the cruiser blocking the street. He rolled down his window to greet the patrolman on duty.

Tyler Morgan had been with the force for about six years after serving in the Marine Corps for four years. "Morning, Sasha. It looks like we caught another one." He motioned in the direction of the scene.

"Appears that way. See ya, Tyler." Sasha rolled up his window, then circled around the cruiser and turned north toward the scene. He passed three more intersections where officers in cruisers blocked the entrance to the area. Todd had quickly gotten the area secured. Sasha pulled up and parked near where

Chris was talking with several patrolmen in front of what he assumed was Ms. Davis's one-story ranch-style home.

"Morning, Sasha." Chris handed Sasha a cup of hot black coffee. "You know Officers Creighton, Butler, and Cavendish, don't you?"

"Yes, I do. They've been on the force for almost as many years as you are old, Chris." Sasha smiled and shook hands with the three patrolmen. "I see Todd sent out the old guys this morning." David Creighton, Mark Butler, and Robert Cavendish all joined the department the same year as Sasha. They were the most experienced officers on the force, and each played a vital role in passing along their experience to new hires. Sadly, Sasha was not as close with them as he was before moving up in the ranks, and he said to himself that he needed to ask the three over for cards sometime soon.

"It's obvious to everybody that Todd went for experience and expertise over youth and full heads of hair," David said. All three of the officers had lost the battle against early onset balding. Sasha, on the other hand, had a full head of hair.

"Obviously." Sasha laughed. He took a drink of the hot coffee. "You can tell that just by looking at you guys."

Chris touched Sasha's elbow to move him toward the scene. "I'd like to take you over to meet Miles Jordan, who found Ms. Davis about forty or so minutes ago." The back passenger door to the cruiser was open, and the man was sitting with his legs out, drinking a cup of coffee. "Mr. Jordan? I'd like to introduce you to Senior Detective Sasha Frank, who is leading the investigation."

Miles Jordan stood up and reached out to shake hands with Sasha. "Good morning, Detective."

"Good morning, Mr. Jordan." Miles towered over Sasha.

"I'm sorry to meet you under these circumstances," Sasha said.

"Me too."

"If you don't mind, I'd like you to tell me what happened this morning, starting with getting into your car to head to work." Sasha watched Chris get out his notebook.

"I live right next door to Steph. I got into my car about 6:10 a.m. to head to my shift, which starts at seven. I have to be there a little early to go over patient records with the other shift, and I always stop for coffee on Veterans on my way." He took another sip of his coffee. Miles looked at Chris. "This isn't as good. But thanks for getting me a cup." Chris nodded.

Sasha smiled. "Go on, Mr. Jordan."

"When I started my car, the headlights automatically came on, and they stayed on as I pulled out onto Mulberry. The sun was up, but with all the trees in the neighborhood, even this time of the year, it still seems dark. When I turned onto Robinson, my headlights shined across the road and that tree." Jordan pointed over to the tree where he found Ms. Davis. "I saw a body on the ground leaning up against the tree. She was, like, just staring straight at me." He closed his eyes.

"I understand this isn't easy, Mr. Jordan."

"It's not just finding a dead body, Detective. No one expects to see a body on your way to work. I see people die at my job every week. It's just that it was Steph." Jordan paused again. "I hit my high beams and pulled forward onto the grass just short of where it drops down to the trail. I was maybe less than forty or fifty feet away. I could clearly see that it was Steph, and she was naked, and her eyes were wide open. She was not blinking even with the high beams shining straight into her face.

"I got out of the car, slid down the embankment, and walked over to her, calling her name. It was silly that I called out to her, as she was obviously dead. Steph was sitting flat on the ground with her legs crossed and her back leaned up to the tree. It seemed like she was looking over at her house. I could tell as I got closer that her eyes weren't clear; they were showing the initial signs of death. I walked over and felt her carotid artery for a pulse. She was cold to the touch, and there was obviously no pulse. I went back up to my car for my mobile when I realized that I had rushed out of the house without it. I ran back to the house and grabbed my mobile and a blanket off the couch and ran back here while calling 911."

Sasha waited to see if Jordan was going to continue. He didn't, so Sasha asked a follow-up question. "Thank you, Mr. Jordan. Can I ask how long you've lived next door to Ms. Davis?"

"We bought our house six years ago." Miles paused. "I live with my part-ner. Steph moved into the house a couple of years ago when her dad bought it for her." He paused. "I don't know how he's going to deal with this. Steph is an only child, and her mother passed away last year. Breast cancer. They were a very close family." Miles looked away and wiped away tears.

"I understand. I'm sorry." Sasha paused and waited for Mr. Jordan to gather himself. "Does Ms. Davis have any roommates, or is she romantically connected with anyone?"

"She doesn't have a roommate. I don't know of anyone she may be involved with." Miles paused. "Well, no one special anyway."

Sasha sensed he was holding back something. "I'm sorry, Mr. Jordan. I apologize for asking you these questions. I understand that there may not have been someone special, but what did you mean by no one special?"

"Like I said, we live right next door. She was a good and fun neighbor. Alex and I—Alex is my partner—we had a lot of fun with Steph. She said she didn't have time for dating." Miles paused again before adding, "At least that's what she told us."

Sasha was never comfortable asking about someone's personal life. He liked it even less when someone asked him about things he considered per-sonal. In a murder investigation, he had to ask difficult questions of family, friends, and coworkers. Quite often people would hold back if they knew something that wasn't complimentary of the person who had died. "I have a couple more questions," he said. "Did Ms. Davis ever mention anyone whom she was afraid of, or did you ever see anyone in the neighborhood who may have wanted to harm her?"

"No, sir. She never mentioned anyone, and I haven't seen or noticed any-one suspicious in the neighborhood. We're a pretty close-knit neighborhood, and we all look out for each other."

"Can you tell me what Ms. Davis did for a living?"

"Steph was a hair stylist at a salon, David Ray's, in Normal off Main Street."

"I appreciate your taking the time to talk with us this morning. I'm going to ask you to accompany Detective Watkins to the police station so that you can provide us a written statement. Do you mind doing that? We can call your employer to let them know that you're helping us with an investigation."

"Yes, I can provide you a written statement. I've already called my employer to let them know that I wouldn't be coming in this morning."

"Thank you for helping us, Mr. Jordan." Sasha turned to Chris. "Chris, please take Mr. Jordan to the station and have him provide us with his written statement." He turned back to Miles. "If you leave us the keys to your car, we will make sure that we return it to your driveway. Is your partner at home?"

"No, he flew yesterday afternoon to Dallas to attend a conference."

"Have you reached out to him?"

"I called him before I left for work. If it's okay, I'd like to call him before I go to the station."

"Certainly. Thank you again for your help. Chris will take you to the station as soon as you finish your call. I apologize, but after you make the call Chris will need to secure your telephone as part of our investigation. I hope you understand?" Miles nodded and shook hands with Sasha.

Sasha walked back to his SUV and opened the rear hatch, grabbed a CSI kit, and ripped it open. He sat down on the rear of the SUV and pulled on the overalls, pulled up the hood, and then grabbed the mask, booties, and latex gloves. He shouted over to the three officers standing nearby: "The ME could be showing up anytime. Keep her and her team back until I'm done, okay?"

Officer Creighton gave Sasha a thumbs-up. "Will do, Sasha."

He pulled on his booties, the latex gloves, and the mask and slowly walked down the embankment. He stopped on the trail about ten feet from the tree where the screens were set up and quickly surveyed the surrounding area. At this point the trail was maybe five to six feet below the street level. To the left and right behind the tree, ground cover had been planted by either the city or a homeowner. A faded white fence about six feet high ran behind the ground cover for probably fifty feet north and south of the tree.

Sasha moved one of the pop-up screens to the side and pulled it back into place behind him. He slowly lifted a corner of the blue-and-orange blanket that was covering the victim. Janet would call her hairstyle edgy. The very short hair on the sides was jet black, and the longer bright blue hair on the top fell across her face.

He looked around to make sure that no one could see as he lifted the blanket completely off the body. Ms. Davis was petite, maybe five feet tall, and probably weighed less than a hundred pounds. Like the others, she was sitting on the ground cross-legged and leaning up against the trunk of the tree. Her eyes were green. There were no apparent signs of glue on her eyelids or face.

There were several empty piercing holes on her face and at the top and bottom of her left ear. Just like the Zumwalts and Greg Bauer, Ms. Davis wasn't wearing any jewelry. Their working theory was that the killer had taken any jewelry they were wearing, along with driver's licenses as trophies.

There were also empty piercing holes at her belly button, and she had a small tattoo of a pair of doves sitting on a tree branch on the inside of her left thigh.

Sasha stood up and walked around the perimeter of the tree, making sure that he stayed at least five feet away from the base of the trunk and Ms. Davis. Nothing appeared out of place, and he didn't see any footprints in the grassy area.

She had been posed with her legs crossed. Her right hand was covering her genitals, while her left hand appeared to be resting on her right shoulder with her arm covering her breasts. Her left hand must be glued down; gravity wouldn't have allowed it to stay in that position. Why did the killer pose her in this way? Sasha wondered.

With his quick review of the scene completed, he moved the screens back into position as several ME vehicles pulled up behind his SUV. He walked up the embankment to the street and over to where Beff was sitting in her SUV talking on her mobile. Beff put her mobile in her coat pocket and stepped out of her SUV. "Hi, Sasha."

"Morning, Beff."

Sasha followed her to the back of her SUV. "Can you give me an update on what we've got here?" Beff asked.

"We have a twenty-eight-year-old female by the name of Stephanie Davis, found by a neighbor as he was driving to work. The neighbor is a nurse. He touched her neck to check for any sign of life. He also covered her with a blanket that had been on a couch in his home."

"Seriously? We'll have to get a DNA swab from him and also get evidence from the couch and his home to eliminate and isolate whatever evidence was transferred from the blanket."

Sasha nodded. "He's at the station, but Chris will bring him back shortly. I just finished a quick review of the scene. Her eyes are wide open, worth noting that there are no visible signs of glue. Ms. Davis is posed in the sitting position, with her legs crossed, her right hand covering her genitals, and her left hand resting on her shoulder with her arm covering her breasts. I'm not sure, but her left hand may be glued to her shoulder." He glanced over, looking at the screens. "She's leaned up against the tree. I didn't touch her, obviously. She has a number of piercings, but no visible jewelry. While you do your thing, I'm going to see if the search warrant for her house is approved. Good luck." Sasha turned and walked over to his SUV and called Todd for an update.

Sasha removed the latex gloves he'd been wearing and opened the back hatch of his SUV. He called Todd on his phone. "You've got the warrant in hand?" He reached in and grabbed a garbage bag, removed his CSI gear while he talked, and put it all in the bag before grabbing another kit.

"I got it just a few minutes ago, Sasha."

"Great. I'm going to check out the house now." He put on the CSI gear and then called to his three friends drinking coffee by their cruisers. "I'd like one of you to stay in position where you're at now, but I'd appreciate two of you coming with me to watch the front and back of her house while I'm inside."

The three talked briefly, and David stayed in place while Mark and Robert joined Sasha. He decided to make a quick walk around the perimeter of the house before entering the front door. The house looked very drab and stark, without any bushes or flower beds like most of the other homes in the neighborhood. There wasn't any outdoor furniture on the deck in the back, but as he got close, he did see an ashtray filled with cigarette butts sitting on the railing. He had friends who were closet smokers who never smoked in their cars or houses.

He next stopped at the driveway, where a car was parked. If this car was Ms. Davis's, Sasha wasn't sure if the search warrant would include it since it wasn't parked inside a garage attached to the house. He quickly called Todd and gave him the license number to confirm that the car was registered to Ms. Davis, and if it was hers, he told Todd to ask the judge to expand the warrant to include the car. He then realized that the house didn't have a garage. Garages had been key to the murders of the Zumwalts and Greg Bauer. That was where the killer had been able to subdue them without being seen. Had the killer this time attacked inside the house?

Sasha walked over to the front steps and then up the two steps to the small porch. He turned the doorknob and found that it was unlocked. "Don't follow me in," he said to Mark, "but please take a position with your weapon drawn here on the front porch." Mark moved forward to take his assigned position as Sasha pulled his gun and pushed the unlocked door open. He turned on his flashlight and stepped inside.

Inside the house was dark. As he shined the flashlight beam around the living room, he could see that it was nicely decorated, and nothing appeared out of place. There was an opening directly in front of him that he assumed led to the back of the house and similar openings to his right and left. He moved forward, leaving the door open, and then turned to his right to the entry of a hallway. He shined the beam of the light down the hallway, which was about twenty feet in length. There were two doors on his left and one doorway on his right.

He walked to the first door on his left, which was open. Inside was a hall bathroom with a sink, toilet, and bathtub. He moved on to the second door on the left and found a small bedroom. After a quick search, he found nothing of interest in the room or closet. Crossing back down the hallway to the single door, he walked into a much larger bedroom, which appeared to be Stephanie's room. The bed had not been used since it was last made. The bedroom was nicely decorated, and there were several pictures on the two bedside tables. He assumed the photos were of her with her parents at different times of her life. She was a beautiful girl. Nothing seemed out of place in her bedroom.

He walked back down the hallway and across the living room to the entry of what might have once been the garage. Inside was a large crafts table similar to one his daughter Emily had in her home. He walked around the table and didn't see anything that looked out of place. The room was very tidy, like the rest of the house.

The kitchen looked as though it had been remodeled recently with new cabinets, countertops, and appliances. He shined his light to the right and saw a doorway that must have led to the small back deck where he had seen the ashtray. He turned and looked to his right and saw a dining table with four chairs. One of the chairs had been pulled away from the table. On top of the table lay a pair of high-heeled black boots, red socks, blue jeans, undergarments, and a red sweater, along with a lightweight jacket, a purse, and a billfold.

The clothing had been cut with scissors, as in the previous murders. He picked up the billfold and quickly looked through it. There was no driver's license. Without touching the open purse, he looked inside and saw makeup, gum, tissues, and a key chain. There were five keys, one of which looked like it would be the key to the car parked outside.

There was a sound behind him, and Sasha quickly turned and crouched, shining his light toward a door he hadn't noticed to the left of the entryway. He slowly approached the door with his flashlight and gun in hand. Sitting on the floor of the doorway was a yellow tennis ball. "Whoever is in there, come out now with your hands up!" No one came out, and he stepped through the door. A calico cat stared at him from atop a clothes dryer. "Hi, kitty." The cat didn't move.

He scanned the room with his flashlight and walked over to the cat. The cat stood up and rubbed up against him. "Nice kitty." Sasha didn't like cats that much, but whenever he was at a friend's house who had one, the cats always liked him. Go figure. "What happened here, kitty?" He walked back to the dining table. The cat jumped down and followed him.

He walked over to the back door and found that, like the front door, it was also unlocked. He opened the door and saw Robert crouching, his gun drawn at the back steps of the deck. Robert relaxed, stood up, and holstered his weapon. Sasha nodded at him. He then shined his flashlight on the outside keyhole and could clearly see there were scratch marks that could have been made from a lockpick. Could this be how the killer gained entry to the house?

The entire house was neat and orderly, with nothing that seemed to be out of place except the one dining table chair that was pulled out of where it would normally be. Sasha thought that the killer could have been sitting in that one chair in the dark, waiting for her to return home.

There was nothing more for him to do in the house, so he headed toward the front door. The cat followed close behind him. He stopped, squatted, and petted it. "I'll be sending someone from animal control over to take you into the shelter before Beff and her team come over, kitty."

Mark was standing outside smoking a cigarette as Sasha walked up. "Do you mind?"

"Here you go." Mark pulled out his pack of cigarettes with a lighter tucked into the open package. Sasha took out the lighter and a cigarette, lit it, and took in a long puff before exhaling.

"I thought you quit, Sasha."

"I did." Sasha laughed. "Stress, I guess. Could you let Robert know that I'd like you both to stand guard in place until the ME's team finishes up?" Mark nodded, and Sasha walked down the sidewalk and across the front of the yard and into the street. He stopped to look at the vehicles that had arrived since he'd been inside. Members of the IBI and FBI stood together about a hundred feet down the street. He'd be talking to them shortly.

Beff was standing outside the pop-up screens. She waved him over.

Sasha stopped at the top of the embankment, about twenty feet from where she was on the trail. "What did you find?"

She removed her mask. "Her eyes were glued open like the others, and I believe that she was suffocated, but other than that and the lack of jewelry, there are no similarities to the other murders. There aren't Taser marks, there aren't abrasions on her wrists or ankles, and there isn't tape residue on her neck."

"Do you think it's because of her size? The killer was able to easily control her because she's petite?"

"I think that's a reasonable assumption." Beff took off her gloves. "I'm estimating that she is less than five feet tall and weighs about ninety-five pounds." She shook her head. "The poor girl would have been very easy to control."

"I just completed a walk-through of her home across the street. You can see there is no garage." Sasha looked over his right shoulder, then looked back to Beff. "I think the killer entered through the back door sometime last night and lay in wait for her to return home. One of the chairs sitting around the dining table was moved, and it looks like the killer could have been sitting there while he waited for her return. Her clothing, shoes, purse, and billfold are lying on the kitchen table. All the clothing appears to have been cut off like the others. There's no driver's license in her billfold. All consistent with the murders of both the Zumwalts and Mr. Bauer."

Beff nodded. "I don't think there's any doubt that the same person did this. We haven't disclosed the fact that the killer has posed the victims, and she most certainly was posed. By the way, you were right about her left hand being glued to her body."

"Geez. Why?"

"Unexplainable. The hand positions must have meaning to the killer."

"Have you established an approximate time of death?"

"Based on body temperature, I'm estimating that time of death was between nine and ten o'clock last night. I'll have a better idea after the autopsy."

"By the way, the mayor and chief are showing up here by ten."

"The team is working her body now, and we will transport the body as soon as they're done, hopefully before they arrive." Beff walked up the bank to where Sasha was standing, and he reached out to help her. "There is something that you can tell the mayor that's important."

"What's that?"

"What amazes me is that like the other murders, I haven't been able to find any physical evidence that points us to a killer. It's very unusual that we find no physical evidence. Whoever is committing these murders is taking extraordinary measures to minimize transference of any possible evidence that would lead us to them. It's highly unusual."

"You're welcome to stay and tell them that, but I'm not going to use your comment as an excuse. I need a cigarette." Sasha turned and walked back to where Mark was standing and motioned for another cigarette. He took another cigarette, and Mark lit it for him. Beff was staring daggers through him.

Sasha walked back. "What?"

"I don't appreciate you walking away from me like that. I'm just trying to help."

"I know you're trying to help, and I apologize for walking away. We are under a lot of pressure to solve these murders for the community. That's all." Sasha waited for Beff to say something, but she just stood there looking at him. "The house is available for the team to begin their investigation. If that's all, I'm going to start my report." Sasha again waited for her to say something. When she didn't, he turned and walked back to his SUV.

Sasha knew that having a good working relationship with Beff was important, but he was tired of it being a one-way street. It was always Beff's way or no way at all. Or maybe he was overreacting. He didn't think he was, but later he'd talk it over with Janet to get her perspective. Her words of wisdom were generally spot-on.

Putting his head back on the headrest, he rubbed his temples and gathered his thoughts; then he reached for a water bottle that was lying in the passenger-side footwell. He took a big drink, reached into his pocket for sinus tablets he hoped would help with his headache. After taking them, he opened the center console and pulled out a bottle of aspirin. What was it that Janet called it when he took this combination of pills to quell a headache? A cocktail. That was it. He hoped that this morning the cocktail of pills would work its magic.

He took the aspirin and began typing his report. He knew most detectives used a technique they developed on their own over the years when writing reports, but he always followed what he was taught in college and the state police academy. A methodical step-by-step, point-by-point report stating precisely what he had done from the minute he was made aware that the body was found. No detail was too small to be included in his initial report, as it was always possible that he could forget some detail that could later prove to be critical to solving the case. When he first became a detective, he thought that the chief had found reading them tiresome, but he had been told that the chief pushed other detectives on the force to adopt his writing style in their reports. And the chief asked him to guide newly promoted detectives through the process. The last several officers promoted worked with Sasha for several months, training with him on cases before they were given the opportunity to be assigned a case of their own. It was a part of the job that he enjoyed the most and knew he'd miss once he retired.

He'd been typing for about forty minutes when his phone rang. Dispatch.

"I just got a call from Tyler Morgan," Todd said. "He's got Stephanie Davis's father at his roadblock."

Sasha bowed his head. With the Zumwalts, Chris had notified the couple's parents of their murders with one of Beff's assistants present. With Greg Bauer, the ME's office had reached out to the police where his ex-wife lived in Arizona, and with their assistance and a member of the clergy jointly gave her the news at her home. Talking with Mr. Davis was going to be very difficult. "Tell Tyler I'll be right there." Sasha saved his report and then powered down his laptop.

It took him a little over a minute to pull up behind the vehicle parked at the roadblock. He got out of his SUV and walked over to where Tyler was standing, attempting to comfort a clearly distraught man.

As Sasha got close, Tyler said something to Mr. Davis, and the man turned to meet him. "My name is Senior Detective Sasha Frank, Mr. Davis."

"What's happened to my daughter!?" Mr. Davis was frantic. "Tell me what's happening."

Sasha answered softly and calmly. "Can we sit in your car, Mr. Davis?"

"I don't need to sit in my car. I know something terrible happened. Just tell me."

"Mr. Davis, I'm sorry to tell you that your daughter has been identified by a neighbor a short while ago as the victim of murder."

"No. No. No. No. No," Mr. Davis screamed and crumpled into Sasha's arms. Tyler struggled to help Sasha get Mr. Davis back on his feet, but he dropped to his knees. "No. No. No." Mr. Davis was sobbing.

Sasha recalled Stephanie's neighbor mentioning that her mother had passed away in the past year. Losing his wife and only child was too much for Mr. Davis to handle. "Is there anyone we can call for you?"

Tyler gave Sasha a helpless look. The two of them considered themselves pretty tough guys, but delivering confirmation of the worst news possible to a parent brought tears to their eyes. Sasha squatted to offer support. "Mr. Davis?"

The father was beginning to calm down. "Yes?"

Sasha looked him in the eyes. "Can you tell me your first name, sir?"

"Lyle. It's Lyle."

"Thank you, Lyle. Can we help you stand up, sir?" Sasha signaled Tyler to help get Mr. Davis to stand.

Mr. Davis accepted the help. "Thank you."

"Lyle? Can we please sit in your car?"

"Yes, Detective."

"Why don't you sit in the front passenger seat? I'll sit behind the wheel." Sasha held Mr. Davis by the arm and helped him into the front seat of his car. "Lyle? Can we get you some water or a soda? Or some coffee?"

"I'd take a bottle of water. Thanks."

Sasha asked Tyler to get a bottle of water from his cruiser, and he walked around to the driver's side door of Mr. Davis's car and sat down inside. Both front doors were open when Tyler returned.

Mr. Davis looked at Sasha. "I want to see my daughter."

"That's not possible right now, Lyle." Sasha watched the man turn and look out his door. He knew that Mr. Davis was trying to hold back tears.

"Why?" Mr. Davis didn't turn to look at Sasha.

"Right now, the medical examiner and her team are at the scene, and they're completing their work and collecting evidence. I don't think it would be a good idea for you to see your daughter now."

Mr. Davis turned to Sasha. "When can I see her?"

Sasha needed to choose his words carefully. "We will need you to positively identify your daughter, Lyle, but not here. Not now." He looked the devasted father in the eyes.

"Okay."

Relieved, Sasha watched him look away and take a drink of water. "I would like to call someone to come be with you, Lyle. Who would you like us to call?"

"My brother Craig."

"Does Craig live locally?"

"Yes. He lives in Towanda."

"Good. Do you have his number with you? If you do, I will give him a call."

"I have his number on my phone." Mr. Davis pulled his mobile phone out from the console and hit the home button. The picture that showed on the home screen was the smiling face of the young dead woman, posed next to a tree across from her home just a few blocks away. "This is my lovely daughter, Stephanie." The father started to weep again. He handed Sasha his mobile phone and managed to speak. "Craig Davis. He's in my favorites."

Sasha took the mobile. "If you'd like, I can get out of the car to make the call. What would you prefer?"

"I'd like to talk with him."

Sasha hit the call button and put the phone up to his ear.

"He may be at work."

Sasha nodded. After three rings the call was answered. "Is this Mr. Craig Davis?"

"Who's calling?"

"I'm Senior Detective Sasha Frank, sir. I'm a detective with the Bloomington Police Department." Sasha paused. "I'm with your brother Lyle."

"Lyle? Why are you with Lyle?"

"I'm sorry to inform you that your niece Stephanie has passed away. Lyle needs you to come be with him."

"What do you mean?"

"Stephanie was found this morning near her home. Lyle needs you to be with him. Now, if possible." Sasha could hear Lyle crying softly. He couldn't imagine hearing the same news if something happened to one of his kids or grandkids.

"Can I please talk to Lyle?"

"Yes, sir, you can, but first I need to know that you're able to come now to be with your brother. Can you do that?"

"Of course I can."

"I'll text you the location. I would suggest that your brother not drive his own car at this time. Can you bring someone to drive his car?"

"Of course. Text me, and I'll be there as quick as I can."

"I'm going to hand the phone to your brother now, and you'll be receiving a text with the intersection we're at now. It's only a few blocks from your niece's home."

Sasha handed his telephone to Lyle and stepped out of the car. He walked over to Tyler, who was standing at the right front fender of Lyle's car. Sasha wrote down Craig Davis's mobile number on a small notepad and handed it to Tyler. "Please send a text to this number with the street intersection we're at. This is Mr. Davis's brother's number. He'll be here shortly to be with Lyle. He'll be bringing someone with him to drive Lyle's car."

Tyler nodded. "I've notified family of deaths before, but that was an exceptionally hard one."

"Stephanie was his only child, and he lost his wife to cancer not very long ago. I can't imagine."

20

APRIL 21, 2018

Sasha was sitting at his desk early Saturday morning rereading his report on the murder of Stephanie Davis and looking through the evidence that Beff and her team had collected. There were distinct similarities to the murders of the Zumwalts and Bauer, but there were also stark differences from the murders of the Zumwalts and Bauer. Ms. Davis had not been Tased, she had not been bound at her wrists and ankles with zip ties, and there was no tape residue on her lips or neck.

As he read through each document, Sasha became more and more frustrated. In most crimes the perpetrator leaves something behind—hair, sweat, saliva, fingerprints.

It was infuriating for Sasha to read each report and see that they had really found nothing. They had identified the model of the Taser used in the first three deaths, which was available online from countless retailers or in stores in and around the area and across the country. The eyes of all four victims had been glued open using a commonly used brand of glue that could be purchased anywhere. Beff had identified the manufacturer of the tape that the killer used on three of the four victims, but the manufacturer sold the tape under five separate brand names. Realistically there was no possible way to determine where the tape had been purchased or which of the brands had been used by the killer.

Beff had written in her report on Ms. Davis that she found it highly unusual to have found no DNA evidence. While each of the victims shared similar fates at the hands of the killer, there was no evidence on any victim that had similarities to any of the other victims. Beff noted in her report that the killer or killers had taken extreme measures to ensure that no evidence was left behind that could be tied back to them.

There was one commonality: Prints made by a pair of men's size ten galoshes had been found at each of the crime scenes on the trail. The impressions could help solidify charges against the killer when he was found. The galoshes had a unique design on the soles, which Beff was able to identify to a single manufacturer. Galoshes weren't used by as many men today as they were in years past, but they were still readily available in stores across the area and in countless stores across the United States. Her report showed that the average shoe size of a male residing in the United States was $10\frac{1}{2}$. The killer had a slightly smaller foot than the average male, which could lead you to believe the killer was probably also shorter than the average male at a height of 5 feet 9 inches. Sasha had a friend who was 6 feet 9 inches and wore a size 11 and another friend who was 5 feet 8 inches who wore a size 13.

Beff had noted that the impressions made by the galoshes indicated damaged areas on both the left and right soles that would allow her to positively identify the shoes if they were found. Hopefully the killer would be wearing them when he was arrested, Sasha thought to himself.

Sasha got up from his desk and walked into the break room. As he poured coffee into his cup and then returned to his desk, he wondered what his next move would be. He and Chris would continue working through the list of family, friends, and coworkers of Ms. Davis, as they had done with the other victims. There was nothing that stood out that provided investigators a motive for the killings. The killings were being committed by someone with serious mental issues, they knew, but whoever it was also was very smart. To plan the murders, to commit the murders, to commit them and not be seen or heard by anyone and then leave no DNA or physical evidence that could be tied to them was, as Beff wrote in her report, "highly unusual."

Chris appeared in the doorway to Sasha's office. "How's it going this morning?" he asked.

Sasha looked up from his desk. "Morning, Chris. Getting nowhere fast, it seems."

"Are you reading Beff's report?" Chris pulled up a chair and sat to the side of Sasha's desk.

"Yep. There's a lot of information in the report, just nothing that can give us a jump start on the investigations. Twenty-four hours after Ms. Davis was found, and we still know nothing. Twenty-one days after the first two murders, and we really don't know anything. Eleven days after the second murder, and we know nothing." Sasha shook his head. "I've been rereading the report on Ms. Davis, and there isn't anything that jumps out at me."

Chris put his cup down on Sasha's desk. "I know. I hardly slept last night. I was lying awake in bed going over and over interviews we've done and looking at the evidence that has been collected and analyzed, and there's nothing for us to chase down."

"But there has to be. We don't seem to be as smart as the killer." Sasha paused. "And if we don't find him, he's not going to stop."

Chris nodded. "I know. With our backs against the wall, I'm going to start working the list that Stephanie's dad and uncle gave us yesterday. I'm also going to talk to the neighbor first thing. His partner is supposed to be back this morning from"—he looked at his notes—"Dallas."

"I'll go through the list with you, and we can split them up and start interviewing those we didn't get to yesterday. I want to find out from her friends if she was seeing someone. You know, dating some guy on a regular basis or whatever."

"A couple of the ladies at the salon yesterday did seem a little hesitant to talk about her social life. It's possible they just don't know."

"True. I don't have any idea what's up with you, for instance, and I see your sorry ass almost every day." Sasha laughed. "Sorry, just kidding."

"No problem. I'm a private person. Maybe Stephanie was as well. Let me go get the list, and I'll be back in a second."

Sasha watched Chris walk away to print out the list of people they either talked to yesterday or planned on talking to today. There were probably forty names on the list. They'd talked to almost half of them the day before and hadn't learned anything helpful. Stephanie kept to herself and worked about fifty or so hours a week. She didn't belong to a gym, and she had a treadmill in the spare bedroom of her house for exercise, the house her dad, Lyle, had bought for her. Sasha remembered that he needed to drive over to see her dad. He knew that Lyle was planning on staying with his brother last night. Poor guy lost his wife to cancer and his only child to a serial killer. Yes, he'd spend some time with Mr. Davis today.

Chris came back and sat down. "You pick out the ones you'd like to interview, and I'll take care of the rest. With any luck we could get them all done today."

The senior detective looked at the list and counted up the outstanding number they needed to interview today and then circled those as he went through the list. "Okay, I'll take these eight, and you take the others. I'm going to make a point of checking in on Mr. Davis this morning to see how he's doing."

"Sounds good. If anything interesting comes up as I do the interviews, I'll circle back to you." Chris stood up. "I'll run off a copy of this so we'll both have it."

As Chris walked toward the copier, Sasha looked back at Beff's report. He said to himself, *Come on, Beff, find us something to go on other than a pair of galoshes.* Surely there had to be something at one of the scenes that could provide them a clue. Something.

Chris dropped off the original to Sasha and kept the copy. "See you later, boss."

Sasha nodded and stood up as Chris walked over to his desk to start his day of interviews. He looked at his watch and saw that it was almost 8 a.m. He was going to run over to LeRoy to watch Aiden's tryout for baseball that started at 8:30. Watching his grandson's tryout would be the highlight of his day and a nice getaway from what had been his sole focus the past three weeks.

21

Cynthia Pope had been an easy target. Somehow Fred knew that she visited her maternal grandmother at a nursing home located in Normal every Sunday night, and she usually left the home around eight o'clock.

Fred's plan called for Brian to park a panel van in the parking lot of the nursing home as close as possible to where Cynthia had parked her car. He'd been able to park the van he was driving next to the driver's side of Cynthia's brand-new Mercedes-Benz GL 63 AMG SUV, which she had parked in the rear lot of the facility, away from the other cars.

Cynthia walked out the back exit of the nursing home just after dark. She unlocked her car with her keyless remote, failing to notice that the sliding door of the van parked next to her Mercedes was wide open. As she reached for the driver's door of the SUV, Brian tased her. She dropped to the ground, and he jumped out, put his hand over her mouth, and pulled her into the van, quickly closing the sliding door. He secured her hands and feet behind her back with zip ties.

He rolled her over on her side, noting the confusion and fear in her eyes. He quickly slid a plastic bag over her head. He gathered the open end of the bag and held it tightly. Brian looked straight into her eyes as she looked back at him in absolute terror. She attempted to scream and then sucked in air, pulling the plastic bag into her mouth.

After he killed her, he shouted, "Damn!" At that moment, he decided that with the next killing he would take his time. He would try to control himself to prolong the exhilaration.

He removed the plastic bag and lifted her head. He pulled her up to him and stared directly into her lifeless eyes. He set her head back down softly on the floor of the van, then reached into the bucket to pull out the tube of fast-drying glue. He first glued open her right eyelid and then her left. He discarded the tube of glue on top of the plastic bag, and then he rolled her over and cut off the zip ties. He removed her shoes and ankle socks, then snipped off her blouse, slacks, and undergarments with scissors. He was getting aroused, but he forced himself to focus on finishing the job.

He removed her rings and diamond earrings and placed them in a bag. He took her driver's license out of her billfold and her passport out of the purse before adding them to the bag.

He quietly opened the sliding door and looked around the parking lot until he felt comfortable that no one was watching. He lifted Cynthia's lifeless body from the floor of the van and then walked between his van and her Mercedes toward the back of the property. He stopped when he reached the trail to look both ways down the dark pathway. He didn't see anyone. Brian turned left and walked to the first tree and gently leaned Cynthia's body against the trunk. He made final adjustments to her arms and legs, as Fred had wanted.

Prior to killing Cynthia Pope, Brian had difficulty looking his victims in the eyes, but tonight had been different. After killing five people, it was clear to him how much he liked it. He was ready for more.

22

Donna Noble's miniature schnauzer, Jazz, pulled her along the trail. Donna was thinking that she needed to make boarding arrangements for Jazz while she was in Oregon for her youngest grandchild's high school graduation at the end of next month. Her thoughts were interrupted when she spotted ahead and to the left side of the path a naked woman sitting on the ground by a tree. She stopped and looked around to see if there was anyone else nearby. Jazz pulled at the leash, and Donna slowly took a few more steps. The lady's eyes were wide open. She appeared to be staring straight down the path at Donna. She assumed the woman was another victim of the serial killer who had already killed four people on the trail.

She called 911, and the operator answered on the first ring. It was only a couple of minutes before Donna could hear police sirens coming from different directions. She turned to see a police cruiser enter the trail two blocks from where she was standing. As the cruiser pulled up, the officer behind the wheel turned off the siren but left the lights on. Jazz was barking like crazy. Another police cruiser approached from the opposite direction.

"Morning, ma'am. Are you the lady who called 911?" Officer Edwards was tall enough that he could see the woman posed at the tree over Donna.

"Yes, sir. I'm still on the line with them." Donna picked up Jazz to calm her down.

"I'm Officer Jeremiah Edwards, ma'am. Do you mind handing me your mobile phone?"

Donna quickly handed it over. "This is Edwards. I'm on scene with the lady who called you." The officer listened for a few more seconds. "Yes. Okay. Thank you. Goodbye."

The second officer, Tommy Ericson, exited his cruiser and stood on the trail about fifteen feet from the woman. "Jeremiah!" he called. "An ambulance is less than one minute out, but it's not needed."

Officer Edwards yelled back at the second officer. "Thanks, Tommy. I'll stay here with the lady." He started asking her a few questions.

As Donna answered the officer's questions, she started to cry.

Jeremiah pulled out a handkerchief. "It's clean, ma'am, and it's never been used."

She took the handkerchief and dabbed her eyes. "I'm sorry. This wasn't how I expected to start my day."

"No one would, ma'am. Take your time. If you're okay, I'm going to step over to talk with Officer Ericson." Donna nodded, and Jeremiah walked over to where Tommy was talking with two Normal Fire Department ambulance personnel who'd just arrived.

Within a few minutes, two more Normal police cruisers arrived. A black sedan drove up behind Jeremiah's cruiser and parked. A man dressed in a suit got out and walked toward where she was standing.

"Morning, ma'am. I'm Detective Al Jalber with the Normal Police Department."

"Good morning, Detective." Donna thought maybe she shouldn't have said "good," as it was far from a good morning.

"I'm assuming that you're Ms. Donna Noble, and you found the body. Am I correct?"

"Yes, Detective, but I'm Mrs. Noble." After years of being Mrs. Noble, she didn't like it when someone call her Ms.

"Sorry, Mrs. Noble." The detective lit up a cigarette. "Would it be possible for you to tell me about how you came upon the body, ma'am?"

Donna stepped a few feet to the side of the detective to avoid the smoke. "I left my home at about 6:50 a.m. to walk my dog, Jazz, and we came across the woman. I knew immediately that it must be another victim of the serial killer."

Al put the cigarette out. "I'm sorry about the smoke, ma'am. How close did you get to the body?"

"I didn't get any closer than where we are right now. She looked dead. She wasn't moving, her eyes were wide open, and she wasn't blinking. That's when I called 911." Donna put Jazz down on the ground, and the dog started pulling on her leash.

"Have you seen anyone else touch the body?"

"One of those men could have, but I didn't see him do it if he did. I need to return to my home."

"I need you to stay here for a bit."

"I have to use the bathroom."

"Well, I'm going to have to ask one of the officers to take you to your home and then bring you back. Is that okay?" Al understood. He had to go every hour, day or night. Getting old wasn't fun.

"Can I leave my dog at home?"

"Absolutely, ma'am." Al called Jeremiah over and asked him to drive Donna home, wait for her, and return.

Al walked over to where the screens had been set up and looked between them at the victim. The lady was sitting on the ground, leaning against the tree with her legs and arms crossed. The lady's head was resting on her left shoulder. She had short blond hair, and her light blue eyes were wide open. Her right ankle and wrist both showed signs of cuts and abrasions, as if she had been bound. Something about her seemed familiar, and he wondered if he'd recently met her somewhere.

"I just got a call from dispatch," Tommy said, walking up next to Al. "They say that Sasha Frank, a Bloomington PD detective, is heading this way. Just a heads-up."

"Thanks, Tommy. I'm sure he is." Al slowly made a 360-degree turn to get a better feel for the area. On the east side of the trail were single-family homes, and on the east side was a parking lot that looked mostly empty.

He walked around the screens and then toward the parking lot, stopping just short of the asphalt surface. Three vehicles were parked in the lot. Two were parked next to the building, about a hundred feet away, and the third was in a parking space next to where he was standing. The top-of-the-line Mercedes-Benz SUV seemed out of place parked in the back of the lot. He stepped to the front of the vehicle and wrote down the license number and then walked back to where the other officers were standing.

"The Bloomington PD detective has arrived," Tommy said, "and they're not letting him in without your okay." He chuckled.

"Let him in. And can you run this plate for me real quick?" Tommy nodded as Al handed him the license number.

Al had known Sasha Frank for years. They had joined the police department around the same time and had first met at the Illinois State Police Academy.

Tommy came back. "The Mercedes is titled to Pope's. You know, the big implement dealership Pope's Farm Stores. I've got a cousin who works over at the location in Peoria. They're in like four states." He looked over at the car in the lot. "That thing was just registered last week. It's gotta cost a hundred or a hundred and fifty thousand. Sweet ride."

"Have somebody call over to Pope's and ask them about it."

"Sure." Tommy headed back to his cruiser.

"And let me know what you find out ASAP."

Al started to walk back over to the parking lot when Jeremiah shouted at him. "Frank's pulling up on the trail now."

Al walked back to the trail and waited for Sasha. "Have somebody run over to the assisted living place and ask if there's anybody named Pope in residence there, okay, Jeremiah?"

Jeremiah called dispatch and did as the detective had asked. "I'll let you know what we find out."

"Good morning, Al," Sasha said. "How long has it been?"

"Maybe last summer at a softball game? Days, weeks, months, and years kinda all run together for me." Al reached out and shook Sasha's hand. "Too long. We should grab a beer sometime soon. How's Janet?"

"Yes, we should. Janet is doing as you'd expect, great. How about Deedee?"

"The same. It's hard to believe she still seems to like being married to me after almost forty years." Al laughed. "At least she says she does. I don't see what she sees in me."

"I don't either. She's too good a woman for you. But aren't they all?" Sasha let out a big laugh. There wasn't much he enjoyed more than messing with Al.

"True." Al tilted his head toward the screens. "Let me show you what we got here."

"Sounds good." Sasha followed Al over to the screens concealing the body from view.

Al lit a cigarette. "I can't place her, but for some reason she looks familiar to me."

Sasha raised two fingers on his right hand, signaling to Al that he'd like to bum one. Al tapped out a cigarette and handed Sasha the lighter.

"Thanks." Sasha lit the cigarette. "Nice-looking lady. When you say she looks familiar, what does that mean exactly?"

"She looks like somebody I've met or seen on TV or something, but I can't place her."

"She doesn't look familiar to me."

Al took a drag on his cigarette. "We're going to extend a professional courtesy to you and the Bloomington PD, Sasha."

Sasha turned to look at Al. "Meaning?"

"We're going to ask that you take the lead in the investigation. I'll be riding shotgun all the way through on this one. I think we'll have a better chance catching the bastard who did this if you run the case. Chief agreed."

"Thanks, Al. That's very generous of you."

"I'm going to assume that you're going to wait for the ME, so walk with me a minute." Al walked toward the parking lot, and Sasha followed him. "This is the parking lot for the assisted living facility right over there." Al pointed to the building across the parking lot from where they were standing. "As you can see, there are only a couple of cars in this lot. The two older models across the way and this brand-spanking-new Mercedes."

"Okay. What are you thinking?"

"Seems odd to me that it's parked here at this hour of the morning. One of the guys thought it might cost around a hundred and fifty thousand or so. Not the type of SUV you'd expect to find sitting by itself in the back lot of an assisted living facility. We ran the license plate. Registered and titled to Pope's Farm Store."

"The farm implement place over on the north side of town?"

"Yes. Big company. Maybe twenty locations in and around Illinois. I asked an officer to call over to Pope's to ask about the vehicle and also sent an officer over to the facility next door to see if anyone named Pope is living there."

"You're not just a pretty face, Al. Great thinking."

"I still got it goin' on." Al laughed out loud. He put out his cigarette on the sole of his shoe and put the butt in his pocket.

"Detective Jalber?" Tommy walked over. "I talked to Pope's. They told me that the owner got the car a couple of weeks ago for his wife."

"Did they give you a name?"

"Initially no, but I pushed a bit, and I got transferred to the general manager of the place. I told him I was with Normal PD, and I could send somebody over to ask officially who drives the car, or he could just tell me." Tommy smiled. "The car was assigned and driven by Cynthia Pope. A gift for Carl Jr.'s wife, he said.

"I then asked the general manager if he could describe Mrs. Pope. I'd be willing to bet that's her up against the tree. Petite blond with short hair and blue eyes. And he said she's thirty-four years old."

"Good work." Al turned to Sasha. "That's why I recognize her. Deedee dragged me to some Christmas charity event that the Popes hosted for disadvantaged children. The lady sits on a number of boards in the community and state too. I read recently that she received an appointment to some commission by the president. I'm sure that's her."

Sasha shook his head. If this really was Cynthia Pope, then the pressure to find the killer just went up exponentially. "Can we ask your officer to pull up her picture on DMV?"

Al turned to Tommy and motioned for him to go check the DMV. He looked back at Sasha. "So why would her SUV be parked in the back lot over there?"

"Good question." Sasha walked over to where the SUV was parked and looked around the lot. A mobile phone rang behind him, and he turned around.

"Detective Jalber. Yes. Okay. Thanks." Al ended the call. "I need to tell you a couple of things quickly."

Sasha walked over to where Al was standing.

"That was dispatch. The officer that I had sent over to check to see if there was someone named Pope living in the facility reported back." Al paused. "The answer is no, there's not, but Cynthia Pope's maternal grandmother does reside in the facility."

"Geez."

"Dispatch also told me that Carl Pope Jr. just called 911 about ten minutes ago saying his wife was missing."

"Missing?" Sasha said. "She must not have come home last night. You'd think he would have called earlier."

"Pope told 911 that his wife was visiting her grandmother last night, as she does every Sunday evening. There's evidently a sing-along each week. The officer I sent over to the facility says they told him that Mrs. Pope was here last night and left when her grandmother fell asleep. They told him the grandmother has Alzheimer's, and they say sometimes Pope stayed the night if her grandmother was having a rough spell. Pope had already called the facility this morning asking about his wife, as she wasn't answering her mobile phone this morning. They told him she left around 8:45 to 9 o'clock last night." Al paused. "Dispatch thinks Carl Jr. is now on his way over to the facility."

Sasha looked back at the building on the other side of the parking lot.

"This is your investigation, Sasha, but it's my town. I think that either I meet Mr. Pope, or you and I meet Mr. Pope and bring him back here. Either way it's going to be bad."

Sasha looked at Al. "Like you say, Al, this is your town. It's your call, my friend."

"If you're okay with it, I'd like us both there to meet him."

"No problem." Sasha turned to see Beff and her team pull up behind the long line of vehicles on the trail. "Can I have just a couple of minutes to talk to the ME?"

"You've got five."

———

Sasha turned and walked quickly over to where Beff had pulled up in her SUV. "Morning, Beff."

"Hi, Sasha. Surprised to see you here."

"Normal PD gave the lead to me."

Beff walked to the back of her SUV. "Mighty generous of them. Al Jalber's call?"

"Evidently." Sasha didn't want to get into a conversation with Beff about jurisdiction and courtesies offered between localities. "I've got a couple of minutes to tell you what we've got."

"Okay. What's the hurry? She's not going anywhere." As soon as Beff said that, she wished she hadn't. Her issues with Sasha shouldn't cause her to say things like that about an innocent victim. "I'm sorry, Sasha."

Sasha looked at her and barely shook his head. "We think we've got Cynthia Pope leaned up against the tree over there. I assume you know the Pope family? Carl Pope Jr. We think he's on his way here now, trying to find out where his wife is. Her grandmother resides in the assisted living facility over there." Sasha put his thumb over his right shoulder. "Mrs. Pope's SUV is parked in the back parking lot. A recent gift from her husband. We also have a tentative ID from a verbal description of her to an officer and confirmation of the picture of her the DMV has on file."

Beff stopped putting on her CSI gear. "What do you need from me?"

"Nothing. I just want you to know that we could have her husband trying to get back to see his wife. Her husband has more pull than anybody you'll ever know in this community. Pope knows everybody. City, state, and probably federal authorities who could make our lives miserable. It's going to be hard to stop him from charging back here and wanting to get his arms around her." Sasha looked back toward to where Mrs. Pope was hidden by the screens. "I know I would. Just wanted you to know."

"Okay. Thanks. Anything I can do?"

"Be nice to him. Just be nice. We could have him positively identify her."

"Will do. I understand."

———

"I sent an officer to wait in the lobby in case Mr. Pope arrives before we can get up there," Al said as he and Sasha headed to the assisted living facility. "I suggest we ask him to identify his wife with the picture I took earlier."

"Can I see the picture?"

Al pulled out his mobile and showed Sasha the headshot he'd taken of the body. "It's not a great picture, but identifying it will be better than asking him to ID her now."

"I agree." As they neared the building, all Sasha could think was that a bad morning was about to get worse.

23

As soon as they found out that the dead woman was socialite Cynthia Pope, unquestionably the fifth person murdered by the trail serial killer, Sasha knew it was going to be a long night. The worst moment of the day was when Al pulled out his mobile phone and showed Carl Pope Jr. the picture of his dead wife. The man dropped to his knees on the lobby floor and started sobbing. The worst part of the job was having to inform a family member that their person was dead. To try to explain to a distraught man that his thirty-four-year-old wife was a victim of murder at the hands of a serial killer made the task even worse.

Detectives from the Bloomington and Normal police departments had worked well into the night with both city mayors and chiefs in attendance. The governor's office had even sent a representative to attend the meetings and take notes. The representative suggested that a task force be formed to take over the investigation, which the politicians in the room quickly embraced. After discussing the suggestion further, everyone agreed that it be tabled for now, but Sasha knew that, if formed, a task force would take over the investigation. The influence and the power of the Pope family was dramatically changing the dynamics of the investigation, and Sasha anticipated political pressure would continue to build over the next few days.

Last night's meeting was more a stage for everyone in the room to say ad nauseum that they all needed to be doing more to find whoever was responsible for the murders. No kidding. Sasha, Chris, Beff, and her team had been expending countless hours working every single tip or lead, regardless of how minor. Sasha thought his longtime friend Al was probably very relieved that Sasha was taking the lead.

Sasha parked in front of the restaurant he'd been coming to for breakfast for many years. "This place brings back a lot of memories," he said to Chris. "Good and bad ones."

The owner was standing by the cash register when they walked in. "Morning, detectives."

"Morning." Sasha knew the owner's name, but neither he nor the owner ever said anything more than "morning" when he entered and "see ya" when he departed. They both seemed to like it that way.

They sat at a booth in the back, and both ordered the breakfast special. "How did you find this place?" Chris marveled that they offered two eggs any style, sausage links, bacon, and ham with hash browns, toast, and a choice of beverage for $4.99.

"You may not have been born the first time I ate here with a couple of the guys." Sasha chuckled thinking back that far. "Whoever they were, I'm guessing they're retired. I wish I was too."

"We're going to figure this out. Let's talk about something else during breakfast. How about those Cubbies?"

Sasha laughed out loud. "How did your dad ever let you grow up to become a Cubs fan?"

That started a lively conversation about baseball. For the next forty minutes the trail murders didn't get brought up during their breakfast conversation. It was good for Sasha to be able to walk away from all of it, even if it was only for a short time. He remembered hearing a politician once say, "Politics is what we do, but it's not who we are." That rang true to how he felt about being in law enforcement. He was not going to let it define who he was, but this case was dragging him down and he needed to change that. He decided he was going to start right now.

As they were leaving the restaurant, the owner said, "See ya."

This time Sasha smiled and nodded.

When they entered the station, Sasha was handed a note letting him know that Detective Al Jalber had called and wanted him to call as soon as he was back.

The two walked into the conference room, and Sasha called Al from his mobile phone and put the call on speaker.

Al answered on the second ring. "It's Chris and Sasha. You're on speaker. Sorry we weren't here when you called. We were out getting breakfast."

"Well, you're both a lot smarter than me. I left the all-nighter we pulled and came straight back to the station to go over everything that we've put together during the past twenty-four hours."

Sasha mouthed, "Really?" "Please tell me the case is solved, Al."

"No, smart-ass. I think we need to talk to every person who visited the assisted living facility on Sunday to see if anyone saw anything hinky."

"Have we interviewed all of the employees?" Chris asked.

"Yes, we have."

"And what did we learn?" Sasha asked.

They could hear Al shuffling papers on his desk. "We didn't find anything that was helpful. Really nothing that we didn't already know."

"What about all the people who were at that sing-along or visiting that night?" Chris asked. "Did you get a list of those people?"

"I don't think that's happened yet."

Sasha asked, "Didn't you agree that you and your team were taking all interviews for employees or visitors of the facility Sunday night?"

There was a long pause. "Well, yes."

"Then where are we on those?"

"Listen, Sasha, my Chris is on vacation, so it's just me and a couple of officers. I could use some help."

Chris motioned to Sasha that he'd like to talk. "I'm not sure I appreciate that comment," Chris said. "Kidding, Al. Just kidding. If you can compile the list, I think I can help you interview them."

Sasha nodded to Chris and gave him a thumbs-up. "Will that work for you?"

"I hope to have a list from the facility within the next hour or so. You want to come over here and pick up a copy? We can then agree on who takes who on the list."

Chris put the phone on mute to ask Sasha a question. "Can't he just email it to me? It's a waste of time to drive over there."

Sasha nodded and took the phone off mute. "How about you put the list together and then evenly split them between you and Chris?" He paused. "Then you can scan and email it to us. That way Chris doesn't have to drive over for you to give it to him."

There was another long pause. "Yeah. I can have somebody do that."

Chris gave Sasha a thumbs-up. "That would be great. Thanks." Sasha waited for Al to say something else, but he was silent. "Have you heard from Mr. Pope?"

"Which one?" Al sounded annoyed. "Yes, I heard from both. Carl Sr. walked in earlier today. He flew up from Florida in a private plane with his wife this morning. He and Carl Jr. came in while you were at breakfast. The mayor and the chief were here too. They want this solved, and they want it solved now."

The two Bloomington detectives shrugged. "I can appreciate your situation," Sasha said. "Can you share with us a little more about the meeting?"

"The Popes called the mayor at 5 a.m. I'm guessing the mayor was just getting to sleep after our all-nighter. The mayor and the chief were here at 7:30 when the Popes arrived with their attorney and some security guy. It wasn't pretty. They insisted I call you. That's why I called the station. I'm no dummy. There was no value in you being brought into the meeting. It was a cluster . . . if you catch my drift."

Sasha smiled. "I catch your drift. Thank you for keeping us out of it." He looked at Chris and mouthed, "Glad we were out." "What do you need from me?"

"Well, I'd ask if you'd do me the favor of sitting down with the Popes, their attorney, and the security guy. It seems like they'd like an update from, what did Pope Sr. call you? Oh yeah, *the man*."

"I'd be happy to. I'm here for you, and I'm willing to do anything that you need me to do. I appreciate all you're doing for the team."

"Thanks, Sasha. I'll call Pope's attorney and set something up. Can I assume that you'd be available anytime that would suit their schedule? Sorry for asking."

"Sure. Sounds good."

"Can I make a suggestion?"

"Go ahead."

"Sorry, Chris, for saying this, but I advise that only Sasha and the chief meet with the Popes. One old-school guy to another."

Chris gave a thumbs-up to Sasha. "No problem here," Sasha said. "Like I said, we're here for you. Whatever you need from us we're happy to accommodate a friend."

"This could happen quickly, as they're interested to meet and get an update."

"Let me know what time when you can." Sasha ended the call.

"This isn't good," Chris said. "It's a waste of time. We appease the rich?"

Sasha gave Chris a withering stare. "When you lose a wife or a daughter-in-law, you can have an opinion." He stood up and walked out of the room.

Chris sat in the conference room, thinking, for almost ten minutes. He wasn't sure how Sasha was dealing with the pressure he was getting from every direction. He needed to work harder and quit complaining and support Sasha every way possible. His phone lit up with a text from Sasha: "Pope's arriving in 15."

———

The small conference room was crowded with Carl Pope Sr., Carl Pope Jr., their attorney Chauncy Jameson McClure, head of security Reggie Collins, Detective Al Jalber, the chiefs of both police departments, the governor's representative, and Sasha. Carl Jr. was distraught, and Carl Sr. was by his side trying to comfort him. Everyone was offered coffee, and then the attorney for the Popes suggested that Sasha provide them an update on the investigation.

Sasha stood up and addressed the room. "On behalf of the Bloomington Police Department, I would like to offer our condolences to the Popes for your loss." Both Popes nodded. "Based on the evidence, Mrs. Pope was murdered by the same person responsible for the murders of the other victims of what the media call the Constitution Trail serial killer." He looked directly at the

Popes. "It's important for you to know that in our investigation each victim is treated equally. All life is precious to us, and we will find the person responsible for these murders."

The Popes' attorney stood. "Detective, we're here to hear what you're doing to find the person responsible for killing Mrs. Pope."

"Is it Mr. McClure?" Sasha watched the attorney nod and take his seat. He turned from the attorney to address the Popes. "Whoever is responsible for this heinous crime will pay. I promise you that. I don't know what you know or don't know. As I said, I can tell you that Mrs. Pope was killed by the same person who killed the other four souls. Someone is targeting and killing them for a reason. At this point the reason is known only by the person responsible for the killings." Sasha sat down. "I believe that the killer has a connection to all five who've died. We haven't found what that connection is yet, but we will. We will find the person who killed Mrs. Pope."

Carl Pope Sr. stood up. "I don't doubt that you're the right person to be leading the investigation into finding my daughter-in-law's murderer." He paused and lowered his head, as he began to tear up. He slowly regained his composure. "If asked, there's no favor I wouldn't give to anyone who finds the person responsible for killing Cynthia. There's no price I wouldn't pay to have the SOB arrested, convicted, and then executed for what he's done. Find the SOB, and I will be forever in your debt, Detective." The older man sat down.

Sasha could see that Carl Sr. was exhausted trying to come to terms with something that no one should ever have to face, and that he was trying to be strong for his son. "I understand, sir," he said. "Please know that you have willing partners, all who are working to find the killer."

Al Jalber stood up. "I want the Popes and their representatives to know that we're utilizing every asset available to solve these murders. We've had help from the FBI, the IBI"—Al turned to look at the governor's representative—"and the governor. I agree with Sasha; we will find the person responsible. We understand that does little to assuage your concerns."

Sasha stood up and addressed the Popes. "Are there any questions you'd like to ask us?"

Carl Pope Sr. shook his head no. Their attorney started to stand up, and the old man shook his head. "No, Chauncy. We're done here."

———

After the meeting, Sasha and Al remained at the conference table. "That went well," Sasha said.

"Ya think?" Al looked at his friend and smiled. "My retirement can't come fast enough."

Chris walked into the room. "How'd the meeting go? And what's our next move?"

"It's your investigation, Sasha," Al said, "and I'm here to support you. You've got a partner in me, my friend."

"Thanks, Al. I know that, but I appreciate you saying it." Sasha looked at Chris. "What's next? We take another look for connections between the Zumwalts, Bauer, and Davis. We obviously need to now look at all the others compared to Pope." He lowered his head and rubbed his temples. The headaches weren't going away. "There has to be a connection here between these victims that provides a motive for the killer to target them. I don't believe these are random acts on random people. The killer has targeted these people for a reason. I say we go back and talk to every-one we've interviewed so far in every investigation to see if we can find a connection."

"I don't disagree, Sasha, but that's hundreds of people," Chris said.

"It is, but we don't have a choice."

Al nodded. "I agree. We ask the same questions worded the same way to each group of family, friends, and coworkers. Did A ever know or have an interaction with B, C, or D? Did B ever know or have an interaction with A, C, or D? Etcetera, etcetera."

"I'm going to put together a document that lays out the questions for each murder related to the others, as Al suggests," Chris said. "I can have it ready in fifteen to twenty minutes." He left the room to work on the document.

"I'm getting old, Sasha," Al said. "I'm going to enjoy sharing a glass from that bottle of thirty-year-old single malt I'm going to buy you." He smiled. "It can't be soon enough, my friend."

"You're not going anywhere until we find the killer." Sasha had similar bets with other friends.

"I didn't say that I was. But when we find 'em, I'm retiring the next day. That's a promise."

24

It had been six days since Cynthia Pope's body had been found, and sleep had become ever more elusive for Sasha. He knew he wasn't the only person dealing with fatigue and added stress, but it was taking a toll on his mind and body.

Anxiety continued to build in the community unabated, as all knew a serial killer was among them, stalking residents. No one wanted to talk about it, but with the latest murder, the investigation took on a new sense of urgency because of Cynthia Pope's social position. The movers and shakers in the community were now shuddering in fear.

Together the chief and mayor had decided that a task force should be formed to find the killer. The task force included local, state, and federal law enforcement agencies. The pressure put on local politicians and law enforcement made it an easy decision for the powers that be. The formation of the task force was a way to bring together greater assets to work more directly on the investigation, as well as the chance to spread the blame of not solving the murders.

While conducting one of the final calls to those previously interviewed, Chris learned more about the connection between two of the victims when reinterviewing one of Maria Zumwalt's relatives. A female cousin who was a year younger and close to Maria told him that Maria Matthews, who had married Warren Zumwalt, and Cynthia Weller, who had married Carl Pope Jr., had been best friends growing up, as well as for some time while attending the University of Illinois. The cousin didn't know the specifics, but for some reason the two friends drifted apart during college.

Armed with this new information, Sasha, Al, and Chris went back again and reinterviewed everyone whom they'd talked to during the Zumwalt and Pope murder investigations. They found several family members or friends of the pair who confirmed that Maria and Cynthia had been close friends when they attended private Catholic schools in Bloomington. Al and Sasha had assumed that with Cynthia marrying into one of the wealthiest families in the area, the orbits of the two women may not have intersected as frequently, resulting in their friendship fading. Without any specifics as to why they didn't stay friends through college and after they returned to Bloomington, Al and Sasha had hit a dead end.

———

Sasha sat at his desk preparing for the next task force meeting, which was scheduled for that afternoon to allow churchgoers the opportunity to attend religious services. The first three meetings had been a waste of time, as half of those in attendance prattled on, jockeying to influence the direction of the investigation. There was very little accomplished. Sasha thought his head was going to explode.

Twenty minutes before the meeting was scheduled to begin, Beff called. Gloria Redman, a serologist at her office, had accessed the FBI's CODIS platform, attempting to find a match for DNA found on Bauer. There were no matches. Sasha was getting annoyed that Beff was wasting his time telling him old news.

"Gloria had an epiphany," Beff said. "She decided to test the female DNA evidence found on Bauer to see if any of the other victims were a match." Beff paused, as she knew that she was about to drop a bombshell into the investigation.

Sasha sat up in his chair. "And?"

"To her surprise, she found it was. Sasha, the vaginal secretions found on Bauer are a match to Stephanie Davis!"

"Seriously?" Sasha stood up, excited with the revelation. "You're absolutely positive it's a match?"

"Yes. An absolute match. Before Gloria informed me of her findings, she ran the test several times to ensure the results were correct. The DNA found on Bauer is a hundred percent match to Davis."

"The meeting starts in about fifteen minutes. I'll call on you to start the meeting off with what Gloria found. Deal?"

"Deal. I'm heading over to the station now."

Sasha sat back down in his chair. This new evidence could blow the investigation wide open and cause it to take a dramatic turn.

As Sasha wheeled the cart holding the four murder books out of the room he and Chris had been using, Chris walked up with a notebook and two cups of coffee, which he'd picked up at the coffee shop on his drive in. Sasha smiled. "Thanks, Chris. Everyone in the meeting this afternoon will be envious of us. Did you order in coffee and doughnuts for today's meeting?"

"You're welcome, and yes, I did. They were supposed to be delivered fifteen minutes ago. I'm guessing that Morgan took care of setting it up." Morgan Smiley was a sergeant with the department and provided support for Chris and Sasha. As he walked alongside Sasha, Chris asked, "Do you think we'll accomplish anything at today's meeting?"

Sasha stopped just outside the door to the conference room. "Yes, I think today's meeting will be different."

Chris gave him a quizzical look. "Why is that?"

"You'll see in a few minutes." Sasha walked inside the room and rolled the cart to one end of the large grouping of tables used by the task force. There would probably be twenty or more people at the meeting today. Beff's news should energize the entire group.

As Sasha and Chris were placing the murder books on the table, Beff walked into the room. She headed directly to Sasha, and they hugged.

"Thanks, Sasha."

"I've got a coffee for you." Sasha handed the coffee Chris had gotten for him to Beff. He winked at Chris, who shook his head with a smile on his face.

"That's so thoughtful." Beff set down her briefcase and took the coffee from him.

As everyone finished getting coffees and finding their seats, Sasha sat down next to Beff. He smiled at her. "Thank you all for your promptness. I'd like to get the meeting started with an important update from Medical Examiner Beff Turner."

Beff stood up holding a manila folder. "As you're all aware, I found vaginal secretions on the genitalia of the third murder victim, Greg Bauer. As I mentioned during our first meeting, we ran the DNA evidence through CODIS without getting a hit. Gloria Redman, staff serologist in my office, took it upon herself to test that DNA evidence against the female victims." That opening got everyone's attention. Beff paused for effect. "Gloria got a match." She paused again, with all eyes in the room on her except Sasha's. "The DNA we found on Bauer matched Stephanie Davis." The room erupted, with half of those in attendance now standing and almost everyone clapping. Although they hadn't found any further information that they could use to move the investigation forward, they now had their first strong connection between two victims.

Throughout the room people were talking to the person sitting beside them or to those across the table from them. "Settle down, everyone." Sasha stood. "Beff, thank you very much, and please thank Gloria for her ingenuity and great find."

Beff nodded. "Certainly, Sasha. That's what we do."

Sasha smiled and said to the room, "What do we do with this new information?"

As soon as he asked the question, he realized he needed to call the chief. Sasha whispered to Chris, "Take over the meeting. I've got to make a quick call." Chris nodded and stood up as Sasha left the room.

"Everyone," Chris said. "One at a time, please."

As he was exiting the conference room, Sasha dialed the chief, who answered on the second ring.

"I have an important update for you." This was the first call Sasha had made to the chief with good news.

"I could use some good news. Let's hear it."

Sasha told him about the DNA match.

"That's interesting, but what does it really tell you?"

"It tells us that we've found the second connection between another two of the five people. There may very well be other connections. When you couple this new evidence with the connection that we already found between Mrs. Zumwalt and Mrs. Pope, I hope this will provide us additional areas to focus our investigation." Sasha realized that he sounded somewhat desperate.

"I think the fact that Bauer and Davis were together before he was killed is interesting, but my gut tells me that it is purely coincidental."

"I understand, but—"

"Let me finish. You've found zero connection between the Zumwalt couple and Bauer. You've found zero connection between the Zumwalts and Davis. Yes, you found an old connection between Mrs. Zumwalt and Mrs. Pope, but there has to be a more direct connection. Again, in my opinion the two connections you've found so far are purely coincidental."

Sasha waited a few seconds to make sure the chief was finished. "I don't disagree, but with this new evidence, we have to drill down more to see if we missed something. I think there must be a connection, and we just haven't connected the dots yet."

"I agree that there's a connection, but I don't believe it is between the people killed. I believe there's a connection with each to the killer. I don't want us to chase this down a rabbit hole."

"I hear you. I'm going back into the task force meeting and see what the FBI and IBI experts think." He knew he needed to be careful talking to the chief. "In my opinion we need to dig deeper, even if we hit a dead end again."

"The investigation is yours to lead, Sasha, until it isn't. Go ahead, dig deeper. Just make sure that you find a killer at the bottom of the hole. Good luck." The chief abruptly ended the call.

As he entered the conference room, Chris said, "Do we all agree that we need to dig deeper and look for connections to the victims? Raise your hands."

Everyone in the room agreed, and Sasha smiled to himself. *Sorry, Chief.* Chris looked over at Sasha and gave him a thumbs-up.

"So we don't step all over each other," Sasha said, "let's determine the best way to divvy up responsibility for uncovering potential connections." Sasha looked over at the most qualified person in the room, FBI Special Agent Lee

Barnes, who was sitting opposite where Chris was standing. "Lee? What's your recommendation for the best way to allocate resources?"

The special agent stood up. "I recommend that we consider having the FBI be responsible for Bauer. The IBI for Davis, and you, Al, and your team responsible for the Zumwalts and Pope."

"Explain why, Lee?" Sasha thought he knew but wanted to make sure everyone on the task force understood the reasoning behind Lee's recommendation.

"Based on what we've found so far, I believe that we know the least about Bauer. Once his wife filed for divorce and she and the kids moved to Arizona, Bauer appears to have withdrawn into a dark place. I think that the FBI and our resources are best suited to delve into Bauer to see what we can find. The IBI has more resources than the Bloomington PD, and Davis is the next person in the victim group that we've learned the least about. Look at the fact that after interviewing Davis's family, and especially her close friends, no one told us that she was looking for hookups."

"Wait a second here," Beff said. "I don't think you can just jump to 'she was looking for hookups.' She and Bauer had sex. You don't know how they found each other or if they had an ongoing relationship based solely on sex."

"Please know that I'm not judging Ms. Davis. Either her close friends are lying to us about their not knowing that she was on apps looking for sex or Ms. Davis was hiding that part of her life for some reason. I'm suggesting that the IBI has more resources to allocate to looking at Ms. Davis."

"I'm assuming that you're thinking the police departments know the most about the Zumwalts and Pope, so you're recommending that we continue to look at them further." Sasha looked over to Al, who nodded. "We agree with all your recommendations." Everyone in the room nodded. "Then we have consensus that the FBI takes Bauer, IBI takes Davis, and Bloomington and Normal PD take the Zumwalts and Pope."

"I suggest that we adjourn today's meeting and get working on our individual assignments," Lee responded. He had the most experience in murder investigations, as he both led and worked on FBI teams investigating a number of high-profile searches for serial killers.

Sasha looked over at IBI Agent Max Duncan, and he nodded to Sasha his agreement. "I think everyone agrees. Let's get to work on finding the SOB."

The meeting broke up, leaving Sasha, Al, Chris, and Beff in the conference room. "I didn't mean to call out Lee like that," Beff said. "It annoyed me that he suggested she was loose or something."

"I don't think that was what he was doing." Beff turned and walked out of the conference room.

"I think that maybe you should have left that gone unsaid," Chris said.

"Yep. Janet tells me I never know when to stop talking. I have to be the last person to talk. Evidently not a trait liked by the ladies." Sasha smiled at Chris. "I'm probably too old to change, so I'm going to embrace it."

Chris laughed. "Good luck with that. I'll check back in a few weeks to see how that's working out for you." He picked up his notepad. "How do you want to begin?"

Sasha started slowly pushing the cart back to the smaller conference room where he and his small team had been working. "First let's go back over each interview with the Zumwalts' and Pope's family, friends, and coworkers to see if there's something we missed. Then tomorrow let's talk to the ones that we agree we should ask a few more pointed questions."

"Are you suggesting asking something like if Warren Zumwalt was looking for something on the side?" Al asked.

"Yes. I think we may have danced around directly asking those kinds of questions. We need to be a little more direct. We probably wouldn't ask his mother that question, though."

"How about asking Mrs. Zumwalt's friends the same kind of questions?" Chris asked.

"I think we first place our focus on Warren. If we get anything, we can then drill down on that information. If we get nothing, then we can look at Maria."

"What about family and coworkers?" Al asked.

"Let's focus first on friends, then coworkers, and last family."

As they entered the small conference room, they removed the murder books from the cart and set them on the table. "I think we should look at each interview together. We should be able to quickly go through them and agree on which ones look the most promising. Deal?"

Both Al and Chris nodded. The three sat down and started going through the interviews. It was going to be another long day for the detectives.

25

ust before noon Brian's burner phone buzzed with a text message from Charlie: "Another one tonight." He'd been looking forward to this next job. Would the target be a man? A woman? A man and woman? He hoped a woman, but it really didn't matter. He texted back a thumbs-up and "After tonight I really need to see you."

Charlie replied: "Ok tonight."

"Cool. Where when."

"Shed. 8pm."

"Deal. Thanks."

Brian knew Charlie was aware of the shed where Fred stored the ten vehicles to be used to drive to the killings, but he wondered how his friend was going to get out to the north side of Normal since Charlie didn't have a car.

Brian appreciated that Charlie was willing to meet with him tonight, as they'd be going against one of Fred's rules. Another one of Fred's rules that he had followed was to not make any friends at work or in the neighborhood where he lived. Fred thought it was better to make new friends when they got to the place each were heading to after the last killing. That advice made sense to Brian.

After tonight he'd be halfway through carrying out Fred's plan. He smiled, thinking that his life was going to be much better in Idaho.

———

Brian thought it was ironic that every night he parked his pickup truck right beside the trail that ran past his apartment. He grabbed a beer from the refrigerator and headed to his bedroom to shower. He'd worked a few hours overtime, which didn't leave him time to fix something for dinner. He'd stop at a convenience store and pick up something to tide him over until his work for the evening was done. Later he planned on having bacon and eggs. He found he was always hungry on a night when he killed someone, and bacon and eggs were easy to fix.

He stepped into the hot shower and thought about how he planned to have a little fun with his victim tonight. He couldn't shake the images going through his head and wasn't sure if what he was going to do would occur before or after the killing.

———

It was just starting to lightly rain as Brian pulled his Dodge Ram into the small parking lot in front of the machine shed. He parked his pickup in front of the overhead door of the shed and left the engine running as he got out to open the shed garage door. Then he pulled into the shed and closed the door and waited.

He walked over to the fifth vehicle in the line of the ten. It was the only pickup in the row and what he would be driving tonight. He did not see a bucket holding the items he would need in the bed of the truck. He reached to open the passenger door of the pickup truck to check to see if the bucket was inside when he heard a voice behind him: "Hey, Brian." Startled, he quickly turned around. It didn't sound like Charlie, and whoever it was pointed a flashlight beam directly at his face, blinding him. He squinted and tried to block the light with his hands.

"Please don't move, Brian. I have a gun pointed at you."

"Who are you and what do you want?" He was scared.

"Don't worry. It's just Fred. I wanted to meet and talk with you."

Brian calmed down a bit. "Okay." He paused quickly, trying to figure out what was happening and why Fred was there. "Charlie told me that you would . . . or I would . . . I would never meet you."

"That was the case, but I wanted to know the specific details of your last kill."

"Cynthia Pope?"

"Yes, and when I say I want details, I mean I want you to start from when you left the shed in this van"—Fred tapped the side of the van, scaring Brian even more—"until you returned and parked it where it's sitting now. I don't want you to leave out a single detail. Nothing. Not one. Do you understand what I'm asking, Brian? Every single detail."

"I can do that." The details of the night were burned into his mind, as that was almost all he'd been thinking about.

Brian began telling Fred each detail of the night, from the moment he left the garage until the point when he was lifting Cynthia's naked body out of the van to pose her by the tree. The scene made him think of what he was planning on doing with tonight's victim.

"Keep going, Brian."

He continued telling Fred about the killing of Cynthia Pope. When he finished, he began wondering where Charlie was. It must be close to their designated meeting time.

"Is there anything you did that night that you now think you would have done differently? Anything at all, Brian?"

Brian hesitated before answering. "Ah, no."

"Nothing? Nothing at all?"

"No, sir. I—we—have followed your plan exactly and haven't changed anything. Not one iota, as you required. I did everything that you wanted and nothing more."

"You're sure you didn't do anything else you're not telling me?"

"What do you mean?"

"It's a straightforward question, Brian. When you killed Cynthia, did you do anything that you're not telling me? Something that wasn't part of the plan."

Brian was beginning to wonder if Fred had been in the parking lot watching him that night. He was beginning to doubt himself and think that maybe he did do something that wasn't part of the plan. "No, I followed the plan."

"Thank you, Brian. I very much appreciate you taking the time to share with me the details of her death. You see, Cynthia Weller was someone who was very important to me." Fred kept the flashlight on Brian's face. "She was very important in my life."

Brian really didn't care how Cynthia or any of the people he had killed were connected to Fred. He didn't care why Fred wanted them killed. Right now, he was scared. Very scared. His only concern was how he was going to get himself out of this place and away from Fred. "I understand." He clearly didn't, but he didn't know what else to say.

"No, you don't, Brian. You couldn't understand. Cynthia was one of my best friends." Fred paused, trying to regain control of his rage. "Key word is *was*."

Brian didn't know what to do or what to say. He offered softly, "Sorry."

"What?"

"I'm sorry."

"You're sorry? Sorry for what? Shut up, Brian. You've done what I wanted you to do. There's nothing more I need from you."

"I don't understand. What do you mean there's nothing more you need from me?"

"There's nothing more you need to do, Brian."

"But I'm not even halfway done."

"No, Brian. You're done. You've done exactly what I wanted you and Charlie to do by killing these five people. Some were just collateral damage. People who had minor parts in the plan."

Brian's eyes darted back and forth, looking for a way out.

"I need you to back up, Brian." Fred watched as Brian stepped past the front of the pickup truck. "You've done a great job. You served your purpose. Sorry." Fred raised his Taser and shot Brian on the left side of his chest. Brian immediately dropped to the floor of the shed. Fred quickly pulled Brian's arms behind him as he lay struggling on the floor. He pulled a zip tie out of the pocket of his hoodie, a hoodie like the ones Brian had been wearing when committing the murders. After securing Brian's hands, Fred pulled Brian's legs together and fastened another zip tie around his ankles. He used another tie to bind together the ties on Brian's hands and feet.

As Fred waited for Brian to recover from being tased, he was thinking how uncomfortably he was dressed—dressed as Brian had been for each kill. He'd finished duct-taping the hoodie sleeves to the gloves and taping his pants legs to the tennis shoes at least twenty minutes before Brian had arrived at the machine shed. He could feel his body temperature rising. Brian had done most of the kills in cooler temperatures; wearing the black sweatpants, hoodie sweatshirt, balaclava, tennis shoes, galoshes, and neoprene gloves probably wasn't as uncomfortable as it was for Fred. He was sweating heavily.

It didn't take long for Brian to recover. "What the hell are you doing?" he screamed.

"Just cleaning up. Like I said. You've served your purpose. Just like Charlie did."

Brian still couldn't see the face of the guy shining the flashlight down at him. "I don't understand."

"Charlie's dead."

"What do you mean Charlie's dead?! He was meeting me here tonight!"

"He died the day after you killed the Zumwalts. As soon as I knew he had chosen the right person in you to do the job, Charlie wasn't really needed anymore. You know, I watched the two of you meet the night of the murder. I thought you'd want to see him. Need to see him, I should say."

Brian didn't know how he could get himself out of the situation, but he needed to do something, and fast.

"He's dead, Brian. Now it's your turn."

"You want your money back? I can give you all the money back." Brian was in a full panic.

"I don't need the money back. I'm sure you'd tell me where you hid it, and I could take it all back from you. But I really don't care."

"But it's like over a quarter mil, man. A quarter mil. I'll give it all back. Just let me go." Brian's eyes continued to dart around the garage looking for a way out.

Fred shook his head. "I have more money than I could spend in a hundred lifetimes. I don't want it back. It would be even better if someone finds your hiding place and decides to keep the money for themselves, don't you think? Let's hope for that." Fred smiled. "Goodbye, Brian. Thanks for your help."

He pulled a clear plastic bag out of his hoodie pocket and placed it over Brian's head and slowly tightened it around his neck. Brian tried to wriggle free, but just like each of his victims, there was really nothing he could do to stop being suffocated. After a couple of minutes, Fred pressed his right index finger and second finger down on Brian's carotid artery to feel for a pulse. There was none.

Fred opened the door of the pickup and pulled out a folded tarpaulin, a garbage bag, a small tube of fast-drying glue, and a pair of scissors. He unfolded the tarp on the floor of the shed, next to Brian. He lifted the limp body and laid it on the tarp. He used the scissors to cut the zip ties from Brian's wrists and ankles. He took Brian's billfold out of his back pocket, removed his driver's license, and then returned the billfold. Fred undid the clasp of Brian's watch and slipped it off his left wrist. He then reached into Brian's pocket and pulled out his burner phone, then rolled the body onto its back. He reached into the pocket of his hoodie and pulled out a Ziploc bag, then dropped the three items into it and put it back in his hoodie pocket.

He removed Brian's tennis shoes and socks and put them into the garbage bag. He used the scissors to cut off the jeans, sweatshirt, and underwear from the body and placed each into the garbage bag. He lifted the body up and laid it on the tailgate of Brian's Dodge Ram. Fred walked back to the cab of the truck and took out four Ziploc bags containing items taken from the others Brian had killed. It took Fred a few minutes to place Brian's fingerprints on each item before putting them back in the appropriate bag. He opened each of Brian's eyelids and took several minutes to glue them open before pushing the body farther into the bed. He put the four Ziploc bags in the truck, then grabbed the tarp off the floor, covered the body in the back of the truck, and then secured the four corners of the tarp before closing the tailgate.

He packed up everything he'd used to kill Brian and then gathered Brian's clothing and put it all into the passenger seat of the pickup. He slid the garage door open about a foot, looked outside to make sure no one was around, and then pulled the door open the rest of the way.

As Fred retraced the route he assumed Brian had taken from his apartment to the shed, he made sure he was driving the posted speed limit. The drive back to the apartment complex took about ten minutes. There were only ten cars parked in the fifteen spaces available on the front side of the apartment building where Brian had lived. There were also fifteen spaces across from the apartments next to the trail. There were no assigned parking spaces, and over the past several months that Fred had been watching Brian, he noticed that Brian had often parked his truck in the same parking place with the tailgate of the truck backed up to the trail. He backed into the space.

There was no moon, and the evening was very dark. A few lights over the front doors of the apartments across from where he parked were on, but with no additional lighting in the parking lot, it would be difficult for anyone to see him.

He waited over an hour and a half before deciding to make his move. Only one car had pulled into the lot, and that was well over an hour ago. He crept out of the truck, walked to the back, and slowly opened the tailgate, making sure that he made as little noise as possible. He released the corners of the tarp and pulled Brian's body onto the tailgate. He looked around the area one more time before lifting the body.

Breathing heavily as he carried Brian's body, Fred went directly to the tree he'd already picked to pose Brian's body against. He lowered it to the ground and leaned his back up against the trunk of the small Japanese maple, the body facing the rear end of Brian's truck. He could feel that the ground was damp from a light rain earlier in the evening. He stood back a few feet from the tree and then moved in to straighten Brian's upper body. He then adjusted the head so that the chin rested on the right collarbone. The initial signs of rigor mortis were just beginning to appear.

He wondered if Brian had followed in detail all the directions that he had provided on precisely posing each of the bodies. There had been little information provided by the police on the deaths. He would probably never know for sure.

Fred squatted and reached for Brian's right hand. He clenched the fist, placed it on the ground alongside the body. He did the same with the left. He then tried to position the index finger of both hands as if they were pointing to the Dodge Ram. As he stood back up to see if Brian was in position, he heard a car pull into the apartment parking lot behind him.

He watched the car slowly drive down the line of parking spaces, past Brian's pickup truck, before it stopped. It looked as if it were going to pull into an open spot next to the truck. Fred didn't believe in God, but he said a quick prayer anyway, asking that the driver not pull into that spot. The driver chose another space farther down the lot.

The car engine was shut off, but the lights stayed on until the driver's door opened. The driver got out and opened the passenger door behind her seat. She reached into the car and a few moments later lifted out a baby. She reached back into the car and pulled out a large bag and put it over her shoulder. Her decision to not park next to Brian's truck certainly saved her life. Tonight was their lucky night.

Fred stood quietly watching the woman walk to the door of an apartment across from where she parked. She paused by the door to unlock it, entered the apartment, and then closed the door behind her. He scanned the area around the body to make sure the scene was exactly as he had wanted.

He walked over to the trail, took off the right galosh, and stepped onto the surface with his right foot. He did the same with the left galosh before putting his left foot on the trail. Fred held on to the pair of galoshes and started walking east. It would take him over an hour to walk the three miles back to his home in Bloomington.

He was looking forward to the next few days, weeks, months, and years. He was about to put into motion the final stage of the payback he had meticulously planned. Fred said out loud one of his father's favorite quotes from the French writer Pierre Choderlos de Laclos. He repeated it in English: "Revenge is a dish that is eaten cold."

26

anice and Alex McMasters recently returned home to Normal after running their first full marathon. They had trained for almost fifteen weeks for the Flying Pig Marathon that they'd run four days before in Cincinnati. They'd been married in Janice's hometown of Cincinnati two years ago this June, and they'd agreed that it would be a great way to have an early anniversary celebration with family and friends. The morning run was going to be the first time they'd run since Sunday's grueling marathon.

They'd left their home a few minutes after seven o'clock. The plan was to run 2.5 miles before turning around and heading home. They were about a quarter of the way into the run when Janice quickly slowed and hit Alex on his left side. "Stop!"

"What the hell, Janice?" Alex stopped but continued jogging in place. She looked scared or shocked about something she was looking at off to the side of the trail. He moved nearer her and followed her gaze. He saw the left side of a man, naked, sitting on the ground against a tree. "Holy crap!"

Janice backed up and started to cry as Alex moved toward the body. He turned back to his wife. "You okay?"

She nodded, trying to process the fact that the serial killer had struck again. She'd never seen a dead body. She wanted to look away, but she also wanted to make sure Alex was okay. "What are you doing?"

"I'm going to check it out." Alex had worked for the Normal Fire Department for the past four years, and he'd seen dead bodies in his job as a firefighter. He needed to check to see if the man was dead or alive. The body was about ten feet off the trail. The man was looking off to his right with his head resting on his right shoulder. He walked around the tree, making sure that he was not getting too close, and stopped when he was standing directly in front of the man.

"What are you doing?" Janice shouted.

Without looking at her, he raised an index finger to his lips, asking her to be quiet. He squatted until his eyes were level with the man's.

The man's chin rested on his right shoulder, and his head was positioned against the tree trunk. The index fingers seemed to be pointed in the same direction that the eyes were looking. Turning slowly, Alex saw the back end of a pickup truck parked about twenty feet away. Was the man looking and pointing at the truck? If not the pickup, maybe he was pointing at the apartments past the parking lot? Alex looked back at the man and the lifeless light blue eyes. He slowly walked to where Janice was standing on the trail.

"Well?" she asked.

"The man is obviously dead. I'm calling 911." Alex pulled out the mobile phone he had zipped into the pocket of the armband he wore on runs. He quickly put in his security code and tapped the number.

"911. Please state your emergency."

"My name is Alex McMasters. I'm a firefighter for the Normal Fire Department and currently off duty. I'm standing on the Constitution Trail, approximately seventy-five feet south of East Lincoln Street in Normal." His training and experience as a firefighter were showing in the way he calmly reported what he and Janice had found. "My wife and I are out for a run, and we discovered a body, a naked male posed against a tree with his eyes open."

"Are you positive that the man is dead?"

"Absolutely," Alex calmly answered. "The eyes are milky. He's absolutely dead."

"Did you touch the body?"

"No. I never got closer than about ten feet." Sirens began wailing in the distance.

"I'm going to ask that you and your wife stay on the line with me until officers arrive at the scene. Can you do that?"

"Yes, we can." Alex muted his mobile. "You doing okay, honey?" Janice was white as a sheet.

Janice nodded. "I'm just a little cold."

"Both the police and fire vehicles will have thermal blankets for us." He hugged his wife.

Alex unmuted the phone. "Do you need anything else from me, ma'am?"

"I just need you to stay on the line with me until the officers arrive."

"No problem." The sirens were very close, and Alex turned to see two police cruisers pull up. One of the cruisers pulled onto the trail and drove up to where they were standing.

A police officer got out. He studied the body for a moment and then walked over to Alex and Janice. "I'm Officer Colby Trent. Are you still on the line with 911?"

"Yes, we are."

"Could you please let me talk with them, sir?" Alex handed him the phone. "This is Officer Colby Trent. I'm with the couple that reported the body." The officer ended the call and handed it back to Alex.

"Can you please give me your names?" The officer pulled out a notepad, ready to write down the answers to the questions he'd be asking. The officer in the second cruiser walked to within fifteen feet of the body. He spoke into the microphone of the mobile radio attached to his left shoulder.

Alex and Janice provided their names and then gave a detailed account of their morning.

"Would you both like to sit inside the cruiser? You'll need to stay until detectives talk with you."

"That would be great, Officer," Alex said.

Officer Trent walked the couple over to the cruiser and took out two rolls of crime scene tape from the back hatch. He walked over to where the other officer and ambulance crew were standing and asked if anyone had contacted dispatch.

Gary Jacobs, a twenty-year veteran with the Normal Police Department and a close friend of Colby's, said he had given them a rundown on the scene.

"They're calling Al Jalber and the senior detective overseeing the case from Bloomington PD."

Both officers began securing the tape at a small tree. They then headed in opposite directions, going from tree to tree securing a wide area around the dead man.

Colby walked back to his cruiser to check on the McMasters. He tapped on the window, and Janice opened the door.

"Would you like some coffee? I can have some brought out, or there should be a crime scene vehicle here shortly and they'll have some."

"No, thank you. We aren't coffee drinkers."

"The lead detective should be here shortly," he said. "I'm sure he'll want to talk to you soon. If you need anything, please give me a shout." Officer Trent walked back over to where Gary was talking with Normal detectives Al Jalber and Samantha Andrews. "Morning, Sam. Al." The three shook hands with one another.

"Morning, Colby. Gary gave us a quick rundown, but he said you talked to the couple that found the body. Can you tell us what they told you?" Sam had out a notepad. Although Sasha Frank was the lead detective heading up the task force, Sam knew that she and Al would play a key role in the investigation, just not a leading role, based on the agreement made between the cities' two mayors and police chiefs when the last victim was found.

Trent shared what Alex had told him, ending with "And he noticed that both index fingers are pointing in the same direction."

"Very observant." Al looked over at the body. "I noticed it too."

"Were those his words, Colby, or your words to describe what he saw?" Sam asked.

Colby chuckled. "I'm not that observant, Sam. Just ask my wife. Those were his observations and words. I'm not embellishing what he told me."

"I'm not suggesting you are. I just wanted to have that on record." Sam made a few more notes.

"How quickly did you show up after they found the body?" Al asked.

"I'd guess under five minutes, but 911 would have specifics. They had Mr. McMasters stay on the call until I showed up."

"You see anything else?" Al asked.

"Like what?"

"What do you see between his left shoulder and collarbone?"

Sam looked closely. "Some redness, but with all the chest hair it's hard to tell from this distance."

"That's what I'm referring to."

A Ford Explorer SUV with its light bars flashing pulled into the apartment parking lot and stopped in front of the pickup truck. Sasha got out of the SUV.

He shook hands with the Normal police officers standing by his cruiser. Sasha walked around the truck and peered through the opening in the screens set up around the body.

He and Al walked toward each other and shook hands. "Long time no see, Sasha."

Sam approached, and she and Sasha exchanged introductions.

"Al speaks highly of you."

"I wouldn't go that far, Sam." Al laughed. "I'm not sure I would have used the word 'highly.'"

"If we can find time for the three of us to have a beer," Sasha said, "we can swap stories about Al. I've got a couple of good ones."

"Whoa, Sasha! What happens in Vegas stays in Vegas." Al laughed.

Sasha smiled and looked over at the screens. "I don't see any reason to go inside the screens or tape, as Beff Turner should be here shortly. I called her on the way over." He'd decided to let Beff have the first look since it wasn't his jurisdiction. "Could one of you call in the tag on that pickup truck and get the owner registration?"

Sam nodded. "I can do that." She wrote down the license number. "I'll be right back."

"How's she doing, Al?"

"Good. Really good. She's under my wing until I retire."

"It's time, isn't it?"

"Yes, it is. After working this case, it's time to let the younger ones do the heavy lifting." Al took out a pack of cigarettes. He tapped on the pack and offered one to Sasha.

"I quit." Sasha then took one and laughed. Al lit the cigarette for Sasha and then got one for himself.

"I can see that. You quit buying, you mean." Al laughed.

Sam returned. "Truck belongs to a Brian Robert Keyes. DMV shows he lives in apartment 2B, right over there." Sam pointed to an apartment across the lot from where the pickup was parked.

"Did you pull his DMV photo?" Sasha asked.

"Yes. The victim distinctly resembles the DMV photo. The license was issued in February of this year. His hair looks a little longer now, but yeah, I'd say that's definitely Brian Robert Keyes."

"Al, can you call and get a search warrant for the truck and apartment?" Sasha asked.

"Yes, I can." Al turned and started for his police sedan.

"Sam, can you get that truck taped off?"

"Yes. I can get the officers to four-corner it with parking cones and tape. Will that work?"

"That would be great. Can you also do a search on Mr. Keyes?"

Sam smiled. "I'm not just a pretty face, Sasha. I already pulled it. Mr. Keyes was released from Menard this past February 1, 2018. He went away on a thirty-year sentence and got released for good behavior after fourteen years. He was convicted on two counts of armed bank robbery, one count of attempted murder. Thirty years seems a light sentence to me."

Sasha wished Sam had joined the Bloomington PD. She might be better than Chris. "Well, I guess if he hadn't behaved so well in prison he might still be alive." Right after Sasha made the comment, he felt bad about it. Brian Keyes was dead, the victim of a serial killer.

Chris pulled up behind the Normal police cruiser parked in the lot. He walked by Sam, who was busy directing two officers taping off the pickup truck.

"Didn't you have a dentist appointment?" Sasha called out.

"I cancelled it when I heard," Chris answered, peering through the screens at the body. "Geez."

Sasha nodded. "Yeah. We've already ID'ed him."

"How so fast?" Chris walked over and stood by Sasha.

"I asked one of the Normal detectives, Sam Andrews, woman over there, to check on the owner of that Dodge pickup truck. Brian Robert Keyes. His truck. His apartment is evidently 2B, right over there." Sasha pointed. "Al's getting warrants now."

"That was quick."

"Look at Mr. Keyes. See how his head and eyes appear to be looking toward the truck and his apartment?" Chris looked and followed the stare of the man's eyes. He nodded. "Now look at his hands. It looks like the killer pointed the index finger of each hand in the same direction his eyes are looking."

"To ensure that we quickly identified the body. What a sick bastard."

"I was just thinking about that. Add a convicted felon and recent parolee to the mix, and it gets weirder."

Chris looked at Sasha. "Convicted felon? Recent parolee?"

"Sam checked the guy out on the computer and found out he got sent to Menard for thirty years for bank robbery, attempted murder. Paroled the first of February this year."

"The pickup truck is secured, Sasha," Sam said, walking toward them. She put her hand out to Chris. "Samantha Andrews, but I go by Sam."

"Detective Chris Watkins. Bloomington PD. Nice to meet you."

Sam looked at Sasha, then back at Chris. "For the record, I'm a detective too. I'm with the Normal PD. I'm going to check on how Al's doing with the warrants."

When she was out of earshot, Sasha said, "She's pretty, don't you think?"

"Sure, she's pretty."

Sasha laughed and then looked back to where Keyes was posed. "See anything else of interest near or on the body?"

Chris studied the body and the area around it for over a minute. "No, I don't see anything. Why?"

"Nothing. Just wanted your opinion." Sasha called out to Sam and pointed to the trail. "I'm going to talk with the two in the cruiser. Care to join us?" Sam gave him a thumbs-up and started walking toward the cruiser. Sasha also started walking toward the cruiser parked on the path. Chris followed close behind.

27

The walk back to his house took Fred a little longer than he'd estimated. He kept getting lost in his thoughts about how well his plan was proceeding. As soon as he walked through the front door, he called his friend José Antonio Arechavaleta in Laredo, Texas. Fred had first traveled down to Laredo last year, looking for a place to sell cars. Now that his plan of revenge was in its final stages, he needed the ten vehicles he'd acquired over the past three years to disappear forever. Once this step in the plan was accomplished, there would be little chance the vehicles would ever be tied to the murders, regardless of the efforts of law enforcement.

José owned a small used-car lot called Vehículos Usados de Aguascalientes in Laredo, just a few miles from the border. It was perfect for what Fred required. On their first meeting, after about thirty minutes talking in Spanish, Fred knew he had found the right person. They later headed to a local bar called La Juanito's, where they shared a bottle of tequila. Fred learned that José went by Papi Chulo. The nickname in Spanish meant a handsome man who had great power over women. Fred was envious, as he seemed unable to connect with women. He had experience with women, but he had been damaged by a relationship with a woman years ago, and he still carried the scars.

During the early-morning call, Fred told Papi that he was ready to ship vehicles in two car carriers that would arrive in Laredo from California by early next week. The vehicles would be across the border into Mexico a few days later.

The vehicles had been purchased and titled under multiple aliases in several Midwestern states, excluding Illinois, over the past three years. He had bought and sold each vehicle several times using ghost addresses he'd set up over five years ago to ensure that it would be impossible for anyone to determine the real owner. Once the vehicles were across the border into Mexico, they would be in another world altogether. Papi would work his magic to mask previous ownership of the vehicles by buying and selling each through Mexican shell companies, and then each would be sold for cash to farms or ranches in central Mexico.

Fred would have the cars shipped from the shed to the California auction yard that he had purchased near Fullerton several years ago under the alias Bob Casey. They would be transferred to two other carriers that would then transport them along with five additional vehicles to Papi.

Later this afternoon the old steel machine shed would be torn down, and the scrap would be hauled to a smelter in eastern Kentucky. The concrete slab that the building had been built on would then be bulldozed and sold for fill. The next step was for a construction company to prepare the land for a new slab to be poured and then erect a larger building on the three-acre property that would be leased to a company that manufactured propane gas tanks. The land trust that held title to the property was owned by Fred. He smiled as another step in his overall plan for revenge fell into place.

28

Sasha, Al, Sam, and Chris had gathered in Beff's office to hear her post-examination report. "Have you found anything different with the killing of Keyes?" Sasha asked.

"Well, the similarities to how the latest victim was killed remain the same as the others. There is no deviation from the pattern we've seen." Beff shuffled through a number of scraps of paper on her desk. "But there was one anomaly."

Sasha looked at Al and then back at Beff. "And?"

"We found cloth fibers on the body that we believe are from some type of tarp or tent material. The fiber has been treated to repel water. We'll know more later, but those fibers are distinct to Keyes."

"What do you think that means?" Sam asked the question the others were thinking.

"It means that at some point he came into contact with the fibers from a tarp or tent. I don't know beyond that what it means. That's for you all to find out. It may mean nothing, or it may mean something."

Al looked at Sasha. "The victim came into contact with a tarp or tent. That doesn't seem helpful to me."

Sasha laughed. "I'm not sure what it tells us either. When Beff can provide us more information on the fiber, we can work to find out where the killer bought the tarp or tent."

"I think that will be difficult, Sasha," Beff said.

"Why do you say that? It's a new lead we can work."

"I don't believe the tarp or tent could have been purchased recently. The fiber appears to be from a material that is perhaps as much as twenty years old. I'll know more later." Beff looked back down at her notes. "By the way, we did not find any tape residue on this victim."

"What does that tell us?" Chris asked.

"I don't know, Detective. I don't think I can answer that."

Sam spoke. "We know that the Zumwalts were confronted in their garage, as was Bauer. We believe that Davis was confronted inside her house, and Pope in a parking lot near her car."

"Yeah," Al said. "So?"

"So some had tape residue on their mouths. I'm just saying the killer needed to put tape over some of their mouths to keep them quiet as he proceeded to kill them, perhaps because of the location where they were killed. No tape residue could mean that Keyes was killed at a location where the killer was unconcerned about anyone hearing him."

Sasha smiled to himself. Sam was going to be a great detective. He needed to see if he could recruit her to his department. "Good thinking, Sam."

"If what Sam is suggesting is right, we can look at camera footage around town and work our way back from the apartment complex parking lot to see if we can find Keyes's truck prior to his murder." Sasha stood up. "Thanks, Beff. If there's really nothing more, I think we'll all head back to the station and start working."

———

"I'd like Chris and Sam to go to the apartment complex and start working their way out from the center to find any business that has cameras." Sasha puffed on his cigarette. "Take a look at the film going back, say, to seven o'clock last night and look for Keyes's pickup truck."

"I agree," Al said. "I'll get some other officers on it as well. I know a few who know which businesses have cameras."

"Excellent." Sasha put his cigarette into the receptacle. "Who knows, maybe we'll get a clear headshot of the killer driving Keyes's truck."

"I'll have Sam send out pictures of the truck to all officers who can start to canvass locations," Al said.

"This is going to be tedious, but it's all we got," Sasha said. "Let me know what we can do. Chris and I will head back to our station and wait to hear from you."

29

Jonathan "JJ" Jennings was a great defense attorney and practiced law in his hometown of Bloomington. He had followed in the footsteps of his father, who was also a local attorney. For as long as he could remember, JJ had wanted to be an attorney, and he fondly remembered growing up watching *Perry Mason* reruns with his father. JJ had graduated from the University of Illinois with a degree in law and then graduated with the highest honors from the University of Chicago Law School. Anyone arrested for a crime and brought into court by a prosecutor with the sole focus of securing a conviction would want JJ to represent him. No prosecutor wanted to be assigned a case where they had to be in a courtroom when JJ was sitting as lead counsel at the defendant's table.

As successful as JJ was as an attorney and named partner at Jennings, Craft & Jones, LLP, he was a failure in marriage. At thirty-four years old, he'd been married and divorced three times. In his first marriage, he was blinded by love and didn't have a prenuptial agreement to limit the cost of alimony. Granted, JJ hadn't achieved the level of success that he enjoyed today, but that first divorce made him a believer in the value of prenuptial agreements. In his next two marriages, prenups saved him his home, his law firm, and the wealth he'd accumulated.

He lived in an eight-thousand-square-foot home that overlooked the country club. He was an avid golfer, and his home provided direct access to the golf course. The parties he threw during the summer at his backyard pool tended to end late at night and were greatly enjoyed by family, friends, and, especially, girlfriends. His current girlfriend, Jodie Paxton, was a recent law graduate from the University of Chicago Law School who worked for the district attorney. Everyone was betting that she was destined to become the fourth Mrs. Jennings, and Jodie was very much looking forward to moving into the home once they married.

The house had been built in the 1950s and had six bedrooms, seven and a half bathrooms, a billiard room, library, wine room, a formal dining room with a table that could seat twenty for dinner parties, and a large outdoor covered patio that opened out onto an Olympic-size pool with a diving well. There was also a pool house that featured an outdoor kitchen and bar area. Suffice it to say, the house JJ had bought just three years ago was the envy of lawyers and doctors in the area.

JJ also enjoyed hunting, especially duck hunting. Since he was a teenager, he had taken pleasure in carving and painting ducks as a hobby. He displayed ten of his hand-carved wooden ducks on the shelves in his library. These were "surprise, it's a box" ducks and different from most of the ducks he carved. Each duck had a secret compartment that he'd carved into them, which was virtually undetectable to the naked eye. He was very proud of his carving skills.

After returning from an afternoon golfing with friends, he was greeted by his dog, Ros, a black female Australian Kelpie that had been his constant companion since he finished law school. JJ petted her on the head, opened a cupboard drawer, and grabbed one of her favorite dog treats. He tossed it into the air, and she jumped up and caught it. JJ walked through the house to the library, where he was planning on reviewing a legal motion that he had dictated earlier in the day to his assistant. The motion needed JJ's final review, as it had to be filed with the district court first thing Monday morning.

JJ had just gotten through the first couple of pages of the motion when Ros began growling. He looked at the dog. "What's up, girl?" he asked. A few seconds later the front doorbell rang. He opened the app on his mobile phone that showed who was standing outside his front door. It was Sasha Frank. He wasn't friends with the detective, but he knew him as a worthy adversary when the two of them sparred in the courtroom. Why would the detective be at his door, especially at this hour?

JJ closed his laptop and got up from his desk. Ros followed him as he began to walk through the opened double doors of the library, but he told her to stay as he walked through the foyer. He opened the massive front door of his house. "Good evening, Detective."

"Good evening, Mr. Jennings." Sasha handed JJ one of his business cards.

"What can I do for you this evening, Detective?"

"I'd like to ask you a few questions, if you don't mind." Sasha was hoping that JJ would quickly agree and invite him inside.

The attorney looked down at Sasha, who was standing two steps below on the outside entry landing. JJ quickly decided that he'd let him ask a few questions, but he wouldn't invite him inside. Neither tried to shake hands. "Sure, I guess so. What questions would you like to ask, Detective?"

Sasha looked around, feigning concern that neighbors might be watching. "Would it be possible for us to talk inside, Mr. Jennings?"

"I'm sorry, but no. I'm right in the middle of reviewing some legal documents. Why don't you just ask me the questions that you have?"

"I understand. Could you tell me where you were on the evening of March thirty-first?" Sasha watched JJ's face closely to discern any note of concern or surprise.

"What is this about?" JJ was puzzled by the detective's question, but his face didn't show it.

"It's a simple question. I would understand if you needed to look at your calendar to answer the question. That's why I thought it would be best if we talked inside."

JJ quickly collected his thoughts, still trying to think through why the detective was at his door. "I know that I was in Bloomington that day. What more do you need to know?"

"Thank you. Could you tell me where you were on the evening of March thirty-first?"

"I have to ask again. Why are you asking me this question?"

"The question relates to an ongoing investigation, Mr. Jennings. That is all I'm prepared to say at this time." JJ was a poker player and an expert at hiding his emotions.

"Since you're not able or willing to provide me a basis for your question other than it's an ongoing investigation, I'm going to respectfully decline to continue this conversation. I wish you a good night, Detective." JJ stepped back, closed the door, and locked the deadbolt. He stood at the door for a few seconds, analyzing the brief conversation.

———

In the SUV in front of Jennings's house, Sasha was also assessing their exchange. The anonymous tip that Jennings was involved in the murders had been called in only a few hours before. Maybe he shouldn't have acted on his own. Maybe he should have shared the tip with Al and come up with a well-thought-out plan before taking action. He probably should alert the chief and the district attorney that he interviewed Jennings before the attorney called one of them. As he drove back to the station, his anger at himself grew for ignoring one of his own key rules—always sleep on big decisions before making them.

———

Ros followed JJ to his office. On the desk was a wooden tray that held a decanter of A. H. Hirsch Reserve sixteen-year-old straight bourbon whiskey, a very expensive gift from a grateful client. He poured three fingers of the liquid into a Simon Pearce lead crystal glass, sat in a leather chair, and took a sip. Ros lay down beside the chair.

JJ's schooling trained him to logically think through myriad issues to determine the best way forward. He took another sip and called his friend Michael Drake.

30

For a more relaxing last thirty minutes of his drive home, Michael changed the music streaming on his mobile from the Sex Pistols to The Eagles and turned it up loud. He grew up with the music of the sixties and seventies that his parents had listened to, and The Eagles were their favorite group. A call on his mobile interrupted the music. When he saw who it was, he answered.

"Sorry to bother you," JJ said, "but do you have a few minutes to talk?" He could tell that Michael was in his car. "Where are you anyway?"

"I've been in Chicago meeting with a new client, and I'm on my way back. The traffic was brutal getting out of the city. One of the guys at the meeting told me to expect a long drive back to Bloomington, especially since Mother's Day is this Sunday. He wasn't kidding. I should've stayed in Chicago for the weekend."

"Sorry to hear about the traffic, but I hope the meeting was successful." JJ was trying to keep his nerves in check.

"I think it was. A Chicago-based restaurant group is looking to enter the Bloomington-Normal market with a few of their restaurants. I'm helping them find the right properties in the area. It's going to be great to have their Chicago-style hot dogs and Italian beef sandwiches available anytime."

"Cool. Congratulations, Michael."

"What's up?"

"I wanted to see if you could drop by the house for a drink on your way home." He petted Ros.

"Sure. Something up?"

"I just need to talk." JJ did not want to tell Michael over the phone what had happened earlier. "I'll have a glass of bourbon waiting for you."

JJ opened the front door as Michael was reaching for the doorbell. JJ was wearing white golf shorts, a blue golf shirt, and the pair of bright red Converse Chuck Taylor 70 low-top custom sneakers he always wore. Ros was standing at his side.

"Hey, man. How was your golf game today? Hey, Ros!" Michael bent down and rubbed the dog's nose.

"Fine. Just fine." JJ reached out and shook Michael's hand, let him into the house, and then closed the door. "Let's go to the library. I've poured us a couple of bourbons."

Michael loosened his tie as he sat down in one of the big leather wing-backed chairs that sat in front of JJ's desk. Ros went around to the back of the desk and lay down. JJ handed Michael his drink, and they clinked glasses. "Thanks. So, what's up?"

JJ reached for two of the Hermès leather coasters on his desk and placed one beside Michael and then one on his side of the polished ebony table that separated the two matching leather chairs. "A police detective stopped by about an hour ago. He knocked on my front door and asked me if I would care to answer a few questions." Michael's eyes narrowed with an inquisitive look.

"Which police detective stopped by and asked what questions?"

"Sasha Frank. He's the lead detective tasked with investigating the Constitution Trail murders." JJ watched Michael tilt his head inquisitively, just like the RCA dog logo on the old 78 rpm records that his father collected.

"Why would Frank stop by and want to ask you questions relating to the murders?"

"My thought exactly. He didn't tell me why. Since he left, that's what I've been trying to figure out, but it's got to be related to the trail murders. He didn't come right out and say that it was. The detective asked me where I was on the evening of March thirty-first. That's the only question he really asked. I told him I was in Bloomington."

"What the hell? Why did you tell him anything?"

"I don't have anything to hide. I don't even know how his question relates to me." JJ took a sip of the bourbon. "At first I thought someone I've defended used me as an alibi. After thinking it through, I think it has to relate to the trail murders."

"You're a defense attorney. What would you tell one of your clients to say if a cop stopped by their house, knocked on their door, and started asking questions? Any first-year law student could answer that question. You'd never allow your client to say anything without his lawyer present."

"I know. But I wasn't thinking it could have anything to do with anything." JJ paused to reflect. "Yeah, I know that was stupid." He shook his head and then took another sip of bourbon.

Michael set his glass on the coaster and stood up. "You shouldn't have provided him any answer to any question without understanding what he was investigating." He looked down at JJ and shook his head. "Seriously, dude. What were you thinking?"

"I wasn't. I wasn't thinking, Michael. I don't have anything to hide, so I saw no harm in answering. At least initially."

"And now?"

Michael looked toward the decanter of bourbon and jiggled his empty glass. "What's a guy got to do to get a drink around here?" JJ laughed, got up, and poured another couple of fingers into the glass, and then poured some more into his glass sitting on the table. "Who do you want to use as an attorney to find out what Frank wanted?"

"I was thinking I'd ask you. That's why I called you."

Michael sat back down in the chair. "Me? Why me?"

"Listen to my logic, as I've really thought this through. You're obviously not a defense attorney, so having an attorney that specializes in real estate reaching out to Frank makes it seem like I'm not worried."

"Are you worried, JJ? Is there something you're not telling me?" Michael put JJ on the defensive with his questions.

"I'm not worried. I've got nothing to hide."

"Why don't you call Frank and let him know that you and I would like to sit down with him?" Michael watched JJ take a sip of the bourbon and consider what he had asked. "And if I'm your attorney, I need you to write me a check for a thousand dollars. Just like you'd ask one of your clients that you represent to do."

"Okay."

"Now that I'm your attorney, I need to ask you, where were you on the evening of March thirty-first?"

JJ looked across the table at Michael. "Screw you."

"I'm serious. I'm not going into a meeting as your attorney of record and not know how you're going to answer the question."

"Sorry. I'm still pissed about Frank. I already looked at my calendar, and I was home that night. Alone."

"Do you remember calling anyone that night?"

"I already looked at my mobile, and I didn't make or receive any calls after seven that night. Emails came in that evening, but I didn't reply to any of them."

"We need to remember that we don't actually know why Frank is asking you about March thirty-first. We've got to understand the why first. Without understanding the context behind the question, we're just spitballing here, man." Michael took another sip of bourbon.

"True. Do you think I should call Frank in the morning?"

"He's not going to contact you over the weekend. I think we should wait until Monday. Don't you think that if Frank had something definitive, he'd have asked you more questions?"

"Probably."

"Plan on calling him on Monday morning, and I'll be there with you."

"That works."

"I'm still not sure I should be your lawyer. I obviously don't have the right experience."

"You're the perfect lawyer, like I told you. I didn't do anything, and nothing says that more than having you at my side. No offense." JJ finally had a smile on his face.

Michael chuckled. "Funny. No offense taken. I get it."

JJ got up from his chair and walked around to the back of his desk. He opened the middle drawer, pulled out his checkbook and a pen, and wrote out a check.

Michael picked up the check. "I'm now your attorney of record. I'm counseling you to not talk with Frank or anyone else unless I'm at your side until we sort this out. Understand?"

They shook hands. "I'm sure that we will sort this out quickly," JJ said.

"I'll be here at nine. We don't need to be in an office where somebody might overhear something."

"I'll have coffee ready." JJ walked around the desk and stood in front of his friend. "Seriously, Michael, I can't tell you how much I appreciate your help."

Michael put his right hand on JJ's left shoulder. "I'm here for you just like you'd be for me. I'm going to head out now. Try to get some rest, okay?"

Michael raised his glass and finished the last sip of bourbon. JJ did the same. They walked around the chairs and headed toward the front door. Ros followed close behind. JJ opened the front door and shook hands again with Michael and watched him head down the front steps to his car.

Michael waved goodbye and got in his car and drove out the circular drive and headed home. He was going to have a good night's sleep. JJ, not so much.

31

ichael backed his car out of his garage and in just a few minutes
pulled into JJ's circle drive in front of his house a bit before 9 a.m.
on Monday morning, as they'd agreed.

JJ opened the front door of his house as Michael was walking up the front
steps. Ros came running out to greet Michael and he pulled out some treats
he had for her in his right front pocket. "Ros seems to like you more than she
does me. She's certainly excited to see you this morning."

"What can I say? All the ladies love me." Michael followed Ros into the
house. "I hope you had a great weekend."

"I golfed and drank a lot, and not in that order."

"I told you to try and not worry about Frank. He's chasing shadows. I
talked with both Lee and Max over the weekend."

"You what? What the hell did you do that for?"

"Calm down. Lee was over, and we played a little pitch-and-putt for
dough in the backyard. And a few scotches as well. We just shot the breeze,
and I asked him if he was involved with the task force looking into the trail
murders."

JJ motioned Michael to follow him to the kitchen. "Let's go to the kitchen
to talk and have a coffee."

Ros was all over Michael. "You and your master both need to calm
down, Ros."

"I don't know what's into her this morning."

Michael pulled out one of the stools that were in front of the massive
island in JJ's kitchen. Ros sat on the floor beside Michael and stared at him.

JJ handed Michael a coffee and made a cup for himself. "I couldn't get my mind off Frank stopping by last Friday. It bugged me all weekend."

"Lee told me that they're chasing their tails. Frank had been running the investigation, but as soon as Cynthia was killed, the pressure skyrocketed, and they formed the task force."

"Why is Frank coming after me?"

"You tell me. So, Maria and her husband were killed on March thirty-first. Then some guy that worked at a dealership. Next a hairdresser."

"Stylist."

Michael shook his head. "Stylist. Then Cynthia, and now some guy who just got out of prison."

"Don't you think it's odd that Maria and Cynthia are two of the ones killed?"

"I do, but both Lee and Max told me they weren't finding solid connections with any of the victims. Lee said they are facing an impossible task of finding the killer." Michael finished his coffee and pushed the cup across to JJ for a refill.

"What do you mean?" JJ turned to make another cup of coffee, and Michael gave Ros another treat.

"Lee told me confidentially that the killer has left no DNA or any other direct clues that point to a suspect. They have no idea what the motive is behind the killings, either. Their biggest concern is that the killings aren't going to stop." Michael took the cup of coffee JJ handed to him. "They're expecting to find another body on the trail six days from now, on the twentieth."

"What would make Frank think I had anything to do with it? It doesn't add up."

"Like I said, Frank is chasing shadows." Michael looked at JJ. "Are you sure you still want a real estate attorney to represent you?"

"Absolutely." JJ fumbled with the business card Sasha had given him the previous Friday. "Should I call now?"

"If you're ready. Put him on speaker and ask for a meeting today."

"Let's get this over with." JJ tapped in Frank's office number and initiated the call, then hit the speaker button on his mobile. After three rings, a man answered and transferred the call to Sasha.

JJ tried to sound upbeat and calm after the detective answered. "Good morning, Detective. I wanted to give you a call to see if we could meet sometime today." There were a few seconds of silence, and JJ felt he needed to fill the void. "As a follow-up to your visit."

Michael shook his head and mouthed, "Stop talking."

"I can certainly set aside some time to do that, Mr. Jennings. When's good for you?"

Michael held up two fingers and JJ nodded. "How about 2 p.m.?"

"Yes, if you could stop by the station at 2 p.m., that would work."

JJ looked at Michael to see if that was okay. Michael shook his head and mouthed, "Here."

"Why don't you stop by my house? We can talk here."

"Okay, I'll see you then. Detective Chris Watkins may join me. I assume you're okay with that?"

Michael nodded, and JJ gave him a thumbs-up and finished the call. "Certainly." JJ and the detective said their goodbyes, and JJ ended the call.

"How'd you think that went?"

"Fine, but you need to learn to say what you need to say and then shut up. The detective might be surprised to meet me since you didn't tell him you'd have counsel present, but that's no biggie."

"How do you suggest we prepare?"

"I'm a real estate attorney, JJ, and you're a defense attorney. I think you can answer that better than I can."

JJ sipped his coffee. "Good point. I picked you because you're not me. No offense."

"None taken. And stop saying that. I know I'm just the pretty face."

JJ came around the island and sat on a stool. "What I'm thinking is that when Frank gets here I invite him in and just flat-out ask him what's going on. And we can take it from there."

"What if he says he's not prepared to ask you any questions at this time?"

"Why would he do that? I'm offering him the opportunity to ask me questions."

"True, but we asked to meet him because we want to know why he was here last Friday night. What if he's not ready to ask you any questions?" Michael stood up and took his coffee cup to the sink. "Let me ask you, when do you ask a question in court when you don't already know the answer? You don't know exactly why Frank was here Friday night. You're just guessing as to the reason why."

"But what else could it be? I need to know. It's driving me crazy."

"Now that I'm your attorney of record, I need to ask if you have any direct knowledge or did you participate in any of the murders that have taken place on the Constitution Trail?"

JJ stood up. "Of course not."

"It's a yes-or-no question, JJ. Remove the emotion from your answer." Michael sat back down on a stool. "Frank is going to ask you questions, and you need to review the question in your mind and answer it with no emotion. Understand?"

"Yes. The answer is no to both." JJ sat down. "What can he ask after I tell him I didn't have anything to do with it?"

"Won't he start asking you who you were with, what you were doing, and where you were type questions before he actually asks you if you killed somebody?"

"Probably. Yes, he'll ease into the questions."

"Just answer the questions with the full knowledge that you weren't involved and have nothing to hide." Michael looked at his watch and stood back up. "What's for lunch?"

"It's only 10:30."

"I didn't have breakfast. The club opens at eleven, and I'm hungry. How much prep time do you need?"

JJ smiled. "You know I appreciate you, right? You're telling me to relax, as I've got nothing to hide. Don't act on edge, don't be defensive, don't act guilty. I get it. You're doing to me what I do to my clients. The only difference is that most of my clients are guilty, so they act on edge, are defensive, and act guilty."

Michael laughed. "Correct. So, don't act like you're any of those things. Can we go now?""

32

After lunch at the country club and a few rounds in a pitching contest on the golf course—in which Michael picked up $3,200 after JJ insisted on betting double or nothing each round—Michael and JJ cleaned up and awaited Sasha Frank's arrival.

"I still want you to answer the door," JJ said. "I'll be in the library standing behind the desk when you bring him in."

"Okay, okay. I'll answer the door." Through the front window of the library, they saw a Ford Explorer SUV drive up and park in the circular drive in front of JJ's house. Sasha Frank and another man got out of the car.

Michael went to the front door to greet the detectives, and Ros was on his heels. The doorbell rang as Michael got to the front door. He told Ros to sit, and she sat off to the side of the double entry doors. Michael opened a door and introduced himself. "Good afternoon, gentlemen. I'm Michael Drake, JJ's attorney. Please come in."

After introductions, Michael said, "If you both could follow me, Jonathan is in the library."

The outside of the house was impressive, but both detectives were amazed at the opulence of the interior of the home. They walked down the hallway that led to the double French door entrance to the home's library. As the three men entered the library, JJ walked out from behind his desk to greet them.

"Good afternoon, Detective." JJ shook hands with Sasha.

"Good afternoon, Mr. Jennings. I'd like to introduce you to Detective Chris Watkins." Chris and JJ shook hands.

"Nice to meet you, Detective. Please be seated. Can I get either of you a bottle of water?"

"No, Mr. Jennings, but thank you for offering." Sasha sat in one of the seats in front of the desk, and Michael sat in the other. Chris stood behind Sasha.

"Jonathan, I introduced myself to the two detectives as your attorney."

"Great. I decided to ask Michael to join me today. Especially since you didn't provide me any information related to the question you asked me last Friday night. I trust you understand."

"That's no problem, Mr. Jennings. I completely understand."

JJ sat in the large chair behind his desk and waited for the detective to speak.

"You called and asked to meet, Mr. Jennings. What would you like to talk about?" Sasha had decided that since it was Jonathan who had reached out, the ball was in his court.

Michael answered on behalf of his client. "Detective Frank, or should I address you as Senior Detective Frank?"

"Detective is fine."

"Thank you. I suggested to Jonathan that he ask to meet with you so you could ask him any questions you'd like, since you posed a question to him last Friday night. The only reason Jonathan didn't provide a more detailed answer to the question you posed to him last Friday night was because you gave him no basis for asking the question."

Sasha smiled. "Well, Mr. Drake, your client can answer the question or not. I'm not required to provide a basis for asking Mr. Jennings questions."

Michael returned Sasha's smile. "We understand that, Detective. We're suggesting that if you did provide your reason for asking Jonathan the question, he'd be more inclined to provide a response." He paused. "Do you mind my asking about your name, Detective?"

"My name, Mr. Drake?"

"Yes, the origin of your first name."

"I was named after my mother's father."

"Sounds Russian."

"Yes, he was Russian, as was my mother. My grandfather was a hero during World War II and was given the honor of Hero of the Soviet Union for his actions during the war. I'm proud to have been named after him."

Whenever he was asked about the origin of his name, he always provided the same answer.

"Very interesting. I can understand why you're so proud," Michael said. "So I assume you're a student of Soviet history?"

"Somewhat, Mr. Drake. Why do you ask?"

"Based on your unwillingness to provide Jonathan with an understanding of the reason you'd like to know his whereabouts on the evening of March thirty-first of this year, it made me think of Lavrentiy Beria."

"I'm not familiar with Lavrentiy Beria."

"He was one of the key heads of Joseph Stalin's secret police." Michael glanced at JJ, who looked at him inquisitively. "Beria served the longest in this position and was also considered the most ruthless. All were ruthless, but Beria set the bar for ruthlessness while he was leading the secret police."

"I'm sorry, Mr. Drake, but I really don't understand why you're bringing this up."

"I bring up Beria because of something he once said, which reminds me of your lack of candor with Jonathan."

"And that is?"

"Beria would say, 'Show me the man, and I'll show you the crime.' I'm suggesting that because you said, and I'm quoting you, 'Your client can answer the question or not. I'm not required to provide a basis for asking Mr. Jennings questions.'"

"Thank you for that history lesson, Mr. Drake. I'm sorry that you feel compelled to compare me to the Soviet Secret Police. I can tell you that no one has ever suggested that prior to today."

"I'm sorry if I offended you, Detective. Jonathan may be willing to answer your questions, but only if he understands the genesis of it. I hope you feel that's reasonable." Michael wasn't necessarily trying to outmaneuver the detective, but he did enjoy these types of discussions. He likened it to foreplay.

"I understand Mr. Jennings's position, and I'm agreeable to your request."

"Thank you, Detective. Please go ahead with your questioning." Michael settled back into the leather chair.

Sasha thought JJ looked very relaxed. He wanted to see if he could rattle him a little. "Mr. Jennings, I had asked you where you were on March thirty-first. As I recall, you mentioned in Bloomington. Is that correct?"

"Yes, I did."

"I'm sure you're aware that I'm leading the investigation into what the media calls the Constitution Trail murders."

JJ looked at Michael and then back to Sasha, nodding. "Yes, I'm obviously aware of that."

On the drive over, the detectives had agreed that Sasha would tell Jennings why he had asked him about his whereabouts that evening. Apparently there was no downside, since Sasha had obviously rattled the attorney at his door last Friday night. "Well, Mr. Jennings, we received an anonymous tip on our 800 hotline that suggested that you are somehow involved with the murders."

JJ leaned forward in his chair. "That's ridiculous."

Sasha smiled and leaned forward in his chair. "I'm not surprised by your answer, sir. Now that you know the reason for my knocking on your door, Mr. Jennings, I'd like to ask where you were *the night* of March thirty-first."

JJ was trying hard not to look at Michael, although he desperately wanted to. "I told you that I recall I was in Bloomington that day, and I know I was at home the *night* of March thirty-first." JJ nodded. "Yes. I was home alone, Detective."

"Can you prove that, Mr. Jennings?" Sasha asked.

"I'm not sure how I could, Detective." JJ looked at Michael. Michael looked back at him.

Chris talked for the first time. "You could allow us access to the GPS data on your cars and mobile phone. That could provide us knowledge as to where your cars and mobile phone were that night."

Michael slowly stood. "My client sees no reason to volunteer that information, detectives." He tried to say that with a strong hint of incongruity. It was preferable that he be the one who got indignant, not JJ.

"If your client has nothing to hide, I'm not sure why he wouldn't agree."

"You don't have probable cause, Detective Watkins. Unless you're not being honest with us."

"Today I know I don't have enough to get a judge to give me a warrant,

Mr. Drake." Sasha turned from Michael to Jonathan. "If I did, this would be a very different discussion."

JJ stood up. "Thank you for coming over, Detective. I know that the police use theatrics when there's no evidence." Michael gave JJ a withering look.

"Very well, Mr. Jennings. Detective Watkins and I appreciate you taking the time to let us ask questions." Sasha stood up, pleased that they had gotten into Mr. Jennings's head and home.

JJ walked around the desk. "Michael will show you and Detective Watkins out."

At the front door Michael watched Detective Watkins walk down the steps of the house to the unmarked SUV parked in the driveway. He shook hands with Frank. "Detective, I know that Jonathan is willing to answer questions, but next time we probably shouldn't allow emotions to come into play, on either side. He has nothing to hide."

"Are you sure about that, Mr. Drake? I was here last Friday because of a tip. You have no idea what more we've learned since that first tip came in. Do you mind my asking if you know if your client ever represented Brian Keyes?" Sasha thought asking the question, even if they hadn't found any connection yet between Keyes and Jennings, would be a nice parting shot across Drake's and his client's bow.

"Brian who?"

"Good day, Mr. Drake." Sasha knew that Drake had to know the name of the last murder victim.

Michael stepped back inside and closed the front door.

JJ was standing in the foyer. "I think that went well."

"You do?" Michael walked past JJ and down the hallway to the library.

"Yes, I think it went very well." JJ followed.

Without asking, Michael took a glass from the bar, got ice out of the refrigerator, and poured himself two fingers of a blended scotch. "I think the detective feels the same, JJ. I'm sure he thought they rattled you, and I'd have to agree that they got into your head." He glanced at the two shelves of carved ducks before turning around to face JJ and taking a sip of his drink. "We had a plan. Remember me saying to let me be the bad guy and for you to stay out of it? All you had to do was answer questions. Nothing more."

"I remember. It's easier to say than to do. You weren't the one being badgered."

"Badgered? You consider that being badgered? That's crap, and you know it. What I know from specializing in real estate is that I live a sheltered life, but you're a criminal defense attorney. You shouldn't be able to get ruffled, certainly not when someone suggests that you let them have access to your mobile and car GPS data. I was going to suggest that an impartial third party look at the GPS data from your phone and car for only the night of March thirty-first. If you're being truthful and you were at home that night, it would have proven that at a minimum your car and phone were at least here."

"This is my area of expertise, Michael. You never give something without getting something in return."

"Seriously? It would have cost you nothing to let them have access to that information. What could they have offered you in return?"

"You never give something without getting something in return. Never. My number one rule."

"Why would Frank ask me if you represented the last murder victim, JJ? He just asked me if you represented Brian Keyes."

"I never represented Keyes."

"Do you know if any of your partners did?"

"I don't know. I doubt they did. I think I read the guy was from Roanoke. My guess is an attorney in Peoria would have represented him."

"Okay, JJ, it's your neck, not mine. I don't get it, but we play by your rules." Michael sat down in one of the leather chairs. Ros came up and sat beside him. "What's next?"

JJ walked over to the bar and got a glass, added ice, and poured himself some scotch. "Nothing. We wait for his next move." He walked over and sat in the other leather chair. "He doesn't have anything. If he had some kind of evidence that I was somehow involved, he wouldn't have agreed to meet here. I've got two things going for me, my friend."

"Like what?" Michael stood up and walked to the bar to refresh his drink.

"First, I didn't do it, and second, he can't prove that I did."

"The last thing that Frank said referred to a tip that brought him to your door Friday night. He suggested that he had learned more since then."

"A tip? I don't know what that means, but I'm not worried." JJ jiggled his glass, asking for a refill.

Michael walked over with the bottle of scotch to pour him another drink. "Ice?"

"Thanks, and no thanks."

"So you're okay with how today worked out with Frank and Watkins?" Michael returned the bottle to the bar and looked up at JJ's carved ducks as he sipped his drink.

"Yes. I obviously got myself in a bad place this weekend after Frank's surprise visit. But after meeting with him today, I feel good. I know he has nothing, so I'm not sure why I let him get into my head last Friday night."

Michael sat in the chair. "It's easy to see how he got into your head, JJ. It's not any different than getting pulled over by a cop while driving. But Frank isn't acting like he has nothing, my friend."

"He has nothing. Tip or no tip. Nothing." JJ was feeling relieved now that the meeting with the two detectives was over.

"I understand what you're saying, but I don't think you're done with this yet." Michael petted Ros's head. "Frank's acting like a dog with a bone, and he's not the type that's going to let go easily."

"Nonetheless, I'm going to roll it down and relax." JJ looked at his watch. "Would you like to join me for nine quick holes of golf? Maybe double or nothing on your earlier winnings? And you get a stroke on hole number six."

"Since you're already paying my hourly rate for the day, I might as well finish by kicking your butt on the course."

33

On their way back to the station, Sasha and Chris debated whether the meeting had gone as they'd hoped. "Do you think we rattled Jennings?" Sasha asked.

"I'm not sure," Chris said, "but his attorney certainly wasn't happy with how his client joined the conversation when I suggested he give us access to the GPS data."

"Jennings seemed a little rattled Friday night when I stopped by. I'm just not sure how to read him this afternoon. He seemed unconcerned."

"What do you think about Drake?"

Sasha turned west on Washington Street. "That's the first time I've met the guy. I've never seen him in a courtroom."

Chris looked up from his mobile phone. "That's because he's a real estate attorney. What's up with that? Why would he be representing Jennings?"

"Maybe Jennings thinks he's signaling to us that he's so innocent even a real estate attorney can represent him? I don't know."

"You saw the ten carved ducks, right?"

"What do you think?"

"The second tip was dead-on as to where they would be, and the number of them was right too."

"What luck was it that they ushered us right into the library to meet, otherwise we wouldn't have been able to see them." Sasha made the final turn toward the station.

"That was lucky. Do you think they're hollow like the tipster said?"

"At this point we've got two tips, and Lee Barnes told me confidentially that the ducks are hollow."

"What's our next step?"

"The first tip, that Jennings was involved somehow, was pretty weak. And the tipster who told us about the ducks could be anyone who had been in Jennings's house." Sasha pulled into his parking space. "The second caller had a different accent from the first one, but I'm thinking the two callers were probably the same person attempting to disguise their voice."

"If the tips aren't enough for a warrant, then we'd have to find some scrap of evidence to tie Jennings to a murder."

"Of course we'd have to, Chris." Sasha looked at him, wondering why he so often felt the need to state the obvious. It was annoying. He was ready to talk with Al about trading Chris for Sam.

"What about asking him to let us search his house?"

"You serious? We just asked the guy if he'd give us access to his GPS data that could prove that his car and mobile were where he said he was, and he got upset. What do you think would happen if we asked him if he minded if we searched his house? Come on, Chris."

"I'm just spitballing."

"Obviously."

"The chief says we need to think outside the box," Chris said. "That's what I'm trying to do."

"Out of the box? You don't get it, do you, Chris? Sorry, I don't mean to snap at you."

Chris got out of the SUV and looked across the roof at Sasha. "I know I say stupid stuff."

Sasha looked at the young detective. "It's okay. The days are all running together. No sleep and living on caffeine isn't helping any of us."

"I'm going to go back to square one and go over every scrap of evidence to see if I can find anything," Chris said.

"We need a miracle," Sasha said. "A frigging miracle."

They walked into the station. Sasha headed straight to the chief's office, and Chris headed to the break room for coffee. Sasha knocked on the chief's door.

"Come on in and take a seat." Chief Boyer leaned back in his desk chair as Sasha walked in and sat across from him. "How did it go with Jennings?"

"It was a fairly short meeting. He had an attorney present, which we expected. Michael Drake, a real estate attorney. He evidently specializes in larger commercial properties."

The chief sipped from his coffee. "Tell me more."

"It started out okay but went upside down when we asked Jennings to provide us access to the GPS data from his mobile and car. You could tell that Drake wanted to be the only person talking on their side, but Jennings couldn't help himself. He let us know that he wouldn't voluntarily provide his GPS data."

"As expected."

"Jennings pretty much ended the meeting shortly after it started."

"So what's your takeaway?"

Sasha considered the chief's question for a few seconds. "On the surface I think Jennings is acting like an innocent man who is being targeted by the police. He's a defense attorney, so he's not going to give up any evidence, even if it is evidence that could confirm that his mobile was in the home and the car was in the garage. With everyone aware of GPS technology and tracking, you'd have to believe that if Jennings did commit the murders, he would have been smart enough to have left his personal mobile and car at home and use a different vehicle. He could've carried a burner when committing the murders."

"I agree. I know Jennings, and he's a smart guy. He's questioned me on the stand. If he's involved, he would know that he should make it appear that he was home that night, and he'd also take steps to not leave any DNA evidence at the scenes. As a criminal defense attorney, he may even know someone who would be willing to commit the killings on his behalf."

"That's an interesting theory," Sasha said.

"I'm not offering it as a theory. I'm just saying the obvious: that a defense attorney knows how criminals commit crimes, how we investigate them, and how the ME's office finds evidence to tie the criminal to the crime."

"Well, the ball is in our court," Sasha said. "The second tip suggested carved wooden ducks on the library shelves are linked to the murders. There were ten of them, just as the tipster told us."

"How do you think they're linked?"

"Chris and I have been noodling on that question. The obvious one is that we've been unable to find the driver's licenses of any of the victims, and none of the victims were wearing any jewelry. We know that both the Zumwalts wore wedding rings. We were told by many of the people who were at the league bowling the night the couple was killed that the wife was wearing a pair of bowling-themed earrings. She wasn't wearing them when she was found, and they weren't found when the house was searched."

"So you're saying that Jennings might have kept the licenses and jewelry as trophies that he is hiding in the carved ducks in his library?" The chief shook his head in disbelief.

Sasha smiled. "That's one theory. He's a very confident man who is so arrogant that he believes he's smarter than the rest of us."

"Do you know for sure that the ducks are hollow?"

"Yes. I confidentially asked Lee Barnes, one of his poker buddies. He told me that Jennings has been a hunter his whole life. Evidently, he especially loves duck hunting. Since he was young, he's carved duck decoys. Inside some of the ducks he carves, he adds secret compartments." Sasha shook his head. "Over the past ten years or so he's carved some number of them. He's kept most of them, but he's given a few as gifts to family and friends."

"How do we convince a judge to give us a search warrant, Sasha, when we've got no solid evidence?"

Sasha breathed a heavy sigh. "We have zero evidence that would convince a judge to give us the warrant. Without some other piece of evidence that can somehow tie Jennings to just one of the murders, we'll never get to look inside the house and those ducks. The entire task force is going back over every piece of evidence and reinterviewing everyone. The proverbial 'we will leave no stone unturned.'"

"I agree. We've got six days until we could see another murder. Find solid evidence, Sasha." The chief stood. "Find it now."

Sasha also stood. "We will, Chief. We will." As he walked to his desk, he said a short prayer asking for divine intervention to help alleviate another innocent person being killed.

34

Sasha woke up early Sunday morning after a restless night. He was averaging four to five hours of sleep a night. Whether he was at work or home, he wasn't fun to be around. The stress of leading the investigation into finding the person responsible for the Constitution Trail murders was bringing him to a breaking point.

He was sitting on a barstool at the kitchen counter, having his third cup of coffee. The clock on the oven said it was 7:13 a.m. It was frustrating waiting for a call he was afraid would be coming. He planned on heading to the station around 9 a.m. to prepare for the daily task force meeting.

Al had been leading the hunt for Keyes's pickup truck's comings and goings on public and private cameras. An officer spotted the truck on a video recording from a camera at a gas station on the corner of Business 51 and Raab Road. The video showed the truck heading west out of Normal on 51 toward Interstate 55 around 7:50 p.m. the night before Keyes was found. A little after 9 p.m., the truck was found on another video recording heading east on Business 51, at the gas station across the street from the one where the officer had first spotted it. Keyes or someone else had driven the pickup west and returned back east a little over an hour later. They couldn't identify the driver. The recordings had been sent to an FBI lab to see if they could clear up the images, but the local FBI didn't believe they'd be able to enhance the recording. Based on the timeline, if the pickup continued heading west it could have been driven as far as the outskirts of Peoria and back, or anywhere in between. Whether the truck continued west or headed north or south on Interstate 55 made looking for the truck's recorded image a daunting task. The number of square miles in the potential areas the truck could have driven made the search for its destination virtually impossible. IBI investigators were also looking, but so far no other images had been found.

With the permission of the chief and the local DA's office, the task force had been tailing Jennings for the past two days. A team consisting of FBI, IBI, Bloomington, and Normal law enforcement undercover officers had been keeping tabs on the attorney around the clock. There were a couple of task force members who played cards with the attorney. Getting them to go along with the surveillance wasn't easy, but with the lack of any solid leads all were in agreement that there was no downside to the decision. Unfortunately, tailing him had uncovered no new evidence.

Sasha heard Janet's alarm go off, and he got up and walked over to the refrigerator to get her a glass of juice. As he walked down the hall to their bedroom with the juice, he thought about the police officers who had been out patrolling the trail the past twelve-plus hours. The task force took a proactive stance and deployed city, state, and federal assets across the many miles of the Constitution Trail. Sasha hoped they'd catch the killer in the act and prior to another murder.

Janet was already in the shower. Sasha placed the juice on the bathroom counter and tapped on the shower door. She turned around and smiled. "I'm making a fresh pot of coffee. It will be ready when you're done with your shower." Janet blew him a kiss.

Sasha wondered if he would be investigating another killing today. If there wasn't a killing, what would that tell them? The task force had debated whether to deploy assets on the trail because if Jennings was involved and no body was found on the trail today, that wouldn't solidly point to him as a suspect. In the end, attempting to keep another murder from taking place won the day.

The mobile phone beside him started to ring. He looked at it for several rings, willing it to stop ringing. "Sasha Frank."

"Good morning, Sasha."

"Morning, Chris."

"I wanted to let you know that as of 7:30 a.m. the patrols on the trail have found nothing to report. I don't think we're going to either."

Sasha rapped his knuckles on the wood cabinet. "I think it's too early to make that prediction, my friend." He knocked the cabinet again.

"Well, we've had people out all night, and the sun's been up for a while, and there are no reports of anything out of the ordinary."

"Okay, thanks for the update, Chris." Sasha abruptly ended the call. He knocked on the cabinet one more time. He wasn't a suspicious man, but he thought it couldn't hurt.

He called task force member Lee Barnes. "Morning, Lee. Is there an update from the surveillance team?" He knew that Lee was a bit touchy over the decision to follow his poker buddy Jennings, but he'd agreed that it needed to be done.

"I'm expecting an update at 8 a.m. You know I'm not part of the team doing the surveillance, but I'm getting updates when the target is on the move. Jennings has been inside his home since 7:04 p.m. last night. He had no visitors. If he had left the home, I would have gotten a call. I'm expecting the next update will be short and sweet and that he's still inside."

"I got a call from Chris, and as of a few minutes ago, there has been no activity on the trail." Sasha paused and let that fact sink in.

"Great news. But that doesn't mean that Jennings is the killer."

"You're right, it doesn't. But it doesn't mean that he didn't somehow figure out he was under surveillance and didn't commit another murder, either."

There was dead silence for at least fifteen seconds. "True. But if there is no body, it's all just circumstantial evidence. No judge is going to give you a warrant to search Jennings's home without hard evidence."

"Yes," Sasha said reluctantly. "But you have to admit that if there is not a body found posed on the trail today, then it doesn't look good for Jennings."

As soon as the call with Lee ended, Sasha's mobile showed that a call was coming in from Chris.

"Hello again. I wanted to let you know that we just got another anonymous tip."

Sasha took a sip of his coffee. "Okay. And?"

"And, like the other two, the call came in with the number blocked, but this time the voice was a male. As we thought with the first two calls, it sounds like the voice may have been altered."

"Okay. And?"

"And the caller left two tips. The first was that Jennings was the reason that Maria and Cynthia ended their friendship in college. Evidently, he and Maria were in a serious relationship, but at some party the three of them were attending, he and Maria got into an argument, she left, and then he hooked up with Cynthia."

Sasha topped off his coffee. "Okay. That's interesting."

"It gets better. The caller also said that Jennings and Davis had a hookup."

"Seriously? You didn't find him when searching dating apps, did you?"

"No, I didn't. I'm just relaying what the informant said. I'll start looking back at the information we found on Davis to see if we missed something."

"Jennings has a girlfriend." Sasha took a sip of coffee.

"Do you think that would stop him? I don't think so. It's possible he met her at a bar somewhere and they hooked up."

"Do you think this could be enough to get a warrant?"

"I don't know, Sasha. All of this is circumstantial, and it came to us anonymously. When you combine them all, it seems significant that he has direct connections to three of the victims."

"Possible direct connections."

"Yes, possible direct connections."

"Tip lines can be helpful, Chris, but let's consider who's calling in these tips." Sasha put down his coffee cup and grabbed a notepad and pen. He drew a triangle. "Work with me for a minute. The tip that he was involved could have come from anyone." Sasha drew a line across the widest part of the triangle. "The next tip about the ducks would have had to have come from a member of his family, former wife, or one of his friends, plus friends of someone who was aware." He drew a second line above the first line. "Today's tip that he was serious with Maria in college and hooked up with Cynthia, which caused the three to no longer be friends, would have probably only been known by a much smaller group." Sasha drew another line above the last, just leaving a smaller triangle inside the larger one he first drew, and shaded it in. "The second tip today, that Stephanie and Jennings hooked up, could have only been known by a close friend of hers or his, which is an even smaller number of people."

"Okay. What are you suggesting?"

"I'm just sayin' that logic would point to the tip having come from a close friend of Jennings's. A very close friend."

"I understand the logic."

Sasha took a drink of coffee. "Why didn't one of Maria's or Cynthia's family members tell us about the two ladies being friends when they were in college? You need to go back and check that out."

"Can do, Sasha."

"I'm going to call Lee and ask him to dig deeper into Bauer to see if he can find a connection with Jennings. We need to dig deeper into whether Jennings knew Keyes or about Keyes somehow. We need to nail down the connection between Jennings and Ms. Davis. Let's get together in an hour or so."

"Sounds good, Sasha. See you in an hour."

"Thanks, Chris." Sasha ended the call and walked back to the bedroom with a cup of coffee for Janet.

"Hi, sweetie. Thanks for the coffee." Janet had a towel wrapped around her, and she was drying her hair.

Sasha kissed her. "We had another tip come in this morning. Actually two tips."

Janet turned off the dryer. "Seriously?"

"Yeah. The tipster says Jennings was somehow involved with both Mrs. Zumwalt and Pope while they were in college. The second tip was that he and Ms. Davis had a hookup."

Janet smiled. "You know this guy has a reputation with the ladies, right? And not a good one. He's been married and divorced like three times."

"Yeah, I know. It happens. I've got to call Lee Barnes to ask him to dig further into Bauer's background for a connection with Jennings."

"Didn't Bauer work at a car dealership in the service department?"

"Yes."

"Maybe he and Jennings had a dustup over a car?"

Sasha smiled. "I love you, Janet." He kissed her and walked back to the kitchen to call Lee again.

Sasha told Barnes about the tips. "We're going to contact some family members to see what they can tell us, but first I'd like to see if you can find out if Bauer and Jennings had some dustup over a car at the dealership he worked at. That was Janet's contribution to the investigation this morning."

"Good thinking. He drives a Mercedes, and Bauer worked for a Mercedes dealership."

"Correct." Sasha waited for Lee to reply. He counted to ten.

"I happen to know that Jennings had issues with the coupe he bought. It cost him a fortune, and I don't think he's ever been happy with the service he got."

"I understand we don't have any facts yet, but if he had an issue and then possibly had a run-in of some sort with Bauer, that could provide us with a possible motive. Tie that together with him hooking up with Ms. Davis and then having some kind of issue during college with Mrs. Pope and Zumwalt; then we're working on solid connections."

"Okay. I'll check that out. Since it's Sunday, I may not be able to access the dealer information until tomorrow morning."

"Sounds good, Lee. Thanks. I look forward to hearing what you find." Sasha had another thought. "Another question. Could he have a connection to the felon? Keyes."

"Don't know." Lee paused for a second. "He's a defense attorney. Maybe he met Keyes somewhere. I recall reading in the murder book on Keyes that J'Quon Sweeney was his parole officer. I'll confidentially check with him to see if he can shed any light."

Sasha chuckled to himself. The chief was probably right. The connection between two victims may be coincidental, but the potential connections between the victims and Jennings were beginning to add up. "Thanks, Lee. I know Jennings is a friend of yours, but he's looking more like a suspect, and I know you'll be handling this professionally."

"Unquestionably. And I wanted to tell you he hasn't left the house this morning."

"Thank you very much. This is the best telephone call I've had for a long while. Talk to you later." Sasha ended the call.

"How's it going, sweetie?" Janet asked, entering the kitchen.

"Fine. Just fine. Better than fine. The building blocks of a case took a positive turn today. The two tips that came in this morning could have just broken this case wide open, putting my prime suspect in play."

"That's big."

Sasha hugged Janet. "Yes, it is. It's huge." He was going to need to head into the station to make sure all the pieces were coming together.

Janet kissed Sasha on the cheek and then turned to put her coffee cup on the counter by the sink. "Listen, Sasha, I know you need to focus on this case. Don't worry about coming to the family dinner today. I'll make the appropriate apologies for your absence. I think everyone will understand."

"Do you know how much I love you?"

"Yes, I know. Let's just say I'm quite the catch for someone like you." Janet smiled, then started to laugh. She tried to keep a straight face, but the "for someone like you" she added caused her to lose it.

"Yeah. Yeah. Yeah. I know how lucky I am. I hear it from my family, your family, the kids. It's true. I know." Sasha walked over to give her another hug. "Thanks for understanding. I feel like I'm getting close."

"I hope you are." Janet lovingly pushed him away. "Now get out of here and solve the case so we both can get some sleep."

Sasha smiled and gave her a kiss on the cheek. "I'll be at the station. Give everyone hugs for me, okay?"

Janet nodded. "Yes, I will. Now get out of here."

35

Chris walked into the conference room where Sasha was reviewing documents. "Morning, Sasha."

"Morning, Chris. What do you have for me?"

"I just talked to Lee Barnes. You had asked him to confidentially check with J'Quon Sweeney on whether Jennings could have had contact with Keyes." Chris sat down across from Sasha.

"I did. What'd he say?"

"Evidently there's a poker game every Thursday night in a downtown bar. Are you aware of it?"

Sasha smiled and nodded. "Go on."

"The weekly game is attended by some pretty high-level people in our judicial and legal community, along with a few law enforcement types."

"And?"

"Lee wouldn't give me any of the names of the people who attended."

"I don't have a problem with that, Chris. You need to let that go." Sasha looked Chris straight in the eye to ensure that his detective understood that the poker game was not part of this inquiry or any future inquiry.

Chris clearly understood. "Evidently Lee attends. J'Quon attends, as does Jennings."

"Okay."

"Like I said, Lee talked with J'Quon confidentially. The players have an unwritten rule they call the cone of silence. You ever hear of that?"

Sasha smiled. "I'm familiar with the term and meaning."

"Evidently it's like the Las Vegas marketing slogan. Those who attend know that whatever happens during the game, anything anybody does or says doesn't leave the room."

"Yes, Chris. I told you I'm familiar with the term. Did Lee find out anything from J'Quon?" Sasha was getting impatient with his young detective.

"Sorry. I get the concept too. Anyway Lee said that J'Quon told him he often talks about felons he and his folks are responsible for overseeing after they're paroled. J'Quon told him that he couldn't remember if he did or didn't talk about Keyes. Evidently Keyes was an unusual parolee, as he had inherited money when his mother passed away while he was in prison. Keyes had plenty of money to buy that Dodge Ram pickup truck that we found at the scene."

"So, what Lee passed along to us was that J'Quon may have talked about Keyes at the poker game and also that in J'Quon's experience most parolees don't have money to buy a vehicle when they get out of prison?"

"Yes. So J'Quon evidently had no problem with Keyes buying a pickup or moving into the apartment off Lincoln. They also had found Keyes a minimum wage job at M & M Trucking & Hauling. It was an entry-level job, but he could be paid pretty good money as a welder at some point if he showed M & M he was a good employee."

Sasha leaned back in his chair. "This is between you and me and doesn't leave the room."

Chris smiled. "A cone of silence?"

"Funny. And yes." The senior detective leaned forward. "The scuttlebutt I've heard is that there could be a judge or two in the game, a few attorneys, law enforcement officials, and evidently a parole officer or two thrown in for good measure. Those in attendance, and I understand that some have been involved in the game for years, feel comfortable saying whatever is on their mind. Then add booze into the equation. Someone could say something during the game and not even remember what they said."

"So, you think that Jennings could have heard J'Quon talk about parolees and one of those parolees could have been Keyes?"

"Let's assume that he did."

Chris leaned back in his chair. "Why would Jennings want or need to kill Keyes? That doesn't make sense."

Sasha nodded. "It just might. I'm testing a theory. Let's say that after hearing J'Quon talk about Keyes at a poker game, Jennings recruited Keyes to commit murders for him that he planned. It's a classic cutout to separate himself from the murders."

"If Jennings recruited Keyes to kill the Zumwalts, Bauer, Davis, and Pope, his intention was to ultimately kill Keyes as a cover-up?"

"It's a theory." As Sasha stood up and stretched, he realized that he'd been stretching a lot lately. With the lack of sleep he'd been getting, more coffee than usual, and not eating regularly, he was feeling old. He'd be turning fifty-six in September, but he was feeling more like a seventy-five-year-old.

"A plausible one, though."

Sasha's phone rang. It was Lee. "One of my guys just got back from talking to Bauer's boss. When he asked if Bauer had ever had an encounter with Jonathan Jennings, the guy hesitated at first, then told him yes."

"Excellent!" Sasha put his phone on speaker so Chris could hear.

"Like I had told you, I knew Jennings had had trouble with the coupe he bought. Bauer's boss said they had trouble isolating a problem with the car. They did finally take care of the problem, and all's good now, but Jennings got in Bauer's face a number of times, and on two occasions they had to separate them."

"Were police called in?"

"They didn't call police, for obvious reasons."

Chris commented, "Obvious reasons?"

"Jennings was a good customer and not somebody you'd want on your bad side. My agent said that Bauer's boss said that looking back, he wished he'd handled it differently and that he should have done more. But he let it slide. After the last incident, though, he made sure that Bauer wasn't around if Jennings had an appointment to get the car serviced."

"With this new info I think we can convince a judge to give us a warrant," Sasha said. "Maybe limited to GPS data and maybe a look at the ducks too. What do you think, Lee?"

"I agree. I think we go to the DA and lay out what we've got, then the three of us go visit a judge the DA thinks we'd have the best chance to convince to give us a warrant." Lee paused. "Sasha, you need to know that there's no way I believe he did it."

"I'm not friends with him, Lee, and I don't know anything other than what we have learned or what we've heard about Jennings." Sasha looked across the conference table to Chris. "But we think that with the couple of tips the caller has given us that we've been able to verify, even if it's circumstantial, it clears the means, motive, and opportunity requirements. If the DA agrees, then we go shopping for a judge."

There was fifteen seconds of quiet before Lee answered. "Agreed."

"I'm going to update the chief," Sasha said, "and tell him what we're doing. Then I'll call the DA to set up a meeting so we can go over what we've got. Then I'll give you a call."

"Sounds good. Thanks, Sasha." Lee disconnected the call.

"While I'm gone," Sasha said, "put together all we've got in a nice and neat package." Chris gave him a thumbs-up, and Sasha headed for the chief's office. He didn't expect it was going to take long to give the chief the additional details. As he knocked on the chief's door, a big smile came across his face. "Got a minute, Chief?"

36

I t was 7:14 p.m. when the surveillance team watched Jonathan Jennings leave the country club. He had been inside the clubhouse for over an hour. Three minutes later Jennings pulled into his driveway and parked his car in the first bay of his garage. At 7:18 p.m. Sasha drove his SUV into the circle drive in front of Jennings's house. The senior detective was backed up by teams from both the Bloomington and Normal police departments, along with agents from the FBI and IBI. The task force members affiliated with law enforcement were walking up behind him as Sasha headed up the front steps of the house.

Sasha rang the doorbell and knocked on the door for emphasis. He was about to knock again when Jennings opened one of the double entry doors. The look on his face was priceless. Sasha hoped that the officer positioned a few steps behind him filming the search got a close-up.

After the initial shock, JJ composed himself. "Good evening, Detective. What can I do for you?" Sensing her master's uneasiness, Ros started to growl. "It's okay, girl."

"Jonathan Jennings, I have a warrant to search your home." Sasha paused. "The search warrant is limited to the home located at this address."

"What's this about, Detective?" JJ calmly asked.

"This search warrant allows us to take into our possession any mobile telephone we find on the premises and to examine only GPS data collected on the phone. It allows us to ask your mobile phone provider to give us access to your movements since March thirty-first, 2018. The search warrant also allows us to examine the GPS data that has been collected on any vehicle located on the premises. Finally, it allows us to examine the ten ducks displayed in your library."

"I don't understand." JJ knew there wasn't anything he could do as he watched Sasha reach out and hand him the search warrant. He took it in his hands and stepped aside.

"Thank you for your cooperation, Mr. Jennings." Sasha stepped inside. "Detective Chris Watkins will stay with you here in the foyer. If you'd like to call an attorney, the detective will allow you to do so. At this time I need you to hand me your mobile phone."

"My mobile is lying on the kitchen island."

Sasha turned to look past the foyer and stairs leading to the second floor of the house. "The kitchen is in the back of the house, Mr. Jennings?"

"Straight back." JJ knew enough that he had to keep calm and fully cooperate. He was looking down and quickly scanning the search warrant. "I'd like to call Michael Drake."

"Thank you, Mr. Jennings. I will ask Al Jalber and Samantha Andrews to secure your mobile telephone." Sasha looked at Al and Sam, who were both standing outside the front door. They both nodded and headed for the kitchen. "Detective Watkins can get you Mr. Drake on his phone." Sasha was being more respectful than he normally was of someone he was serving a warrant to, a request by Judge Robert Mayo. "Could you also please hand me the keys to your car?"

"My key fob is with my mobile, Detective."

"Thank you, Mr. Jennings." Sasha called out, "Could you please secure the key fob as well, Detective Jalber?" Al nodded.

Sasha turned to the officer filming. "Could you please step inside, Marcus?"

"Chris, stay with Mr. Jennings. He'd like to talk with his attorney. I'd like you to provide Mr. Jennings your mobile phone so he can make the call." Sasha motioned for Lee Barnes and Max Duncan to come inside. The two would accompany Sasha to the library to search the ten ducks.

Lee and Max walked in and both nodded to JJ as they passed him. It was an uncomfortable moment for the three of them. Even with an officer filming the search, Sasha wanted the FBI and IBI agents to witness him checking the ducks.

As Sasha, Lee, Max, and the officer with the camera walked toward the hallway that led to Jennings's library, he could hear the start of the conversation between Jennings and his attorney. Jennings told Drake he needed him to get over to his house as soon as possible. With Sasha in the lead, the four men entered the library.

"You're filming, right, Marcus?" Sasha had known Marcus Livingston for almost ten years when he joined the force after graduating from Illinois State.

"Yes, sir. I started filming when I stepped out of my vehicle."

"Excellent. Thanks." Sasha planned on talking through every move that he made, even if it was being filmed. "Before I start, I'd like to ask FBI Agent Lee Barnes and IBI Agent Max Duncan if they have anything to say before I begin to execute this portion of the search warrant."

"I identify myself as FBI Agent Lee Barnes, and I'm here to observe the execution of the search warrant signed by Judge Robert Mayo."

"I identify myself as IBI Agent Max Duncan, and I am also here to observe the execution of a search warrant signed by the Honorable Judge Robert Mayo."

Sasha nodded. "I'm beginning the limited search of the ten ducks now. The first duck I'm examining is located on the lower of the two shelves containing the ten ducks. I'm going to go from left to right as I'm facing the shelves." He reached for the first duck. Sasha didn't know much about the different types of ducks. In his mind a duck was a duck, but he could tell that Jennings had a unique talent in not only being able to carve the decoys but also to then paint them to look amazingly alive. Sasha used both hands to remove the redhead drake from the shelf. "The first duck, as you can see, has a red head." He turned and set the duck on the surface of a portable table that Max had carried in with him.

Looking at Marcus to make sure the camera was pointed at the duck and not just at him, he said, "The duck appears to be approximately fifteen inches long by seven inches high and four and a half to five inches wide. The bottom of the duck is flat. Visible on the gray back of the duck is a line that is rectangular in shape, which could be what we understand is a secret compartment." He looked up at Lee and Max. "I shouldn't say it's a secret compartment, because it's clearly visible."

Lee nodded. "I can clearly see the lines of the compartment."

"The compartment seems to be approximately four inches by three inches in size. There's no way to tell its depth. As you can see, there is no handle, and I'm not sure how the compartment is accessed. I'm going to turn the duck over to see if there's a cover that will fall out." He slowly rotated the duck with the red head while placing one hand on what he assumed was a cover. As he lowered his hand, the cover dropped into his palm, along with two Illinois driver's licenses, and assorted pieces of jewelry fell onto the table.

"Holy crap." Max couldn't believe his eyes. He looked at Lee and shook his head in disbelief.

The senior detective looked inside to see that the compartment had nothing else inside. Sasha then set the body of the duck down on the table and placed the wooden cover on the table next to the duck. Sasha picked up the two licenses one by one and showed them to the camera. "This driver's license is in the name Maria Matthews Zumwalt." He set it down and picked up the other license. "The second license is her husband's, Warren I. Zumwalt." Sasha was told that Warren's friends called him Wiz, and now he knew why. He put down the second license. "We're looking at a plain silver or platinum wedding ring along with a diamond engagement ring and a wedding ring. There's also a pair of silver-and-black pierced earrings that are in the shape of a bowling pin and bowling ball. There's also a small single ring." He pointed at a small ring. "I recall the ME telling us that Mrs. Zumwalt had a ring mark on one of her toes."

Lee stepped to the open French doors that led into the library and yelled, "Paul! Evidence bags! Now!"

FBI Agent Paul Pritchard walked down the hallway leading from the foyer to the library, carrying a large box filled with a variety of sizes of evidence bags. "Somebody must have found something!" the agent said. JJ wondered what they could have possibly found.

"You can put the box beside the table we set up in here, Paul." Lee motioned the agent to where he wanted him to put the box.

"This is a really great place, Lee! Tall doors that I don't have to bend my head down to keep from hitting," the 6'9" agent said.

Max smiled at the big agent. "Maybe you can buy it cheap sometime soon."

"Camera's recording," Sasha said.

Paul put the box on the floor next to the table. Max reached down and took out the first bag. He used a marker to write down key information that would establish the chain of custody of the evidence recovered from the first duck. Each bag would be marked with what the bag contained, along with when and where the item was discovered.

Max couldn't believe that his friend could have killed the Zumwalts, but that was exactly what the evidence was telling him.

After the duck and its contents were bagged, Sasha said, "Okay, let's look at the second duck on the first shelf."

Sasha had been patiently waiting for Lee and Max to do their respective tasks before examining the next duck on the shelf. It was hard for the detective to keep calm, as he anticipated finding the belongings of Greg Bauer in the next duck. "I'm now taking down the second duck off the lower shelf. This duck is brown, gray, and black with a white stripe." As he lowered the duck, he could see a similar line on its back, which he now knew was the compartment cover. What he didn't know was that this duck was carved by JJ seven years ago and was a northern pintail. This was one of JJ's favorite decoys. "The duck is larger than the first one and is approximately twenty inches long by eight inches high by, say, six inches wide. It has a flat bottom, as we found with the first duck."

Paul moved to his right to get a better view of Sasha as the senior detective turned the duck slowly upside down.

"I'm now rotating the duck to allow access to the compartment." The cover fell into his open palm. Sasha smiled as a driver's license fell down onto the table along with the adornment that Bauer was known to have worn in his left ear. "We've just seen a driver's license fall out of the compartment." The detective picked it up and turned it over. "You can see that this is Gregory Adam Bauer's Illinois driver's license. We also see what I believe is called a barbell hoop. It is a type of ear adornment that Bauer was known to have worn in his pierced left ear."

Max marked the first evidence bag, and Lee put Greg Bauer's driver's license in the bag and closed it. The barbell hoop was placed into the second evidence bag. As Lee and Max described what they were doing for the camera, Sasha wondered why Jennings hadn't moved the trophies, especially after his second visit to the house. It made no sense.

"This third duck is the most colorful duck of them all," Sasha said, reaching for the carved waterfowl. "It has very distinctive colors. The eyes of this duck are red. It has a white neck and blue, yellow, white, and black markings." It was beautiful. Sasha didn't have any artistic talents, and he was amazed by Jennings's ability to carve and paint the details that made each duck a masterpiece. He wondered what kind of a person could make something so beautiful yet do something as ugly as kill a human being.

"Does this duck have a compartment carved into it, Detective?" Lee asked. It was difficult to see if there was or was not.

"Yes, there is, Agent Barnes. As you can see, there is an almost invisible line that follows the carved feathers." Sasha marveled at Jennings's skill. If you didn't know that there was a compartment in this duck, you may have never seen it. "I'm going to roll this duck over so the cover will drop." He rolled it over and found that the cover didn't drop into his hands like the others. Sasha patted the flat bottom of the decoy, and he watched the cover drop. "Here it comes." The senior detective grabbed the edge of the cover with his thumb and fingers and pulled it from the duck. Out came a driver's license and several pieces of jewelry and assorted earrings.

Sasha picked up the license and stared at it for a few seconds. The picture on the license was of Stephanie Davis, but she didn't look at all like she did when he saw her by the tree on the trail across from her house. The photo was probably taken when she was in her early twenties. A beautiful young woman. Sasha realized he wasn't talking. "This driver's license belonged to Stephanie Ann Davis." Her initials spelled SAD. It was indeed sad that she was killed.

On the table were pieces of jewelry that presumably filled the piercings that Beff had cataloged during Stephanie's autopsy. "There is one ear cuff chain post that her friends said she had been wearing when she left work the evening she was murdered. There is also a navel ring that has a small blue crystal skull that friends told us she usually wore." Sasha looked at Lee and Max and shook his head. "There's also a septum ring that is known as a hoop, along with two stud earrings."

A commotion came from somewhere in the front of the house. Sasha motioned for Paul to go out and check what was happening. Paul entered the foyer and saw Chris standing between Jennings and another man he didn't recognize who was wearing a pair of shorts, a T-shirt, and flip-flops.

"What's going on, Detective Watkins?"

Chris turned to Paul. "Agent Pritchard, this is Mr. Jennings's attorney, Michael Drake."

"Evening, Mr. Drake. Pleased to make your acquaintance." Paul reached out his hand.

Michael declined the gesture. "It's Agent Pritchard, right? I'd like to talk with my client, and the detective isn't letting me do so."

"Until we've completed the search that's taking place in the library, your client needs to remain where he is. If you'd like, you're welcome to stay right where you are, but we're not obligated to allow you to be one-on-one with your client at this time."

"He's correct, Michael," JJ said. "I don't know what's going on, but the search warrant has been properly served. What and why they're in the library executing a search I can't answer."

"Who is in the library, Agent?" Michael knew just enough about criminal law to be dangerous.

"Senior Detective Sasha Frank is leading the search. Beyond that I'm not obligated to tell you."

"Lee and Max are with him, Michael. There's also a guy that's got a camera recording whatever it is they're doing in there." JJ was very famil- iar with the process they were following, as he'd defended countless people whose homes had been searched. He also had experience with clients who had search warrants executed on their properties followed by their arrest once investigators found the evidence they were looking for.

"Lee and Max? What the hell, JJ? What are they looking for?"

"I don't know, Michael. But I get the sense they came here knowing exactly what it was they were looking for. They've been in there for a while. Agent Pritchard is the first to come back out."

"Let us do our work and everything will become clear after we've finished," Paul said. He winked at Chris. As he reentered the library, he saw Sasha bringing down the fourth duck.

"Due to its coloring," Sasha said, "I believe this is a female duck. Its coloring is less distinctive from the first three carved ducks, which were male. The color has various shadings, but primarily the color is brown. It has a black beak. As with the other ducks, the bottom of the duck is flat." The detectives didn't know that this was a canvasback, which was known for diving underwater for its primary food source.

"As with the last duck, the compartment cover is very well disguised. I'm turning it over now." The cover fell into his open palm as he turned it over. On this duck the cover was barely a quarter inch thick and had fit snugly into the compartment opening.

Onto the table fell a driver's license, passport, and several diamond rings and earrings. The license fell picture side up. "The driver's license is that of Cynthia Weller Pope." Sasha handed it to Lee.

"We're looking at the diamond engagement and wedding rings she was wearing the last time she was seen alive. We also see the large five-carat diamond ring that Mrs. Pope received as a gift from her husband to celebrate their tenth wedding anniversary. There's also two one-carat diamond pierced earrings that her husband gave her as a gift on her thirtieth birthday." Sasha thought the gifts he'd given Janet really paled compared to what Carl Pope Jr. gave his wife, but he also didn't have Pope's bank account.

After the agents had finished bagging the evidence from the fourth duck, Sasha reached for the last duck on the first shelf. "This duck's primary color is white, but it also has blue, black, and green feathers and markings. It's smaller than the other four ducks that we've examined."

Sasha raised the duck so Marcus could get a good shot of the back, where the compartment was concealed. The senior detective showed the others the minute line that separated the cover from the back of the duck.

"I'm turning the duck over in my hand now to allow the cover to drop."

The five men saw the cover fall into Sasha's hand, followed by a driver's license and a silver watch. The detective waved to Marcus and the others. "Inside the compartment is a mobile phone that appears to be stuck." He set the duck on the table.

Picking up the driver's license, he faced the picture side of it to the camera. "This driver's license belongs to Brian Robert Keyes." Sasha handed the license to Lee. "You will also see on the table a silver wristwatch." He handed the watch to Lee and then carefully removed the phone from the compartment.

"You could see that the mobile phone was wedged into the compartment. The phone is black and is made by a manufacturer by the name D. I'm not familiar with this manufacturer." Sasha showed it to Lee.

Lee took the phone from Sasha. "It's a low-cost phone that is used primarily as a prepaid mobile. You can use it like any other mobile phone, except there is no camera, and it doesn't have much storage. Most use it solely for calling and texting." Lee showed the phone to Max.

"I agree with Lee," Sasha said. "We see this phone used especially in the drug trade. It is known as a burner phone."

Paul had been mostly quiet. "I didn't want to disturb the flow of your search, but Jennings evidently had Chris call his personal attorney, and he's arrived." He laughed. "And Jennings has been explaining to him how search warrants work."

Sasha nodded. "Drake can wait. Don't you think it's interesting that the only mobile phone kept as a trophy was Keyes's?"

"Only the person who put it there will know." Lee certainly had doubts that JJ was the killer.

"I'm now going to take down the first duck on the second row," Sasha said. "As with the first row, I'm going to move from left to right down the shelf."

"This duck has a green head and is mostly white and black. You can see the line through the feathers on the back of this duck, where we assume we'll find a hidden compartment."

Sasha turned the duck over so the cover dropped. "I'm looking inside the carved compartment of the duck, and there is nothing there." Lee had already picked up and bagged the cover and had handed it to Max for identification.

Nothing was hidden in the secret compartments of the remaining ducks. "It is now 9:24 p.m. on Monday, May 21, 2018. This ends our search authorized by Judge Robert Mayo of the ten ducks in the library. We will now be ending the recording of this part of the search by FBI Agents Lee Barnes and Paul Pritchard, IBI Agent Max Duncan, Bloomington Police Department Filmographic Officer Marcus Livingston, and myself, Senior Detective Sasha Frank with the Bloomington Police Department."

Marcus turned off the camera.

"Thanks, guys," Sasha said. "I really appreciate all your help in this search."

"No problem, Sasha. I have to tell you, I still can't believe what we found." Lee looked at Max. "What about you, Max?"

"I'm in shock. I find it very hard to believe that JJ did this, but the evidence is obviously damning."

"Paul and Marcus, do you two mind stepping out of the library and closing the door behind you, please?" Marcus got his camera equipment together and headed for the door. Paul followed. "Please change out the memory card in the camera, Marcus. We may have more filming." Sasha waited until the door to the library closed.

"What's up, Sasha?"

"The evidence is damning, as you say, Max, but I can't wrap my head around why Jennings did this. You know him. What could drive him to do something like this?"

Lee shook his head. "I've been wondering the same since you first asked me about him. This isn't the JJ Jennings I know. And I've known him for five or six years."

"This isn't the JJ I know either." Max looked down at the box full of evidence. "But all of the trophies in this box point to him as the murderer."

"We have enough evidence to put him away forever," Sasha said, "and if the DA gets his way, the death penalty. There's no way Pope Sr. won't influence how this is going to end."

"We've finished step one of the search warrant. Now we need to have technicians look at his mobile device and the GPS in his car." Lee turned to Max. "I'm guessing we're going to find that both of them were in this house the nights the killings took place."

Max nodded. "I agree."

"If he's so smart, why would he keep the trophies in his house?" Lee asked.

"I hear what you're saying," Sasha said, "but almost every serial killer wants to keep trophies close by. Everything I've read on serial killers is that they think they're the smartest people in the room. Always."

"I haven't known JJ as long as Lee," Max said. "I only see him at poker night. He is a very smart guy. He's got a lot of relationship issues. But it's hard not to look at everything in this box and not believe he did it."

"I agree." Sasha nodded. "Would the two of you mind taking the box of evidence out to the CSI vehicle? I need to get Marcus ready for filming the next phase of the search."

37

ichael Drake immediately approached Sasha in the foyer. "I read the search warrant, Detective. Why did you want to inspect the ducks?"

"I think your client will be able to tell you that, Mr. Drake."

"I'm asking you, Detective."

Sasha looked back down the hallway and saw Jennings standing by himself at the bottom of the stairs. "Five of the ten ducks contained trophies."

Michael had a confused look on his face. "Trophies?"

This back-and-forth was getting tedious. "You're a close friend of Mr. Jennings. I assume that you're aware of his hobby of carving ducks." Michael nodded. "I'm sure you're aware that the ten ducks he has displayed in the library also have hidden compartments carved into them?"

"I'm aware of the ducks. I have no knowledge as to whether all ten have hidden compartments or not."

"Five of the ten ducks contained personal effects taken from the six murder victims that were found along the trail."

Michael's expression conveyed that he grasped the gravity of the situation. "There's no way JJ is responsible for those murders." He moved closer to Sasha. "No way."

"Back up and calm down, Mr. Drake."

Michael quickly regained his composure and apologized as he stepped back.

"Since the ducks were carved by your client, displayed in a room in the home of your client, I would suggest to you that your client is responsible for the deaths of three women and three men."

"That's just not possible. JJ couldn't kill anyone."

"The evidence would suggest that he could and did, counselor."

"Can I please speak privately with my client, Detective?"

"You can wave your client over to where we're standing, and I'll give you five minutes alone with him." Sasha motioned to JJ to come over. "Mr. Jennings, you've got five minutes to confer with your attorney, and then I'm going to take you into custody and then to the station for your booking."

There was a look of surprise on JJ's face. "Arrest me for what?"

"Murder, Mr. Jennings. Actually six murders." Sasha walked away.

"What's going on, Michael?"

"I've never done this before. Can I stop them from arresting you?"

"They're arresting me for the six murders that were committed along the trail? On what evidence?"

"Seriously, JJ? They found trophies they believe you took from each of the victims the nights they were killed."

"Trophies? What trophies?"

"Frank told me they found personal effects taken from each of the six victims at the time they were killed. Jewelry and driver's licenses." Michael glanced at Sasha. "What do you want me to do next?"

"First, I didn't do this," JJ said. "Second, if they found evidence that was taken from the victims in my ducks, I'm being set up. I don't know why or by who, but someone is setting me up."

"I believe you. Regardless, Frank is going to arrest you for murder. What do I do next?"

"I'm going to be given a bail hearing. At this hour, that won't take place until tomorrow. They believe that I killed six people, so the DA will be able to convince a judge that I should be held with no chance for bail. Totally understandable, considering I killed six people." JJ looked over at Sasha, who was watching him. "The warrant was also for GPS data from my mobile and Merc. I promise you they're not going to find any incriminating information on either the phone or the car. That won't help in getting me out on bail, as they'll just say that I left both here at the house the night of the murders."

Michael couldn't believe how calm JJ was, considering he would be arrested in a minute or two. "But what do I do to defend you, JJ?"

JJ looked at Michael. "I appreciate what you've done so far to help me, and I want you by my side until I'm released. But I'll get a criminal defense attorney to represent me once we've gotten past the initial questioning." JJ looked back at Sasha. "They'll now be able to search the entire house, hoping to find anything else connected to the murders. They could find more incriminating evidence inside the house or at my office. They'll probably try to get a search warrant for my office at the firm if they don't find anything here."

"I'm asking again, what do you want me to do?"

"I want you to call Gray and Sig as soon as I'm arrested and tell them what's happened. We have got an action plan that we put together if something like this ever happened to one of us. They can start on that immediately. One of them will probably be my lead attorney unless we think there's someone better I can get." JJ watched the senior detective and another detective, holding the evidence bag containing his mobile phone, walk his way. "We've just got a few seconds. Call my partners, and we'll figure out the strategy in the morning. Nothing much is going to happen until then."

"Excuse me, gentlemen. Mr. Drake, we're going to be placing your client, Mr. Jennings, under arrest for suspicion of murder." Sasha waited for either attorney to say something, but neither did. He proceeded by asking JJ to turn around so he could be handcuffed, and then Sasha began reading the criminal defense attorney his Miranda rights. Once finished, he asked, "Do you understand your rights as I've explained them to you, Mr. Jennings?"

JJ nodded and answered. "Yes, I understand."

"I assume you're fully aware that I'm going to take you to the McLean County Detention Center for processing."

"Can you explain to me what's going to happen next with my client?" Michael asked.

Sasha was looking at JJ when he responded. "Your client knows what comes next as well as anyone, Mr. Drake." He turned to Michael. "Mr. Jennings will be put in a holding cell before being processed. He'll be asked a few questions, and he'll be asked to fully identify himself; then we'll ask him if he has any medical issues we should be concerned about before the jail will issue him an inmate identification number."

JJ looked at Michael. "Next they'll take my fingerprints and a couple of mug shots. Any personal effects will be taken from me and placed in a bag until I get bail."

"Sorry, Mr. Jennings, but you've got no chance of getting out on bail." Sasha always enjoyed telling someone he'd arrested that bail would be denied.

JJ breathed a heavy sigh and prepared himself mentally for what was coming. Little did he know how bad it would be.

38

I t had been over three weeks since JJ had been arrested. There was never any consideration for his making bail, based on the evidence that was presented to the judge at the hearing the morning after his arrest. JJ had spent the past three-plus weeks settling into the daily routine at the detention center where, in addition to helping with his own defense, he was continually asked questions from other inmates about their own cases. Everyone inside liked JJ because he was known as a great defense attorney, but they were also in fear of him as the only suspect in the trail murders.

Since JJ had been in jail, Michael took care of Ros. She was his constant companion wherever he went. JJ's two partners, Gray and Sig, had taken over handling the charges. Michael was still on the defense team, because JJ greatly valued his opinions.

The DA had given JJ's attorneys an overview of the case he'd been preparing against the local defense attorney. Gray and Sig had learned that the DA did have compelling statements from several relatives and friends of two of the victims. Those statements provided information that Maria Matthews Zumwalt and Cynthia Weller Pope had a serious falling out over a sexual encounter between JJ and Cynthia when JJ was dating Maria.

It was perplexing to JJ's defense team how initial information that was provided had become even more damning after JJ was charged. The attorneys had learned that one family member had recently embellished the information she provided in her first interview with police. It was now Janice Weller's recollection that JJ had threatened to kill Maria for not taking him back while also threatening Cynthia for causing his breakup with Maria. The attorneys believed JJ's version of what took place, but Maria's cousin was sticking to what she said the two murder victims had told her separately over fourteen years ago.

Another cousin came forward to say that she remembered a conversation she had with Maria Weller years ago that confirmed what her cousin Janice had told police. In addition, the DA's team supposedly found a couple of other college friends who, when asked about what had taken place, remembered something similar to what the cousins were told. All four potential witnesses were solid citizens, and the legal team feared that the stories the four would tell would be very damaging in front of a jury.

The police had also investigated the fight JJ had with Greg Bauer over problems JJ had experienced with a new car. Everyone who had witnessed the altercation told essentially the same story of what transpired, including JJ. He told his attorneys that he'd gone ballistic, and Bauer had just stood there while he hit him several times before other employees pulled him off the service writer. Also very damning.

After the police and the DA's office had talked with a number of friends of Stephanie Davis, they discovered that the hair stylist had told them of a fling she was having with a wealthy local attorney. Stephanie told her friends it wasn't anything more than sex, and she had attempted several times to end the relationship. Her attempts to end the relationship evidently had really upset the attorney; at least that was the story being told by her friends. One of the friends had told investigators that Ms. Davis told her in confidence that the attorney was into rough sex and had hit her a number of times. Stephanie was scared, and that was why she ended the relationship. That was not what JJ said happened, but his attorneys knew it would be difficult, if not impossible, to get that testimony barred from the jury. Even Stephanie's father had come forward, telling investigators that his only child had told him of a man she met who was an attorney who lived by the country club and was physically and sexually abusive to her.

J'Quon Sweeney told investigators that he recalled talking about Brian Keyes during a Thursday night poker game that JJ had attended. The poker game talk was always done in confidence, and he often shared stories about parolees he oversaw. J'Quon often guessed correctly whether a parolee would make it or not, and he remembered expressing doubt that Keyes would make it as a parolee. J'Quon also told investigators that in early April Keyes became less respectful to him and had caused a few problems at his place of work. It was apparent to J'Quon that the change in attitude by Keyes meant that he'd probably fallen back into his old ways and life of crime.

During the investigation it came out that another one of J'Quon's parolees, and a friend of Keyes while in prison at Menard, had been missing since the night of the first murder. Charlie Cole was someone who J'Quon expected would quickly find his way back into crime and back into prison. J'Quon heard from Cole's employer that late on the evening of April 2 the parolee failed to show up for his graveyard shift. The rules required the company to report tardiness or if Cole was a no-show at work as soon as possible. J'Quon's records showed that the night manager at Higgins had left a message for him during the early-morning hours of April 3 to report that Cole didn't clock in as required. J'Quon reported that no one had seen or heard from Charlie Cole since his last shift, including his sister. It was assumed that Cole had decided to skip town, but JJ's attorneys thought that perhaps Cole was somehow involved. Investigators had looked into the missing man, but up until now they had been unable to find anything to support that theory.

Gray, Sig, and Michael had been meeting every day for the past four weeks at the offices of Jennings, Craft & Jones trying to find a crack in the charges brought against their friend. There was a cadre of private investigators working to find anything that would lead to a crack in the solid case that was being built by police investigators and the DA's office, but they'd found nothing that could help defend JJ. None of his attorneys really believed that JJ could have planned out and taken part in the killings he was charged with, but the evidence was clearly damning.

———

JJ and his three attorneys met in the drab conference room at the detention center late in the afternoon. It was the same beige room with a barred window where he had previously met with his own clients countless times. As JJ looked out the window, he realized that the conference room offered a different view of Bloomington's downtown versus the view he saw from his cell. For the first time JJ understood the reason why his clients spent so much time looking out the window of the conference room while he met with them.

"JJ? JJ?" The four attorneys had been going over the case and the strategy they thought would give their client the best defense against the murder charges he was facing.

"Sorry, guys." JJ looked back at the papers lying on the table in front of him.

"We're hoping to poke some holes in the evidence that the DA plans on presenting at trial," Gray said.

"Like what?"

"You know that over the past two weeks we've had investigators stop at hundreds of businesses, showing a photo array of headshots of those who were murdered or we feel may have had some involvement, along with your picture." JJ nodded. Gray looked at Sig and Michael before continuing. "We've had investigators asking employees of bars, restaurants, or coffee shops if they recognized any of the men or women meeting with you. Except for the bartender at a bar across from the airport, who told an investigator that he recalled seeing you with a woman who looked similar to Stephanie Davis, we've found no one who saw you with any of them."

"Okay. So?"

"One of the investigators decided to check out some small towns outside the twin cities. He struck gold today when he stopped at a small restaurant in Minier, twenty-five to thirty minutes west of Bloomington-Normal. When the investigator showed Shirley Barton, a waitress who worked at the restaurant, the photo array, she identified Brian Keyes as a man who had dinner several times at the restaurant during the month of March." Gray paused to emphasize what he was next going to tell JJ. "What got us excited was that when he showed her additional headshots, Barton immediately identified one of the pictures as someone she recognized as having dinner with Keyes several times. That man was Charlie Cole."

"What do you think it means?" JJ asked.

"We don't know yet, so don't get your hopes up. The investigator is just starting to work on the lead and what it could mean. What's most important is that none of the investigators has found anyone that saw Keyes meeting with you." Gray wanted to give JJ some positive news, but until they were able to put meaning on why the two parolees were having dinner together, it was just something of interest. JJ's partner knew that you never knew where a lead could take you. One lead could take you in a new direction that could help solve a case or to a dead end that wasted precious time.

"I've got to hold on to hope that someone out there is going to find something that will get me out of here."

Gray looked at Sig and then back to JJ. "Listen, JJ, the evidence that the DA has is damning. You know that only your fingerprints were found on the five ducks. Keyes's fingerprints were found on a number of the items recovered from those ducks. Not every piece, but each driver's license had Keyes's prints on them, and his prints were found on some of the other pieces of jewelry."

Sig looked at JJ. "You know that when your garage was searched, police found the pair of size ten galoshes that are an exact match to the impressions collected at the murder scenes. Every single one, including Keyes."

Gray added, "And you know they also found a gym bag containing latex gloves, zip ties, duct tape, tubes of glue, a pair of scissors, and clear plastic bags, along with two Tasers hidden in another cabinet in your garage. The gym bag had only your prints on the outside."

"Another problem, JJ." Sig leaned back in his chair. "Only your fingerprints were found on the latches and doors of the cabinets in the garage."

"You think I don't know all that, guys?" JJ stood up and looked out the window. He walked over to the barred window and leaned up against the wall under it. "Keyes wore a size nine, and I wear a size ten."

This time Michael talked for the three attorneys. "The pair of galoshes found in your home left impressions at each murder scene. Whether they were worn by Keyes or you, it points to you since they were found in your garage, hidden behind some of the carving equipment in the cabinets on the west wall. It looks bad, JJ. Really bad."

"I didn't wear the damn galoshes. You all have to believe that I had nothing to do with this." JJ walked back to the table and sat down.

Gray stood up from his chair and started walking around the room. "We believe you, JJ. As with any case, it is the totality of the evidence. What the evidence tells us is that we've got to come up with an effective strategy to defend you against all of it. We've said it several times: It's obviously damning. Very damning." The partner looked at Michael and Sig before looking back at JJ. "Any of us, excluding Michael, when we've defended a client up against the kind of evidence that the DA has assembled against you, would tell our client to consider looking at cutting a deal."

Sig, who had been mostly quiet, leaned forward in his chair. "The DA's working theory is that you got Keyes to commit the first murders and then you killed him to cover them all up."

"I'm being set up, damn it. I didn't do this, and you know it. There has to be something out there that will show that I'm being set up." JJ slammed his fist on the table. "I'm not going to plead guilty to something I didn't do."

"We have ten private investigators trying to find something. You know every one of these PIs, as they've all done work for you." Michael stood. "They're chasing down every lead and talking to anyone connected to the victims, and they're working day and night to find someone else who had the means, motive, and opportunity to commit these murders."

JJ turned and looked up at his friend. "I know. I know. It's just infuriating that I could be set up so easily. I didn't do this, and I'm going to go to trial with no defense. Just me sitting in the witness chair saying I didn't do it. The jury isn't going to believe me. I wouldn't believe a client who faced this evidence. At best, Michael, I am looking at spending the rest of my life in prison, at worst getting the death penalty."

Sig was looking through his notepad, then looked over at JJ. "You've got solid alibis for two of the first four murders, but the DA is saying that doesn't matter. He's saying that you hired Keyes to commit the murders of the Zumwalts, Bauer, Davis, and Pope. But the DA's got no direct proof you paid Keyes."

"I didn't know the SOB."

"The DA thinks that you became aware of Keyes from J'Quon at poker night. J'Quon says he was sure he talked about him because he thought the guy could be different from other parolees. You know the DA doesn't have any direct knowledge of your meeting with Keyes, but the other evidence builds a case where he believes that he doesn't have to prove that to the jury. The rest of the evidence is strong enough on its own. More than enough. You know that." Sig looked back down at his notepad.

Gray walked around the conference table in the center of the room and stood next to his friend. "And you don't have an alibi for the night Keyes was killed. The DA's case says that Keyes is the only one you killed, to cover up the other killings."

"So, my partners are throwing in the towel? Neither of you believe that I'm innocent?"

Gray put his hand on JJ's shoulder. "I believe you."

Michael walked back to the table and sat down. "All of us believe you're innocent. What we're doing is talking about what you're up against. We've been at this for weeks, and we really haven't found a crack in what we know the DA is going to present to a jury. Nothing."

"Sorry, guys," JJ said. "I'm just running out of ideas here."

"You're the one we look to for ideas," Sig said. "If you're running out of ideas, then we're in trouble."

"We're in trouble, Sig? We're in trouble? I'm in trouble. I'm the one in trouble." JJ leaned back in his chair. "Listen, guys. Let's call it a day. It's Friday, and you guys should enjoy the weekend. I'm shot, and I know you've got to be too."

JJ's partners and friend started packing up their paperwork. "Listen, JJ," Gray said, "we're going to keep digging until we find something that will clear your name."

"Thanks, Gray, but I don't know how much longer I can keep believing that. Whoever did this to me did too good of a job. The connections I have to every victim, all but Keyes, have been firmly established. What's crazy is that I'm positive I didn't tell anyone about the hookups with Stephanie Davis. I didn't want Jodie to find out. I didn't expect that she'd be anything more than a one-night stand. I just don't see how anyone could have known about us. So that's one more thing that's going to be hard to explain to a jury."

"We'll be back at it tomorrow," Sig said.

"You guys need to take a few days off."

JJ's three attorneys looked at one another and each signaled their agreement. "We agree with you that it would probably be best to take the weekend off and start fresh Monday morning," Gray said.

"I think I need and deserve a few days off from you guys," JJ said. All four attorneys laughed.

39

J was waiting to be taken back to his cell after meeting with his attorneys when there was a knock on the door to the conference room, and then someone opened it. Standing in the doorway was Senior Detective Sasha Frank. "Good afternoon, Mr. Jennings. I know that your attorneys have left, but would it be possible for us to talk for a minute?"

"Sure, Detective." JJ thought this could be an interesting diversion, as he hadn't seen the detective for several weeks. He sat up straight in his chair. A detective asking to talk with someone accused of a crime, especially when the crime was killing six people, without their lawyer present was certainly unusual.

Sasha walked in and closed the door behind him. He sat down across from JJ.

"I'll get right to it. I don't believe that you're responsible for killing these people."

JJ leaned back in his chair. "Do tell. Your actions to date would say otherwise."

Sasha nodded. "I understand. I don't know what you know or don't know, Mr. Jennings. I'm going out on a limb just talking to you. The DA would certainly not be happy to know that I'm here. Your attorneys wouldn't be happy to find me talking to you either. Let's say this is a conversation just between you and me."

"At this moment I don't see any downside in listening to what you have to say. Please go on."

"As you may know, we received a number of tips regarding your involvement with the murders."

"I knew someone was telling you things that got you to focus so hard on me."

"I'm going to lay it out for you. We got the first tip from an unidentified woman who told us that you were somehow involved. That's why I stopped by your home that first night." JJ nodded. "The second tip also came in from an unidentified woman. She told us that the carved ducks in your library were somehow involved. Then we get a tip from a man, also unidentified, who told us that we should dig deeper into the relationships among you, Mrs. Zumwalt, and Mrs. Pope when you three were in college. We were told that something important happened. The same man gave us a tip that you were hooking up with Ms. Davis." Sasha let all that sink in.

"So two women and one man provided you with these tips?"

"Yes. It's odd, though, that no one has come forward to collect the reward money that was offered. Even after Carl Pope Sr. offered an additional $100,000 for information that would lead to your conviction. We got inundated with meaningless tips we had to chase down, but you'd think someone would like to collect that reward."

"There's still time." JJ smiled at the detective.

"True." Sasha reached for one of the Styrofoam cups that still had coffee in it to use as an ashtray. "I think all the tips came from the same person who used a device to alter their voice. We've tried to find similarities in the recorded voices, but we have no conclusive evidence that it was one person. Just my gut."

"So, why is your gut telling you this, Detective?"

"I was suspicious from the first tip. Whoever killed these six people put together one hell of a plan. It took a lot of time and money to execute, in my opinion. We have evidence that suggests you're connected to each one of them, and the DA feels one hundred percent positive that he can convict you of all six murders." Sasha leaned back in his chair and pulled out a cigarette. He lit it and offered the pack to JJ. "Let me correct that. The DA is not only one hundred percent positive. According to him, it's a slam dunk, Mr. Jennings."

JJ reached for the pack of cigarettes and took one. "Thanks. You know we're breaking the law, Detective?"

Sasha smiled and tossed JJ his lighter. "I think they'll let it slide."

As JJ lit his cigarette, he smiled. "So you think I'm innocent?"

The senior detective took a drag of his cigarette. "We have more than enough evidence to convict you, Mr. Jennings, but there are a few things that just don't add up. By the way, no one knows that I don't think it adds up."

"It's good that I've got you in my corner. What things don't add up?"

"The single biggest issue for me is how could anyone know that the ducks were somehow involved?"

"It bothers me too. Getting a limited search warrant that included the ducks was highly unusual. I had no idea what you were doing in the library. When I saw the big FBI agent walk out with a box with my carved ducks, I was even more confused. I gave that one some serious thought."

"Gave what serious thought? That we searched the ducks?"

"Yes. I was surprised the judge allowed it, but you must have found incriminating evidence that caused him to give you a search warrant, albeit a limited one." JJ took a drag of his cigarette. "I started thinking about the search and finally figured it was like a math problem, Detective."

"I don't follow."

"Well, there are some number of people that know I carve ducks as a hobby. Then there's a subset of that number that know I carve hidden compartments into some of those ducks. I've given away twelve of the ducks with the hidden compartments as gifts." JJ tapped his ashes into the Styrofoam cup sitting on the table between them. "Ten of the twelve went to ten family members, and the other two to friends."

Sasha nodded. "We were wondering how many of them there were."

"Doing the math, you now know that I've carved twenty-two ducks with hidden compartments. You have to figure that both family and friends have shown others the ducks I've given them." JJ smiled at Sasha. "You know I'm pretty good, and they're works of art."

"I can tell you that I was impressed." It was hard not to like this guy. He was kind of funny.

"There's no way to tell how many people knew I carved hidden compartments into the ducks. I'm assuming that you would agree?"

"Yeah."

"So the question we should be asking ourselves is who had access to my house to plant the evidence in the ducks?" JJ put out his cigarette in the cup. "It's a subset of the larger group."

"That's a question I've been asking myself. Some number of people know you carve ducks, some number of people know you carve hidden compartments into those ducks, and some number of people have access to your house. That's got to narrow the field down quite a bit, Mr. Jennings."

JJ nodded and motioned to Sasha, asking for another cigarette. Sasha pushed the pack across the table. "You can call me JJ if you'd like."

Sasha nodded. "You can call me Sasha. And like I said, that's got to narrow the field quite a bit, JJ."

"Yes, it would. I'm an only child, and my parents live in Florida year-round. They've got one set of keys. There are two ladies who clean my home once a week, and they have a set of keys. There's also a set of keys in the safe at the office."

"Anyone at your office have access to your house?" Sasha acted surprised.

"Yes and no. Each of the partners keeps a key to their home in the safe. The keys to my house are inside an envelope, as are keys to the homes of both Craft and Jones. Those three envelopes were sealed and then were placed inside a legal envelope that was also sealed. We each signed our names across the flap of our own envelope, and then all three of us signed across the flap of the larger envelope." JJ shook his head and laughed. "Funny. It sounded smart when we did it, but as I just told you what we did, it sounds pretty stupid."

"Not really. There's really no reason for any of you to get inside the others' house unless something happened to one of you. I follow the logic. I'm guessing that you believe the big envelope is intact?"

"Absolutely. It should be checked, though, and I obviously am not in a position to do that." JJ smiled at Sasha as he lit the cigarette.

"I'm sure you'll see your partners soon. Tell them to bring the envelope so you can check it." Sasha lit another cigarette. "You okay with that?"

"Yeah. It's not like I'm accusing them. It's just something that needs to be ticked off the list."

"Assuming that it's intact, that leaves only your parents and the cleaning ladies with access."

JJ took a drag of his cigarette. "You need to talk to the cleaning ladies, but I trust them unequivocally."

"With your life?"

"Yes. There has to be some other way somebody got in." JJ paused to think. "Somebody had to have picked the locks or made a copy of my key somehow."

Sasha nodded. "What about your dog?"

"She doesn't have a key."

Sasha laughed. "Funny." It had to be hard to keep your sense of humor in jail. Sasha was really beginning to like JJ. "Where's your dog kept while you're not in the house?"

"She stays in the mudroom between the garage and the kitchen. There's a dog door between the mudroom and garage so she can do her business in the garage if she really needed to, if I was running late or something." JJ leaned back in his chair. "Ros would tear someone up who didn't belong there."

"Okay. So who belongs there?"

"Who belongs there?"

"Yes. Who would the dog let into the house besides the cleaning ladies? Who else does the dog like?"

JJ gave Sasha's question some thought, then put out the cigarette. "That would be a much smaller subset of the subset." He tilted his head back, then slowly forward. "Actually, the only person I can think of that Ros wouldn't have a problem with outside of the cleaning ladies and maybe my mother is Michael Drake."

"Does he know about the hidden compartments in the carved ducks?"

"Yes. He's one of the friends I gave one to."

"Let's go down the list of victims. Does he know Maria Matthews Zumwalt?"

"Yes. He was at the U of I when we were there."

"So he knew Cynthia Weller Pope?"

"Yes. All four of us knew each other at the U of I. Michael and I were roommates our first two years."

Sasha leaned back. "Did he know about the altercation with Greg Bauer?"

"I may have told him."

"May have?"

"Probably told him. I can't be sure."

"Stephanie Davis?"

"Definitely not."

Sasha leaned forward and lit another cigarette. "Definitely not?"

"Definitely. Definitely not." JJ leaned back into his chair, giving Michael some thought. "I didn't want anyone to know, for fear that Jodie would find out. So definitely not. I'm not a kiss-and-tell kinda guy, Detective."

"It's Sasha. Try to remember." They both smiled. Sasha took a drag of his cigarette. "What about Keyes? Was Drake playing poker the night Sweeney says he talked about Keyes?"

"I'm sure that he would have been there. He and J'Quon are very close friends, by the way. Much closer than I am with Michael, and definitely he's more of a friend with J'Quon than I am."

"That's interesting. Does Drake have access to your house keys?"

"No."

"You sure about that?"

"Absolutely. I've never given him a key."

"Could Drake have had access to your house keys at some point in time?"

"I can't imagine how, but anything is possible, Detective."

"You can call me Sasha, remember." Gaining JJ's trust was something that was important for Sasha, especially since he was firmly believing in JJ's innocence.

"Sorry, Sasha." JJ smiled. "Are we becoming friends, Sasha?"

This time Sasha smiled. "Maybe."

"Well, I can use all the friends I can find." JJ reached across the table, offering his hand to Sasha. They shook.

"Back to Drake getting access to your keys."

"Okay."

"There are ways to duplicate a key in seconds by first making an impression in clay. If you've got the key, it's easy."

JJ looked at Sasha. "There's one thing that doesn't add up."

"What's that?"

"All we're doing is talking about someone who may have had the means and opportunity. What's Michael's motive?"

"Remember we started this conversation with me saying I didn't believe you committed these murders? By your own admission you said that Drake knew a minimum of four of the six people that were murdered. Maybe you did tell him about Ms. Davis, and he was at a poker game when Sweeney says he talked about Keyes. You with me?"

"Yes."

"You said there were two friends that you gave one of your special ducks with a hidden compartment to, and one of them was Michael Drake."

"Correct."

"You said he was the only person that could have gained access to your house with your dog inside. If nothing else, Drake provides you some level of reasonable doubt." Sasha leaned back in his chair.

JJ leaned forward. "Nice try, Sasha. Reasonable doubt has limitations. You can't just merely say that Michael could have done it. Does he have means and opportunity? Yes and maybe. My attorney would have to show that Michael had a motive to not only plan the deaths of six people but also frame me for those same murders. I appreciate you trying to help me, but it's really hard for me to believe Michael would be capable of what you're suggesting."

"By process of elimination, we came up with his name. Drake wasn't even on my radar." Sasha stood up and stretched. "You want something to eat or drink?"

"Sure. I'd like an old-fashioned." JJ started laughing.

"We can smoke some cigarettes, but the guards wouldn't let me go that far. How about a soda?"

"Sure. How about a root beer? I'm not really hungry."

Sasha walked over to the door and knocked loudly several times. A guard came and opened the door, and Sasha told him what he wanted. The door closed; Sasha stretched again before turning back to JJ. "Let's stick with Drake. I know you're friends, but have the two of you ever had a disagreement?"

JJ shook his head. "Nothing that comes to mind. We first met when we were assigned to the same dorm room at the U of I."

"You said you were roommates for the first year?"

"The first two years. Then he got an apartment with some friends in an investment club he was in."

"Why didn't you two keep living together?"

"We were interested in different things. Both of us were in prelaw, but he was big into his investments."

"What can you tell me about Drake?"

"He's from Springfield. His parents died the summer after he graduated from high school, before he started at Illinois. Both of Michael's parents were attorneys, and I think all four of his grandparents were attorneys. He was an only child. Maybe the only grandchild too. I'm pretty sure he has no living relatives. I think he told me that once."

"How did he become such good friends with Sweeney?"

"Like I said, they met in an investment club. They became fast friends. They seemed like the odd couple to me." JJ stood up. "You know J'Quon played football at Illinois. Many thought he'd go pro. As I understand it, J'Quon was interested in helping kids in trouble and rehabilitating convicted felons. He had twin older half brothers who joined gangs in Chicago and were both killed when he was young. The brothers' parole officer had become like a father to J'Quon."

There was a knock at the door. Sasha opened it, and the guard handed Sasha two cans of root beer. The door closed, and Sasha walked back to the table and handed one to JJ. "Here you go."

"Thanks, Sasha." JJ sat back down and opened the root beer. "You know Michael's the one who got J'Quon to move here and take the job that got him where he is today?"

"I didn't know that." The conversation with JJ wasn't providing anything concrete that would lend solid credence to Drake being the person behind setting JJ up. Sasha sat back down at the table. "What about Maria and Cynthia?"

"What about them?"

"You went to school with them both, and we heard you supposedly were going to get engaged to Maria Matthews. Then you did something that messed that up, and it involved Cynthia Weller."

JJ looked across the table at Sasha. "Where are you going with this? I'm pretty sure my attorney wouldn't think having this conversation with you would be a good idea, Sasha."

"I understand. You need to trust me that I'm your only friend in law enforcement today. Lee Barnes and Max Duncan are done with you. I think you've lost most of your judge friends too. You're toxic, JJ. Toxic. I'm your best hope."

It wasn't easy to hear Sasha tell him that, but JJ couldn't disagree. "Yes, Maria and I started dating our first year at the U of I. That led us to talk about getting engaged. We didn't get engaged, but that's where we were heading." JJ took a drink of soda. "We were at a party one night our sophomore year, and we got into a silly disagreement over something. I don't remember what. She got mad and left. Cynthia was there, and the two of us got really drunk and hooked up. Not one of my better moments."

"Maria found out?"

JJ laughed. "Yeah. Maria knocked on Cynthia's door in the dorm they lived in the morning after the party. Cynthia opened the door, and there I was lying in her bed. You're a detective. I think you can imagine what happened next."

Sasha looked across the table at JJ. "Yeah. I can see why it wasn't one of your better moments. What about Drake?"

"What about him?"

"Was he at this party?"

"I don't remember."

The detective stood up. "I think it's time for me to leave, but I do suggest that you give some more thought to Drake setting you up. Think back to anything you may have done that would cause him to target you. And if you do not think that's a possibility, think of others who you've pissed off who could have set you up. You say you're innocent. I think you're innocent. So, it's really up to you to come up with who could have done this to you."

JJ stood up. "I appreciate the conversation and soda, Detective."

"No problem. The soda was free, as was my time. I don't know how much more I can do to help you, JJ. Like I said, I'm out on a limb talking with you about how I think you're innocent. It's really not my job."

"I understand. I appreciate you believing in me."

"The fact that I believe you, and this entire conversation, stays between the two of us. Nobody should know about it." Sasha reached out to shake JJ's hand.

JJ took the detective's outstretched hand, and the two shook hands. "Thank you again. I'm going to work through all we talked about. Can we talk again?"

"Sure. I'll stop back by in a couple of days." Sasha knocked on the door, and it quickly opened. "Good luck, Mr. Jennings. I think you'll need it." He turned and walked out of the room.

40

After spending the past two hours discussing the status of his case with his partners, Gray and Sig, and Michael, JJ lowered his head in defeat. "Based on what I'm seeing and hearing again today, my chances at trial are zilch. Is that your opinion, guys?"

Gray was the first to respond. "Based on what we know today, I would agree with that assessment, JJ." He looked over at Sig and Michael and motioned for them to offer their views.

"Our investigators haven't found anything that's going to give us a chance to discredit any witness from their testimony, JJ," Sig said. "All the evidence the DA has seems to be rock solid. Sadly, I must concur with your and Gray's view."

Michael waited until JJ looked up from the table. "I obviously have no experience as a defense attorney. You know I've been working on this since the day you were arrested, and based on my limited experience, I'm sorry to say that if the trial was taking place today, I don't know how we could defend you successfully."

JJ lowered his head again. "I appreciate you not sugarcoating your views, guys. Like I said, I'm not seeing or hearing anything that leads me to believe I've got a chance for a positive outcome at trial. I have to consider a plea deal with the DA."

Gray stood up. "No. At this point there's no advantage for you to consider a plea deal."

"That's much harder to do if you agree to a plea," Sig said. "What's the incentive for anyone to continue to look for any exculpatory evidence if you've pled out?"

"I have to agree with Sig on this one, JJ," Gray said. "Once you go down the plea path, your long-term options are limited. Very limited."

JJ wished he had a cigarette. He'd found that smoking seemed to lower his stress. Medical evidence probably refuted that, but with what he was facing, it wasn't something that concerned him. "So, the legal advice is to go to trial and hope for a miracle?"

"The only person who can really answer that question is you," Gray said.

"I know that. I'm just asking for your advice. What would you do, Gray?"

"It's possible that we can push for a continuance. Then ask for another and then another. You know the drill."

"That's not answering my question."

"If I were you and faced the onslaught of evidence and witnesses pointing to me as the only person on earth with the means, motive, and opportunity to commit these murders, I'd cut a deal and not go to trial." Gray sat down and leaned back in his chair. "But I'm not the one about to face a jury."

"So, you're advising that I plead out to take the death penalty off the table?"

"You asked what I'd do, JJ. I told you." Gray leaned forward in his chair. "One of my law school professors used to ask, what does a defendant do when his lawyer has no more options? Find a new lawyer. It sounds to me like you've reached that point, but only you can decide."

As he stood up to stretch, JJ saw how late it was. "Let's call it a day. I'm beat and need time to think."

His three attorneys stood up. "Would you mind staying for a little while to talk, Michael?"

"Sure. No problem." Michael turned to shake hands with Sig and Gray and then watched them both give JJ a fist bump before they knocked on the door to exit the conference room.

JJ sat in his chair and reached under the table to adjust his pants legs. "None of this makes sense to me. None of it."

"I can see that." Michael sat across from his friend.

"I'm not sure what I should do. You believe I didn't do this, right?"

Michael looked across the table and saw that for the first time his friend looked defeated. "I know you didn't do it."

"I'm tired. I'm not sure how much more of this I can handle." JJ lowered his head.

"I don't think I've ever heard you talk like this."

"I've never been beaten down like this. My life has been pretty easy up until now. I'm beginning to think that I actually deserve all that is happening." JJ stood up and walked around the conference room table.

"I can't disagree."

JJ looked at his friend. "What do you mean? You think I deserve what's happening?"

Michael had been concealing his resentment of Cynthia, Maria, and JJ since he returned from spring break in 2004. The actions of the three had changed Michael's life forever. The ease with which they had so casually disrespected him, especially his roommate, was difficult for Michael to comprehend. The fact that he'd been able to hide those feelings from everyone around him for so long, in spite of the injustice they wrought on him, was a testament to how his parents raised him. "You've always been a narcissist, JJ. I've never known anyone in my life who cares more about themselves than you. Your constant need for self-gratification in every facet of your life pushes people away from you. My needs over others. That could be your motto. My needs over others." It felt good to let JJ know exactly how he felt. Seeing him morphing into a defeated shell of his normally egotistical self was certainly gratifying.

"Where's this coming from? You think I'm a narcissist?" JJ had never heard Michael talk like this before.

"Think back to college, JJ. Everything you did showed that you didn't care for the feelings or needs of others around you. You always thought you were the smartest person in the room, the best-looking guy in the room. Your own proclamations of your prowess and power over women, any woman, all women. You're so arrogant, so manipulative. You can't see how many lives you've either hurt or destroyed by your actions. And you don't care, because you only live in your own world. JJ's world, where everything is about you, to the detriment of all others." Michael stood up.

"What's going on here, Michael? We've been friends for almost sixteen years. How long have you felt like this? Felt this way about me?"

Michael walked around the room. "Probably since the day I met you."

"You okay?" JJ thought Michael seemed calm, but the things he was saying sounded more like a man in rage. There was something incongruent about what his friend was saying and how he was acting.

"Never felt better, JJ. Never felt better." Michael stopped and was standing across from JJ. "Do you remember the party that we went to back in 2004?"

JJ laughed. "You'll have to be more specific. We went to a lot of parties."

"You really don't remember?"

"If you can't be more specific than just a party we went to back in 2004, then no. How could I? How could you, Michael?"

"The party where you and Maria had the big fight. She left, and then you decided that Cynthia would be another one of your conquests, regardless of how many people you hurt. Remember?"

"Sure I remember. Maria and I had a fight, and then Cynthia and I hooked up. So what?"

"What did you say?" Michael glared at JJ. "So what?"

"We weren't that serious. It wasn't a big deal. Maria found Warren, and Cynthia found Carl. Everybody was happy. Things happen. Why are you making such a big deal out of this?" JJ wasn't sure where this conversation was going.

"You take advantage of people. You always have. You've never cared about anyone but yourself. As long as you get what you want, you're fine with how others are hurt by your arrogance."

"I'm not sure what I did exactly that offended you so much, Michael, but if I did offend you, I apologize."

"I don't want or need your apology." Michael started slowly walking around the room again. "I've lived with what you did that night, and every night since." JJ was so full of himself that he couldn't see the damage he'd done.

"I didn't do anything to you that night."

"How about we circle back to where we started this conversation? Why you're so deserving of what's now happening to you." Michael leaned up against the wall under the barred window.

JJ was wishing he could have a cigarette. "I'm going to be spending the rest of my life in prison because somebody is smarter than I am. Much smarter."

"You're right about that. Somebody much smarter than you executed a foolproof plan that culminates in you being found guilty of murder. Actually guilty of murdering six people, with no way out. It doesn't get any better than this."

"Let me get this straight. You agree with me that I've been set up. Then you take it further by saying that I deserve what's happening to me now?" JJ sensed that Michael was on the verge of telling him something but at the same time was struggling to say it. "If you've got something to tell me, Michael, just tell me. The drama is killing me."

Michael sat down. "It took a great deal of time, effort, and money to put the plan into place, but it was really easy."

"What plan? What was easy?"

"The murders." It wasn't enough that JJ was behind bars for the murders. Now the only way Michael would be able to stop obsessing about JJ ruining his life was for JJ to know what he had done. "The reason you find yourself where you are today is because of how you ruined my life. I've remained your friend for all these years just to savor this moment."

JJ told himself that continuing to act indifferent to the obvious pain and resentment Michael had been harboring was going to pay off. "I guess I'm dense, as I'm still not following you." Michael's eyes widened, and his nostrils flared.

"You're such a narcissist that you're blinded by anything other than what has meaning to you." Michael tried in vain to remain calm. "Because you were so caught up in yourself, you were unable to comprehend anyone else's feelings. I started considering how I could inflict the same kind of pain on you as you did to me with what you did on March twelfth, 2004. We've already talked about the heavy responsibility you bear for that night, but over time I came to realize that Maria and Cynthia bore a similar responsibility." Michael paused to see if JJ was understanding the importance of this moment. "From the day I met you, I should have recognized what you were. I had mistakenly thought you cared for me. It took me time to clearly understand that you were incapable of change, but when you, Maria, and Cynthia did what you did, the plans we had were destroyed."

"Plans? The plans we had were destroyed? We who?"

Michael was incensed. "My plans with Cynthia."

"Cynthia barely could tolerate you. She didn't even like you."

Michael laughed incredulously. "My point is made. In your mind, everything has always been about you, and not the things around you that everyone else could see. How you saw yourself and how you could not see what you ruined. You didn't see what Cynthia and I shared. Everyone but you saw it." He thought to the bodies posed on the trail. "In the end, everyone's eyes were open. Everyone saw it."

"What was it you and Cynthia had, Michael? What was it I didn't see?"

"We were going to get married, have children, and live our lives happily together."

What Michael was saying was so far from reality that JJ was not sure how to reply. "You're wrong, Michael. I already told you what Cynthia thought of you. You pretend that you and Cynthia had a thing, that you two were close, and that you were going to get married? That couldn't be any further from the truth, and you know it. You're delusional if you think any of that is true." JJ stood up from the table. "If you recall, Cynthia didn't date anyone in college. Did she like to party and mess around? Absolutely, but she didn't want to establish a relationship with someone until after she graduated. She said that hundreds of times when someone asked her out on a date. Maria, on the other hand, not only wanted a relationship; she wanted a husband. That was more important to her than school. She was the complete opposite of Cynthia. You're acting like I was the only person she had sex with in college." JJ started walking around the room. "Did Cynthia like to have sex? Yes. I can tell you that I wasn't the first or the last guy. Did you and Cynthia ever hook up? I can answer that. No, you didn't. Why? I don't know why, because everyone knew that she had sex with a lot of other guys."

As he walked around the conference room, Michael stared straight ahead as if he was in a trance. "You couldn't know what we shared."

JJ laughed. "You shared nothing. Any idea that you two were going to get married is a joke, and obviously conjured up in your mind."

All of the detailed plans that Michael had made to set JJ up, and which he successfully executed now, seemed to be in the distant past and had no meaning to him. JJ appeared not to have learned anything from what had happened, and he showed no remorse for his past actions. He hadn't changed at all. "I told you, JJ, that it became very clear to me while I was on spring break that you, Maria, and Cynthia acted together to hurt me. I decided then to embark on the road that led us to this day. You've got to admire what I've done."

"What have you done?" JJ sat down at the table. "Can you explain it to me?"

Michael needed to take back control and to regain the feelings he had enjoyed since the night JJ was arrested but was at risk of losing now. "You've got to admire that I was able to set all this up. You have to admit that the depth of planning required to put all that happened into play was genius. Pure genius. You talk about drama. What could be more dramatic than watching Sasha Frank placing the handcuffs on you in the foyer of your home? In a word, it was incredible." He leaned back in his chair and felt like he was regaining control. "You could never understand what all it took to make this happen. It was like I was a grifter setting up a sting. I played all the parts against the mark, you."

"You're right. I'm not smart enough."

"When I started putting this plan together, I knew that Maria would play a key role in exacting the revenge I so deserved. Warren was never supposed to be a part of the plan, but he became an integral part after I followed them for months. I was able to quickly determine that one of the nights of bowling league offered me the best opportunity for them to play their parts. Warren was just collateral damage. I didn't know him very well. I thought it would be better for Maria's husband to not have to endure the pain of loss that I did." Michael sat up in his chair.

JJ shook his head. "Who are you?"

Michael smiled. "As with Maria, you also chose Greg Bauer to play a key part, due to your actions. Your fight with the service writer at a dealership over your new car was a perfect example to the police of your capability to hurt someone. I was so happy when they found that all on their own. I had hoped that Lee and Max would recall that you'd talked about the incident with Bauer at poker night and then bring it to Frank's attention. I was beginning to think that the investigators weren't smart enough to look for potential suspects that had interacted with Bauer at his job. I was afraid I was going to have to give them a nudge in that direction, but they finally figured it out." Michael laughed. "I didn't even have to provide them a tip pointing that out to investigators."

JJ hadn't been sure how his asking Michael to stay after the earlier meeting that included Gray and Sig was going to play out, but it was obvious that Michael had strong feelings bottled up inside him that he needed to get out. "What are you trying to say, Michael?"

Michael shook his head. "Greg Bauer played a perfect part, as his death pointed to how the anger inside you could boil up to the surface given the right set of circumstances. It showed how unstable you could be and gave credence to your need to exact revenge on someone who'd stood up to you. Someone who made you look like a fool." He leaned back again in his chair. "Stephanie Davis also played a vital role in the plan. In reality, it could have been anyone that you were hooking up with and treated poorly over the past years, but you cannot imagine how pleased I was when I found out that she was also hooking up with Greg Bauer. That was totally unplanned." Michael smiled. "What's the word that best describes your meeting up with her at the bar across from the airport? Kismet. That's it! Then she and Bauer find each other on a sex app. Investigators thought they had only hooked up once, but Bauer was having sex with her while you were having sex with her, JJ. I had Keyes pose them covering themselves like Adam and Eve in the garden hiding their sins. As it turned out, no one better could have been chosen. I was looking through the DA's evidence, and I saw that Davis had hooked up with Bauer within hours before he was killed. It was an unexpected bonus that added to the complexity that I had already devised, as it had the police chasing their tails. Having DNA found on him, the investigators' inability to identify who the DNA belonged to and then having some low-level nobody in the DA's office come up with the idea to check if Stephanie Davis was a match was a gift. A spectacular gift." Michael stood up.

JJ sat silently, showing no emotion.

"Being able to pay Cynthia back for her infidelity and who, like Maria, was complicitous in your deeds was, shall we say, satisfying. I had only wished that I could have been the one to kill her. I thought about killing her quite a bit but decided it would add a layer of risk that I wasn't willing to accept." Michael walked over to the door and turned back to JJ. "You're probably wondering why I didn't also kill Cynthia's husband, Carl Jr."

"Based on what you said drove you to kill Warren? Yes, I am."

"The Zumwalts had no children. Cynthia and Carl Jr. had children, and as she was breathing her last breath, she would have realized that she was never going to see them again. She would have realized that her husband would have to comfort them after their mother was brutally murdered. Children old enough to understand what had happened and old enough that the experience would be burned into their brains. And poor Carl Jr. will always ask himself why he wasn't there for Cynthia at her time of need. He didn't call her or even send a text when she failed to come home that night. Carl Jr. will think every remaining day of his life that his dead wife lay naked on the trail for anyone to see. He deserves that for his part in keeping her from me."

"I can't believe any of this is true, Michael. You've got to be making this all up."

Michael walked back to the table and stood across from JJ. "It's all true. Now let's move on to a principal character, Brian Keyes, who obviously played the pivotal role in executing the plan. Without him, or someone like him, none of this would have been possible." Michael started walking around the room again. "There was another minor character, but his role ended shortly after the Zumwalts were killed."

"A minor character? Who was that?"

"Charlie Cole. He dangled the bait to catch Brian Keyes. Once Brian found he was capable of killing two people in cold blood, I knew I had him. The money that he could so easily make for killing hooked him. Sadly, Charlie was no longer needed, and his existence would add risk to executing the plan. He had to go."

JJ looked at Michael as he paced the room. "So, if I'm hearing this right, Michael, you orchestrated all of this because of something that happened"— JJ straightened up in his chair—"something that had nothing to do with you when we were in college?"

"*La vengeance est un plat qui se mange froide.*" Michael stopped across from where JJ was sitting. "All of this is your fault. Seven people are dead because of you."

JJ stood up. "You're crazy. I don't believe you. I don't know why, but you're making all this crap up."

"Let it sink in. It will all make sense when you work through the logic. Like I said, the beautiful thing about my plan was how easy it was to set you up to take the fall. When J'Quon told investigators that he remembered talking about Brian Keyes at poker night, that was also a gift. I actually don't recall him talking specifically about Keyes. He opens up at poker night like you all do, drinking too much and letting your guards down. J'Quon did talk about Charlie Cole, though." Michael sat down. "I had met and talked with a number of parolees the past couple of years, trying to find the perfect one that could help me execute my plan. Charlie fit the bill perfectly. He had recently been paroled from Menard and served as a cutout for the person that he recruited for me that would be willing to do what needed done. Once Charlie did what was required, he then became a liability. Just as Brian Keyes became a liability once Cynthia was dealt with. My plan had originally called for filling all ten of your sacred carved ducks with the personal effects of people who could be tied to you, but I became bored."

"I still don't believe you could do this, Michael. Especially to me."

"You don't know anything about what I could or couldn't do. You don't know me. You've never known me. No one really knows me or what I'm capable of. I can see by the look on your face that you need more proof of how I did this. Sure." Michael began walking around the room again. "You know how much we've all tried to figure out who put the personal effects into the ducks, since you were clearly innocent?"

JJ nodded. "Of course."

"Of course you remember. My name had to have come up, as you had to be thinking about who could get past Ros. Gray and Sig could never have figured that out. Since you first got Ros, I brought treats for her whenever I came over. I think she likes me more than she likes you. She's doing great, by the way, and loves my house." Michael smiled and winked at JJ. "I'm sure that right now your mind is racing, thinking about how I got into your house. It's probably hard for you to remember, since you always drink too much at poker night. I doubt you have any idea how many times J'Quon and I got you home after you got drunk at poker night. Let me save you the time to think on that one. At least twenty times in the past year, JJ. When the two of us had to get you and your car home, I'd just drive up to your garage door, and it would automatically open. I would pull in to park, and I'd look over at you in the passenger seat in a drunken sleep. Do you know it only takes seconds to make a clay impression of your house key? And mere minutes for me to make a duplicate. Because you have Ros in your house, you never turn on your alarm, but even if you had, I could have easily turned the alarm off after it was triggered." JJ looked at Michael inquisitively. "You can't even remember telling me your passcode one night when you were drunk. As we drove up to your garage door, I asked you if the alarm was on, and you weren't sure, so you told me the passcode. $9 - 6 - 1 - 9 - 5 - 2$."

JJ looked at Michael with disbelief. "So, the genesis of what you've done was because I slept with Cynthia once in 2004? In your madness you believed that the two of you would be together one day? What's wrong with you?"

"Nothing's wrong with me. You ask about the genesis of all this? You're the genesis, JJ."

"I'm supposed to believe that you think I'm the one responsible for the deaths of seven innocent people?"

"Yes."

"Only in the screwed-up alternate universe you occupy can you place responsibility on me for something that you're responsible for planning and for which you've admitted responsibility for executing."

"I freely admit that it was me and me alone who carefully planned and executed the events that find you behind bars. You are the intended consequence of my plan. What I find exceptionally rewarding is that there's no way out for you. You may be thinking that now you can tell the DA of my taking full responsibility for the murders."

JJ shook his head. "I just don't understand."

"Nothing exists that could point back to me. Nothing. I've established multiple levels of cutouts that separate me entirely from any of this. No one could ever prove that I was responsible."

"Thank you for all of that, Michael." JJ stood up from the table. "I promise you they're certainly going to try."

"Try what?"

The door to the conference room slowly opened. Michael turned to see Senior Detective Sasha Frank standing in the doorway, flanked by two detention center officers. Behind them stood the DA.

"Good evening, Mr. Drake. I'm arresting you for the murders of Maria Zumwalt, Warren Zumwalt, Greg Bauer, Stephanie Davis, Cynthia Pope, Brian Keyes, and Charles Cole."

Michael looked at JJ and then back at the senior detective. "What evidence could you possibly have to arrest me, Detective?" Michael interrupted. Sasha began reading him his rights. "What are you doing?"

"Reading you your rights. By admitting your responsibility, Mr. Drake, I am arresting you," Sasha said.

"You can't be serious." Michael turned to JJ. "I've been talking with my client on the charges that you've already charged him with committing. The conversation that we've been having is covered under attorney-client privilege."

Gerry Frump, who'd been the DA for the past ten years, stepped forward past Sasha. "Good afternoon, Mr. Drake. I'm sorry to inform you that Mr. Jennings waived his attorney-client privilege. You of all people should know that your discussions with your client don't protect you from self-incrimination. No one compelled you to disclose your involvement and the details of the murders for which you're being charged today. Detective?"

"Please turn around, Mr. Drake." Sasha stepped forward and placed handcuffs on Michael.

Michael looked at JJ. "What's going on here, JJ?"

"Sasha and I talked a couple of weeks ago. The senior detective"—JJ looked over at Sasha—"Sasha knocked on the door and asked if we could talk a few minutes after you, Gray, and Sig left one evening. I saw no harm in talking. After all, my attorneys had just told me that there was no viable defense for the charges against me. The evidence clearly showed that only I, Jonathan Jennings, could have committed these heinous crimes." JJ moved closer to Michael. "Sasha didn't believe I committed the murders. He felt I was being set up. We talked through the evidence, and it came down to means, motive, and opportunity. You were the only person that I could think of who could have set me up."

"Why, JJ? Why me?"

JJ laughed. "That's funny, after you just spent the last thirty-plus minutes telling us that you did it. You set me up, Michael. You admitted that you did, and you admitted responsibility for the deaths of seven people. Now get the hell away from me, you SOB."

Sasha pulled Michael backward and moved him toward the two police officers who were with him. "Get him out of here."

The DA reached out his hand to JJ, and the two shook. Frump walked out behind Michael and the two police officers who were walking alongside him. The DA stopped again, turned to look at JJ. "I'm sorry, sir." He then left the room and the door closed.

"Thank you, Sasha."

"It was all you, JJ. You played that perfectly."

"I didn't know we could get him to admit all that he did. I still don't understand why he did it. He's obviously a sick man."

Sasha reached out and gave JJ a fist bump. "It's not your problem. The DA wants you out of here, Mr. Jennings. It's going to take him an hour or so to unwind the charges and officially charge Drake, but he's requested an emergency hearing with Mayo to request that you be released and charges against you be completely dropped."

JJ smiled. "That's mighty nice of Gerry. I need to close out some pro bono work I've been doing with some of my friends in here before I leave, Sasha. Tell the DA to take his time. There's no rush."

Sasha was amazed that JJ wasn't throwing a chair around demanding to be let out immediately. "Okay, then. How about a cigarette and soda?"

"Now you're talking, Sasha." JJ sat down at the table. "After all, we have to start talking about you becoming the newest member of the country club and taking up golf so you can hit the course with your new best friend."

Sasha smiled and took out his cigarettes. "Your decision to wear a wire worked."

"Yes, it did. I plan on making a habit of making good decisions for the rest of my life." He reached out to shake hands again with Sasha. "I couldn't have done this without you, my friend."

"Sure you could have. You just needed somebody to believe in you." Sasha looked at his watch. "I know you want me to stay for a soda and cigarettes, but the DA is going to execute a search warrant on Drake's home. I want to be there to get Ros. She can hang with me until you're released." Sasha smiled. "I just need to remember to bring along some of those treats."

"Thanks, Sasha."

Sasha put his hand on JJ's shoulder. "You're very welcome." Sasha smiled at JJ again and walked to the door of the room with one of the chairs in his hand and knocked twice. The door opened quickly, and Sasha told the officer standing outside, "I'm going to leave this chair in the door to keep it propped open. Please don't touch it." The officer nodded.

Sasha walked through the door, stopped to prop it open with the chair, and looked back to tell JJ one more thing. "I'll be back to take you home shortly. Maybe we could even stop by the club for a drink on the way. I'm just sayin' I think we could both use one."

"Great idea, my friend." JJ smiled as he sat back down in his chair and lit one of the cigarettes from the pack Sasha had left on the table. "That's a truly exceptional idea."

EPILOGUE

JJ had spent almost two months as a guest of McLean County. Since being in jail, he had missed Ros, playing golf, his home, and his girl-friend, Jodie—in that order. He had eased back into his life quickly once exonerated from being accused as the mastermind behind the Constitution Trail murders.

After walking out of jail with Senior Detective Sasha Frank, the two headed to the country club for a quick drink. As Sasha drove, JJ called his partners, Sig and Gray, to let them know of his release. Unlike some friends who believed the damning evidence found in his home that tied him to the six killings, Sig and Gray never wavered in believing in his innocence.

Once JJ arrived at the club, word spread quickly of his release. He was joined by more friends who came to celebrate. The club even allowed Ros inside the bar. Old-fashioneds were the drink of choice that night, and there were as many toasts to Sasha as there were to JJ.

The following evening JJ walked into Maggie's Bar & Grill with his new friend Sasha for the Thursday night poker game he had missed since his arrest. Everyone welcomed JJ back to the table, especially Lee Barnes and Max Duncan. After witnessing Sasha's inspection of the ten carved ducks displayed on JJ's library shelves, the two had reluctantly come to believe in their poker-playing friend's guilt. They had quickly renewed their friend-ship with JJ once Michael Drake admitted his responsibility in the murders. When JJ walked into Maggie's, he presented two of his carved ducks to the pair of agents.

As a thank-you gift to the detective, JJ sponsored and paid the club mem-bership fees for the detective and Janet. The couple, who had spent the last ten years together, decided to get married and chose the country club to exchange vows in early September.

Michael Drake had initially been found incompetent to stand trial after doctors examined him. The same doctors determined that he was competent almost four months after his arrest on July 11, 2018. His trial for the seven murders was to begin on March 19, 2019.

Sasha decided that he would definitely not retire upon hitting the thirty-five-year mark with the force. After talking with Janet, he thought he should wait at least until Janet was ready to retire. There would be more opportunities for the senior detective to solve future crimes and, more importantly, help train other detectives.

Deliberate Duplicity

David Rohlfing

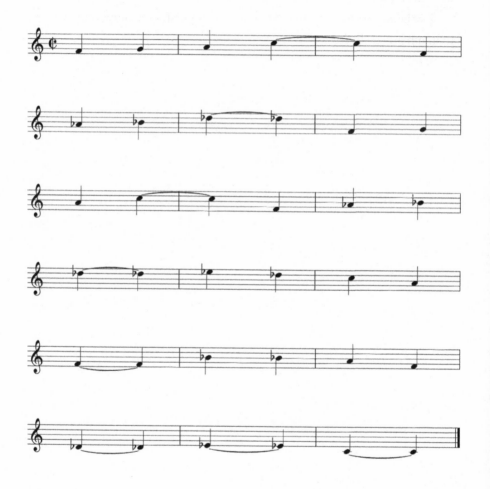

AUTHOR'S NOTE

I hope that you enjoyed reading *Deliberate Duplicity*. I've enjoyed writing blogs for a number of years, and they were germane to views or experiences I had during my business career. I've had the desire to write a book for some time, and a few years ago while having a drink with a friend in Nashville, he suggested I write a book on leadership, which I could then use as a stepping-stone into a career as a motivational speaker. Evidently, I wasn't motivated enough to do that, as I was never able to get past a few pages in a book that could potentially start me down that path.

I've read countless works of fiction over the years, and I certainly learned how much time is consumed in writing a novel. I decided on the title before I wrote a single word. I then started thinking about how I could weave a murder mystery based on the area that I live. In developing the protagonist Senior Detective Sasha Frank, I wanted him to be flawed, but relentless in his drive to find the person or persons responsible for the Constitution Trail murders.

Again, I hope that you enjoyed reading my first book. I'm writing a follow-up to *Deliberate Duplicity* based on another case headed by Senior Detective Sasha Frank. If you found this book interesting, I hope that you'll look for the next book in the series, where Sasha will be working to solve another string of murders.

You can learn more about Sasha Frank and me at www.davidrohlfing.com.

Thanks.

QUESTIONS FOR DISCUSSION

At the beginning of the book you see a jaded J'Quon who tries to guess at the life trajectories of his parolees. How did this impact your initial impression of the character, as well as the characters around him?

With each character's introduction into the story, you are given a brief summary of their background and history. How does this information color your relationship with the characters? Are you able to sympathize or identify with some of these characters better than others? Why or why not?

What do you make of Charlie and Brian's quick turn back to crime? Charlie was shown as dissatisfied early in the story, but Brian was initially driven to stay on the straight and narrow. Why do you think the job offer changed his mind so quickly?

Does the third-person point of view and omniscience of the narrator affect the genre of the story, perhaps pushing it slightly away from a traditional mystery story? Did you enjoy this shifting perspective? Why or why not?

Fred's introduction into the story is the only character introduction not associated with any amount of background information, thus providing the story with mystery. How did this affect your interpretation of him and the direction in which the story would be moving?

Both the murder of the Zumwalts and the subsequent investigation are detailed to you explicitly. How does having both sides of the story affect your reading? What are some of the similarities and differences in the recounting of the two scenes?

As the killings continue, you see less of Brian and Fred. As a reader you have already been given insight into not only the "how," but also the "who" of the murders. Giving the reader this much information deviates from some traditional crime drama tropes. Does this create more or less anxiety as you read? Why or why not?

As Brian continues killing under Fred's direction, you begin to see him devolve from a hired killer to a psychotic serial killer. How did it make you feel to read Brian's fall, especially given that he was initially presented as a character who could be redeemed?

What assumptions or guesses did you make about Fred's motives as you read the book? What details led you to these guesses?

Sasha quickly becomes the central figure of the story. What did you make of the character? Did his light joking humanize this hardened and determined detective? Were you able to relate to him?

After spending so much time with Sasha and the investigation team, were you expecting J'Quon's friends, JJ and Michael, to be pulled back into the story in such a dramatic way?

Did you expect or predict Michael, a.k.a. Fred, to be the mastermind behind the killings? If so, what evidence was provided that led you to thinking that Michael was the killer?

What did you think of Michael's confession? Did you believe that he would be so willing to tell JJ everything? Did you believe and understand his motives for committing the crimes?

The story has multiple depictions of murder and death. Were those scenes difficult to read? Did they affect how you approached the book?

When you first meet Sasha, you find a detective who often spends time alone trying to solve the crime in his head; however, as the story progresses, he begins to trust the help of others more, eventually cracking the case. How does this important lesson that Sasha learns resonate with you? Do you think Sasha will carry this lesson with him and seek help before things get desperate?

AUTHOR Q & A QUESTIONS

Q. What was your inspiration for writing this story?

A: I have enjoyed reading murder mystery novels for years. As many novels in this genre take place in larger cities, I thought it would be an interesting twist to read about a police detective investigating murders in a small Midwestern city.

Q. The narrator provides the reader with a lot of information from both sides of the killings. How did you find the right balance of information that the reader would and would not learn from the narrator?

A: As I wrote *Deliberate Duplicity*, I generally used the narrator to provide more detailed or technical information related to the killings to the reader while using characters to relay information solely from their own perspective.

Q. You mention that you are already working on another book with Sasha as the protagonist. Are there any more details or insights you can give into the next book?

A: The draft of my second book in the series featuring Senior Detective Sasha Frank has been finished. The book begins with the murder of a young woman in Bloomington, Illinois, in 2013, five years before the Constitution Trail murders detailed in *Deliberate Duplicity*. Sasha is assigned the case, and with no physical evidence pointing to potential suspects, he keeps hitting brick walls slowing the initial investigation. As the senior detective keeps looking for suspects who could have killed the young woman, additional murders quickly take place. Sasha never gives up in his pursuit of justice for the young woman and her family.

Q. Are there any characters that you particularly identify with? What characters did you enjoy developing and writing the most?

A: My career in business was spent as a senior executive in national and multinational companies having traveled to six of the seven continents. Although I have no background in law enforcement, I identify with Sasha in his unrelenting pursuit of justice for those killed by Brian and Michael. That persistence in ensuring that he delivers on the promise of justice while facing adversity is a trait I identify with. I especially enjoyed JJ as a character. Understanding that JJ cared only about himself up until he found himself in jail facing murder charges, the reader sees him change for the better when he realizes that he's going to be convicted of a crime he did not commit.

Q. As Michael reveals his actions, the reader begins to see how twisted his mind is. Was it difficult or uncomfortable to write such a dark character?

A: I found the writing of Michael's character relatively easy, much to the surprise to my wife, family, and friends who read the first draft of the book. Even though Michael and I share no similar traits or qualities, I found no difficulty writing about someone with such a dark and flawed mind while building his character.

Q. What scenes did you enjoy writing the most? What scenes did you find challenging to write?

A: I enjoyed writing the entire book, so picking out a favorite section is difficult. That being said, developing the background of Fred as Michael provided readers an opportunity to learn of the farm where Charlie's body is disposed, trips to Laredo, Texas, to meet with José Antonio Arechavaleta that gave further hints that Fred was a person of means, as well as describing Michael's home and items inside that home was fun to write. The details of the murders were unquestionably a challenge to write. The manner of which each murder was planned by Michael and then committed by Brian was at times difficult.

Q. The scenes that focus on the investigation of the murders are very well detailed. Did it require a significant amount of research to develop these scenes as an accurate portrayal of a police investigation? If so, where did you first look for information? Were there any sources that were particularly useful?

A: Prior to writing *Deliberate Duplicity* I read a number of articles on police and law enforcement tactics. I think that watching television shows about police and crime scene investigations over the years was also helpful.

Q. What were some of the biggest challenges in weaving a mystery story? How did you overcome these challenges?

A: Before I began writing the book I read several articles on must do's on how to start writing a novel. A similar theme in all the articles I read was that I needed to outline the book and build the main characters before I began writing. I didn't follow that recommendation at all. I started with Sasha Frank as the main character and the murder of the Zumwalts, then began to add other events and characters as I developed the book. The sequence of chapters as they appear in the book changed while I wrote the book. I would add or delete chapters as I worked toward a final draft weaving what I hoped was a suspenseful murder mystery keeping the reader searching for clues to the identity of the mastermind directing the murders.

Q. Do you have a particular method for writing, such as writing at a certain time or location? Did you ever face writer's block? What tactics did use to push past it?

A: I wrote the book during a few winter months in 2018/2019 sitting at a couch in my great room. I semiretired in June 2018 and would typically write during morning and afternoons. On nights I had trouble sleeping I found myself at times writing for hours in the great room in the dark on my laptop. I never suffered writer's block. Since *Deliberate Duplicity* was my first attempt at writing a book, I did have problems understanding that at times less is more. It was hard to write less and not be too detailed in describing places or events.

Q. You mentioned that the title came to you before you began writing the book. Did this affect your writing of the story or where you wanted the story to go?

A: The working title of the book was *Intended Consequence*, but after talking with my publisher I decided to change the title to *Deliberate Duplicity*. The working title gave away too much to the reader. The title portrays the plan of the mastermind, who is a deeply flawed narcissist, delusional, and a psychopath.

Q. What books or authors have influenced your writing style? Are there any books, podcasts, or shows that you enjoy that you would recommend to your audience?

A: Over the years I've greatly enjoyed Michael Connelly and his books on Detective Harry Bosch. I have also enjoyed Lee Child's Jack Reacher series. I would recommend both these authors to anyone who enjoys reading these types of novels.

Q. If you could go back in time to when you first began writing this book, what piece of advice would you give yourself?

A: The most important advice I would have liked to have given myself would be that less is more. My initial draft had too many details that did not add anything to the story. I did heed that advice while writing the second book in the Sasha Frank series.

Q. In writing and developing these characters, did you find that they taught you any lessons? Is there a lesson you learned from the process of writing as a whole?

A: As I mentioned earlier I identify with Sasha. His persistence in finding ways over, under, or through walls that he hit during murder investigations are good lessons for all to learn in life. Never give up.

Q. All of the characters have detailed histories, many of which are interconnected. Was it difficult to develop these backstories and connections? If so, how did you craft this complex web of characters?

A: I wrote the book adding characters and events as I developed the story. By writing the book in this manner, I did not have that much difficulty providing connections and histories to other characters in the book. I hoped that readers would find it rewarding trying to pick out who the killer really was via subtle hints while reading the book and effectively help Sasha solve the Constitution Trail murders.

ABOUT DAVID ROHLFING

After a long career in business that gave him the opportunity to travel to all but one continent and countless countries around the globe, David decided to write his first novel, *Deliberate Duplicity*.

He lives in Illinois with his wife. When he's not writing, he spends as much time as possible with his wife and family and working on his golf game.

He's currently working on his second novel, and if you'd like to know when his next book will be published, please visit his website at www.davidrohlfing. com, where you can sign up to receive updates on future book releases.

Made in the USA
Las Vegas, NV
08 February 2021